KT-165-990

'Barclay succeeds in both banging the gong and serving up a riveting, rewarding and ... plausible three courses, though you may need to take a deep breath somewhere around the coffee stage' *Guardian*

'In a world of staggering choice when it comes to your reading material, this chilling little book sits right at the top of the genre – anyone not riveted by this tale and the emotional punch it carries must be made of stone, because despite its dark premise, it has real heart. I loved it'

Shots Magazine

'A genuinely mystifying puzzle with tense moments'

Sunday Telegraph

'Nerve-racking until the very end' *Herald*

'A thoughtful study of relationship paranoia and an engrossing whodunnit' *Esquire*

'This is the thriller equivalent of shooting down a sheet of ice clinging to a bobsleigh as it slews round tricky corners and hurtles to a climax' *Peterborough Evening Telegraph*

'One of the top delights in book reviewing is discovering a gem; a book that pushes the bar just a little higher, and this is exactly what *No Time for Goodbye* does'

Deadly Pleasures

'Impossible to put down' Crimesquad.com

'With *No Time for Goodbye*, Linwood Barclay is now firmly in the major league of thriller writers'

Yorkshire Evening Post

Linwood Barclay is married with two children and lives in Toronto. He has written a popular column for the *Toronto Star* since 1993.

By Linwood Barclay

No Time for Goodbye
Too Close to Home

No Time For Goodbye

LINWOOD BARCLAY

An Orion paperback

First published in Great Britain in 2007
by Orion
This paperback edition published in 2008
by Orion Books Ltd,
Orion House, 5 Upper St Martin's Lane,
London WC2H 9EA

An Hachette UK company

33 35 37 39 40 38 36 34 32

Copyright © Linwood Barclay 2007

The right of Linwood Barclay to be identified as the author of this work has been asserted by him in accordance with the Copyright, Designs and Patents Act 1988.

All rights reserved. No part of this publication may be reproduced, stored in a retrieval system, or transmitted, in any form or by any means, electronic, mechanical, photocopying, recording or otherwise, without the prior permission of the copyright owner.

All the characters in this book are fictitious, and any resemblance to actual persons, living or dead, is purely coincidental.

A CIP catalogue record for this book is available from the British Library.

ISBN 978-0-7528-9368-6

Typeset by Deltatype Ltd, Birkenhead, Merseyside
Printed and bound in Great Britain by
Clays Ltd, St Ives plc

The Orion Publishing Group's policy is to use papers that are natural, renewable and recyclable products and made from wood grown in sustainable forests. The logging and manufacturing processes are expected to conform to the environmental regulations of the country of origin.

www.orionbooks.co.uk

This is for my wife, Neetha

Acknowledgements

As a guy who dropped out of high school chemistry, I am most grateful to Barbara Reid, a DNA technologist with the Centre of Forensic Sciences in Toronto, for helping me with some pertinent details in this manuscript. If anything's wrong, I'm afraid I'm not going to be able to blame Barbara.

I want to thank Bill Massey at Orion, Irwyn Applebaum, Nita Taublib and Danielle Perez at Bantam Dell, and my wonderful agent, Helen Heller, for their continued support and confidence.

Last but not least, the home team: Neetha, Spencer and Paige.

May 1983

When Cynthia woke up, it was so quiet in the house she thought it must be Saturday.

If only.

If there'd ever been a day that she needed to be a Saturday, to be anything but a school day, this was it. Her stomach was still doing the occasional somersault, her head was full of cement and it took some effort to keep it from falling forward or on to her shoulders.

Jesus, what the hell was that in the waste-paper basket next to the bed? She couldn't even remember throwing up in the night, but if she needed evidence, there it was.

She had to deal with this first, before her parents came in. Cynthia got to her feet, wobbled a moment, grabbed the small plastic container with one hand and opened her bedroom door a crack with the other. There was no one in the hall, so she crept past the open doors of her brother's and parents' bedrooms and slipped into the bathroom, locking the door behind her.

She emptied the bucket into the toilet, rinsed it in the tub, took a bleary-eyed look at herself in the mirror. So, this is how a fourteen-year-old girl looks when she gets hammered, she thought.

Not a pretty sight. She could barely remember what Vince had given her to try the night before, stuff he'd snuck out of his house. A couple of cans of Bud, some vodka, gin, an already opened bottle of red wine. She'd promised to bring some of her dad's rum, but had chickened out in the end.

Something was niggling at her. Something about the bedrooms.

She splashed cold water on her face and dried off with a towel. Cynthia took a deep breath, tried to pull herself together, in case her mother was waiting for her on the other side of the door.

She wasn't.

Cynthia headed back to her room, the walls plastered with posters of Kiss and other soul-destroying entertainers that sent her parents into fits, feeling the broadloom under her toes. Along the way, she glanced into her brother Todd's room, then her parents'. The beds were made. Her mother didn't usually get around to making them until later in the morning – Todd never made his own, and their mother let him get away with it – but here they were, looking as though they'd never been slept in.

Cynthia felt a wave of panic. Was she already late for school? Just how late was it?

She could see Todd's clock on his bedside table from where she stood. Just ten before eight. Nearly half an hour before she usually left for her first class.

The house was still.

She could usually hear her parents down in the kitchen about this time. Even if they weren't speaking to each other, which was often the case, there'd be the faint sounds of the fridge opening and closing, a spatula scraping against a frying pan, the muffled rattling of dishes in the sink, someone – her father usually – leafing through the pages of the morning newspaper, grunting about something in the news that irritated him.

Weird.

She went into her room, closed the door. Pull it together, she told herself. Show up for breakfast like nothing ever happened. Pretend there wasn't a screaming match the night before. Act like her father hadn't dragged her out of her much older boyfriend's car and taken her home.

She glanced at her ninth grade math text sitting atop her open notebook on her desk. She'd only managed half the questions before she'd gone out the night before, deluded herself into thinking that if she got up early enough she could finish them in the morning.

Todd was usually banging around this time of the morning. In and out of the bathroom, putting Led Zeppelin on his stereo, shouting downstairs to his mother asking where his pants were, burping, waiting until he was at Cynthia's door to rip one off.

She couldn't remember him saying anything about going into school early, but why would he tell her anyway? They didn't often walk together. She was a geeky Ninth Grader to him, although she was giving it her best shot to get into as much bad stuff as he was. Wait until she told him about getting really drunk for the first time. No, wait, he'd just rat her out later when he was in the doghouse himself and needed to score points.

OK, so maybe Todd had to go to school early, but where were her mother and father?

Her dad, maybe he left on another business trip before the sun even came up. He was always heading off somewhere, you could never keep track. Too bad he hadn't been away the night before.

And her mother, maybe she'd driven Todd to school or something.

She got dressed. Jeans, a sweater. Put on her make-up. Enough not to look like shit, but not too much that her mother started making cracks about her going to 'tramp tryouts'.

When she got to the kitchen, she just stood there.

There were no cereal boxes out, no juice, no coffee in the coffee maker. No plates out, no bread in the toaster, no mugs. No bowl with a trace of milk and soggy Rice Krispies in the sink. The kitchen looked exactly as it had after her mother had cleaned up from dinner the night before.

Cynthia glanced about for a note. Her mom was big about leaving notes when she had to go out. Even when she was angry. A long enough note to say, 'On your own today', or 'Make yourself some eggs, have to drive Todd', or just 'Back later'. If she was really angry, instead of signing off with 'Love, Mom', she'd write 'L, Mom'.

There was no note.

Cynthia worked up the nerve to shout, 'Mom?' Her own voice suddenly sounded strange to her. Maybe because there was something in it she didn't want to recognize.

When her mother didn't answer, she called out again. 'Dad?'

Again, nothing.

This, she surmised, must be her punishment. She'd pissed off her parents, disappointed them, and now they were going to act like she didn't exist. Silent treatment, on a nuclear scale.

OK, she could deal with that. It beat a huge confrontation first thing in the morning.

Cynthia didn't feel she could keep down any breakfast,

so she grabbed the school books she needed and headed out the door.

The *Journal Courier*, rolled up with a rubber band like a log, lay on the front step.

Cynthia kicked it out of her way, not really thinking about it, and strode down the empty driveway – her father's Dodge and mother's Ford Escort were both gone – in the direction of Milford South High School. Maybe, if she could find her brother, she'd learn just what was going on, just how much trouble she might actually be in.

Plenty, she figured.

She'd missed curfew, an early one of eight o'clock. It was a school night, first of all, and then there'd been that call earlier in the evening from Mrs Asphodel about how if she didn't hand in her English assignments, she wasn't going to pass. She told her parents she was going to Pam's house to do homework, that Pam was going to help her get caught up on her English stuff, even though it was stupid and a total waste of time.

'OK, but you still have to be home by eight.'

'Come on,' she said.

'That's barely enough time to get one assignment done. Do you want me to fail? Is that what you want?'

'Eight,' her father said. 'No later.'

Well, screw that, she thought. She'd be home when she got home.

When Cynthia wasn't home by 8.15, her mother phoned Pam's house, got Pam's mother, said, 'Hi, it's Patricia Bigge? Cynthia's mom? Could I talk to Cynthia please?'

Pam's mother said, 'Huh?' Not only was Cynthia not there, but Pam wasn't even home.

That was when Cynthia's father grabbed the faded Fedora hat he never went anywhere without, got in his Dodge and started driving around the neighborhood, looking for her. He suspected she might be with that Vince Fleming boy, the seventeen-year-old from the eleventh grade, the one who had his license, who drove around in a rusted 1970 red Mustang. Clayton and Patricia Bigge didn't much care for him. Tough kid, troubled family, bad influence. Cynthia had heard her parents talking one night, about Vince's father, that he was some bad guy or something, but she figured it was just bullshit.

It was just a fluke that her dad spotted the car at the far end of the parking lot of the Connecticut Post Mall, out on the Post Road, not far from the theaters. The Mustang was backed up to the curb, and her father parked in front, blocking it in. She knew it was him instantly when she saw the Fedora.

'Shit,' said Cynthia. Good thing he hadn't shown up two minutes earlier, when they'd been making out, or when Vince was showing her his new switchblade. Jesus, you pressed this little button, and zap! Six inches of steel suddenly appeared. Vince had held it in his lap, moving it around and grinning, like maybe it was something else. Cynthia tried holding it, sliced the air in front of her and giggled.

'Easy,' Vince had said cautiously. 'You can do a lot of damage with one of these.'

Clayton Bigge marched right over to the passenger door, yanked it open. It creaked on its rusty hinges.

'Hey, pal, watch it!' Vince said, no knife in hand now, but a beer bottle – almost as bad.

'Don't "hey pal" me,' he said, taking his daughter by

the arm and ushering her back into his own car. 'Christ almighty, you reek,' he told her.

She wished she could have died right then.

She wouldn't look at him or say anything, not even when he started going on about how she was becoming nothing but trouble, that if she didn't get her head screwed on right she'd be a fuck-up her whole life, that he didn't know what he'd done wrong, he just wanted her to grow up and be happy and blah blah blah, and, Jesus, even when he was pissed off he still drove like he was taking his driver's test, never exceeding the speed limit, always using his turn signal, the guy was unbelievable.

When they pulled into the driveway, she was out of the car before he had it in park, throwing open the door, striding in, trying not to weave, her mother standing there, not looking mad so much as worried, saying, 'Cynthia! Where were—'

She steamrolled past her, went up to her room. From downstairs, her father shouted, 'You come down here! We got things to discuss!'

'I wish you were dead!' she screamed and slammed her door.

That much came back to her as she walked to school. The rest of the evening was still a bit fuzzy.

She remembered sitting down on her bed, feeling woozy. Too tired to feel embarrassed. She decided to lie down, figuring she could sleep it off by the morning, a good ten hours away.

A lot could happen before morning.

At one point, drifting in and out of sleep, she thought she heard someone at her door. Like someone was hesitating just outside it.

Then, later, she thought she heard it again.

Did she get up to see who it was? Did she even try to get out of bed? She couldn't remember.

And now she was almost to school.

The thing was, she felt remorseful. She'd broken nearly every household rule in a single night. Starting with the lie about going to Pam's. Pam was her best friend, she was over to the house all the time, slept over every other weekend. Cynthia's mother liked her, maybe even trusted her, Cynthia thought. Bringing Pam's name into it, Cynthia had thought somehow that would buy her some time, that her mother wouldn't have been so quick to phone Pam's mother. So much for that plan.

If only her crimes ended there. She'd broken curfew. Gone parking with a boy. A *seventeen-year-old* boy. A boy they say broke school windows the year before, took a joyride in a neighbor's car.

Her parents, they weren't all bad. Most of the time. Especially her mom. Her dad, shit, even he wasn't too bad, when he was home.

Maybe Todd did get a lift to school. If he did have practice, and he was pressed for time, her mom might have given him one, then decided to go grocery shopping after. Or to the Howard Johnson's for a coffee. She did that once in a while.

First period history was a write-off. Second period math was even worse. She couldn't focus, her head still hurt. 'How did you do on those questions, Cynthia?' the math teacher asked. She didn't even look at him.

Just before lunch, she saw Pam, who said, 'Jesus, if you're going to tell your mom you're at my house, you wanna fucking let me know? Then maybe I could tell my mom *something*.'

'Sorry,' Cynthia said. 'Did she have a fit?'

'When I came in,' Pam said.

At lunch, Cynthia slipped out of the cafeteria, went to the school pay phone, dialed home. She'd tell her mother she was sorry. Really, really sorry. And then she'd ask to come home, say she felt sick. Her mother would look after her. She couldn't stay mad at her if she was sick. She'd make soup.

Cynthia gave up after fifteen rings, then thought maybe she'd dialed wrong. Tried again, no answer. She had no work number for her dad. He was on the road so much of the time, you had to wait for him to check in from wherever he was staying.

She was hanging out front of the school with some friends when Vince Fleming drove by in his Mustang. 'Sorry about all that shit last night,' he said. 'Jeez, your dad's a prize.'

'Yeah, well,' Cynthia said.

'So, what happened after you went home?' Vince asked. There was something in the way he asked, like he already knew. Cynthia shrugged and shook her head, didn't want to talk about it.

Vince asked, 'Where's your brother today?'

Cynthia said, 'What?'

'He home sick?'

Nobody had seen Todd at school. Vince said he'd been going to ask him, quiet like, how much trouble Cynthia was in, whether she was grounded, because he was hoping she wanted to get together Friday night or Saturday. His friend Kyle was getting him some beer, they could go up to that spot, the one on the hill, maybe sit in the car awhile, look at stars, right?

Cynthia ran home. Didn't ask Vince for a ride, even though he was right there. Didn't check in at the school office to tell them she was skipping off early. Ran the whole way, thinking, please let her car be there, please let her car be there.

But when she rounded the corner from Pumpkin Delight Road to Hickory, and her two-storey house came into view, the yellow Escort, her mother's car, was not there. But she shouted out her mother's name anyway, when she got inside, with what little breath she had left. Then her brother's.

She started to tremble, then willed herself to stop.

It made no sense. No matter how angry her parents might be at her, they wouldn't do this, would they? Just leave? Take off without telling her? And take Todd with them?

Cynthia felt stupid doing it, but rang the bell at the Jamison house next door. There was probably a simple explanation for all this, something she forgot, a dental appointment, something, and any second her mother would turn into the driveway. Cynthia would feel like a total idiot, but that was OK.

She started blathering when Mrs Jamison opened the door about how when she woke up no one was home and then she went to school and Todd never showed up and her mom still wasn't—

Mrs Jamison said, 'Whoa, everything's OK. Your mother's probably out doing some shopping.' Mrs Jamison walked Cynthia back home, glanced down at the newspaper that still had not been taken in. Together they looked upstairs and down and in the garage again and out in the backyard.

'That sure is odd,' Mrs Jamison said. She didn't quite know what to think, so, somewhat reluctantly, she called the Milford Police.

They sent around an officer, who didn't seem all that concerned, at first. But soon there were more officers and more cars, and by evening, there were cops all over the place. Cynthia heard them putting out descriptions of her parents' two cars, calling Milford Hospital. Police were going up and down the street, knocking on doors, asking questions.

'You're sure they never mentioned anything about going any place?' asked a man who said he was a detective and didn't wear a uniform like all the other police. Named Findley, or Finlay.

Did he think she'd forget something like that? That she'd suddenly go, 'Oh yeah, now I remember! They went to visit my mom's sister, Aunt Tess!'

'You see,' the detective said. 'It doesn't look like your mom and dad and brother packed to go away or anything. Their clothes are still here, there are suitcases in the basement.'

There were a lot of questions. When did she last see her parents? When had she gone to bed? Who was this boy she was with? She tried to tell the detective everything, even admitted she and her parents had had a fight, although she'd left out how bad it was, that she'd gotten drunk, told them she wished they were dead.

This detective seemed nice enough, but he wasn't asking the questions Cynthia was wondering. Why would her mom and dad and brother just disappear? Where would they go? Why wouldn't they take her with them?

Suddenly, in a frenzy, she began to tear the kitchen apart. Lifting up and tossing place mats, moving the toaster, looking under the chairs, peering down into the crack between the stove and the wall, tears streaming down her face.

'What is it, sweetheart?' the detective asked. 'What are you doing?'

'Where's the note?' Cynthia asked, her eyes pleading. 'There has to be a note. My mom never goes away without leaving a note.'

ONE

Cynthia stood out front of the two-storey house on Hickory. It wasn't as though she was seeing her childhood home for the first time in nearly twenty-five years. She still lived in Milford. She'd driven by here once in a while. She showed me the house once before we got married, a quick drive-by. 'There it is,' she'd said and kept on going. She rarely stopped. And if she did, she didn't get out. She'd never stood on the sidewalk and stared at the place.

And it had certainly been a very long time since she'd stepped through that front door.

She was rooted to the sidewalk, seemingly unable to take even one step toward the place. I wanted to go to her side, walk her to the door. It was only a thirty-foot driveway, but it stretched a quarter century into the past. I was guessing, to Cynthia, it must have been like looking through the wrong end of some binoculars. You could walk all day and never get there.

But I stayed where I was, on the other side of the street, looking at her back, at her short red hair. I had my orders.

Cynthia stood there, as though waiting for permission to approach. And then it came.

'OK, Mrs Archer? Start walking toward the house. Not too fast. Kind of hesitant, you know, like it's the first time you've gone inside since you were fourteen years old.'

Cynthia glanced over her shoulder at a woman in jeans and sneakers, her ponytail pulled down and through the opening at the back of her baseball cap. She was one of three assistant producers. 'This *is* the first time,' Cynthia said.

'Yeah yeah, don't look at me,' ponytail girl said. 'Just look at the house and start walking up the drive, thinking back to that time, twenty-five years ago, when it all happened, OK?'

Cynthia glanced across the street at me, made a face, and I smiled back weakly, a kind of mutual *what-are-you-gonna-do?*

And so she started up the driveway, slowly. If the camera hadn't been on, is this how she would have approached? With this mixture of deliberation and apprehension? Probably. But now it felt false, forced.

But as she mounted the steps to the door, reached out with her hand, I could just make out the trembling. An honest emotion, which meant, I guessed, that the camera would fail to catch it.

She had her hand on the knob, turned it, was about to push the door open, when ponytail girl shouted, 'OK! Good! Just hold it there!' Then, to her cameraman, 'OK, let's set up inside, get her coming in.'

'You're fucking kidding me,' I said, loud enough for the crew – a half dozen or so people, plus Paula Malloy, she of the gleaming teeth and Donna Karan suits, who was doing all the on-camera stuff and voiceovers – to hear.

Paula herself came over to see me.

'Mr Archer,' she said, reaching out with both hands and touching me just below my shoulders, a Malloy trademark. 'Is everything OK?'

'How can you do that to her?' I said. 'My wife's walking in there for the first time since her family fucking vanished, and you basically yell "Cut"?'

'Terry,' she said, insinuating herself closer to me. 'May I call you Terry?'

I said nothing.

'Terry, I'm sorry, we have to get the camera in position, and we want the look on Cynthia's face when she comes into the house after all these years, we want that to be genuine. We want this to be honest. I think that's what both of you want as well.'

That was a good one. That a reporter from the TV news/entertainment show *Deadline*, which, when it wasn't revisiting bizarre, unsolved crimes from years past, was chasing after the latest drinking-and-driving celebrity, or hunting down a pop star who'd failed to buckle her toddler into a seatbelt, would play the honesty card.

'Sure,' I said tiredly, thinking of the bigger picture here, that maybe after all these years, some TV exposure might finally provide Cynthia with some answers. 'Sure, whatever.'

Paula displayed some perfect teeth and went briskly back across the street, her high heels clicking along the pavement.

I'd been doing my best to stay out of the way since Cynthia and I had arrived here. I'd arranged to get the day off from school. My principal and long-time friend, Rolly Carruthers, knew how important it was to Cynthia to do this show, and he'd arranged a substitute teacher to take my English and creative writing classes. Cynthia took the day off from Pamela's, the dress shop where she worked. We'd dropped off our eight-year-old daughter

Grace at school along the way. Grace would have been intrigued, watching a film crew do its thing, but her introduction to TV production was not going to be a segment on her own mother's personal tragedy.

The people who lived in the house now, a retired couple who'd moved down here from Hartford a decade ago to be close to their boat in the Milford harbor, had been paid off by the producers to clear out for the day so they could have the run of the place. Then the crew had gone about removing distracting knick-knacks and personal photos from the walls, trying to make the house look – if not the way it looked when Cynthia lived there – at least as generic as possible.

Before the owners took off for a day of sailing, they'd said a few things on the front lawn for the cameras.

Husband: 'It's hard to imagine what might have happened here, in this house, back then. You wonder, were they all cut up into bits in the basement or something?'

Wife: 'Sometimes, I think I hear voices, you know? Like the ghosts of them are still walking around the house. I'll be sitting at the kitchen table, and I get this chill, like maybe the mother or the father, or the boy, has walked past.'

Husband: 'We didn't even know, when we bought the house, what had happened here. Someone else had got it from the girl, and they sold it to someone else, and then we bought it from them, but when I found out what happened here, I read up on it at the Milford library, and you have to wonder, how come she was spared? Huh? It seems a bit odd, don't you think?'

Cynthia, watching this from around the corner of one of the show's trucks, had shouted, 'Excuse me? What's that supposed to mean?'

One of the crew had whirled around and said, 'Shush!' But Cynthia would have none of it.

'Don't you fucking shush me,' she'd said. To the husband, she'd called out, 'What are you implying?'

The man had looked over, startled. He must have had no idea that the person he was talking about was actually present. The ponytail producer had taken Cynthia by the elbow and ushered her gently, but firmly, around the back of the truck.

'What kind of horseshit is that?' Cynthia had asked. 'What's he trying to say? That I had something to do with my family's disappearance? I've put up with that shit for so—'

'Don't worry about him,' the producer had said.

'You said the whole point of doing this was to help me,' Cynthia had said. 'To help me find out what happened to them. That's the only reason I agreed to do this. Are you going to run that? What he said? What are people going to think when they hear him saying that?'

'Don't worry about it,' the producer had assured her. 'We're not going to use that.'

They must have been scared Cynthia was going to walk at that point, before they had even a minute of her on film, so there had been plenty of reassurances, cajoling, promises that once this piece went on TV, for sure someone who knew something would see it. Happened all the time, they'd said. They'd closed cold cases for the cops all over the country, they'd said.

Once they had again persuaded Cynthia that their intentions were honorable, and the old farts who lived in the house had been whisked away, the show went on.

I followed two cameramen into the house, then got

out of the way as they positioned themselves to catch Cynthia's expressions of apprehension and déjà vu from different angles. I figured that once this was on TV, there'd be lots of fast editing, maybe they'd turn the image all grainy, dig around in their bag of tricks to bring more drama to an event that TV producers in decades past would have found plenty dramatic on its own.

They led Cynthia upstairs to her old bedroom. She looked numb. They wanted footage of her walking into it, but Cynthia had to do it twice. The first time, the cameraman was waiting inside her bedroom with the door closed, to get a shot of Cynthia entering the room, ever so tentatively. Then they did it again, this time from the hall, the camera looking over her shoulder as she went into the room. When it aired, you could see they'd used some fish-eye lens or something to make the scene spookier, like maybe we were going to find Jason in a goalie mask hiding behind the door.

Paula Malloy, who'd started out as a weather girl, got her make-up retouched and her blonde hair repouffed. Then she and Cynthia had those little microphone packs attached to the backs of their skirts, the wires running up and under their blouses and clipped just below their collars. Paula let her shoulder rub up against Cynthia's, like they were old friends reminiscing, reluctantly, about the bad times instead of the good.

As they came into the kitchen, cameras rolling, Paula asked, 'What must you have been thinking?' Cynthia appeared to be walking through a dream. 'You hadn't heard a sound in the house so far, your brother's not upstairs, you come down here into the kitchen and there's no sign of life at all.'

'I didn't know what was happening,' Cynthia said quietly. 'I thought everyone had left early. That my dad was gone to work, that my mother must have taken my brother to school. I thought they must be mad at me, for misbehaving the night before.'

'You were a difficult teen?' Paula asked.

'I had ... my moments. I'd been out the night before, with a boy my parents didn't approve of. I'd had something to drink. But I wasn't like some kids. I mean, I loved my parents, and I think ...' Her voice broke a bit here, '... they love me.'

'The police reports from the time indicate that you'd had an argument with your parents.'

'Yes,' Cynthia said. 'About not being home when I promised, lying to them. I said some awful things.'

'Like what?'

'Oh.' Cynthia hesitated. 'You know. Kids can say pretty hateful things to their parents that they don't really mean.'

'And where do you think they are, today, two and a half decades later?'

Cynthia shook her head sadly. 'It's all I ask myself. There's not a day goes by I don't wonder.'

'If you could say something to them, right now, here on *Deadline*, if somehow they are still alive, what would it be?'

Cynthia, nonplussed, looked somewhat hopelessly out the kitchen window.

'Look into the camera there,' Paula Malloy said, putting her hand around Cynthia's shoulder. I was off to the side, and it was all I could do not to step into the frame and peel Paula's artificial face off. 'Just ask them what you've been waiting all these years to ask them.'

Cynthia, her eyes shiny, did as she was told, looked to the camera and managed, at first, to say nothing more than, 'Why?'

Paula allowed for a dramatic pause, then asked, 'Why what, Cynthia?'

'Why,' she repeated, trying to compose herself, 'did you have to leave me? If you're able to, if you're alive, why haven't you gotten in touch? Why couldn't you have left just a simple note? Why couldn't you have at least said goodbye?'

I could feel the electricity among the crew, the producers. No one was breathing. I knew what they were thinking. This was their money shot. This was going to be fucking awesome TV. I hated them for exploiting Cynthia's misery, for milking her suffering for entertainment purposes. Because that's what this was, ultimately. Entertainment. But I held my tongue, because I knew Cynthia probably understood all this, too, that they were taking advantage of her, that she was just another story to them, a way to fill up another half-hour show. She was willing to be exploited if it meant someone watching would step forward with the key to unlock her past.

At the show's request, Cynthia had brought with her two dented cardboard shoeboxes of memories. Newspaper clippings, faded Polaroid photos, class pictures, report cards, all the bits and pieces that she'd managed to take from her house before she moved from it and went to live with her aunt, her mother's sister, a woman named Tess Berman.

They had Cynthia sit at the kitchen table, the boxes open in front of her, taking out one memory and then another, laying them out as if starting to begin a jigsaw puzzle, looking for all the pieces with straight edges, trying to assemble the border, then work toward the middle.

But there were no border pieces in Cynthia's shoeboxes. No way to work toward the center. Instead of having a thousand pieces to a single puzzle, it was like she had a single piece from a thousand different puzzles.

'This is us,' she said, showing off a Polaroid, 'on a camping trip we took up in Vermont.' The camera zoomed in on a disheveled looking Todd and Cynthia standing on either side of their mother, a tent in the background. Cynthia looked about five, her brother seven, their faces smudged with earth, their mother smiling proudly, her hair wrapped in a red-and-white checked kerchief.

'I don't have any pictures of my father,' she said mournfully. 'He always took the pictures of the rest of us, so now, I just have to remember how he looked. And I still see him, standing tall, always in his hat, that Fedora, that little hint of a moustache. A handsome man. Todd took after him.'

She reached for a yellowed piece of newsprint. 'Here's a clipping,' Cynthia said, unfolding it gingerly, 'from some things I found in my father's drawer, what little there was there.' The camera moved in again, scanned the square of newspaper. It was a faded, grainy black and white picture of a school basketball team. A dozen boys faced the camera, some smiling, some making stupid faces. 'Dad must have saved it because Todd was in it, when he was littler, although they left his name out of the caption. He was proud of us, Dad was. He told us all the time. He liked to joke that we were the best family that he'd ever had.'

They interviewed my principal, Rolly Carruthers.

'It's a mystery,' he said. 'I knew Clayton Bigge. We went fishing together a couple of times. He was a good man. I can't imagine what happened to them. Maybe there was some kind of serial killer, you know, heading across country, and Cynthia's family, they were just in the wrong place at the wrong time?'

They interviewed Aunt Tess.

'I lost a sister, a brother-in-law, a nephew,' she said. 'But Cynthia, her loss was so much greater. She managed to beat the odds, to still turn out to be a great kid, a great person.'

And while the producers kept their promise and didn't air the comments of the man who now lived in Cynthia's house, they got someone else to say something almost as sinister.

Cynthia was stunned, when the segment aired a couple of weeks later, to see the detective who'd questioned her in her house after her neighbor Mrs Jamison called the police. He was retired now, living in Arizona. At the bottom of the screen it said: 'Retired detective Bartholomew Finlay'. He'd led the initial investigation and finally moved it off his desk after a year when he wasn't getting anywhere. The producers got a crew from one of their affiliates out in Phoenix to get some comments from him sitting outside a gleaming Airstream trailer.

'The thing that always nagged at me was, why'd she survive? Assuming, of course, that the rest of the family was dead. Because I just never bought into the theory that a family would up and leave a kid behind. I could see kicking a kid out of the house who was difficult, that kind of thing happens all the time. But to go to the trouble to disappear just to be rid of one of your children? It didn't make any sense. Which had to mean some sort of foul play. Which always brought me back to the original question. Why did she survive? There aren't that many possibilities.'

'What do you mean by that?' came the voice of Paula Malloy, although the camera never wandered from Finlay. Malloy's questions had been edited in later because she hadn't been sent to Arizona to interview this guy.

'Figure it out,' Detective Finlay said.

'What do you mean, figure it out?' Malloy's voice asked.

'That's all I'll say.'

When she saw that, Cynthia was furious. 'Jesus, this again!' she shouted at the television. 'That son of a bitch is implying I had something to do with it. I've heard these whispers for years. And that Paula fucking Malloy said they weren't going to run anything like that!'

But I managed to calm her down, because the segment had been, on balance, pretty positive. The parts where Cynthia was on screen, walking through the house, telling Paula what had happened to her that day, she'd come across as sincere and believable. 'If there's someone who knows something,' I assured her, 'they're not going to be influenced by what some boneheaded retired cop says. In fact, what he said might make it even more likely for someone to step forward to contradict him.'

And so the program ran, but it was up against the season finale of some reality show featuring a bunch of overweight, aspiring rock stars who had to live under the same roof and compete to see who could shed the most pounds and win a recording contract.

Cynthia waited by the phone the moment the show finished, figuring someone would see it, someone who knew something, and call the station immediately. The producers would be in touch before the sun came up the next day, the mystery solved. Finally, she'd know the truth.

But there were no calls, other than one from a woman who said her own family had been abducted by aliens, and a man who theorized that Cynthia's folks had stepped through a tear in the fabric of time, and were either on the run from dinosaurs, or having their minds erased in some *Matrix*-like future.

No credible tips came in.

Evidently no one who knew anything saw the show. Or if they did, they weren't talking.

For the first week, Cynthia called the *Deadline* producers every day. They were nice enough, said that if they heard anything, they'd be in touch. The second week, Cynthia held off to every other day, but now the producers were getting short with her, said there was no point calling, they'd had no responses, and that if anything did come up they'd be in touch.

They were on to other stories. Cynthia quickly became old news.

TWO

Grace's eyes were pleading, but her tone was stern.

'Dad,' she said. 'I'm. Eight. Years. Old.' Where had she learned this? I wondered. This technique of breaking down sentences into individual words for dramatic effect. As if I needed to ask. There was more than enough drama to go around in this household.

'Yes,' I said to my daughter. 'I'm aware.'

Her Cheerios were getting soggy and she hadn't touched her orange juice. 'The kids make fun of me,' she said.

I took a sip of my coffee. I'd only just poured it but it was already verging on cold. The coffee maker was on the fritz. I decided I would pick up a cup at the Dunkin' Donuts on the way to school.

'Who makes fun of you?' I asked.

'Everybody,' Grace said.

'Everybody,' I repeated. 'What did they do? Did they call an assembly? Did the principal stand up there and tell everyone to make fun of you?'

'Now *you're* making fun of me.'

OK, that was true. 'I'm sorry. I'm just trying to get an idea how widespread this problem is. I'm guessing it's not *everybody*. It just feels like everybody. And even if it's only a few, I understand that can still be pretty embarrassing.'

'It *is*.'

'Is it your friends?'

'Yeah. They say Mom treats me like I'm a baby.'

'Your mom's just being careful,' I said. 'She loves you very much.'

'I know. But I'm *eight*.'

'Your mom just wants to know that you get to school safely, that's all.'

Grace sighed and bowed her head defeatedly, a lock of her brown hair dropping in front of her brown eyes. She used her spoon to move some Cheerios around in the milk. 'But she doesn't have to walk me to school. Nobody's mom walks them to school unless they're in kindergarten.'

We'd been through this before, and I'd tried talking to Cynthia, suggested as gently as possible that maybe it was time for Grace to fly solo now that she was in fourth grade. There were plenty of other kids to walk with, it wasn't as though she'd be walking all by herself.

'Why can't *you* walk me instead?' Grace asked, and there was a bit of a glint in her eye.

The rare times when I had walked Grace to school, I'd fallen behind the better part of a block. As far as anyone knew, I was just out for a stroll, not actually keeping an eye on Grace, making sure she got there safely. And we never breathed a word of it to Cynthia. My wife took me at my word, that I'd walked with Grace, right alongside her, all the way to Fairmont Public School, and stood on the sidewalk until I'd seen her go inside.

'I can't,' I said. 'I have to be at my school by eight. If I walk you to school before I go, you have to hang around outside for an hour. Your mom doesn't start work till ten, so it's not a problem for her. Once in a while, when I get a first period spare, I can walk you.'

In fact, Cynthia had arranged her hours at Pamela's so

that she'd be around each morning to make sure Grace was off to school safely. It had never been Cynthia's dream to work at a women's clothing store owned by her best friend from high school, but it allowed her to work part-time, which meant she could be home by the time school let out. In a concession to Grace, she didn't wait for her at the school door, but down the street. Cynthia could see the school from there, and it didn't take her long to spot our often pigtailed daughter in the crowd. She had tried persuading Grace to wave, so that she could pick her out even sooner, but Grace had been stubborn about complying.

The problem came when some teacher asked the class to stay after the bell had gone. Maybe it was a mass detention, or some last-minute homework instructions. Grace would sit there, panicking, not because her mom would be worrying, but because it might mean that she, worried by the delay, would come into the school and hunt her down.

'Also, my telescope's broken,' Grace said.

'What do you mean, it's broken?'

'The thingies that hold the telescope part to the standy part are loose. I sort of fixed it, but it'll probably get loose again.'

'I'll have a look at it.'

'I have to keep a lookout for killer asteroids,' Grace said. 'I'm not going to be able to see them if my telescope is broken.'

'OK.' I said. 'I'll look at it.'

'Do you know that if an asteroid hit the earth it would be like a million nuclear bombs going off?'

'I don't think it's that many,' I said. 'But I take your point, that it would be a bad thing.'

'When I have nightmares about an asteroid hitting the earth, I can make them go away if I've checked before I go to bed to make sure there isn't any coming.'

I nodded. The thing was, we hadn't exactly bought her the most expensive telescope. It was a bottom-of-the-line item. It wasn't just that you didn't want to spend a fortune on something you weren't sure your child was going to stay interested in; we simply don't have a lot of money to throw around.

'What about Mom?' Grace asked.

'What about her?'

'Does she have to walk with me?'

'I'll talk to her,' I said.

'Talk to who?' Cynthia said, walking into the kitchen.

Cynthia looked good this morning. Beautiful, in fact. She was a striking woman and I never tired of her green eyes, high cheekbones, fiery red hair. It was no longer long like when I first met her, but no less dramatic. People think she must work out, but I think it's anxiety that's helped her keep her figure. She burns off calories worrying. She doesn't jog, doesn't belong to a gym. Not that we could afford a gym membership anyway.

Like I've mentioned, I'm a high-school English teacher, and Cynthia works in retail – even though she has a family studies degree and worked for a while doing social work – so we're not exactly rolling in dough. We have this house, big enough for the three of us, in a modest neighborhood that's only a few blocks from where Cynthia grew up. You might have thought Cynthia would have wanted to put some distance between herself and that house, but I think she wanted to stay in the neighborhood, just in case someone came back and wanted to get in touch.

Our cars are both ten years old, our vacations low key. We borrow my uncle's cabin up near Montpelier for a week every summer, and three years ago, when Grace was five, we took a trip to Disney World, staying outside the park in a cheap motel in Orlando where you could hear, at two in the morning, some guy in the next room telling his girl to be careful, to ease up on the teeth.

But we have, I believe, a pretty good life, and we are, more or less, happy. Most days.

The nights, sometimes, can be hard.

'Grace's teacher,' I said, coming up with a white lie about who Grace wanted me to talk to.

'What do you want to talk to Grace's teacher for?' Cynthia asked.

'I was just saying, when it's one of those parent-teacher nights, I should go in and talk to her, to Mrs Enders,' I said. 'Last time, you went in, I had a parent-teacher thing at my school the same night, it always seems to happen that way.'

'She's very nice,' Cynthia said. 'I think she's a lot nicer than the teacher last year, what's-her-name, Mrs Phelps. I thought she was a bit mean.'

'I hated her,' Grace concurred. 'She made us stand on one leg for hours when we were bad.'

'I have to go,' I said, taking another sip of cold coffee. 'Cyn, I think we need a new coffee maker.'

'I'll look at some,' Cynthia said.

As I got up from the table Grace looked at me despairingly. I knew what she wanted from me. Talk to her. Please talk to her.

'Terry, you seen the spare key?' Cynthia asked.

'Hmm?' I said.

She pointed to the empty hook on the wall just inside the kitchen door that opened on to our small backyard. 'Where's the spare?' It was the one we used if we were taking a walk, maybe a stroll down to the sound, and didn't want to take a ring loaded with car remotes and workplace keys.

'I don't know. Grace, you got the key?' Grace did not yet have her own house key. She hardly needed it with Cynthia around to take her to and from school. She shook her head, glared at me.

I shrugged. 'Maybe it's me. I might have left it next to the bed.' I sidled up next to Cynthia, smelled her hair as I walked past. 'See me off?' I said.

She followed me to the front door. 'Something going on?' she asked. 'Is Grace OK? She seems kind of quiet this morning.'

I grimaced, shook my head. 'It's, you know. She's eight years old, Cyn.'

She moved back a bit, bristling. 'She complains about me to you?'

'She just needs to feel a bit more independent.'

'That's what that was about. She wants you to talk to me, not her teacher.'

I smiled tiredly. 'She says the other kids are making fun of her.'

'She'll get over it.'

I wanted to say something, but felt we'd had this discussion so many times, there weren't any new points to make.

So Cynthia filled the silence.

'You know there are bad people out there. The world is full of them.'

'I know, Cyn, I know.' I tried to keep the frustration, and the tiredness, out of my voice. 'But how long are you going to walk her? Till she's twelve? Fifteen? You going to walk her to high school?'

'I'll deal with that when it comes,' she said. She paused. 'I saw that car again.'

The car. There was always a car.

Cynthia could see in my face that I didn't believe there was anything to this. 'You think I'm crazy,' she said.

'I don't think you're crazy.'

'I've seen it two times. A brown car.'

'What kind of car?'

'I don't know. An average car. With tinted windows. When it drives past me and Grace it slows down a bit.'

'Has it stopped? Has the driver said anything to you?'

'No.'

'Did you get a license plate?'

'No. The first time, I didn't think anything of it. The second time, I was too flustered.'

'Cyn, it's probably just somebody who lives in the neighborhood. People have to slow down. It's a school zone up there. Remember that one day, the cops set up a speed trap? Getting people to stop speeding through there, that time of day.'

Cynthia looked away from me, folded her arms in front of her. 'You're not out there everyday like I am. You don't know.'

'What I do know,' I said, 'is that you aren't doing Grace any favors if you don't let her start fending for herself.'

'Oh, so you think, if some man tries to drag her into that car, that she's going to be able to defend herself? An eight-year-old girl?'

'How did we get from some brown car driving by to a man trying to drag her away?'

'You've never taken these things as seriously as I do.' She waited a beat. 'And I suppose that's understandable, for you.'

I puffed out my cheeks, blew out some air. 'OK, look, we're not going to solve this now,' I said. 'I have to get going.'

'Sure,' Cynthia said, still not looking at me. 'I think I'm going to call them.'

I hesitated. 'Call who?'

'The show. *Deadline*.'

'Cyn, it's been what, three weeks since the show ran? If anyone was going to call in with anything, they'd have done it by now. And besides, if the station gets any interesting calls, they're going to get in touch. They'll want to do a follow-up.'

'I'm going to give them a call anyway. I haven't called for a while, so maybe they won't get so pissed off this time. They might have heard something, figured it wasn't important, that it was some crank, but it might be something. We were lucky, you know, that some researcher even remembered what had happened to me, decided it was worth a look back.'

I turned her gently, lifted her chin so that our eyes could meet. 'OK, whatever you want to do, do,' I said. 'I love you, you know.'

'I love you, too,' she said. 'I – I know I'm not easy to live with about this stuff. I know it's hard on Grace. I know my anxieties, that they kind of rub off on her.

But lately, with that show, it's made it all very real for me again.'

'I know,' I said. 'I just want you to be able to live for the present, too. Not always fixate on the past.'

I felt her shoulders move. 'Fixate?' she said. 'Is that what you think I do?'

It was the wrong word. You'd think an English teacher could come up with something better.

'Don't patronize me,' Cynthia said. 'You think you know, but you don't. You can't ever know.'

There wasn't much I could say to that, because it was true. I leaned in and kissed her hair and went to work.

THREE

She wanted to be comforting in what she had to say, but it was just as important to be firm.

'I can understand you might find the idea a bit unsettling, really, I do. I can see where you might be feeling a bit squeamish about the whole thing, but I've been here before, and I'm telling you, I've given this a lot of thought, and this is the only way. That's the way it is with family. You have to do what you have to do, even if it's difficult, even if it's painful. Of course, what we have to do to them is going to be difficult, but you have to look at the bigger picture. But it's a bit like when they said – you're probably not old enough to remember this – that you have to destroy a village to save it. It's something like that. Think of our family as a village. We have to do whatever it takes to save it.'

She liked the 'we' part. That they were a kind of team.

FOUR

When she was first pointed out to me at the University of Connecticut, my friend Roger whispered, 'Archer, check it out. That is one seriously fucked up chick. She's hot – she's got hair like a fire engine – but she's majorly screwed up.'

Cynthia Bigge was sitting down in the second row of the lecture theatre, taking notes on literature of the Holocaust, and Roger and I were up near the top, close to the door, so we could make a break for it as soon as the professor was done droning on.

'What do you mean, fucked up?' I whispered back.

'OK, you remember that thing, a few years ago, there was this girl, her whole family disappeared, nobody ever saw them again?'

'No.' I didn't read the papers or watch the news at that time in my life. Like many teens, I was somewhat self absorbed – I was going to be the next Philip Roth or Robertson Davies or John Irving; I was in the process of narrowing it down – and oblivious to current events, except for when one of the more radical organizations on campus wanted students to protest about something or other. I tried to do my part because it was a great place to meet girls.

'OK, so her parents, her sister, or maybe it was a brother, I can't remember, they all disappeared.'

I leaned in closer, whispered, 'So what, they got killed?'

Roger shrugged. 'Who the fuck knows? That's what makes it so interesting.' He tipped his head in Cynthia's direction. 'Maybe she knows. Maybe she offed the bunch of them. Haven't you ever wanted to kill off your entire family?'

I shrugged. I guessed it crosses everyone's mind at some point.

'What I think is that she's just stuck up,' Roger said. 'She won't give you the time of day. Sticks to herself, you see her in the library all the time, just working, doing stuff. Doesn't hang out with anybody, doesn't go out to things. Nice rack, though.'

She was pretty.

It was the only course I shared with her. I was in the school of education, preparing to become a teacher, in case the whole bestselling-writer thing didn't happen immediately. My parents, retired now and living in Boca Raton, had both been teachers, and had liked it well enough. At least it was recession-proof. I asked around, learned Cynthia was enrolled in the school of family studies at the Storrs campus. It included courses in gender studies, marital issues, care of the elderly, family economics, all kinds of shit like that.

I was sitting out front of the university bookstore, wearing a UConn Huskies sweatshirt and glancing at some lecture notes, when I sensed someone standing in front of me.

'Why you asking around about me?' Cynthia said. It was the first time I'd heard her speak. A soft voice, but confident.

'Huh?' I said.

'Somebody said you were asking about me,' she repeated. 'You're Terrence Archer, right?'

I nodded. 'Terry,' I said.

'OK, so, why are you asking about me?'

I shrugged. 'I don't know.'

'What do you want to know? Is there something you want to know? If there is, just come out and ask me, because I don't like people talking about me behind my back. I can tell when it's going on.'

'Listen, I'm sorry, I only—'

'You think I don't know people talk about me?'

'God, what are you, paranoid? I wasn't *talking* about you. I just wondered whether—'

'You wondered whether I'm the one. Whose family disappeared. OK, I am. Now you can mind your own fucking business.'

'My mom's hair is red,' I said, cutting her off. 'Not as red as yours. Sort of a blondie-red, you know? But yours is really beautiful.' Cynthia blinked. 'So yeah, maybe I asked a couple of people about you, because I wondered if you were seeing anybody, and they said no, and now I guess I can see why.'

She looked at me.

'So,' I said, making a big thing of stuffing my notes into my backpack and flinging it over my shoulder. 'Sorry and all.' I stood up and turned to go.

'I'm not,' Cynthia said.

I stopped. 'You're not what?'

'I'm not seeing anybody.' She swallowed.

Now I was feeling I'd been too abrupt. 'I didn't mean to be an asshole there,' I said. 'You just seemed a bit, you know, touchy.'

We agreed that she'd been touchy and that I had been an asshole, and somehow ended up having a coffee at a campus snack bar, where Cynthia told me that she lived with her aunt when she wasn't attending university.

'Tess is pretty decent,' Cynthia said. 'She didn't have any kids of her own, so my moving in, after the thing with my family, that kind of turned her world upside-down, you know? But she was OK with it. I mean, what the hell was she going to do? And she was sort of going through a tragedy too, her sister and brother-in-law and nephew just disappearing like that.'

'So what happened to your house? Where you lived with your parents and brother?'

That was me. Mr Practical. Girl's family vanishes and I come up with a real estate question.

'I couldn't live there alone,' Cynthia said. 'And like, there was no one to pay the mortgage or anything anyway, so when they couldn't find my family the bank sort of took it back and these lawyers got involved, and whatever money my parents had put into the house went into this trust thing, but they'd hardly made a dent in the mortgage, you know? And now, it's been so long, they figure everyone is dead, right? Legally, even if they aren't.' She rolled her eyes and grimaced.

What could I say?

'So, Aunt Tess, she's putting me through school. Like, I've had summer jobs and stuff, but that doesn't cover much. I don't know how she's managed it, really, raising me, paying for my education. She must be in debt up to her eyeballs, but she never complains about it.'

'Boy,' I said. I took a sip of coffee.

And Cynthia, for the first time, smiled. 'Boy,' she said. 'That's all you have to say, Terry? *Boy?*' As quickly as it had appeared, the smile vanished. 'I'm sorry. I don't know what I expect people to say. I don't know what the fuck I'd say if I was sitting across from me.'

'I don't know how you handle it,' I said.

Cynthia took a sip of her tea. 'Some days, I just want to kill myself, you know? And then I think, what if they showed up the day after?' She smiled again. 'Wouldn't that be a kick in the head?'

Again, the smile drifted away as though carried off by a gentle breeze.

A lock of her red hair fell forward across her eyes, and she tucked it back behind her ear.

'The thing is,' she said, 'they could be dead, and they never had a chance to say goodbye to me. Or they could still be alive, and couldn't be bothered.' She looked out the window. 'I can't decide which is worse.'

We didn't say anything for another minute or so. Finally, Cynthia said, 'You're nice. If I did go out with someone, I might go out with someone like you.'

'If you get desperate,' I said, 'you know where to find me.'

She looked out the window, at other students strolling past, and for a moment, it was like she had slipped away.

'Sometimes,' she said, 'I think I see one of them.'

'What do you mean?' I asked. 'Like a ghost or something?'

'No no,' she said, still looking outside. 'Like, I'll see someone I think is my father, or my mother. From behind, say. There's just something about them, the way they hold their head, the way they walk, it seems familiar somehow, and I'll think it's them. Or, you know, I'll see a boy, maybe a year older than me, who looks like he could be my brother, seven years later. My parents, they'd still look pretty much the same, right? But my brother, he could look totally different, but there'd still be something about him that would be the same, wouldn't there?'

'I guess,' I said.

'And I'll see someone like that, and I'll run after them, cut in front of them, maybe grab their arm or something and they turn around and I get a good look.' She turned away from the window, gazed down into her tea, as though searching for an answer there. 'But it's never them.'

'I guess, someday, you'll stop doing that,' I said.

'If it's them,' Cynthia said.

We started hanging out. We went to movies, we worked together in the library. She tried to interest me in playing tennis. It had never been my game, but I gave it my best shot. Cynthia was the first to admit she wasn't a great player, just a fair player with a magnificent backhand. But it was enough of an advantage to make mincemeat out of me. When I served and saw that right arm of hers swing back over her left shoulder, I knew I had little hope of sending that ball back across the net to her. If I even saw it.

One day, I was hunched over my Royal typewriter, even then approaching antique status, a hulking machine forged out of steel and painted black, heavy as a Volkswagen, the 'e' key producing a letter that was more like a 'c' even with a fresh ribbon. I was trying to finish an essay on Thoreau I honestly didn't give a flying fuck about. It didn't help any that Cynthia was under the blanket, fully clothed, on the single bed in my dorm room, having fallen asleep reading a tattered paperback copy of *Misery* by Stephen King. Cynthia wasn't an English major and could read whatever the hell she wanted, and found comfort sometimes in reading about people who had gone through worse things than her.

I had invited her to come over and watch me type an essay.

'It's quite interesting,' I said. 'I use all ten fingers.'

'At the same time?' she asked.

I nodded.

'That does sound amazing,' she said.

So she brought some work of her own to do, and sat quietly on the bed, her back up against the wall, and there were times when I felt her watching me. We'd been hanging out but we'd barely touched each other. I'd let my hand brush across her shoulder as I'd moved past her chair in the coffee shop. I'd taken her hand to help her off the bus. Our shoulders had bumped looking up into a night sky.

Nothing more.

I thought I heard the blanket get tossed aside, but I was consumed with setting up a footnote. Then she was standing behind me, her presence somehow electric. She slipped her hands around my chest and leaned down and kissed my cheek. I turned so that she could place her lips on mine. Later, under the blanket, before it happened, Cynthia said, 'You can't hurt me.'

'I don't want to hurt you,' I said. 'I'll take it slow.'

'Not that,' she whispered. 'If you dump me, if you decide you don't want to be with me, don't worry. I can't be hurt any more than what's already happened.'

She would turn out to be wrong about that.

FIVE

As I got to know her, and as she began to let me into her heart, Cynthia told me more about her family, about Clayton and Patricia and her older brother Todd, whom she loved and hated, depending on the day.

Actually, when she'd talk about them, she'd often retract her tenses. 'My mother's name was – my mother's name *is* Patricia.' She was at odds with the part of herself that had accepted they were all dead. There were still sparks of hope, like embers in an untended campfire.

She was a part of the Bigge family. It was, of course, a kind of constant joke, given that their extended family, at least on her father's side, was pretty much non-existent. Clayton Bigge had no brothers or sisters, his parents died when he was young, no aunts or uncles to speak of. There were never any family reunions to attend, no disputes between Clayton and Patricia over which family they'd go see at Christmas, although sometimes work kept Clayton out of town during holidays.

'I'm it,' he liked to say. 'The whole family. There are no more.'

He wasn't much of a sentimentalist, either. No dusty family albums of previous generations to linger over, no snapshots of the past, no old love letters from former flames for Patricia to throw out when she married him. And back when he was fifteen, a kitchen fire got out of control and burned his family house down. A couple generations of mementoes went up in smoke. He was a day-at-a-time kind of guy, living for the moment, not interested in looking back.

There wasn't that much family on Patricia's side, either, but at least there was a history of it. Lots of pictures – in shoeboxes if not in albums – of her own parents and extended family and friends from her childhood. Her father died of polio when she was young, but her mother was still alive when she met Clayton. Thought he was charming, if a bit quiet. He'd talked Patricia into slipping away to get married, so there was no formal wedding, and that disappointed Patricia's limited family.

Her sister Tess certainly wasn't won over. She didn't think much of the way Clayton's work took him on the road more than half the time, leaving Patricia to raise her children alone for so many long stretches. But he provided for them, he was decent enough, and his love for Patricia seemed deep and genuine.

Before she met Clayton, Patricia Bigge had a job in a drugstore in Milford, on North Broad Street, looking out on the town green, just down from the old library, where she would take out classical records from the library's extensive music collection. She stocked shelves, worked the cash register, helped the pharmacist, but only with the most basic things. She didn't have the proper training, and knew she should have taken more school, learned some sort of trade, something, but mostly she had to get out there and support herself. Same for her sister Tess, who worked in a factory in Bridgeport that made parts for radios.

Clayton walked into the drugstore one day, looking for a Mars bar.

Patricia liked to say, if her husband hadn't been hit

by a Mars bar craving that day in July, 1967, as he passed through Milford on a sales trip, well, things would have turned out very differently.

As far as Patricia was concerned, they turned out fine. It was a speedy courtship, and within a few weeks of getting married she was pregnant with Todd. Clayton found them an affordable house on Hickory, just off Pumpkin Delight Road, a stone's throw from the beach and Long Island Sound. He wanted his wife and child to have a decent home to live in while he was on the road. He had responsibility for the corridor that ran roughly between New York and Chicago and up to Buffalo, selling industrial lubricants and other supplies to machine shops all along the way. Lots of regulars. Kept him busy.

A couple of years after Todd was born, Cynthia arrived.

I was thinking about all this as I drove to Old Fairfield High School. Whenever I daydreamed, I found it was often about my wife's past, her upbringing, about the members of her family I never knew, would in all likelihood never be able to know.

Maybe, if I could have had the chance to spend any time with them, I'd have more insights into what made Cynthia tick. But the reality was, the woman I knew and loved had been shaped more by what had happened since she'd lost her family – or since her family had lost her – than by what had occurred before.

I popped into the doughnut shop for a coffee, resisting the urge to buy a lemon-filled doughnut while there, and was carrying it with me into the school, a satchel full of student essays slung over my shoulder, when I saw Roland Carruthers, the principal, and probably my best friend here at this institution.

'Rolly,' I said.

'Where's mine?' he said, nodding at the paper cup in my hand.

'If you'll take my period one class I'll go back and get you one.'

'If I take your period one class I'm going to need something stronger than coffee.'

'They're not that bad.'

'They're savages,' Rolly said, not even cracking a smile.

'You don't even know what my period one class is or who's in it,' I said.

'If it's made up of students from this school, then they're savages,' Rolly said, staying in deadpan.

'What's happening with Jane Scavullo?' I asked. She was a student in my creative writing class, a troubled kid with a messed-up family background that was vague at best as far as the office was concerned, who spent nearly as much time down there as the secretaries. She also happened to write like an angel. An angel who'd happily punch your lights out, maybe, but an angel just the same.

'I told her she's this close to a suspension,' Rolly said, holding his thumb and forefinger a quarter-inch apart. Jane and another girl had gotten into an all-out, hair-pulling, cheek-scratching brawl out front of the school a couple of days earlier. A boy thing, evidently. Was it ever anything else? They attracted a sizeable cheering crowd – no one much cared who won as long as the fight kept going – before Rolly ran out and broke it up.

'What'd she say to that?'

Rolly pretended to chew gum in an exaggerated fashion, including 'snapping' sound effects.

'OK,' I said.

'You like her,' he said.

I opened the tab on the top of my takeout cup and took a sip. 'There's something there,' I said.

'You don't give up on people,' Rolly said. 'But you have good qualities, too.'

My friendship with Rolly was what you might call multi-layered. He's a colleague and friend, but because he's a couple of decades older than I am, he's something of a father figure, too. I found myself looking for him when I was in need of some wisdom, or, as I liked to say to him, perspective of the ages. I got to know him through Cynthia. If he was an unofficial father figure for me, he was an unofficial uncle to Cynthia. He had been a friend to her father, Clayton, before he went missing, and outside of her aunt Tess, was about the only person she knew with any connection to her past.

His retirement was imminent, and there were times when you could tell he was coasting, counting the days till he was out of there and down in Florida, living in his newly purchased mobile home someplace outside Bradenton, out on the water fishing for marlin or swordfish or whatever it was they pulled out of the water down there.

'You around later?' I asked.

'Yeah, sure. What's up?'

'Just ... stuff.'

He nodded. He knew what that meant. 'Drop by, after eleven would probably be good. I've got the superintendent in before that.'

I went into the staff room, checked my cubbyhole for any mail or important notices and found none, and as I turned to head back into the hall, bumped shoulders with Lauren Wells, who was also checking her mail.

'Sorry,' I said.

'Hey,' Lauren said before she realized who'd bumped into her, and then when she saw me, smiled with surprise. She was decked out in a red tracksuit and white running shoes, which made sense since she taught physical education. 'Hey, how's it going?'

Lauren had come to Old Fairfield four years ago, having transferred from a high school in New Haven where her former husband taught. When that marriage fell apart she didn't want to work in the same building with him, or so went the gossip. Having garnered a reputation for being an outstanding track and field coach whose students had won several regional competitions, she was able to pick and choose among several schools whose principals were happy to add her to their staff.

Rolly won. He told me, privately, that he hired her for what she could bring to the school, which also happened to include 'an awesome body, flowing auburn hair and gorgeous brown eyes'.

First, I said, 'Auburn? Who says auburn?'

Then, I must have given him a look because he felt obliged to say, 'Relax, it's merely an observation. The only pole I can get up these days I use to catch bass.'

In all the time Lauren Wells had been at this school I'd never been on her radar until the show about Cynthia's family had aired. Now, whenever she saw me, she asked how things were going.

'Any nibbles?' she asked.

'Huh?' I said. For a second, I thought she was asking whether anyone had brought snacks to the staff room. Some days, doughnuts miraculously appeared.

'From the show,' she clarified. 'It's been a couple of

weeks, right? Has anyone called in with any tips about what happened to Cynthia's family?'

It seemed funny, her using Cynthia's name. Not 'your wife's' family. It was like Lauren felt she knew Cynthia, even though they'd never met, at least as far as I knew. Or maybe they had at some school function where teachers brought their spouses.

'No,' I said.

'Cynthia must be *so* disappointed,' she said, laying a sympathetic hand on my arm.

'Yeah, well, it would be nice if someone came forward. There has to be somebody out there who knows something, even after all these years.'

'I think about you two all the time,' Lauren said. 'I was telling my friend about you just the other night. And you, how are you holding up? You doing OK?'

'Me?' I acted surprised. 'Yeah, sure, I'm good.'

'Because,' and Lauren's voice softened, 'sometimes you look, I don't know, maybe it's not my place to say, but sometimes I see you in the staff room, and you look kind of tired. And sad.'

I wasn't sure which struck me as more significant. That Lauren thought I'd been looking tired and sad, or that she had been watching me in the staff room.

'I'm OK,' I said. 'Really.'

She smiled. 'Good, that's good.' She cleared her throat. 'Anyway, I've got to get to the gym. We should talk some time.' She reached out, touched my arm again and held her hand there a moment before taking it away and slipping out of the staff room.

Heading to my first period creative writing class, it struck me that anyone who'd construct a high-school timetable in such a way as to make anything 'creative' come first thing in the morning either had no understanding of high-school students, or was possessed of a wicked sense of humor. I had mentioned this to Rolly, whose response was, 'That's why they call it creative. You have to be, to find a way to get kids to care that early in the day. If anyone can do it, Terry, you can.'

There were twenty-one bodies in the room as I walked in, about half of them sprawled across their desks as if someone had surgically removed their spines during the night. I set down my coffee and let my satchel hit the desk with a 'fwump'. That got their attention, because they knew what had to be inside.

At the back of the room, seventeen-year-old Jane Scavullo was sitting so low in her desk I almost couldn't see the bandage on her chin.

'OK,' I said. 'I've marked your stories and there's some good stuff here. Some of you even managed to go entire paragraphs without using the word "fuck".'

A couple of snickers.

'Can't you get fired for saying that?' asked a kid named Bruno sitting over by the window with white wires running down from his ears and disappearing into his jacket.

'I sure fucking hope so,' I said. I pointed to my own ears. 'Bruno, can you lose those for now?'

Bruno pulled out the earbuds.

I riffled through the pile of papers, most done on computer, a few handwritten, and pulled out one.

'OK, you know how I talked about how you don't necessarily have to write about people shooting each other or nuclear terrorists or aliens bursting out of people's chests for something to be interesting? How you can find stories in the most mundane of environments?'

A hand up. Bruno. 'Mun-who?'

'Mundane. Ordinary.'

'Then why didn't you say ordinary? Why you have to use a fancy word for ordinary when an ordinary word would do?'

I smiled. 'Put those things back in your ears.'

'No no, I might miss something mun-dane if I do.'

'Let me read a bit of this,' I said, holding out the paper. I could see Jane's head rise a notch. Maybe she recognized the lined paper, how the handwritten sheets had a different look to them than paper pumped out of a laser printer.

'"Her father – at least the guy who'd been sleeping with her mother long enough to think he should be called that – takes a carton of eggs out of the fridge, breaks open two of them, one-handed, into a bowl. There's bacon already sizzling in a pan, and when she walks into the room he tips his head, like he's telling her to sit down at the kitchen table. He asks how she likes her eggs and she says she doesn't care because she doesn't know what else to say because no one's ever asked her before how she likes eggs. All her mom's ever made her that's even remotely egg-like is an Eggo waffle out of a toaster. She figures whatever way this guy makes them, there's a pretty good chance they'll be better than a goddamn Eggo."'

I stopped reading and looked up. 'Comments?'

A boy behind Bruno said, 'I like my eggs runny.'

A girl on the opposite side of the room said, 'I like it. You want to know what this guy is like, like, if he cares about her breakfast, maybe he's not an asshole. All the guys my mom hooks up with are assholes.'

'Maybe the guy's making her breakfast because he wants to do her *and* her mother,' Bruno said.

Laughter.

An hour later, as they filed out, I said, 'Jane.' She sidled over to my desk reluctantly. 'You pissed?' I said.

She shrugged, ran her hand over the bandage, making me notice it by trying to keep me from noticing it.

'It was good. That's why I read it.'

Another shrug.

'I hear you're flirting with a suspension.'

'That bitch started it,' Jane said.

'You're a good writer,' I said. 'That other story you did, I submitted it to the library's short story contest, the one they have for students.'

Jane's eyes did a little dance.

'Some of your stuff, it reminds me a bit of Oates,' I said. 'You ever read Joyce Carol Oates?'

Jane shook her head.

'Try *Foxfire: Confessions of a Girl Gang*,' I said. 'Our library probably doesn't have it. Bad words. But you could find it at the Milford Library.'

'We done?' she asked.

I nodded, and she headed out the door.

I found Rolly in his office, sitting at his computer, staring at something on the monitor. He pointed at the screen. 'They want more testing. Pretty soon, we won't have any time to teach them anything. We'll just test them from the moment they get here to the moment they go home.'

'What's that kid's story?' I asked. He needed to be reminded who I was talking about.

'Jane Scavullo, yeah, shame about her,' he said. 'I don't even think we have a current address for her. The last one we have for her mother has to be a couple of years old, I think. Moved in with some new guy, brought her daughter along, too.'

'The fight aside,' I said, 'I think she's actually been a bit better the last few months. Not quite as much trouble, a little less surly. Maybe this new guy, maybe he's actually been an improvement.'

Rolly shrugged. He opened up a Girl Guide cookie box on his desk. 'Want one?' he asked, holding the box out to me.

I took a vanilla.

'It's all wearing me down,' Rolly said. 'It's not like it was when I started. You know what I found out behind the school the other day? Not just beer cans – if only – but crack pipes, and you won't believe this, a gun. Under the bushes, like it had fallen out of someone's pocket, or maybe it had been hidden there.'

I shrugged. This wasn't exactly new.

'How you doin', anyway?' Rolly asked. 'You look, I don't know, off today. You OK?'

'Maybe a bit,' I said. 'Home stuff. Cyn's having a hard time giving Grace any kind of taste of freedom.'

'She still looking for asteroids?' he said. Rolly had been over to the house with his wife, Millicent, a few times and loved talking with Grace. She'd shown him her telescope. 'Smart kid. Must get that from her mother.'

'I know why she does it. I mean, if I'd had the kind of life Cyn's had, maybe I'd hold on to things a bit tight, too, but shit, I don't know. She says there's a car.'

'A car?'

'A brown car. It's been by a couple of times when she's been walking Grace to school.'

'Has anything happened?'

'No. A couple months ago, it was a green SUV. Last year, Cyn said there was some guy with a beard on the corner, three days in one week, looked at them funny.'

Rolly took another bite of cookie. 'Maybe, lately, it's the TV show.'

'I think that's part of it. Plus this is twenty-five years since her family vanished. It's taking a bit of a toll on her.'

'I should talk to her,' Rolly said. 'Time to hit the beach.' In the years after her family's disappearance, Rolly would occasionally take Cynthia off Tess's hands for a while. They'd get an ice cream at the Carvel at Bridgeport Ave. and Clark St., then stroll the shore of Long Island Sound, sometimes talking, sometimes not.

'That might be a good idea,' I said. 'And we're seeing this psychiatrist, this woman, you know, once in a while, to talk about things. Dr Kinzler. Naomi Kinzler.'

'How's that going?'

I shrugged, then said, 'What do you think happened, Rolly?'

'How many times you asked me this, Terry?'

'I just wish this could end for Cyn, that she could get some sort of answer. I think that's what she thought the TV show would do.' I paused. 'The thing is, you knew Clayton. You went fishing with him. You had a handle on the type of person he was.'

'And Patricia.'

'They seem like the types to just walk out on their daughter?'

'No. My guess is, what I've always believed in my

heart, is that they were murdered. You know, like I told the show, a serial killer or something.'

I nodded slowly in agreement, although the police had never put much stock in that theory. There was nothing about the disappearance of Cynthia's family that was consistent with anything else they had on their books. 'Here's the thing,' I said. 'If some kind of serial killer did come to their house, took them away and killed them, why not Cynthia? Why did he leave her behind?'

Rolly had no answer for me. 'Can I ask you something?' he asked.

'Sure,' I said.

'Why do you think our fabulously engineered gym teacher would put a note in your cubbyhole, then go back a minute later and take it out again?'

'What?'

'Just remember, Terry, you're a married man.'

SIX

After Rolly finished telling me what he had observed while sitting on the far side of the staff room, supposedly reading a newspaper, he had some good news for me. Sylvia, the theatre arts teacher, was doing an early morning rehearsal the following day for the school's big annual production, which this year was 'Damn Yankees'. Half the kids from my creative writing class were involved, so my first period class was effectively wiped out. With that many missing, those who were still obliged to show up would not.

So the next morning, as Grace picked at her toast and jam, I said, 'Guess who's walking you to school today?'

Her face lit up. 'You are? Really?'

'Yeah. I already told your mom. I don't have to be in first thing today, so it's OK.'

'Are you really going to walk with me, like, right next to me?'

I could hear Cynthia coming down the stairs so I put an index finger to my lips and Grace immediately went quiet.

'So, Pumpkin, your dad's walking you today,' she said. Pumpkin. It had been Cynthia's own mother's pet name for her. 'That OK with you?'

'Sure!'

Cynthia raised an eyebrow. 'Well, I see. You don't like my company.'

'Mom,' said Grace.

Her mother smiled. If she was actually offended, she showed no signs of it. Grace, less sure than I, backtracked. 'It's just fun to walk with Dad for a change.'

'What are you looking at?' Cynthia asked me. I had the newspaper open to the real estate ads. Once a week the paper had a special section filled with houses for sale.

'Oh, nothing.'

'No, what? You thinking of moving?'

'I don't want to move,' Grace said.

'Nobody's moving,' I said. 'Just, sometimes, I think we could use a place with a little more space.'

'How could we get a place with more space – hey, that rhymes – without moving?' Grace asked.

'OK,' I said. 'So we'd have to move to get more space.'

'Unless we added on,' Cynthia said.

'Oh!' Grace said, overcome with a brainwave. 'We could build an observatory!'

Cynthia let loose with a laugh, then said, 'I was thinking more along the lines of another bathroom.'

'No no,' Grace said, not giving up yet. 'You could make a room with a hole in the ceiling so you could see the stars when it was dark out and I could get a bigger telescope to look straight up instead of out the window which totally sucks.'

'Don't say "sucks",' Cynthia said, but she was smiling.

'OK,' she said. 'Did I commit a fox pass?'

Around our house, that was the deliberately dumb pronunciation of *faux pas*. It had been an in-joke between Cynthia and me for so long, Grace had genuinely come to believe this was how you described a social misstep.

'No, honey, that's not a fox pass,' I said. 'That's just a word we don't want to hear.'

Switching gears, Grace asked, 'Where's my note?'

'What note?' her mother asked.

'About the trip,' she said. 'You were supposed to do a note.'

'Honey, you never said anything about any note for any trip,' Cynthia said. 'You can't spring these things on us at the last minute.'

'What's it for?' I asked.

'We're supposed to visit the fire station today, and we can't go if we don't have a note giving us permission.'

'Why didn't you tell us about this soon—'

'Don't worry about it,' I said. 'I'll bang off a note.'

I ran upstairs to what would be our third bedroom, but was a combined sewing room and office. Tucked into the corner was a desk where Cynthia and I shared a computer and I did my marking and lesson planning. Also sitting on the desk was my old Royal typewriter from university days, which I still used for short notes since my handwriting is terrible, and I find it easier to roll a piece of paper into a typewriter than turn on the computer, open up Word, create and write a document, print it out, etc.

So I typed a short note to Grace's teacher giving our daughter permission to leave school grounds to tour the fire station. I only hoped the fact that the 'e' key resembling a 'c' didn't create any confusion, especially when my daughter's name came out looking like 'Gracc'.

I came back downstairs, handed Grace the note, folded, and told her to tuck it into her backpack so she wouldn't lose it.

At the door, Cynthia said to me, 'Make sure you see

her go into the building.' Grace, out of earshot, was in the driveway, twirling around like a post-hole digger.

'What if they play outside for a while first?' I said. 'They see some guy like me loitering around the schoolyard, aren't they going to call the cops?'

'If I saw you out there I'd arrest you in a minute,' Cynthia said. 'Just get her to the schoolyard then. That's all.' She pulled me closer to her. 'So when exactly do you have to be to school?'

'Not till start of second period.'

'So you've got almost an hour,' she said, and she gave me a look that I did not get to see quite as often as I'd like.

'Yes,' I said very evenly. 'You are correct, Mrs Archer. Did you have something in mind?'

'Perhaps I do, Mr Archer.' Cynthia gave me a smile and kissed me very lightly on the lips.

'Won't Grace seem suspicious when I tell her we have to run the whole way to school?'

'Just go,' she said and ushered me out the door.

'So, what's the plan?' Grace asked as we started off down the sidewalk, next to each other.

'Plan?' I said. 'There's no plan.'

'I mean, how far are you going to walk me?'

'I'd thought I'd go right in with you, maybe sit in class with you for an hour or so.'

'Dad, don't joke.'

'Who says I'm joking? I'd like to sit in class with you. See if you're doing your work properly.'

'You wouldn't even fit in the desk,' Grace pointed out.

'I could sit on top of it,' I said. 'I'm not particular.'

'Mom seemed kind of happy today,' Grace said.

'Of course she did,' I said. 'Mom's happy lots of times.' Grace gave me a look to suggest that I was not being totally honest here. 'Your mom has a lot on her mind these days. This hasn't been an easy time for her.'

'Because it's been twenty-five years,' Grace said. Just like that.

'Yeah,' I said.

'And because of the TV show,' she said. 'I don't see why you guys won't let me see it. You taped it, right?'

'Your mother doesn't want to upset you,' I said. 'About the things that happened to her.'

'One of my friends taped it,' Grace said quietly. 'I've sort of already seen it, you know.' A kind of 'so there' tone in her voice.

'How did you see it?' I asked. Cynthia kept our daughter on such a short leash that she would know if Grace went to a friend's house after school. Had Grace smuggled home a tape, watched it with the volume down while we were up in the study?

'I went to her house at lunch,' Grace said.

Even when they were eight, you couldn't keep a lid on things. Five years and she'd be a teenager. Jesus.

'Whoever let you see it shouldn't have,' I said.

'I thought the cop was mean,' she said.

'What cop? What are you talking about?'

'The one on the show? He lives in a trailer? One of those shiny ones? Who said it was weird that Mom was the only one left? I could tell what he was hinting. He was hinting that Mom did it. That she killed everybody.'

'Yeah, well, he was an asshole.'

Grace whipped her head around and looked at me. 'Fox pass,' she said.

'Just swearing isn't a fox pass,' I said, shaking my head, not wanting to get into it.

'Did Mom like her brother? Todd?'

'Yes. She loved him. She had fights with him, just like lots of brothers and sisters do, but she loved him. And she didn't kill him or her mother or her father, and I'm sorry you saw that show and heard that asshole – yes, asshole – detective suggest such a thing.' I paused. 'Are you going to tell your mother that you saw the show?'

Grace, still a bit dumbstruck by my shameless use of a bad word, shook her head no. 'I think she'd freak out.'

That was probably true, but I didn't want to say so. 'Well, maybe you should talk to her about it some time, when everyone's having a good day.'

'Today's going to be good,' Grace said. 'I didn't see any asteroids last night, so we should be OK at least until tonight.'

'Good to know.'

'You should probably stop walking with me now,' Grace said. Up ahead, I saw some school kids about her age, maybe even her friends. More kids were funneling onto our street from side streets. The school was visible three blocks up.

'We're getting close,' Grace said. 'You can watch me from here.'

'OK,' I said. 'Here's what we're going to do. You start pulling ahead of me. I'll do my old man walk. Like Tim Conway.'

'Who?'

I started shuffling and Grace giggled. 'Bye, Dad,' she said, and quickened her pace. I kept my eyes on her as I took my tiny steps, being overtaken by other children walking and on bikes and skateboards and inline skates.

She didn't glance back. She was running to catch up with friends, shouting, 'Wait up!' I slipped my hands into my pockets, thought about getting back to the house and having a few private moments with Cynthia.

That was when the brown car drove past.

It was an older North American model, fairly generic, an Impala I think, a bit of rust around the wheel wells. Windows tinted, but it was one of those cheap tint jobs, the glass covered with air bubbles, like the car had measles or something.

I stood and watched as it headed down the street, down to the last corner before the school, where Grace was chattering away with two of her friends.

The car stopped at the corner, a few yards away from Grace, and my heart was in my mouth for a moment.

And then one of the brown car's rear tail-lights started to flash, the car turned right, and disappeared down the street.

Grace and her friends, aided by a crossing guard in a bright orange vest and wielding a huge STOP sign, made it across the street and on to school property. To my amazement, she looked back and waved at me. I raised my hand in return.

So, OK, there was a brown car. But no man jumped out of it and ran after our daughter. No man jumped out and ran after anyone else's kid, either. If the driver happened to be some crazed serial killer – as opposed to a perfectly sane serial killer – he wasn't up to any serial killing this morning.

It appeared to be some guy going to work.

I stood there another moment, watching as Grace was swallowed up by a throng of fellow students, and felt a sadness wash over me. In Cynthia's world, everyone was plotting to take away your loved ones.

Maybe, if I hadn't been thinking that way, I'd have had a bit more of a spring in my step as I walked back in the direction of home. But as I approached our house, I tried to shake off my gloominess, to put myself into a better frame of mind. My wife, after all, was waiting for me, very likely under the covers.

So I sprinted the remainder of the last block home, walked briskly up the driveway, and as I came through the front door I called out, 'I'm baaaaaack.'

There was no response.

I thought that had to mean Cynthia was already in bed, waiting for me to come upstairs, but as I hit the base of the stairs I heard a voice from the kitchen.

'In here,' Cynthia said. Her voice was subdued.

I stood in the doorway. She was sitting at the kitchen table, the phone in front of her. Her face seemed drained of color.

'What?' I asked.

'There was a call,' Cynthia said quietly.

'Who from?'

'He didn't say who he was.'

'Well, what did he want?'

'All he said was he had a message.'

'What kind of message?'

'He said they forgive me.'

'What?'

'My family. He said they forgive me for what I did.'

SEVEN

I sat down next to Cynthia at the kitchen table. I put one hand over hers and could feel her shaking. 'OK,' I said. 'Just try to remember what he said exactly.'

'I told you,' she said, clipping her words. She bit into her upper lip. 'He said – OK, wait a minute.' She pulled herself together. 'The phone rang and I said hello, and he said, "Is this Cynthia Bigge?" Which threw me, calling me by that name, but I said it was. And he said, I couldn't believe he said this, he said, "Your family, they forgive you."' She paused. '"For what you did."

'I didn't know what to say. I think I just asked him who he was, what he was talking about.'

'Then what did he say?'

'He didn't say anything else. He just hung up.' A solitary tear ran down Cynthia's cheek as she looked into my face. 'Why would he say something like that? What does he mean, they forgive me?'

'I don't know,' I said. 'It's probably some nut. Some nut who saw the show.'

'But why would a person call and say something like that? What would the point be?'

I pulled the phone over closer to me. It was the only hi-tech one we had in the house, with a small caller-ID display screen.

'Why would he say my family forgives me? What does my family think I did? I don't understand. And if they think I did something to them, then how can they even tell me they forgive me? It doesn't make any sense, Terry.'

'I know. It's crazy.' My eyes were on the phone. 'Did you see where the call was coming from?'

'I looked and it didn't say, and then when he hung up I tried to check the number.'

I pressed the button that displayed the call history. There was no record of a call in the last few minutes.

'It's not showing anything,' I said.

Cynthia sniffed, wiped the tear from her cheek and leaned over the phone. 'I must have ... what did I do? When I went to check where the call came from I pressed this button to save it.'

'That's how you delete it,' I said.

'What?'

'You deleted the last call from the history,' I said.

'Oh shit,' Cynthia said. 'I was so flustered, I was upset, I just didn't know what I was doing.'

'Sure,' I said. 'So, this man, what did he sound like?'

Cynthia wasn't listening to my question. She had a vacant look on her face. 'I can't believe I did that. I can't believe I deleted the number. But nothing showed up on the screen anyway. You know when it says it's an unknown number?'

'OK, let's not worry about that any more. But the man, what did he sound like?'

Cynthia half raised her hands in a gesture of futility. 'It was just a man. He was talking kind of low, like maybe he was trying to disguise it, you know. But there wasn't really anything.' She paused, then her eyes flashed with an idea. 'Maybe we should call the phone company. They might have a record of the call, maybe they'd even have a recording of it.'

'They don't keep recordings of everybody's phone calls,' I said. 'No matter what some people may think. And what are we going to tell them? It was one isolated call, from a nut who probably saw the show. He didn't threaten you, he didn't even use obscene language.'

I slipped an arm around Cynthia's shoulder. 'Just ... don't worry about it. Too many people know about what happened to you. It can make you a target. You know what we should look into?'

'What?'

'An unlisted number. We could get an unlisted number, then we wouldn't get calls like this.'

Cynthia shook her head. 'No, we're not doing that.'

'I don't think it costs that much more, and besides—'

'No, we're not doing it.'

'Why not?'

She swallowed. 'Because when they are ready to call, when my family finally decides to get in touch, they have to be able to reach me.'

I had a free period after lunch, so I slipped out of the school, drove across town to Pamela's and went inside the store with four takeout cups of coffee.

It's not what you'd call a high-end clothing store, and Pamela Forster, at one time Cynthia's best friend in high school, was not aiming for a young, hip clientele. The racks were filled with fairly conservative apparel, the kind of clothes, I liked to joke with Cynthia, preferred by women who wear sensible shoes.

'OK, so it's not exactly Abercrombie & Fitch,' Cynthia would concede. 'But A&F wouldn't let me work whatever hours I want so I can pick up Grace after school, but Pam will.'

There was that.

Cyn was standing at the back of the shop, outside a change room, talking to a customer through the curtain. 'Do you want to try that in a twelve?' she asked.

She hadn't spotted me, but Pam had, and she smiled from behind the register. 'Hey.' Pam, tall, thin and small-chested, carried herself well on three-inch heels. Her knee-length turquoise dress was stylish enough to suggest that it had not come from her own stock. Just because she was appealing to a clientele unfamiliar with the pages of Vogue didn't mean she had to completely tone it down herself.

'You're too kind,' she said, looking at the four cups of coffee. 'But it's just me and Cyn holding down the fort at the moment. Ann's on a break.'

'Maybe it'll still be warm by the time she gets back.'

Pam prized off the plastic lid, sprinkled in a packet of Splenda. 'So, how's things?'

'Good.'

'Cynthia says still nothing. From the show.'

Was this what everyone wanted to talk about? Lauren Wells, my own daughter, now Pamela Forster?

'That's right,' I said.

'I told her not to do it,' Pam said, shaking her head.

'You did?' This was news to me.

'Long time ago. When they first called about doing it. I told her, honey, let sleeping dogs lie. No sense stirring up that shit.'

'Yeah, well,' I said.

'I said, look, it's been twenty-five years, right? Whatever happened, it happened, if you can't move on with your life after this much water's gone under the bridge, well, where are you going to be in another five years, or ten?'

'She never mentioned this,' I said. Cynthia had caught sight of us talking and waved, but didn't move from her post outside the change room curtain.

'The lady in there, trying shit on she can't hope to fit into?' Pamela whispered. 'She's walked out of here before with stuff she didn't pay for, so we keep an eye on her when she's here. Lots of personal service.'

'She shoplifted?' I said, and Pamela nodded.

'If she stole, why don't you charge her? Why do you let her back in?'

'Can't prove it. We just have our suspicions. We kind of let her know we know, without saying it, never let her out of our sight.'

I started forming an image of the woman behind the curtain. Young, a bit rough-looking, kind of cocky. The kind of person you'd pick out of a lineup as a shoplifter, with maybe a tattoo on her shoulder.

The curtain slid back and a short, stocky woman in her late forties, early fifties maybe, stepped out, handing several outfits to Cynthia. If I had to stereotype her, I would have said librarian. 'I just don't see anything today,' she said politely and walked past Pamela and me on her way out.

'Her?' I said to Pamela.

'A regular Catwoman,' Pamela said.

Cynthia came over, kissed me on the cheek and said, 'A coffee run? What's the occasion?'

'I had a free period,' I said. 'Just figured, you know.'

Pamela excused herself to the back of the store, taking her coffee with her.

'Because of this morning?' Cynthia asked.

'You were kind of shook up after the phone call. I wanted to see how you were doing.'

'I'm good,' she said, with limited conviction, and took a sip of her coffee. 'I'm OK.'

'I never knew Pam tried to talk you out of doing *Deadline*.'

'You spoke against it, too, at first.'

'You just never mentioned her talking against the idea.'

'You know Pam's never been one to keep her opinion to herself. She also thinks you could lose five pounds.'

She'd blown the wind out of my sails. 'So, that lady, the one who was trying on clothes? She's a shoplifter?'

'You think you can spot the bad guy, but you can't always,' Cynthia said, taking another sip.

This was the day where we met with Dr Naomi Kinzler after work. Cynthia had arranged to drop Grace off at a friend's house after school, and then we headed over. We'd been seeing Dr Kinzler once every two weeks for the last four months, after being referred to her by our family physician. He'd been trying, without success, to help Cynthia deal with her anxieties, and felt it would be better for her to talk to someone – for both of us to talk to someone – rather than see her becoming dependent on a prescription.

I'd been skeptical from the beginning whether there was anything a psychiatrist could accomplish, and after coming here for almost ten sessions, I hadn't become any more convinced. Dr Kinzler had an office in a medical building in the east end of Bridgeport that had a view of the turnpike when she didn't have the blinds closed, as she did today. I suppose she had noticed me looking out the window during previous visits, my mind drifting as I counted tractor trailers.

Sometimes Dr Kinzler met with us together, other times one of us would step out to allow her some one-on-one with the other.

I'd never been to a shrink before. About all I knew came from watching *The Sopranos*' Dr Melfi help Tony work through his problems. I couldn't decide whether ours were more or less serious than his. Tony had people disappearing around him all the time, but he was often the one who'd arranged it. He had the advantage of knowing what had happened to these people.

Naomi Kinzler wasn't exactly Dr Melfi. She was short and plump with gray hair pulled back and pinned into submission. She was pushing seventy, I guessed, and had been at this kind of thing long enough to figure out how to keep everyone else's pain from burrowing under her own skin and staying there.

'So, what's new since our last session?' she asked.

I didn't know whether Cynthia was going to mention the crank call from that morning. At some level, I guess I didn't want to get into it, didn't really think it was that big a deal, felt we'd smoothed it over during my visit to the shop, so before Cynthia could say anything, I said, 'Things are good. Things have been very good.'

'How's Grace?'

'Grace is good,' I said. 'Walked her to school this morning. We had a nice talk.'

'About what?' Cynthia asked.

'Just a chat. Just talking.'

'Is she still checking the night skies?' Dr Kinzler asked. 'For meteors?'

I waved my hand dismissively. 'It's nothing.'

'You think?' she replied.

'Oh yeah,' I said. 'She's just very interested in the solar system, in space, other planets.'

'But you did buy her the telescope.'

'Sure.'

'Because she's worried an asteroid will destroy the earth,' Dr Kinzler reminded me.

'It's helped put her fears at ease, plus she uses it to look at the stars and the planets,' I said. 'And the other neighbors, for all I know.' I smiled.

'How about her anxiety level overall? Would you say it's still somewhat heightened, or is it dissipating?'

'Dissipating,' I said. 'Still up there,' Cynthia said at the same time.

Dr Kinzler's eyebrows went up a notch. I hated it when they did that.

'I think she's still anxious,' Cynthia said, glancing at me. 'She's very fragile at times.'

Dr Kinzler nodded thoughtfully. She was looking at Cynthia when she asked, 'Why do you think that is?'

Cynthia wasn't stupid. She knew where Dr Kinzler was going. She'd gone down this road before. 'You think it's rubbing off me.'

Dr Kinzler's shoulders raised a fraction of an inch. A conservative shrug. 'What do you think?'

'I try not to worry in front of her,' Cynthia said. 'We try not to talk about things in front of her.'

I guess I made a noise, a snort or a sniff or something, enough to get their attention.

'Yes?' Dr Kinzler said.

'She knows,' I said. 'Grace knows a lot more than she lets on. She's seen the show.'

'What?' Cynthia said.

'She saw it at a friend's house.'

'Who?' Cynthia demanded. 'I want a name.'

'I don't know. And I don't think there's any point beating it out of Grace.' I glanced at Dr Kinzler. 'That was just a figure of speech.'

Dr Kinzler nodded.

Cynthia bit her lower lip. 'She's not ready. She doesn't need to know these things about me. Not now. She needs to be protected.'

'That's one of the toughest things about being a parent,' Dr Kinzler said. 'Realizing that you can't protect your children from everything.'

Cynthia let that sink in a moment, then said, 'There was a phone call.'

She gave Dr Kinzler the details, offered up a near-verbatim account. Dr Kinzler asked a few questions that were similar to mine. Did she recognize the voice? Had he ever called before? That kind of thing. Then, 'What do you think the caller meant by that, that your family wants to forgive you.'

'It doesn't mean anything,' I said. 'It was just a crank call.'

Dr Kinzler gave me a look that I took to mean, 'Shut up.'

'That's the part I keep thinking about,' Cynthia said. 'What's he saying they forgive me for? For not finding them? For not doing more to find out what happened to them?'

'You could hardly be expected to,' Dr Kinzler said. 'You were a child. Fourteen is still a child.'

'And then I wonder, do they think it was my fault that it happened in the first place? Was it my fault that they left? What could I have done that would make them leave me in the middle of the night?'

'There's part of you that still believes that it was somehow your responsibility,' Dr Kinzler said.

'Look,' I said before Cynthia could respond. 'It was a *crank call*. All sorts of people saw that show. It shouldn't be a surprise that a few nutcases would come out of the woodwork.'

Dr Kinzler sighed softly and looked at me. 'Terry, maybe this would be a good time for Cynthia and me to speak one on one.'

'No, it's OK,' Cynthia said. 'He doesn't have to go.'

'Terry,' Dr Kinzler said, trying so hard to be patient that I could tell she was pissed. 'Of course it may have been a crank call, but what the caller said can trigger feelings in Cynthia just the same, and by understanding her reaction to those feelings we have a better chance of working through this.'

'What is it, exactly, we're working through?' I asked. I wasn't trying to be argumentative: I really wanted to know. 'I'm not trying to be a jerk here, I guess I've just lost sight of the goal for the moment.'

'What we're attempting to do here is help Cynthia deal with a traumatic incident in her childhood that's resonating to this day, not just for her own sake, but for the sake of the relationship the two of you share.'

'Our relationship is fine,' I said.

'He doesn't always believe me,' Cynthia blurted.

'What?'

'You don't always believe me,' she said again. 'I can tell. Like when I told you about the brown car. You don't think there's anything to it. And when that man called this morning, when you couldn't find it in the call history, you wondered whether there'd even been a call.'

'I never said that,' I said. I looked at Dr Kinzler, as if she were a judge and I a defendant desperate to prove his innocence. 'That's not true. I never said anything like that at all.'

'But I know you were thinking it,' Cynthia said, but there was no anger in her voice. She reached over and touched my arm. 'And honestly, I don't entirely blame you. I know what I've been like. I know I've been hard to live with. Not just these last few months, but ever since we got married. This has always hung over us. I try to put it away, like trying to put it in the closet, but every once in a while, it's like I open that door by mistake and everything spills out. When we met—'

'Cynthia, you don't—'

'When we met I knew getting close to you would only bring you some of the pain I'd been feeling, but I was selfish. I wanted to share your love so desperately, even if that meant you'd have to share my pain.'

'Cynthia.'

'And you've been so patient, you really have. And I love you for it. You have to be the most patient man in the world. If I were you, I'd be exasperated with me, too. Get over it, right? It happened a long time ago. Like Pam said. Just get the fuck over it.'

'I'd never say anything like that.'

Dr Kinzler watched us.

'Well, I've said it to myself,' Cynthia said. 'Hundreds of times. And I wish I could. But sometimes, and I know this is going to sound crazy ...'

Dr Kinzler and I were both very quiet.

'Sometimes, I hear them. I can hear them talking, my

mother, my brother. Dad. I can hear them like they're right here in the room with me. Just talking.'

Dr Kinzler spoke up first. 'Do you talk back?'

'I think so,' Cynthia said.

'Are you dreaming when this happens?' Dr Kinzler asked.

Cynthia pondered. 'I must be. I mean, I don't hear them right now.' She cracked a sad smile. 'I didn't hear them in the car on the way over.'

Inside, I breathed a sigh of relief.

'So, maybe it's when I'm sleeping, or daydreaming. But it's like they're around me, like they're trying to talk to me.'

'What are they trying to say?' Dr Kinzler asked.

Cynthia took her hand off my arm and linked her own fingers together in her lap. 'I don't know. It varies. Sometimes, it's just talk. About nothing in particular. About what we're having for dinner, or what's on TV, nothing important. And then other times ...'

I must have looked as though I was about to say something, because Dr Kinzler shot me another look. But I wasn't. My mouth had opened in anticipation, wondering what Cynthia was going to say. This was the first I'd heard her speak about hearing members of her family speak to her.

'Other times, I think they're asking me to join them.'

'Join them?' Dr Kinzler said.

'To come and be with them, so that we can all be a family again.'

'What do you say back to them?' Dr Kinzler asked.

'I tell them I want to go, but I can't.'

'Why?' I asked.

Cynthia looked into my eyes and smiled sadly. 'Because where they are, I might not be able to take you and Grace with me.'

EIGHT

'What if I skipped all this other stuff, and just did it right away?' he asked. 'Then I could come home.'

'No no no,' she said, almost in a scolding tone. She took a moment, tried to let the calm wash over her. 'I know you'd like to come back. There's nothing I'd like more. But we need to get these other things out of the way first. You mustn't be impatient. There were times, when I was younger, when I was a bit impetuous, too impulsive. I know now it's better to take the time to do something right.' She could hear him sigh at the other end of the line.

'I don't want to screw it up,' he said.

'And you won't. You've always been a pleaser, you know. It's nice to have at least one in the house.' Half a chuckle. 'You're a good boy and I love you more than you'll ever know.'

'I'm not really a boy any more.'

'And I'm no little girl any more either, but I'll always think of how you were when you were younger.'

'It's going to feel weird . . . doing it.'

'I know. But that's what I'm trying to tell you. If you're patient, when the time comes, once the stage is set, it'll seem like the most natural thing in the world.'

'I suppose.' He didn't sound convinced.

'That's the thing you need to remember. What you're doing, it's all part of a grand cycle. That's what we're a part of. Have you seen her yet?'

'Yeah. It was strange. Part of me wanted to say hello, say to her, hey, you won't believe who I am.'

NINE

The next weekend, we went up to see Cynthia's aunt Tess, who lived in a small, modest house about halfway up to Derby, just off the heavily wooded Derby Milford Rd. She lived less than twenty minutes away, but we didn't get up to see her nearly as often as we should. So when there was a special occasion, like Thanksgiving or Christmas, or, as was the case this particular weekend, her birthday, we made a point of getting together.

That was fine with me. I loved Tess nearly as much as I did Cynthia. Not just for being such a great old gal – when I called her that I ran the risk of a dirty yet playful look – but for what she had done for Cynthia in the wake of her family's disappearance. She'd taken in a young teenage girl who was, Cynthia would be the first to admit, a handful at times.

'There was never any choice,' Tess told me once. 'She was my sister's daughter. And my sister was gone, along with her husband, and my nephew. What the hell else could I have done?'

Tess had a way of being cantankerous, slightly abrasive, but it was an act she'd developed to protect herself. She was all marshmallow below the surface. Not that she hadn't earned the right, over the years, to be a bit cranky. Her own husband had left her, before Cynthia had come to live with her, for a barmaid from Stamford, and, as Tess told it, they'd fucked off to some place out west never to be heard from again, and thank Christ for that. Tess, who had left her job with the radio factory years earlier, found a job with the county, clerical work in the roads department, and made just enough to support herself and pay the utilities. There wasn't much left to raise a teenage girl, but you did what you had to do. Tess had never had children of her own, and with her no-good husband gone, it was nice to have someone to share her home with, even if the circumstances that brought Cynthia to her were shrouded in mystery, and undoubtedly tragic.

Tess was in her late sixties now, retired, getting by on social security and her county pension. She gardened and pottered about, took the occasional bus trip like the one she took last fall up through Vermont and New Hampshire to look at the changing leaves – 'Jesus, a bus full of old people, I thought I'd kill myself' – but she didn't have much of a social life. Not a joiner, not inclined to attend retirement association meetings. But she kept up with the news, maintained her subscriptions to *Harper's* and *The New Yorker* and *The Atlantic Monthly* and was not bashful about offering her left-of-center political opinions. 'That president,' she said to me on the phone one day. 'He makes a bag of hammers look like a Nobel Prize winner.'

Spending most of her teenage years with Tess had helped shape Cynthia's attitude and perspective as well, and no doubt contributed to her decision to pursue, in the early years of our marriage, a career in social work.

And Tess did love to see us. Especially Grace.

'I was going through some boxes of old books in the basement,' Tess said, flopping into her La-Z-Boy after we'd done the hug thing. 'And look what I came across.'

She leaned forward in her chair, moved aside a copy of *The New Yorker* that had been hiding something else, and handed Grace an oversized hardcover book, *Cosmos*, by Carl Sagan. Grace's eyes went wide, looking at the kaleidoscope of stars on the cover.

'It's a pretty old book,' Tess said, as if apologizing for her thoughtfulness. 'Nearly thirty years, and the guy who wrote it, he's dead now, and there's lots better stuff now on the Internet, but there might be something in there to catch your interest.'

'Thank you!' Grace said, taking the book in her hands and nearly dropping it, not expecting it to be quite so heavy. 'Is there anything in here on asteroids?'

'Probably,' Tess said.

Grace ran down to the basement, where I knew she'd cuddle up on the couch in front of the TV, maybe wrap a blanket around herself while she leafed through the pages of the book.

'That was sweet,' Cynthia said, leaning over and giving Tess probably her fourth kiss since we'd arrived.

'Didn't make any sense to throw the damn thing out,' Tess said. 'I could have donated it to the library, but you think they want thirty-year-old books? How are you, sweetheart?' she asked Cynthia. 'You look tired.'

'Oh, I'm fine,' Cynthia said. 'You? You look kind of beat today too.'

'Oh, I'm OK, I guess,' Tess said, peering at us over her reading glasses.

I held up a loaded shopping bag with twine handles. 'We have some things.'

'Oh, you shouldn't have,' Tess said. 'Hand me my loot.'

We called Grace back up so she could see Tess receive

some new gardening gloves, a red and green silk scarf, a package of fancy biscuits. Tess oohed and ahed over each thing as it came out of the bag.

'The cookies are from me,' Grace announced. 'Aunt Tess?'

'Yes, sweetheart?'

'Why do you have so much toilet paper?'

'Grace!' Cynthia scolded.

'That,' I said to Grace, 'is a fox pass.'

Tess waved dismissively, suggesting it would take more than that to embarrass her. Like a lot of older people, Tess tended to stockpile certain staples. Her basement storage cupboards were loaded with two-ply. 'When it's on sale,' Tess said. 'I pick up extra.'

As Grace retreated again to the basement, Tess quipped, 'When the apocalypse comes, I'll be the only one left who can wipe her ass.' The gift presentations seemed to have exhausted her, and she leaned back into her chair with a deep sigh.

'You alright?' Cynthia asked.

'I'm peachy,' she said. Then, as if she'd just remembered something, 'Oh, I can't believe it. I meant to buy some ice cream for Grace.'

'That's OK,' Cynthia said. 'We thought we'd take you out for dinner, anyway. How about Knickerbocker's? You love the potato skins.'

'I don't know,' Tess said. 'I suppose I am a bit off today, tired. Why don't we have dinner here? I have some things. But I really wanted some ice cream.'

'I can go,' I said. I could drive up to Derby and find a grocery store or a 7-Eleven.

'I could use a couple of other things,' Tess said.

'Cynthia, maybe you should go, you know if we send him he'll just get it all wrong.'

'I suppose,' Cynthia said.

'And there's some things I'd like Terry to carry down to the basement from the garage while he's here, if you don't mind, Terry.'

I said sure. Tess made up a short list, handed it to Cynthia, who said she probably wouldn't be gone more than thirty minutes. I wandered into the kitchen as Cynthia went out the door, glanced at the bulletin board next to the wall-mounted phone where Tess had pinned a picture of Grace taken at Disney World. I opened the freezer compartment of the refrigerator, looking for some ice to put in a glass of water.

In the front of the freezer was a container of chocolate ice cream. I took it out, prized off the lid. It had one scoop out of it. Getting a bit absent-minded in her old age, I figured.

'Hey, Tess,' I said. 'You've already got ice cream here.'

'Is that a fact?' she said from the living room.

I put the ice cream back, closed the freezer, and took a seat on the couch by Tess. 'What's going on?' I asked.

'I've been to the doctor,' Tess said.

'What? What's wrong?'

'I'm dying, Terry.'

'What do you mean? What's wrong?'

'Don't worry, it's not going to happen overnight. I might have six months, I might have a year. You never really know. Some people, they can hang on quite a while, but I'm not looking forward to some long, drawn out kind of thing. That's no way to go. Tell you the truth, I'd like to go fast, just like that, you know? Lot simpler that way.'

'Tess, tell me what's wrong.'

She shrugged. 'Doesn't really matter. They've done some tests, they've got a couple more they have to do to be sure, but they'll probably just tell me the same thing. The upshot is, I can see the finish line. And I wanted to tell you first, because Cynthia, she's been going through a lot lately. Twenty-five years, the TV show.'

'There was an anonymous call the other day,' I said. 'That shook her up pretty bad.'

Tess closed her eyes briefly and shook her head. 'Nuts. They see something on TV, they get out the phone book.'

'That's the way I figure it.'

'But Cynthia's going to have to know eventually, that I'm not well. I guess it's a matter of finding the right time.'

We heard noises on the stairs. Grace emerged from the basement, lugging her new book with both hands. 'Did you know,' she said, 'that even though the moon looks like it's been hit with way more asteroids than the earth, the earth has probably been hit with just as many, but because the earth has atmosphere, the atmosphere smoothes the land so you don't see all the craters, but there's not any air or anything on the moon, so when it gets hit by an asteroid, it just looks that way for ever?'

'Good book, huh?' said Tess.

Grace nodded. 'I'm hungry,' she said.

'Your mother has gone to pick up a few things,' I said.

'She's not here?'

I shook my head. 'She'll be back soon. But there's some ice cream in the freezer. Chocolate.'

'Why don't you take the whole container downstairs,' Tess said. 'And a spoon.'

'For real?' Grace asked. This violated every rule of etiquette she knew.

'Go for it,' I said.

She ran into the kitchen, dragged a chair over to reach the freezer compartment, grabbed the ice cream and a spoon from the drawer, and ran back downstairs.

Tess's eyes were moist when I looked back at her.

'I think you should be the one to tell Cynthia,' I said.

She reached out and held my hand. 'Oh, of course, I wouldn't make you do that. I just needed to tell you first, so when I tell Cynthia, you'll be ready to help her through it.'

I said, 'She'll have to help me through it, too.'

Tess grinned at that. 'You turned out to be a pretty good catch for her. I wasn't so sure at first, you know.'

'So you've said.' I smiled.

'You seemed a bit serious to me. Very earnest. But you turned out to be perfect. I'm so glad she found you, all the heartache she's had.'

Then Tess looked away, but squeezed my hand a little harder. 'There's something else,' she said.

The way she said it was as though the thing she still had to tell me was bigger than the fact that she was dying.

'There are some things I need to tell, while I'm still able to, to get off my chest. You understand what I mean?'

'I suppose so.'

'And I've only got so much time left to tell it. What if something happens and I go tomorrow? What if I never get a chance to tell you what I know? Thing is, I don't know whether Cynthia's ready to hear all this, I don't even know if it does her any service to know, because what I have to say only raises more questions than it answers. It may torment her more than help her.'

'Tess, what is it?'

'Just hold your horses and hear me out. You need to know this, because it might be an important piece of the puzzle someday. On its own, I don't know what to make of it, but maybe, in the future, you'll find out a bit more about what happened to my sister and her husband, and Todd. And if you do, this might be useful.'

I was breathing, but it felt as though I was holding my breath, waiting for Tess to say what she had to say.

'What?' Tess said, looking at me like I was stupid. 'You don't want to know?'

'Jesus Christ, Tess, I'm waiting.'

'It's about the money,' she said.

'Money?'

Tess nodded tiredly. 'There was money. It would just show up.'

'Money from where?'

Her eyebrows went up. 'Well, that's the question, isn't it? Where was it coming from? Who was it coming from?'

I ran my hand over the top of my head, starting to feel exasperated. 'Just start at the beginning.'

Tess breathed in slowly through her nose. 'It wasn't going to be easy, raising Cynthia. But like I've said, I didn't have any choice. She was my niece, my sister's flesh and blood. I loved her like she was my own child, so when it happened, I took her in.

'She'd been a bit of a wild kid there, up until her folks upped and vanished, and in some ways, that calmed her down. She started to get a little more serious about things, started paying attention at school. She had her moments, of course. The cops brought her home one night, found her with marijuana.'

'Really?' I said.

Tess smiled. 'Let her off with a warning.' She put a finger to her lips. 'Not a word.'

'Sure.'

'Anyway, a thing like that happens to you, losing your family, you think you've got license to do whatever the hell you want, to cut loose, stay out late, that you're owed. You know?'

'I think so.'

'But there was a part of her wanted to get herself together. In case her parents came back, she wanted to make something of herself, that she didn't turn out to be useless. Even though they were gone, she wanted them to be proud of her. So she decided to go to school, to college.'

'The University of Connecticut,' I said.

'That's right. Good school. Not cheap. I wondered how I was going to be able to afford it. Her marks, they weren't bad, but they weren't scholarship material, if you get my meaning. I was going to have to look into loans for her, that kind of thing.'

'OK.'

'I found the first envelope in the car, on the passenger seat,' Tess said. 'It was just sitting there. I'd come out from work, got in, there was this white envelope on the seat next to me. Thing is, I'd locked the car, but I'd left the windows open half an inch, it was pretty hot out and I wanted to let a little air in. There was enough room to fit in the envelope, but only just. It was pretty thick.'

I cocked my head to one side. 'Cash?'

'Just under five thousand dollars of it,' Tess said. 'All sorts of bills. Twenties, fives, some hundreds.'

'An envelope full of cash? No explanation, no note, nothing?'

'Oh, there was a note.'

She got up from her chair and took a few steps over to an antique roll-top desk off to one side of the front door, opened the single drawer. 'I found all this when I started cleaning up in the basement, going through those boxes of books and everything else. I need to start paring things down now, make it easier for you and Cynthia to sort through my stuff when I'm gone.'

Held together with a rubber band was a small stack of envelopes, maybe a dozen or more. Together, they weren't half an inch thick.

'They're all empty now of course,' Tess said. 'But I always kept the envelopes just the same, even though there's nothing written on them, no return address, no postmark, of course. But I thought, what if they've got fingerprints on them or something that might be useful to someone someday?'

Tess's hands were all over them, so it was doubtful how much evidence they contained. But then again, forensic science wasn't exactly my area of expertise. You didn't see me teaching chemistry.

Tess worked a piece of paper out from under the rubber band. 'This was the only note I ever got. With the first envelope. All the others that followed, they had cash in them, too, but never another word.'

She handed me a standard-sized piece of typewriter paper, folded in thirds. It had yellowed slightly with age.

I unfolded it.

The message was printed, very deliberately, in block letters. It read:

THIS IS TO HELP YOU WITH CYNTHIA. FOR HER EDUCATION, FOR WHATEVER ELSE YOU NEED. THERE WILL BE MORE, BUT YOU MUST FOLLOW THESE RULES. NEVER TELL CYNTHIA ABOUT THIS MONEY. NEVER TELL ANYONE ABOUT IT. NEVER TRY TO FIND OUT WHERE IT'S COMING FROM. NEVER.

That was it.

I must have read it three times before I looked at Tess, standing in front of me.

'I never did,' she said. 'I never told Cynthia. I never told anyone. I never made any attempt to find out who had left it in my car. I never knew when, or where, it would show up. One time, I found it tucked into the *New Haven Register* on the front step one evening. Another time, I came out of the Post Mall, there was another one in the car.'

'You never saw anyone.'

'No. I think, whoever left it, was watching me, making sure I was far enough away for it to be safe. You want to know something? I always made sure, whenever I parked the car, to leave the window open a crack, just in case.'

'How much, altogether?'

'Over about six years, $42,000.'

'Jesus.'

Tess reached out her hand. She wanted the note back. She folded it up, slipped it under the rubber band with the envelopes, got up and put everything back into the desk drawer.

'So, nothing for how many years?' I asked.

Tess thought a moment. 'About fifteen, I guess. Nothing since Cynthia finished school. It was a blessing, I'll tell you that. I'd have never got her through school without it, not without selling this house or taking out a new mortgage or something.'

'So,' I said. 'Who left it?'

'It's the $42,000 question,' Tess said. 'It's all I've ever wondered, all these years. Her mother? Her father? Both of them?'

'Which would mean they were alive all those years, or at least one of them was. Maybe still alive even now. But if one or the other of them was able to do that, to watch you, to leave you money, why wouldn't they be able to get in touch?'

'I know,' Tess said. 'It doesn't make any goddamn sense. Because I've always believed my sister is dead, that they're all dead. That they all died the night they disappeared.'

'And if they are dead,' I said, 'then whoever sent you that money, it's someone who feels responsible for their deaths. Who's trying to make it right.'

'You see what I mean?' Tess said. 'It just raises more questions than it answers. The money, it doesn't mean they're alive. And it doesn't mean they're dead.'

'But it means something,' I said. 'After it stopped, when it was clear there wasn't any more coming, why didn't you tell the police? They might have reopened the investigation.'

Tess's eyes grew weary. 'I know you might think I've never been afraid to stir up a bit of shit, but where this was concerned, Terry, I just didn't know whether I wanted to know the truth. I was scared, and I was afraid of how much the truth might hurt Cynthia, if we were able to find it. It's taken its toll on me. The stress of it. I wonder if that's why I'm sick. They say stress'll do that to you, affect your body.'

'I've heard that.' I paused. 'Maybe you need to talk to somebody.'

'Oh, I gave that a try,' Tess said. 'I saw your Dr Kinzler.'

I blinked. 'You did?'

'Cynthia mentioned going to her, so I gave her a call, saw her a couple of times. But you know, I'm just not prepared to open up to a stranger. There are some things you only tell family.'

We heard a car pull into the driveway.

'It's up to you whether to tell Cynthia,' Tess said. 'About the envelopes, that is. The stuff about me, I'll tell her myself, soon enough.'

A car door opened, closed. I peeked out the window, saw Cynthia going around to the back of the car, the trunk open.

'I have to think about this,' I said. 'I don't know what to do. But thank you for telling me.' I paused. 'I wish you'd told me sooner.'

'I wish I could have.'

The front door opened and Cynthia burst in with

a couple of shopping bags at the same time Grace re-appeared from the basement, holding the container of chocolate ice cream to her chest like it was a stuffed toy, her mouth smeared with chocolate.

Cynthia eyed her curiously. I could see the wheels turning, that she was thinking she'd been sent on a fool's errand.

Tess said, 'Right after you left, we suddenly realized we had ice cream after all. But I still needed all those other things. It's my goddamn birthday. Let's have a party.'

TEN

When I went into Grace's bedroom to kiss her goodnight it was already in darkness, but I quickly saw her silhouetted against the window, where she was peering at the moonlit sky through her telescope. I was just barely able to see that she had crudely wrapped masking tape around the scope where it was supported by the stand to hold it together.

'Sweetheart,' I said.

She twinkled some fingers but didn't prize herself away from the telescope. As my eyes adjusted, I could see her *Cosmos* book open on her bed.

'Whatcha see?' I asked.

'Not much,' she said.

'That's too bad.'

'No it's not. If there's nothing coming to destroy earth, that's a good thing.'

'Can't argue with that.'

'I don't want anything to happen to you and Mom. If an asteroid was going to hit our house by morning, I'd be able to see it coming by now, so you can rest easy.'

I touched her hair, ran my hand down to her shoulder.

'Dad, you're bumping my eye,' Grace said.

'Oh, sorry,' I said.

'I think Aunt Tess is sick,' she said.

Oh no. She'd been listening. Instead of being down in the basement, she'd been hiding at the top of the stairs.

'Grace, were you—'

'She just didn't seem very happy for her birthday,' she said. 'I'm way happier than that on my birthday.'

'Sometimes when you get older, having a birthday isn't quite such a big deal,' I said. 'You've already had a lot of them. The novelty kind of wears off after a while.'

'What's novelty?'

'You know how when something's new, it's exciting? But then after some time, it gets kind of boring? When it's new, it's a novelty.'

'Oh.' She moved her telescope a bit to the left. 'The moon is really shiny tonight. You can see all the craters.'

'Get to bed,' I said.

'In a minute,' she protested.

'Sleep tight, and don't worry about asteroids tonight.'

I decided not to be heavy-handed and demand that she get under the covers immediately. Letting a kid stay up past her bedtime to study the solar system didn't strike me as a crime worthy of intervention by the child welfare authorities. After giving her a gentle kiss on her ear, I slipped out of her room and back down the hall to our bedroom.

Cynthia, who'd already said goodnight to Grace, was sitting up in bed, looking at a magazine, just turning the pages, not paying any real attention to them.

'I have some errands to run at the mall tomorrow,' she said, not taking her eyes away from the pages. 'I've got to find Grace some new running shoes.'

'Hers don't look worn out.'

'They're not, but her toes are jammed up in them. You joining us?'

'Sure,' I said. 'I might cut the grass in the morning. We could grab some lunch there.'

'That was nice today,' she said. 'We don't see Tess enough.'

'Why don't we make it a weekly thing?' I said.

'You think?' She smiled.

'Sure. Have her here for dinner, take her to Knickerbocker's, maybe out to that seafood place along the sound. She'd like that.'

'She'd love it. She seemed a bit preoccupied today. And I think she's starting to get a bit absent-minded. I mean, she already had ice cream.'

I took off my shirt, hung my pants over the back of a chair. 'Oh well,' I said. 'That's not a big thing.'

Tess held off telling Cynthia about her health problems. She wouldn't have wanted to spoil her own birthday celebrations for Cynthia. And while it was certainly up to Tess to decide when to break the news to Cynthia, it felt wrong to know while my wife was kept in the dark.

But an even greater burden was suddenly knowing about the money that had been sent anonymously to Tess over several years. What right did I have to keep that information to myself? Surely Cynthia was more entitled to know about it than I. But Tess had held back from telling because she thought Cynthia was fragile enough these days, and I couldn't disagree. And yet.

I'd even have liked to ask Cynthia whether she knew her aunt had paid a couple of visits to Dr Kinzler, but then she'd want to know why Tess had mentioned that to me and not her, so I left it alone.

'You OK?' Cynthia asked.

'Yeah, good. Just kind of beat, that's all,' I said as I

stripped down to my boxers. I brushed my teeth and got into bed, lying on my side, my back to her. Cynthia threw her magazine onto the floor and turned off the light, and a few seconds after that, her arm slipped around me and she stroked my chest, and then she took me in her hand.

'How beat are you?' she whispered.

'Not that beat,' I said, and turned over.

'I want to be safe with you,' she said, pulling my mouth down to hers.

'No asteroids tonight,' I said, and if the lights had been on, I think I might have seen her smile.

Cynthia fell asleep quickly. I wasn't so lucky.

I stared at the ceiling, turned over onto my side, glared at the digital clock. When it turned over to a new minute, I started counting to sixty, seeing how close I could come. Then I rolled onto my back and stared at the ceiling some more. Around three in the morning, Cynthia sensed my restlessness and said groggily to me, 'You OK?'

'Fine,' I said. 'Go back to sleep.'

It was her questions I couldn't face. If I knew the answers to the questions Cynthia would have about the cash-stuffed envelopes that had been left for Tess to help pay for her upbringing, I might have told her about it right away.

No, that was not true. Having some of the answers would only spark more questions. Suppose I knew the money was being left by someone from her family? Suppose I even knew which one?

I still wouldn't be able to answer why.

Suppose I knew the money was being left by someone

outside her family? But who? Who else would feel responsible enough for Cynthia, about what had happened to her mother and father and brother, to leave that kind of money to care for her?

And then I wondered whether I should tell the police. Get Tess to turn over the letter and the envelopes. Maybe, even after all these years and after the amount of handling they'd had they still held some secrets that someone with the right kind of forensic equipment could unlock.

Assuming, of course, that there was anyone still in the police department who cared about this case. It had gone into the 'cold' file a very long time ago.

When they were doing the TV show, they had a hard time even finding anyone still on the force who'd investigated the incident. Which was why they'd had to track down that guy in Arizona, sitting out front of his Airstream, so he could insinuate that Cynthia had had something to do with the disappearance of her brother and her parents – the prick.

And so I lay awake, haunted by the information I had not shared with Cynthia, and how it only served to remind me of how much we still didn't know.

I killed some time in the bookstore while Cynthia and Grace looked at shoes. I had an early Philip Roth in my hand, one that I'd never gotten around to reading, when Grace came running into the store. Cynthia trailed behind her, a shopping bag in hand.

'I'm starving,' Grace said, throwing her arms around me.

'You got some shoes?'

She took a step back and modeled for me, sticking

out one foot and then the other. White sneakers with a pink swoosh.

'What's in the bag?' I asked.

'Her old ones,' Cynthia said. 'She had to wear them right away. You hungry?'

I was. I put the Roth book back and we took the escalator up to the food court level. Grace wanted McDonald's so I gave her enough money to buy herself something while Cynthia and I went to a different counter to get soup and a sandwich. Cynthia kept glancing back over to the McDonald's, making sure she could see Grace. The mall was busy on this Sunday afternoon, as was the food court. There were still a few tables free, but they were filling up fast.

Cynthia was so occupied watching Grace that I moved both our plastic trays along, gathered together cutlery and napkins, loaded the sandwiches and soup as they became ready.

'She's got us a table,' Cynthia said. I scanned the court, spotted Grace at a table for four, waving her arm back and forth long after we'd caught sight of her. She already had her Big Mac out of the box when we joined her, her fries dumped into the other side of the container.

'Eww,' she said when she saw my cream of broccoli soup. A kindly looking woman of about fifty in a blue coat, sitting alone at the next table, glanced over, smiled, and went back to her own lunch.

I sat across from Cynthia, Grace to my right. I noticed that Cynthia kept looking over my shoulder. I turned around once, looked where she was looking, turned back.

'What?' I said.

'Nothing,' she said, and took a bite of her chicken salad sandwich.

'What were you looking at?'

'Nothing,' she said again.

Grace pushed a fry into her mouth, biting it into quarter-inch segments at a furious rate.

Cynthia was looking over my shoulder again.

'Cyn,' I said. 'What the hell are you looking at?'

She didn't immediately deny this time that something had caught her eye. 'There's a man over there,' she said. I started to turn around and she said, 'No, don't look.'

'What's so special about him?'

'Nothing,' she said.

I sighed, and probably rolled my eyes, too. 'For crying out loud, Cyn, you can't just stare at the guy for—'

'He looks like Todd,' she said.

OK, I thought. We've been here before. Just be cool. 'All right,' I said. 'What is it about him that makes him look like your brother?'

'I don't know. It's just something about him. He just looks like Todd would probably look today.'

'What are you talking about?' Grace asked.

'Never mind,' I said. To Cynthia, I said, 'Tell me what he looks like, and I'll just casually turn around and get a look at him.'

'He's got black hair, he's wearing a brown jacket. He's eating Chinese food. Right now, he's eating an egg roll. He looks like a younger version of my dad, an older version of Todd, I'm telling you.'

I swiveled slowly on my backless chair, made like I was taking in the various food kiosks, thinking about going to get something further to eat. I saw him, catching some sprouts with his tongue that were falling out of the half-eaten egg roll. I'd seen a few pictures of Todd from Cynthia's shoebox of mementoes, and I suppose it was possible, had he grown up to be in his late thirties, early forties, that he might look a bit like this guy. Slightly overweight, a doughy face, black hair, maybe six foot, although it was hard to tell with him sitting down.

I turned back. 'He looks like a million other people,' I said.

'I'm going to get a closer look,' Cynthia said.

She was on her feet before I could protest. 'Honey,' I said as she walked by me, making a half-hearted attempt to grab her by the arm and failing.

'Where's Mommy going?'

'To the washroom,' I said.

'I'm going to have to go too,' Grace said, swinging her legs back and forth so she could catch glimpses of her new shoes.

'She can take you after,' I said.

I watched as Cynthia took the long way around the food court, heading in the opposite direction from where the man sat. She walked past all the fast-food outlets, approaching him from behind and to the side. As she came up alongside him, she walked straight ahead, went to the McDonald's and joined the line, glancing occasionally, as casually as possible, at the man she felt bore an amazing resemblance to her brother Todd.

When she sat back down she presented Grace with a small chocolate sundae in a clear plastic cup. Her hand was shaking as she put it on Grace's tray.

'Wow!' said Grace.

Cynthia showed no reaction to her daughter's expression of gratitude. She looked at me and said, 'It's him.'

'Cyn.'

'It's my brother.'

'Cyn, come on, it's not Todd.'

'I got a good look at him. It's him. I'm as sure that's my brother as I am that that's Grace sitting there.'

Grace looked up from her ice cream. 'Your brother's here?' She was genuinely curious. 'Todd?'

'Just eat your ice cream,' Cynthia said.

'I know what his name is,' Grace said. 'And your dad was Clayton, and your mother was Patricia.' She rattled off the names like it was a classroom exercise.

'Grace!' Cynthia snapped.

I felt my heart begin to pound. This could only get worse.

'I'm going to talk to him,' she said.

Bingo.

'You can't,' I said. 'Look, it doesn't make any sense that it's Todd. For Christ's sake, if your brother was just out and about, going to the mall, eating Chinese food in public, you think he wouldn't have gotten in touch with you? And he'd have spotted you, too. You were practically Inspector Clouseau there, wandering around him as obvious as all hell. It's just some guy, he's got some passing resemblance to your brother. You go over to him, start talking to him like he's Todd, he's going to freak—'

'He's leaving,' Cynthia said, a hint of panic in her voice.

I whirled around. The man was on his feet, wiping his mouth one last time with a paper napkin, crumpling it in his hand and dropping it onto the paper plate. He left the tray sitting there, didn't take it over to the waste basket, and started walking in the direction of the washrooms.

'Who's Inspector Cloozoo?' Grace asked.

'You can't follow him into the can,' I cautioned Cynthia.

She sat there, frozen, watching the man as he wandered down the hall that led to the men's and ladies' rooms. He'd have to come back, and she could wait.

'Are you going into the men's room?' Grace asked her mother.

'Eat your ice cream,' Cynthia said again.

The woman in the blue coat at the table next to us was picking at her salad, trying to pretend she wasn't listening to us.

I felt I only had a few seconds to talk Cynthia out of doing something we'd all regret. 'Remember what you said to me, when I first met you, that you were always seeing people you thought might be your family?'

'He's got to show up again soon. Unless there's another way out. Is there another way out back there?'

'I don't think so,' I said. 'It's perfectly normal to feel this way. You've spent your whole life looking. I remember, years ago, I was watching Larry King, and they had that guy on, the one whose son was killed by O.J. Simpson, Goldman I think it was, and he told Larry that he'd be out driving, and he'd see someone driving a car like his son used to drive, and he'd chase the car, check the driver, just to be sure it wasn't his son, even though he knew he was dead, knew it didn't make any sense . . .'

'You don't know that Todd is dead,' Cynthia said.

'I know. I didn't mean it to come out that way. All I'm saying is—'

'There he is. He's heading for the escalator.' She was on her feet and moving.

'For fuck's sake,' I said.

'Daddy!' Grace said.

I turned to her. 'You stay right here and do not move, you understand?' She nodded, a spoonful of ice cream stopped frozen en route to her mouth. The woman at the next table glanced over again and I caught her eye. 'Excuse me,' I said, 'but would you mind keeping an eye on my daughter, just for a moment?'

She stared at me, unsure what to say.

'Just a couple of minutes,' I said, trying to reassure her, then got up, not giving her a chance to say no.

I went after Cynthia. I managed to spot the disappearing head of the man she was pursuing as he descended the escalator. The food court was so crowded it had slowed Cynthia down and there were half a dozen people between her and the man as she got on to the top step of the escalator, and another half dozen between Cynthia and me.

When the man got off at the bottom he started walking briskly in the direction of the exit. Cynthia was straining to get past a couple ahead of her, but they were precariously balancing a stroller on the steps, and she couldn't.

When she hit the bottom she broke into a run after the man, who was nearly at the doors.

'Todd!' she shouted.

The man was oblivious. He shoved open the first door, let it swing shut behind him, threw open the second, proceeded on to the parking lot. I'd nearly caught up with Cynthia as she went through the first door.

'Cynthia!' I said.

But she was giving me no more attention than the man was giving her. Once she was out the door, she called 'Todd!' again to no effect, then caught up to the man, grabbing him by the elbow.

He turned around, startled by this out-of-breath, wild-eyed woman.

'Yes?' he said.

'Excuse me,' Cynthia said, taking a second to catch her breath. 'But I think I know you.'

I was at her side now, and the man looked at me, as if to ask, 'What the hell's going on?'

'I don't think so,' the man said slowly.

'You're Todd,' Cynthia said.

'Todd?' He shook his head. 'Lady, I'm sorry, but I don't know—'

'I know who you are,' Cynthia said. 'I can see my father in you. In your eyes.'

'I'm sorry,' I said to the man. 'My wife thinks you look like her brother. She hasn't seen him in a very long time.'

Cynthia turned angrily on me. 'I'm not losing my mind,' she said. To the man, she said, 'OK, who are you then? Tell me who you are.'

'Lady, I don't know what the fuck your problem is, but keep me out of it, OK?'

I tried to position myself between the two of them, and using as calm a voice as possible, said to the man, 'This is a lot to ask, believe me, I understand, but maybe, if you could tell us who you are, it would help put my wife's mind at ease.'

'This is crazy,' he said. 'I don't have to do that.'

'You see?' Cynthia said. 'It's you, but for some reason, you can't admit it.'

I took Cynthia aside and said, 'Give me a minute.' Then I turned back to the man and said, 'My wife's family went missing many years ago. She hasn't seen her brother in years and you, evidently, bear a resemblance to him. I'll understand if you say no, but if you were to show me some ID, a driver's license, something like that, it would be a tremendous help. It would settle this once and for all.'

He studied my face a moment. 'She needs help, you know that,' he said.

I said nothing.

Finally, he sighed, shook his head and took his wallet from his back pocket. He flipped it open and withdrew a plastic card. 'There,' he said, handing it to me.

It was a New York State license for Jeremy Sloan with an address up in Youngstown. It had his picture right on it.

'May I have this for one moment?' I asked. He nodded. I moved over to Cynthia and handed it to her. 'Look at this.'

She took the license tentatively between her thumb and index finger, examined it through the start of tears. Her eyes went from the picture on the license to the man in person. Quietly, she handed the license back to him.

'I'm very sorry,' she said. 'I'm – I'm so sorry.'

The man took the license back, slid it into his wallet, shook his head again disgustedly, muttered something under his breath – although the only word I caught was 'loony' – and headed off into the parking lot.

'Come on, Cyn,' I said. 'Let's get Grace.'

'Grace?' she said. 'You left Grace?'

'She's with someone,' I said. 'It's OK.'

But she was running back into the mall, across the main court, up the escalator. I was right behind her, and we threaded our way back through the maze of busy tables to where we'd had our lunch. There were the three trays with our unfinished Styrofoam bowls of soup and sandwiches, Grace's McDonald's trash.

Grace was not there.

The woman in the blue coat was not there.

'Where the hell ...'

'Oh my God,' Cynthia said. 'You left her here? *You left her here alone?*'

'I'm telling you, I left her with this woman, she was sitting right here.' What I wanted to tell her was that if she hadn't run off on a wild goose chase I wouldn't have been faced with the choice of leaving Grace on her own. 'She must be around somewhere,' I said.

'Who was she?' Cynthia asked. 'What did she look like?'

'I don't know. I mean, she was an older woman. She had on a blue coat. She was just this woman sitting here.'

She had left her unfinished salad sitting on her tray, along with a paper cup half filled with Pepsi or Coke. It was like she'd left in a hurry.

'Mall security,' I said, trying to keep panic from taking over. 'They can watch for a woman, blue coat, with a little girl ...' I was scanning the food court, looking for anyone official.

'Did you see our little girl?' Cynthia asked people at surrounding tables. They looked back, their faces blank, shrugging. 'Eight years old? She was sitting right here?'

I felt overwhelmed with helplessness. I looked back

toward the McDonald's counter, thinking, maybe the woman lured her away with the promise of another ice cream. But surely Grace was too smart for that. She was only eight, but she'd been through the whole street-proofing thing.

Cynthia, standing in the middle of the crowded food court, started to shout our daughter's name. 'Grace!' she said. 'Grace!'

And then, behind me, a voice.

'Hi Dad.'

I whirled around. 'Why's Mom screaming?' Grace asked.

'Where the hell were you?' I asked. Cynthia had spotted us and was running over. 'What happened to that woman?'

'Her cell rang, and she said she had to go,' Grace said matter-of-factly. 'And then I had to go to the bathroom. I told you I had to go to the bathroom. Don't everybody freak out.'

Cynthia grabbed Grace, held her close enough to smother her. If I'd been having qualms about keeping to myself the information about those secret payments to Tess, I was over them now. This family did not need any more chaos.

No one spoke the whole way home.

When we got there, the message light on the phone was flashing. It was one of the producers, from *Deadline*. The three of us stood in the kitchen and listened to her say that someone had gotten in touch with them. Someone who claimed to know what might have happened to Cynthia's parents and brother.

Cynthia phoned back immediately, waited while someone tracked down the producer, who'd slipped out for a coffee. Finally, the producer was on the line. 'Who is it?' Cynthia asked, breathless. 'Is it my brother?'

She was convinced, after all, that she had just seen him. It would have made sense.

'No,' the producer said. Not her brother. It was this woman, a clairvoyant or something. But very credible, as far as they could tell.

Cynthia hung up and said, 'Some psychic says she knows what happened.'

'Cool!' said Grace.

Yeah, terrific, I thought. A psychic. Absolutely fucking terrific.

ELEVEN

'I think we should at least hear what she has to say,' Cynthia said.

It was that evening, and I was sitting at the kitchen table, marking papers, having a hard time concentrating. Cynthia had been able to think of nothing else since the producer's call about the psychic. I, on the other hand, had been somewhat dismissive.

I didn't have much to say through supper, but once Grace had gone up to her room to do some homework of her own, and Cynthia was loading the dishwasher, her back to me, she said, 'We need to talk about this.'

'I don't see much to talk about,' I said. 'So a psychic phoned the show. That's only a step up from the guy who thought your family disappeared into some rip in the fabric of time. Maybe this woman, maybe she'll have a vision of them all riding atop a brontosaurus or something, or pedaling a Flintstone car.'

Cynthia turned around. 'That's hateful,' she said.

I looked up from a dreadfully written essay on Whitman. 'What?'

'What you said. It was hateful. You're being hateful.'

'I am not.'

'You're still pissed with me. About today. About what happened at the mall.'

I didn't say anything. There was some truth to what she said. There were things I had wanted to say on the way home but felt I could not. That I had had enough. That it was time for Cynthia to move on. That she had to accept the fact that her parents were gone, her brother was gone, that nothing had changed just because this was the twenty-fifth anniversary of their disappearance, or because some second-rate news show had shown some interest. That while she might have lost a family long ago, and that it was undeniably tragic, she had another family now, and that if she wasn't willing to live in the moment for us, instead of in the past for a family that was in all likelihood gone, then ...

But I'd said nothing. I couldn't bring myself to say those things. And yet I'd found myself unable to offer comfort once we got home. Then the call from the psychic hotline, by way of *Deadline*, had just pissed me off even more. I'd gone into the living room, turned on the TV, flipped through the channels, never settling on anything for more than three minutes. Cynthia had gone into a tidying frenzy, vacuuming, cleaning the bathroom, rearranging soup cans in the pantry. Anything to keep her too busy to have to talk to me. There wasn't much good that came out of a fight between us, but at least the house ended up looking ready for a spread in *Home & Garden*.

But I said, 'I'm not pissed,' riffling my finger through the stack of papers I still had to mark.

'I know you,' she said. 'And I know when you're angry. I'm sorry about what happened. I'm sorry for you, I'm sorry for Grace. I'm sorry for that man, for what I put him through. I embarrassed myself, I embarrassed all of us. What more do you want from me? What more can I say? Aren't I already going to see Dr Kinzler? What do you want me to do? Go every week instead of every other week? You want to put me on some sort of drug, something that will numb the pain, make me forget everything that's ever happened to me? Would that make you happy?'

I threw down my red marking pen. 'Jesus Christ,' I said.

'You'd be happier if I just left, wouldn't you?' Cynthia asked.

'That's ridiculous.'

'You can't take any more of this, and you know something? Neither can I. I've had enough of it, too. You think I like the idea of meeting with a psychic? You think I don't know how desperate it looks? How pitiful it makes me look, to go down there and have to listen to what she has to say? But what would you do? What if it was Grace?'

I looked at her. 'Don't even say that.'

'What if we lost her? What if she went missing some day? Suppose she'd been gone for months, for years? And there wasn't a clue as to whatever happened to her?'

'I don't want you talking like this,' I said.

'And then suppose you got a call, from some person who said she had a vision or something, that she'd seen Grace in a dream, that she knew where she was. Are you telling me you'd refuse to listen?'

I ground my teeth together and looked away.

'Is that what you would do? Because you didn't want to look like a fool? Because you were afraid of looking embarrassed, of looking desperate? But what if, what if there was just one chance in a million that maybe this person knew something? What if she wasn't even psychic, but just thought she was, but had actually seen something, some clue that she interpreted as a vision or something? And what if finding out what that was actually led to finding her?'

I put my head in my hands, my eyes landing on: 'Mr Whitman's most famous writing was *Leaves of Grass*, which some people think is probably about marijuana, but it was not, although it's hard to believe that a guy who wrote something called *I Sing The Body Electric* wasn't stoned at least some of the time.'

The next day, when I ran into Lauren Wells, I noticed she wasn't wearing her traditional tracksuit. She was in a snug black T-shirt and a pair of designer jeans. Cynthia would have known, at twenty paces, what kind they were. We were watching *American Idol* one night, on our tiny, non-high-definition screen, when she pointed to a contestant screeching out her own version of Bette Midler's 'Wind Beneath My Wings', and said, 'She's wearing Sevens.'

I didn't know whether Lauren was wearing Sevens or not, but she looked nice, and the male students were craning their necks around, getting a peek at her from behind as she made her way up the hall.

I was coming the other way and she stopped me. 'How you doing today?' she asked. 'Better?'

I couldn't recall admitting to feeling anything less than perfect the last time we'd spoken, but said, 'Yeah, I'm good. You?'

'OK,' she said. 'Although I almost took today off. This girl, who was in my senior class in high school, she was killed in a car accident up in Hartford a couple of days ago, and this other friend I keep in touch with on MSN, she told me, and I just felt so bad about it.'

'She was a close friend, was she?' I asked.

Lauren offered up half a shrug. 'Well, she was in my year. It took me a couple of minutes to place her when my friend mentioned the name. We didn't actually hang out or anything. She sat behind me in a couple of classes. But it's still a shock, you know, when something like that happens to someone you know. It makes you think, makes you reassess, which is why I almost didn't come in.'

'To reassess,' I said, not sure Lauren's predicament warranted an outpouring of sympathy. 'These things happen.' I feel as bad as the next guy when someone dies in a traffic accident, but Lauren was using up my time to discuss a tragedy involving someone whom not only did I not know, but whom, it was becoming evident, she didn't know all that well herself.

Kids shuffled past, dodged and weaved around us as we stood in the middle of the hall.

'So,' Lauren said. 'What's she really like?'

'Who?'

'Paula Malloy,' Lauren said. 'From *Deadline*. Is she as nice as she seems on TV? Because she seems very nice.'

'She has wonderful teeth,' I said. I reached up, touched her arm, motioned her toward the wall of lockers so that we weren't blocking traffic.

'Listen, um, you and Mr Carruthers, you're pretty tight, right?' she asked.

'Rolly and I? Yeah, we've known each other a long time.'

'This is kind of awkward to ask, but in the staff room the other day, he was there, and, well, I think he might have, what I'm saying is, did he mention seeing me put something in your cubbyhole and taking it out later?'

'Uh, well, he …'

'Because, OK, I did leave something there, but then I thought about it, and thought maybe it was a bad idea, so I took it back, but then I thought, oh great, Mr Carruthers, Roland, if he saw me, he'd probably tell you anyway, and then I thought, shit, I might as well have left it there because at least then you'd know what it said instead of wondering what it said …'

'Lauren, don't worry about it. It's no big deal.' I wasn't sure I wanted to know what the note said. I didn't want any further complications to my life at the moment. And I was certain I didn't want complications with Lauren Wells, even if the rest of my life was as smooth as glass.

'It was just a note to you and Cynthia, that maybe you'd like to come over some time. I was thinking of having some friends over, and thought maybe it would be a nice break for the two of you, with all you've got to think about. But then I thought, maybe I was being a bit pushy, you know?'

'Well, that's very thoughtful,' I said. 'Maybe some time.' Thinking to myself, not a chance.

'Anyway,' Lauren said, her eyebrows bobbing up for a second. 'You going to the Post Mall tonight? They're having some of the stars from the latest *Survivor*, signing autographs.'

'I had no idea,' I said.

'I'm going,' she said.

'I'll have to pass. Cynthia and I, we have to go into New Haven. It's about the TV show. No big deal. Just a follow-up.'

I immediately regretted telling her.

She brightened and said, 'You'll have to tell me all about it tomorrow.'

I just smiled, said I had to get to class and once I was away from her gave my head an invisible shake.

We had dinner early to give us time to drive to the Fox affiliate in New Haven, and had intended to get a sitter for Grace, but Cynthia said she had called around and been unable to get any of our regulars.

'I could stay home on my own,' Grace said as we were getting ready to go. Grace had never stayed home on her own, and we certainly weren't going to make this her first night for going solo. Maybe in five or six years.

'Not a chance, pal,' I said. 'Bring your *Cosmos* book or some homework or something else to do while we're there.'

'Can't I hear what the lady says?' Grace said.

'No,' Cynthia said, before I could say the same thing.

Cynthia was edgy through dinner. I'd gotten over being pissed off, so it wasn't my doing. I attributed it to anxiety over what the psychic would have to say. Having someone read your palm, tell your fortune, lay out some Tarot cards on a table before you could be entertaining, even when you didn't believe in it. That was under normal circumstances. This was going to be different.

'They want me to bring one of the shoeboxes,' Cynthia said.

'Which one?'

'Any. She says she just needs to hold it, maybe hold some of the things inside, to pick up more vibrations or whatever about the past.'

'Sure,' I said. 'And they're going to be filming all this, I suppose?'

Cynthia said, 'I don't see how we can tell them not to. It was their story that brought this woman forward. They're going to want to follow it through.'

'Do we even know who she is?' I asked.

'Keisha,' Cynthia said. 'Keisha Ceylon.'

'Really.'

'I looked her up on the Internet,' Cynthia said, then added, 'she has a webpage.'

'I'll just bet she does,' I said, and gave her a rueful smile.

'Be nice,' Cynthia said.

We were all in the car, backing out of the drive, when Cynthia said, 'Hold it! I can't believe it. I forgot the shoebox.'

She had taken from the closet one of her boxes of family mementoes and left it on the kitchen table so she wouldn't forget.

'I'll go get it,' I said, putting the car in park.

But Cynthia already had her keys out of her purse, the car door open. 'I'll just be a second,' she said. I watched her go up the drive, unlock the door and run inside, the keys left dangling from the lock. She seemed to be in there for a while, longer than it would take to grab the shoebox, but then she reappeared, shoebox tucked under her arm. She locked up, took the keys out of the door, got back in the car.

'What took so long?' I asked.

'I took an Advil,' she said. 'My head's pounding.'

At the station, we were met at reception by the ponytailed producer, who led us into a studio and to a talk-show set with a couch, a couple of chairs, some fake plants, some cheesy background lattice work. Paula Malloy was there and she greeted Cynthia like an old friend, oozing charm like a runny sore. Cynthia was reserved. Standing next to Paula was a black woman, late forties I guessed, dressed impeccably in a navy blue suit. I wondered if she was another producer, maybe a station manager.

'I'd like to introduce you to Keisha Ceylon,' Paula said.

I guess I was expecting someone who looked like a gypsy or something. A flower child, maybe. Someone in a floor-length tie-dyed skirt, not someone who looked like she could be chairing a board meeting.

'Pleased to meet you,' Keisha said, shaking hands with us. She caught something in my look and said, 'You were expecting something different.'

'Perhaps,' I said.

'And this must be Grace,' she said, bending down to shake hands with our daughter.

'Hi,' Grace said.

'Is there some place Grace could go?' I asked.

Grace said, 'Can I stay?' She looked up at Keisha. 'Have you, like, seen Mom's parents in a vision or something?'

'Maybe, what do you call it, a green room?' I interrupted.

'Why is it green?' Grace asked as she was led away by some assistant.

After they'd put some make-up on Cynthia and Keisha, they were seated on the couch with the shoebox between them. Paula got herself into a chair opposite them while a couple of cameras were wheeled noiselessly into position. I retreated back into the darkness of the studio, far enough to be out of the way, but close enough to watch.

Paula did some setup stuff, a recap of the story they'd broadcast a few weeks earlier. They'd be able to edit more into the segment later. Then she told her audience of a startling development in the case. A psychic had stepped forward, a woman who believed she could offer some insights into the disappearance of the Bigge family in 1983.

'I had seen your show,' said Keisha Ceylon, her voice low and comforting. 'And of course I found it interesting. But I didn't think much more about it after that. And then, a couple of weeks later, I was helping a client attempt to communicate with a lost relative, and I was not having the success I normally do. It's as though there was some kind of interference, like I was on one of those old party lines and someone else is picking up the phone when you're trying to make a call.'

'Fascinating,' breathed Paula. Cynthia remained expressionless.

'And I heard this voice, she said to me, "Please get a message to my daughter."'

'Really? And did she say who she was?'

'She said her name was Patricia.'

Cynthia blinked.

'And what else did she say?'

'She said she wanted me to reach her daughter Cynthia.'

'Why?'

'I'm not entirely sure. I think she wanted me to contact her so that I could learn more. That's why I wanted you,' she smiled at Cynthia, 'to bring some mementoes, so that I could hold them, perhaps understand better what happened.'

Paula leaned in toward Cynthia. 'You brought some things, didn't you?'

'Yes,' Cynthia said. 'This is one of the shoeboxes I showed you before. Pictures, old clippings, just bits and pieces of things. I can show you what's inside and—'

'No,' said Keisha. 'That's not necessary. If you would just give me the entire box ...'

Cynthia let her take it, let her set it on her lap. Keisha put a hand on each end of the box and closed her eyes.

'I feel so much energy coming from this,' she said.

Give me a fucking break, I thought.

'I feel ... sadness. So much sadness.'

'What else do you feel?' Paula asked.

Keisha furrowed her brow. 'I sense ... that you are about to receive a sign.'

'A sign?' said Cynthia. 'What kind of sign?'

'A sign ... that will help answer your questions. I'm not sure I can tell you more.'

'Why?' asked Cynthia.

'Why?' asked Paula.

Keisha opened her eyes. 'I ... I need you to turn the cameras off for a moment.'

'Huh?' said Paula. 'Fellas? Can we hold off for a second?'

'OK,' said one of the guys manning a camera.

'What's the problem, Keisha?' said Paula.

'What is it?' Cynthia asked, alarmed. 'What is it you didn't want to say on camera? Something about my mother? Something about what she wanted you to tell me?'

'Sort of,' Keisha said. 'But I just wanted to get straight, before we go any further, how much I'm getting paid to do this.'

Here we go.

'Uh, Keisha,' said Paula. 'I think it was explained to you that while we would cover your expenses, put you up in a hotel for the night if necessary, I know you had to come down from Hartford, we weren't paying you for your services in any sort of professional sense.'

'That wasn't my understanding,' she said, getting a bit huffy now. 'I've some very important stuff to tell this lady, and if you want to hear it, I'm going to need to be financially compensated.'

'Why don't you tell her what you have to say and we'll go from there?' Paula suggested.

I walked forward to the set, caught Cynthia's eye. 'Hon,' I said, tipping my head, the international 'let's go' gesture.

She nodded resignedly, unclipped the microphone from her blouse and stood up.

'Where are you going?' Paula asked.

'We're outta here,' I said.

'What do you mean?' Keisha asked, outraged. 'Where are you going? Lady, if this show isn't going to pay to hear what I know, maybe you should.'

Cynthia said, 'I'm not going to be made a fool of any more.'

'A thousand dollars,' Keisha said. 'I'll tell you what your momma told me to tell you for a thousand dollars.'

Cynthia was rounding the couch. I reached out my hand for hers.

'OK, seven hundred!' Keisha said as we went to find our way to the green room.

'You really are a piece of work,' Paula told Keisha. 'You could have been on TV. All the free advertising in the world, but you've got to shake us down for a few hundred bucks.'

Keisha gave Paula the evil eye, looked at her hair. 'That's one bad dye job, bitch.'

'You were right,' Cynthia said on the drive home.

I shook my head. 'You were good, walking away like that. You should have seen the look on that so-called psychic's face when you took off your mike. It's like she was watching her meal ticket walk away.'

Cynthia's smile was caught in the glare of some oncoming headlights. Grace, after a flurry of questions we declined to answer, had fallen asleep in the backseat.

'What a waste of an evening,' Cynthia said.

'No,' I said. 'What you said was right, and I'm sorry I gave you a hard time about this. Even if there's only a one in a million chance, you have to check it out. So we checked it out. And now we can cross it off and move on.'

We pulled into the drive. I opened the back door, unbuckled Grace and carried her into the house, following Cynthia into the living room. She walked ahead of me, turned on the lights in the kitchen as I headed for the stairs to carry Grace up to bed.

'Terry,' Cynthia said.

Ordinarily, I might have said, 'Be there in a sec' and taken Grace upstairs first, but there was something in my wife's voice that said I should come into the kitchen immediately.

So I did.

Sitting in the center of the kitchen table was a man's black hat. An old, worn, shiny with wear, Fedora.

TWELVE

She tried to move in a bit closer, got as near to him as she could, and whispered, 'For heaven's sake, are you even listening to me? I come all this way and you won't even open your eyes. You think it's easy getting here? The things you've put me through. I make the effort, seems the least you could do is stay awake a few minutes. You've got the whole day to sleep, I'm only here for a little while.

'Well let me tell you something. You're not quitting on us. You're going to be with us for a while longer, that's for sure. When it's time for you to go, believe me, you'll be the first to know.'

And then he seemed to be trying to say something.

'What's that?' she said. She was just able to make out a question. 'Oh, him,' she said. 'He couldn't come tonight.'

THIRTEEN

Gently, I set Grace down on the couch in the living room, tucked a throw pillow under her head, and went back into the kitchen.

The Fedora might as well have been a dead rat, the way Cynthia was staring at it. She was standing as far away from the table as possible, her back to the wall, and her eyes were full of fear.

It wasn't the hat itself that scared me. It was how it got there. 'You watch Grace for a minute,' I said.

'Be careful,' Cynthia said.

I went upstairs, flicked on the lights in each room and poked in my head as I did so. Checked the bathroom, then decided to check the other rooms again, looking in closets, under beds. Everything looked the way it should.

I came back down to the main floor, opened the door to our unfinished basement. At the bottom of the steps I waved my hand around, caught the string and turned on the bare bulb.

'What do you see?' Cynthia called from upstairs.

I saw a washer and dryer, a workbench piled with junk, an assortment of nearly empty paint cans, a folded-up spare bed. Nothing much else.

I came back upstairs. 'The house is empty,' I said.

Cynthia was still staring at the hat. 'He was here,' she said.

'Who was here?'

'My father. He was here.'

'Cynthia, someone was here and left that on the table, but your father?'

'It's his hat,' she said, more calmly than I might have expected. I approached the table, reached out to grab it. 'Don't touch it!' she said.

'It's not going to bite me,' I said, and grabbed one of the peaks between my thumb and forefinger, then grabbed it with both hands, turning it over, looking inside.

It was an old hat, no question. The edges of the brim were tatty, the lining darkened from years of sweat, the nap worn down to a shine in places.

'It's just a hat,' I said.

'Look inside,' she said. 'My father, years ago, he lost a couple of hats, people took his by mistake at restaurants, one time he took somebody else's, so he got a marker and he wrote the letter 'C' on the underside of the band inside. For Clayton.'

I ran my finger along the inside of the band, folding it back. I found it on the right side, near the back. I turned the hat around so that Cynthia could see.

She took a breath. 'Oh my God.' She took three tentative steps toward me, reached her hand out. I extended the hat toward her, and she took it, holding it as though it was something from King Tut's tomb. She held it reverently in her hands for a moment, then slowly moved it toward her face. For a moment, I thought she was going to put it on, but instead, she brought it to her nose, took in its fragrance.

'It's him,' she said.

I wasn't going to argue. I knew that the sense of smell was perhaps the strongest when it came to triggering memories. I could recall going back to my own childhood home once in adulthood – the one my parents moved from when I was four – and asking the current owners if they'd mind my looking around. They were most obliging, and while the layout of the house, the creak of the fourth step as I climbed to the second floor, the view of the backyard from the kitchen window, were all familiar, it was when I stuck my nose into a crawlspace and caught a whiff of cedar mixed with dampness, that I felt almost dizzy. A flood of memories broke through the dam at that moment.

So I had an idea of what Cynthia was sensing as she held the hat so close to her face. She could smell her father.

She just knew.

'He was here,' she said. 'He was right here, in this kitchen, in our house. Why, Terry? Why would he come here? Why would he do this? Why would he leave his goddamn hat but not wait for me to come home?'

'Cynthia,' I said, trying to keep my voice even. 'Let's say it is your father's hat, and if you say it is I believe you, the fact that it's here doesn't mean that it was your father who left it.'

'He never went anywhere without it. He wore it everywhere. He was wearing that hat the last night I saw him. It wasn't left behind in the house. You know what this means, don't you?'

I waited.

'It means he's alive.'

'It might, yes, it might mean that. But not necessarily.'

Cynthia put the hat back on the table, started to reach

for the phone, then stopped, then reached for it again, and again stopped herself.

'The police,' she said. 'They can take fingerprints.'

'Off that hat?' I said. 'But you already know it's your father's. Even if they could get his prints off it, so what?'

'No,' Cynthia said. 'Off the knob.' She pointed to the front door. 'Or the table. Something. If they find his fingerprints in here, it'll prove he's alive.'

I wasn't so sure about that, but I agreed that calling the police was a good idea. Someone – if not Clayton Bigge, then *somebody* – had been in our house while we were out. Was it breaking and entering if nothing appeared broken? It was definitely entering.

I called 911. 'Someone ... was in our house,' I told the dispatcher. 'My wife and I are very upset, we have a little girl, we're very worried.'

There was a car at the house about ten minutes later. Two uniforms, a man and a woman. They checked the doors and windows for any obvious signs of entry, came up with nothing. Grace, of course, had woken up during all the excitement and was refusing to go to bed. Even when we sent her back to her room and told her to get ready for bed, we spotted her at the top of the stairs, peering through the railings like an underage inmate.

'Was anything stolen?' the woman cop asked, her partner standing alongside her, tipping his hat back and scratching his head.

'Uh, no, not as far as we can tell,' I said. 'I haven't had a close look, but it doesn't seem like it.'

'Any damage done? Any vandalism of any kind?'

'No,' I said. 'Nothing of that sort.'

'You need to check for fingerprints,' Cynthia said.

The male cop said, 'Ma'am?'

'Fingerprints. Isn't that what you do when there's a break-in?'

'Ma'am, I'm afraid there's no real evidence here that there's been a break-in. Everything seems in order.'

'But this hat was left here. That shows someone broke in. We locked the house up before we left.'

'So you're saying,' the male cop said, 'someone broke into your house, didn't take anything, didn't break anything, but they got in here just so they could leave that hat on your kitchen table?'

Cynthia nodded. I could imagine how this looked to the officers.

'I think we'd have a hard time getting someone out to dust for prints,' the woman said. 'When there's no evidence of a crime having been committed.'

'This may be nothing more than a practical joke,' her partner said. 'Chances are it's someone you know having a bit of fun with you is all.'

Fun, I thought. Look at us, falling down laughing.

'There's no sign of the lock being messed with,' he said. 'Maybe someone you've given a key to came in, left this here, thought it belonged to you. Simple as that.'

My eye went to the small, empty hook where we usually keep an extra key. The one I'd noticed missing the other morning.

'Can you have an officer park out front?' Cynthia asked. 'To keep an eye on the house? In case anyone tries to get in again? But just to stop them, see who it is, not hurt them. I don't want you hurting whoever it is.'

'Cyn,' I said.

'Ma'am, I'm afraid there's no call for that. And we

don't have the manpower to put a car out front of your house, not without good reason,' the woman cop said. 'But if you have any more problems, you be sure to give us a call.'

With that, they excused themselves. And in all likelihood, got back in their car and had a good laugh at our expense. I could see us on the police blotter. Responded to report of strange hat. Everyone at the station would get a good chuckle out of that.

Once they were gone, we both took a seat at the kitchen table, the hat between us, neither of us saying a word.

Grace came into the kitchen, having slipped down the stairs noiselessly, pointed to the hat, grinned, and said, 'Can I wear it?'

Cynthia grabbed the hat. 'No,' she said.

'Go to bed, honey,' I said, and Grace toddled off. Cynthia didn't release her grip on the hat until we went up to bed.

That night, staring at the ceiling again, I thought about how Cynthia had forgotten, at the last minute, to take along her shoebox to the station for that disastrous meeting with the psychic. How she'd had to run back into the house, just for a minute, while Grace and I waited in the car.

How, even though I'd offered to run in and get the box for her, she beat me to it.

She was in the house a long time, just to grab a box. Took an Advil, she told me when she got back into the car.

Not possible, I told myself, glancing over at Cynthia, sleeping next to me.

Surely not.

FOURTEEN

I had a free period so I poked my head into Rolly Carruthers' office. 'I'm on a prep. You got a minute?'

Rolly looked at the stack of stuff on his desk. Reports from the board office, teacher evaluations, budget estimates. He was drowning in paperwork. 'If you only need a minute, I'll have to say no. If you need at least an hour, however, I might be able to help you out.'

'An hour sounds about right.'

'You had lunch?'

'No.'

'Let's go over to the Stonebridge. You drive. I may decide to get smashed.' He slipped on his sport jacket, told his secretary he'd be out of the school for a while but she could reach him on his cell if the building caught fire. 'So I'll know that I don't need to come back,' he said.

His secretary insisted he speak to one of the superintendents, who was holding, so he signaled to me that he would be just a couple of minutes. I stepped outside the office, right in the path of Jane Scavullo, who was bearing down the hall at high speed, no doubt for a date to beat the shit out of some other girl in the schoolyard.

The handful of books she was carrying scattered across the hallway.

'Fucking hell,' she said.

'Sorry,' I said, and knelt down to help her pick them up.

'It's OK,' she said, scrambling to get to the books before I did. But she wasn't quick enough. I already had *Foxfire*, the Joyce Carol Oates book I'd recommended to her, in my hand.

She snatched it away from me, tucked it in with the rest of her stuff.

I said, without a trace of I-told-you-so in my voice, 'How are you liking it?'

'It's good,' Jane said. 'Those girls are seriously messed up. Why'd you suggest I read it? You think I'm as bad the girls in this story?'

'Those girls aren't all bad,' I said. 'And no, I don't think you're like them. But I thought you'd appreciate the writing.'

She snapped her gum. 'Can I ask you something?'

'Sure.'

'What do you care?'

'What do you mean?'

'What do you care? About what I read, about my writing, that shit?'

'You think I'm a teacher just to get rich?'

She looked as though she was almost going to smile, and then caught herself. 'I gotta go,' she said, and did.

The lunch crowd had thinned by the time Rolly and I got to the Stonebridge. He ordered some coconut shrimp and a beer to start, and I settled on a large bowl of New England clam chowder with extra crackers, and coffee.

Rolly was talking about putting their house on the market soon, that they'd have a lot of money left over after they paid for the mobile home in Bradenton. There'd be money to put in the bank, they could invest it, take the odd trip. And Rolly was going to buy a boat so he could fish along the Manatee River. It's like he was already finished being a principal. He was someplace else.

'I got stuff on my mind,' I said.

Rolly took a sip of Sam Adams. 'This about Lauren Wells?'

'No,' I said, surprised. 'What made you think I wanted to talk about Wells?'

He shrugged. 'I noticed you talking to her in the hall.'

'She's a wingnut,' I said.

Rolly smiled. 'A well-packaged wingnut.'

'I don't know what it is. I think, in her world, Cynthia and I have achieved some sort of celebrity status. Lauren rarely spoke to me until we appeared on that show.'

'Can I have your autograph?' Rolly asked.

'Bite me,' I said. I waited a moment, as if to signal that I was changing gears here, and said, 'Cynthia's always thought of you like an uncle, you know? I know you looked out for her, after what happened. So I feel I can come to you, talk to you about her, when there's a problem.'

'Go on.'

'I'm starting to wonder whether Cynthia's losing it.'

Rolly put his glass of beer down on the table, licked his lips. 'Aren't the two of you already seeing some shrink, what's-her-name, Krinkle or something?'

'Kinzler. Yeah. Every couple of weeks or so.'

'Have you talked to her about this?'

'No. It's tricky. I mean, there are times when she talks to us separately. I could bring it up. But, it's not like it's any one thing. It's all these little things put together.'

'Like what?'

I filled him in. The anxiety over the brown car. The anonymous phone call from someone saying her family had forgiven her, how she'd accidentally erased the call. Chasing the guy in the mall, thinking he was her brother. The hat in the middle of the table.

'What?' Rolly said. 'Clayton's *hat*?'

'Yeah,' I said. 'Evidently. I mean, I suppose she could have had it tucked away in a box all these years. Regardless, it did have this little marking inside, his first initial, under the lining.'

Rolly thought about that. 'If she put the hat there, she could have written in the hat herself.'

That had never occurred to me. Cyn had let me look for the initial, rather than take the hat away from me and do it herself. Her expression of shock had been pretty convincing.

But I supposed what Rolly was suggesting was possible.

'And it doesn't even have to be her father's hat. It could be any hat. She could have bought it at a second-hand store, said it was his hat.'

'She smelled it,' I said. 'When she smelled it, she said for sure it was her father's hat.'

Rolly looked at me like I was one of his dumb high-school students. 'And she could have let you smell it, too, to confirm it. But that proves nothing.'

'She could be making everything up,' I said. 'I can't believe my mind's going there.'

'Cynthia doesn't strike me as mentally unbalanced,' Rolly said. 'Under tremendous stress, yes. But delusional?'

'No,' I said. 'She's not like that.'

'Or fabricating things? Why would she be making

these things up? Why would she pretend to get that phone call? Why would she set up something like the hat?'

'I don't know.' I struggled to come up with an answer. 'To get attention? So that, what? The police, whoever, would reopen the case? Finally find out what happened to her family?'

'Then why now?' Rolly asked. 'Why wait all this time to finally do this?'

Again, I had no idea. 'Shit, I don't know what to think. I just wish it would all end. Even if that meant we found out they had all died that night.'

'Closure,' Rolly said.

'I hate that word,' I said. 'But yeah, basically.'

'And the other thing you need to consider,' Rolly said, 'is that if she *didn't* leave that hat on the table, then you actually had an intruder in your house. And that doesn't necessarily mean it was Cynthia's father.'

'Yeah,' I said. 'I've already decided we've got to get deadbolts.' I pictured a stranger moving about through the rooms of our house, looking at our things, touching our stuff, getting a sense of who we were. I shuddered.

'We try to remember to lock the house up every time we go out. We're pretty good about it, but the odd time, I guess we must slip up. The back door, I guess it's possible we've forgotten that once in a while, especially if Grace was in and out and we didn't know it.' I thought about that missing key, tried to remember when I first noticed it wasn't on the hook. 'But I know we locked everything up the night we met with that nutjob psychic.'

'Psychic?' Rolly said.

I brought him up to speed.

'When you get deadbolts,' Rolly said, 'look into those bars you can put across basement windows. That's how a lot of kids get in.'

I was quiet for the next few minutes. I hadn't gotten to the big thing I wanted to discuss. Finally, I said, 'The thing is, there's more.'

'About what?'

'Cyn's in such a delicate frame of mind, there's stuff I'm not telling her.' Rolly raised an eyebrow. 'About Tess,' I said.

Rolly took another sip of his Sam Adams. 'What about Tess?'

'First of all, she's not well. She told me she's dying.'

'Ah, fuck,' Rolly said. 'What is it?'

'She didn't want to get into specifics, but I'm guessing it must be cancer or something like that. She doesn't look all that bad, mostly just tired, you know? But she's not going to get any better. At least that's the way it looks at the moment.'

'Cynthia'll be devastated. They're so close.'

'I know. And I think it has to be Tess who tells her. I can't do it. I don't *want* to do it. And before long, it's going to become obvious that something's wrong with her.'

'What's the other thing?'

'Huh?'

'You said "first of all" a second ago. What's the other thing?'

I hesitated. It seemed wrong to tell Rolly about the secret payments before I told Cynthia, but that was one of the reasons why I was telling him – to get some guidance on how to break this to my wife.

'For a number of years, Tess was getting money.'

Rolly set down his beer, took his hand off the glass. 'What do you mean, getting money?'

'Someone left money for her. Cash, in an envelope. A number of times, with a note that it was to help pay for Cynthia's education. The amounts varied, but it added up to more than $40,000.'

'Fucking hell,' Rolly said. 'And she'd never told you this before?'

'No.'

'Did she say who was it from?'

I shrugged. 'That's the thing. Tess had no idea, still has no idea, although she wonders whether the envelopes the money came in, the note, whether you could still get fingerprints off them after all these years, or DNA, shit, what do I know about that stuff? But she can't help but think it's linked to the disappearance of Cynthia's family. I mean, who would give her money, other than someone from her family, or someone who felt responsible for what had happened to her family?'

'Jesus Christ,' Rolly said. 'This is huge. And Cynthia doesn't know anything about this?'

'No. But she's entitled to know.'

'Sure, of course she is.' He wrapped his hand around the beer again, drained the glass, signaled the waitress that he wanted another. 'I suppose.'

'What do you mean?'

'I don't know. I have the same concerns you do. Suppose you do tell her. What then?'

I moved my spoon around in the clam chowder. I didn't have much of an appetite. 'That's the thing. It raises more questions than it answers.'

'And even if it did mean that maybe someone from Cynthia's family was alive then, it doesn't mean they're alive now. The money stopped showing up when?'

'Around the time she finished at university,' I said.

'What's that, twenty years?'

'Not quite. But a long time ago.'

Rolly shook his head in wonderment. 'Man, I don't know how to advise you. I mean, I think I know what I would do if I were in your shoes, but you've got to decide yourself how to handle this.'

'Tell me,' I said. 'What would you do?'

He pressed his lips together and leaned forward over the table. 'I'd sit on it.'

I guess I was surprised. 'Really?'

'At least for the time being. Because it's only going to torment Cynthia. It'll make her think that, at least back when she was a student, that had she known about the money, maybe there was something she could have done, that she could have found them if she'd only been paying attention and asking the right questions, that she could have found out what happened. But who knows whether that's even possible now.'

I thought about that. I thought he was right.

'And not only that,' he said. 'Just when Tess needs all the support and love she can get from Cynthia, when she's in poor health, Cynthia's going to be mad at her.'

'I hadn't considered that.'

'She's going to feel betrayed. She's going to feel her aunt had no business keeping this information from her all these years. She's going to feel it was her right to know about this. Which it was. And, arguably, still is. But not telling her back then, it's water under the bridge now.'

I nodded, but then stopped. 'But I've only just found

out. If I don't tell her, aren't I betraying her the same way she may feel Tess did?'

Rolly studied me and smiled. 'That's why I'm glad it's your decision instead of mine, my friend.'

When I got home, Cynthia's car was in the drive, and there was a vehicle I didn't recognize parked at the curb. A silver Toyota sedan, the anonymous kind of car you'd look at and never remember a moment later.

I stepped in through the front door, and saw Cynthia sitting on the couch in the living room across from a short, heavyset, nearly bald man with olive-colored skin. They both got to their feet and Cynthia moved toward me.

'Hi honey,' she said, forcing a smile.

'Hi sweetheart.' I turned toward the man and extended a hand, which he took confidently in his and shook. 'Hello,' I said.

'Mr Archer,' he said, his voice deep and almost syrupy.

'This is Mr Abagnall,' Cynthia said. 'This is the private detective we're hiring to find out what happened to my family.'

FIFTEEN

'Denton Abagnall,' the detective said. 'Mrs Archer here has filled me in on a lot of the particulars, but I wouldn't mind asking you a few questions as well.'

'Sure,' I said, holding a 'hang on just a second' finger up to him and turning to Cynthia to say. 'Can I talk to you a minute?'

She gave Abagnall an apologetic look and said, 'Could you excuse us?' He nodded. I steered Cynthia out the front door and on to the top step. Our house was small enough that I figured Abagnall would hear us if we had this discussion – which I was worried might become a bit heated – in the kitchen.

'What the hell's going on?' I asked.

'I'm not waiting around any more,' Cynthia said. 'I'm not going to wait for something to happen, wondering what's going to happen next. I've decided to take charge of this situation.'

'What do you expect him to find out?' I asked. 'Cynthia, it's a very old trail. It's been twenty-five years.'

'Oh, thanks,' she said. 'I'd forgotten.'

I winced.

'Well, that hat didn't appear twenty-five years ago,' she said. 'That happened this week. And that phone call I got, that morning you walked Grace to school, that wasn't twenty-five years ago, either.'

'Honey,' I said. 'Even if I thought hiring a private

detective was a good idea, I don't see how we can afford it. How much does he charge?'

She told me his daily rate. 'And any expenses he has are on top of that,' she said.

'OK, so how long are you prepared to let him go?' I said. 'Are you going to keep him on this a week? A month? Six months? Something like this, he could spend a year on it and still be getting nowhere.'

'We can skip a mortgage payment,' Cynthia said. 'You remember, that letter the bank sent us before last Christmas? That offer to let you skip a payment in January, so you can pay off your Christmas Visa bill? They tack the missed payment onto the end of the mortgage? They might do that again, and this can be my Christmas present. You don't have to get me anything this year.'

I looked down at my feet and shook my head. I really didn't know what to do.

'What's happening with you, Terry?' Cynthia asked. 'One of the reasons I married you is because I knew you'd be a guy who was always there for me, who knew the kind of fucked-up history I had, who'd support me, who'd be in my corner. And for years, you've been that guy. But lately, I don't know, I'm getting this vibe, that maybe you aren't that guy any more. That maybe you're getting tired of being that guy. That maybe you're not even sure you believe me all the time any more.'

'Cynthia, don't—'

'Maybe that's one of the reasons why I'm doing this, why I want to hire this man. Because he's not going to judge me. He's not going into this thinking I'm some sort of crackpot.'

'I never said I think you're a—'

'You don't have to,' Cynthia said. 'I could see it in your eyes. When I thought that man was my brother. You thought I'd lost my mind.'

'Jesus Christ,' I said. 'Hire your fucking detective.'

I never saw the slap coming. I don't think Cynthia did either, and she was the one swinging. It just happened. An explosion of anger, like a thunderclap, standing out there on the step. And all we could do for a couple of seconds was look at each other in stunned silence. Cynthia appeared to be in shock, both hands poised just over her open mouth.

Finally, I said, 'I guess I can be grateful it wasn't your backhand. I wouldn't even be standing now.'

'Terry,' she said. 'I don't know what happened. I just, I just kind of lost my mind there for a second.'

I pulled her close to me, whispered into her ear, 'I'm sorry. I'll always be that guy in your corner, I'll always be here for you.'

She put her arms around me and pressed her head into my chest. I had a pretty good feeling that we'd be throwing our money away. But even if Denton Abagnall didn't find out anything, maybe hiring him to try was exactly what Cynthia needed to do. Maybe she was right. It was a way to take control of the situation.

At least for a while. For as long as we could afford it. I did some quick calculations in my head and figured that a month's mortgage payment, plus dipping into the movie rental fund for the next couple of months, would buy us a week of Abagnall's time.

'We'll hire him,' I said. She hugged me a bit more tightly.

'If he doesn't find anything soon,' she said, still not looking at me, 'we'll stop.'

'What do we know about this guy?' I asked. 'Is he reliable? Is he trustworthy?'

Cynthia pulled away, sniffed. I handed her a tissue from my pocket and she dabbed her eyes, blew her nose. 'I called *Deadline*. Got the producer. She got all defensive when she knew it was me, figured I was going to give her shit about that psychic, but then I asked her if they ever used detectives to find out stuff for them, and she gave me this guy's name, said they hadn't used him, but they did a story on him once. Said he seemed on the up and up.'

'Then let's go talk to him,' I said.

Abagnall had been sitting on the couch, looking through Cynthia's shoeboxes of mementoes, and got up when we came in. I know he spotted my red cheek, but he did a good job of not being too obvious about it.

'I hope you don't mind,' he said. 'I was having a look at your things here. I'd like to spend some more time looking at them, provided you've reached a decision about whether you want my help.'

'We have,' I said. 'And we do. We'd like you to try to find out what happened to Cynthia's family.'

'I'm not going to give you any false hopes,' Abagnall said. He spoke slowly, deliberately, and jotted down the occasional thing in his notebook. 'This is a very cold trail. I'll start with reviewing the police file on this, talking to anyone who remembers working on the case, but I think you should have low expectations.'

Cynthia nodded solemnly.

'I don't see a lot here,' he said, motioning to the shoeboxes, 'that jumps out at me, that offers any sorts of clues, at least right away. But I wouldn't mind hanging on to these, for a while, if you don't mind.'

'That's fine,' Cynthia said. 'Just so long as I get them back.'

'Of course.'

'What about the hat?' she asked. The hat she believed to be her father's sat on the couch next to him. He'd been looking at it earlier.

'Well,' he said. 'The first thing I would suggest is that you and your husband review your security arrangements here, perhaps upgrade your locks, get deadbolts on your doors.'

'I'm on it,' I said. I had already called a couple of locksmiths to see who could fit us in first.

'Because whether this hat is your father's or not, someone got in here and left it. You have a daughter. You want this house to be as secure as it can possibly be. As far as determining whether this is your father's,' he said, his voice low and comforting, 'I suppose I could take it to a private lab and they could attempt to do a DNA test on it, to find hair samples from it, sweat from the inside lining. But that won't be cheap, and Mrs Archer, you'd need to provide a sample for comparison purposes. If there turned out to be a link between your DNA and what they might find on this hat, well, that might confirm that this was indeed your father's, but it won't tell us where he is or whether he's alive.'

I could tell, looking at Cynthia, that she was starting to feel overwhelmed.

'Why don't we just leave out that part of it for now,' I suggested.

Abagnall nodded. 'That would be my advice, at least for the time being.' Inside his jacket, his cell phone rang. 'Excuse me one second.' He opened the phone, saw who was calling, answered it. 'Yes, love?' He listened, nodded. 'Oh, that sounds wonderful. With the shrimp?' He smiled. 'But not too spicy. OK, I'll see you in a bit.' He folded the phone and put it away. 'My wife,' he said. 'She gives me a call about this time to let me know what she's making for dinner.'

Cynthia and I exchanged glances.

'Shrimp with linguini in a hot pepper sauce tonight,' he said, smiling. 'Gives me something to look forward to. Now, Mrs Archer. I wonder, do you have any photos of your father? You've provided some of your mother, and one of your brother, but I have nothing for Clayton Bigge.'

'I'm afraid not,' she said.

'I'll check with the Department of Motor Vehicles,' he said. 'I don't know how far back their records go, but maybe they have a photo. And perhaps you could tell me a bit more about the route he traveled for work.'

'Between here and Chicago,' Cynthia said. 'He was in sales. He took orders, I think it was, for machine shop supplies. That kind of thing.'

'You never knew his exact route?'

She shook her head. 'I was just a kid. I didn't really understand what he did, only that it meant he was on the road a lot of the time. One time, he showed me some pictures of the Wrigley building in Chicago. There's a Polaroid shot of it in the box, I think.'

Abagnall nodded, folded his notebook shut and slipped it into his jacket, then handed each of us a business card. He gathered up the shoeboxes and got to his feet. 'I'll be in touch soon, let you know how I'm progressing. How about you pay me now for three days of my services. I wouldn't expect to find the answers to your questions in that time, but I might have an idea whether I think it's reasonable to think that such a thing is possible.'

Cynthia went for her checkbook, which was in her purse, wrote out a check and handed it to Abagnall.

Grace, who had been upstairs all this time, called down, 'Mom? Can you come up here for a second? I spilled something on my top.'

'I'll walk Mr Abagnall to his car,' I said.

Abagnall had his door open and was about to plop down into his seat when I said, 'Cynthia mentioned that you might want to talk to her aunt, to Tess.'

'Yes.'

If I didn't want Abagnall's efforts to be a complete waste, it made sense for him to know as much as possible.

'She recently told me something, something she's not yet disclosed to Cynthia.'

Abagnall didn't beg, but waited. I told him about the anonymous donations of cash.

'Well,' he said.

'I'll tell Tess to expect you. And I'll tell her she should tell you everything.'

'Thank you,' he said. He dropped into the seat, pulled the door shut, powered down the window. 'Do you believe her?'

'Tess? Yes, I do. She showed me the note, the envelopes.'

'No. Your wife. Do you believe your wife?'

I cleared my throat before responding. 'Of course.'

Abagnall reached over his shoulder for the seatbelt, snapped it in place. 'One time I had a woman call me up, wanted me to find someone, went to see her, and can you guess who she wanted me to locate?'

I waited.

'Elvis. She wanted me to find Elvis Presley. This was around 1990, I think it was, and Elvis had been dead about thirteen years at that point. She lived in a big house, had lots of money, and she had a few screws loose as I'm sure you might have guessed, and she'd never so much as met Elvis in her entire life and had no connection to him whatsoever, but she was convinced that the King was still alive and just waiting for her to find and rescue him. I could have worked for her for a year, trying to track him down for her. She could have been my early retirement plan, this lady, bless her heart. But I had to say no. She was very upset, so I explained to her that I'd been hired once before to find Elvis, and that I'd found him, and he was fine, but wanted to live the rest of his life in peace.'

'No kidding. And did she accept that?'

'Well, she seemed to at the time. Of course, she might have called some other detective. For all I know, he's still working on the case.' He chuckled softly to himself. 'Wouldn't that be something.'

'What's your point, Mr Abagnall?' I asked.

'I guess the point I'm making is, your wife really wants to know what happened to her parents, and her brother. I wouldn't take a check from someone I thought was trying to string me a line. Your wife isn't trying to string me a line.'

'No, I don't think she is, either,' I said. 'But this woman who wanted you to find Elvis, was she trying to string you a line? Or did she really believe, in her heart, that Elvis was still alive?'

Abagnall gave me a sad smile. 'I'll report back to you folks in three days, sooner if I learn anything interesting.'

SIXTEEN

'Men are weak – not you of course – and they let you down, but just as often it's the women who'll really betray you,' she said.

'I know. You've said this before,' he said.

'Oh, I'm sorry.' Getting sarcastic. He didn't like it when she got like that. 'Am I boring you, sweetheart?'

'No, it's OK. Go ahead. You were saying. Women will betray you, too. I was listening.'

'That's right. Like that Tess.'

'Yeah, her.'

'She stole from me.'

'Well . . .' Technically speaking, he was thinking, then decided it wasn't worth getting into a debate.

'That's basically what she did,' she said. 'That money was mine. She had no business hanging on to it herself.'

'It's not like she spent it on herself. She did use it to—'

'Enough! It makes me crazy, the more I think about it. And I don't appreciate you defending her.'

'I'm not defending her,' he said.

'She should have found a way to tell me and make things right.'

And how would she have done that? he wondered. But he said nothing.

'Are you there?' she said.

'I'm still here.'

'Was there something you wanted to say?'

'Nothing. Just . . . well, that would have been a bit tricky, don't you think?'

'I can't talk to you sometimes,' she said. 'Call me tomorrow. If I need some intelligent conversation in the meantime, I'll talk to the mirror.'

SEVENTEEN

After Abagnall left, I called Tess from my cell to give her a heads-up.

'I'll help him any way I can,' Tess said. 'I think Cynthia's doing the right thing, having someone private look into this. If she's willing to take this kind of step, she's probably ready for me to tell her what I know.'

'We'll all get together again soon.'

'When the phone rang, I was actually thinking about calling you,' Tess said. 'But I didn't want to call you at the house, it would seem odd, my asking for you if Cynthia answered, and I don't think I have your cell phone number around here anywhere.'

'What is it, Tess?'

She took a breath. 'Oh Terry, I went for another test.'

I felt my legs going weak. 'What did they say?' She'd told me earlier that she might have six months to a year left. I wondered if that timetable had been shortened.

'I'm going to be OK,' she said. 'They said the other tests, they were fairly conclusive, but they turned out to be wrong. This last one, it was definite.' She paused. 'Terry, I'm not dying.'

'Oh my God, Tess, that's such wonderful news. They're sure?'

'They're sure.'

'That's so fabulous.'

'Yeah, if I were the kind of person who ever prayed,

I'd have to say my prayers were answered. But Terry. Tell me you didn't tell Cynthia.'

'I never told her,' I said.

When I went inside, Cynthia spotted a tear running down my cheek. I thought I'd wiped my cheeks dry, but evidently I'd missed one. She reached up and brushed it away with her index finger. 'Terry,' she said. 'What? What's happened?'

I threw my arms around her. 'I'm so happy,' I said. 'I'm just so happy.'

She must have thought I was losing my mind. No one was ever this happy around here.

Cynthia was more at ease than I had seen her for some time the next couple of days. With Denton Abagnall on the case, a sense of calm washed over her. I was afraid she'd be calling his cell every couple of hours, like with the *Deadline* producers, wanting to know what progress, if any, he was making. But she did not. Sitting at the kitchen table, just before we headed up for bed, she asked me whether I thought he'd learn anything, so his progress was very much on her mind, but she was willing to let him do his job without being hounded.

After Grace was home from school the following day, Cynthia suggested they go over to the public tennis courts behind the library, and she said sure. I'm no better at tennis now than I was in university, so I rarely, if ever, pick up a racket, but I still enjoy watching the girls play, particularly to marvel at Cynthia's mean backhand. So I tagged along, bringing some papers to mark, glancing up every few seconds to watch my wife and daughter run and laugh and make fun of each other. Of course, Cynthia didn't use her backhand to pummel Grace, but was always offering her friendly tips on how to perfect her own. Grace wasn't bad, but after half an hour on the court, I could see her tiring, and I was guessing she'd rather be home reading Carl Sagan, like all the other eight-year-old girls.

When they were done, I suggested grabbing some dinner on the way home.

'Are you sure?' Cynthia asked. 'What with ... our other expense of the moment?'

'I don't care,' I said.

Cynthia gave me a devilish smile. 'What is it with you? Ever since yesterday, you're the most cheerful little boy in town.'

How could I tell her? How could I let her know how thrilled I was by Tess's good news when she'd never been privy to the bad? She'd be happy that Tess was OK, but hurt that she'd been kept out of the loop.

'I just feel ... optimistic,' I said.

'That Mr Abagnall is going to find out something?'

'Not necessarily. I just feel as though we've turned a corner, that you – that we – have gone through some stressful times of late, and that we're coming out of them.'

'Then I think I'll have a glass of wine with dinner,' she said.

I returned her playful smile. 'I think you should.'

'I'm going to have a milkshake,' Grace said. 'With a cherry.'

When we got home from dinner, Grace vanished to watch something on the *Discovery* channel about what Saturn's rings are really made of, and Cynthia and I plunked ourselves down at the kitchen table. I was writing down numbers on a scratch pad, adding them up, doing them another way. This was where we always sat when faced with weighty financial decisions. Could we afford that second car? Would a trip to Disney World break the bank?

'I'm thinking,' I said, looking at the numbers, 'that we could probably afford Mr Abagnall for two weeks instead of just one. I don't think it would put us in the poor house, you know?'

Cynthia put her hand over the one I was writing with. 'I love you, you know.'

In the other room, someone on the TV said 'Uranus' and Grace giggled.

'Did I ever tell you about the time,' Cynthia asked, 'when I ruined my mother's James Taylor cassette?'

'No.'

'I must have been eleven or twelve, and Mom had lots of music. She loved James Taylor, Simon and Garfunkel, Neil Young and lots of others, but most of all she liked James Taylor. She said he could make her happy, and he could make her sad. One day, Mom made me mad about something, there was something I wanted to wear to school that was in the dirty clothes pile and I mouthed off because she hadn't done her job.'

'That must have gone over well.'

'No kidding. She said if she wasn't cleaning my clothes to my satisfaction I knew where the washing machine was. So I popped open the cassette player she had in the kitchen, grabbed whatever tape was in there and threw it on the floor. It busted open and the tape spilled out and the thing was ruined.'

I listened.

'I froze, I couldn't even believe I'd done it, and I thought she'd kill me. But instead, she stopped what she was doing, went over, picked up the tape, calm as could be, had a look at which one it was, and said, "James Taylor. This is the one with 'Your Smiling Face' on it. That's my favorite. You know why I like that one?" she asks me. "Because it starts off how every time I see your face, I have to smile myself, because I love you." Anyway, something like that. And she said, "That's my favorite because every time I hear it, it makes me think of you, and how much I love you. And right about now, you need me to hear that song more than ever."'

Cynthia's eyes were wet.

'So, after school, I took the bus over to the Post Mall and I found the cassette. *JT*, it was called. I bought it and brought it home, and I gave it to her. And she got all the cellophane wrapping off it and put the cassette into her player and asked me if I wanted to hear her favorite song.'

A single tear ran down her cheek and dropped onto the kitchen table. 'I love that song,' Cynthia said. 'And I miss her so much.'

Later, she phoned Tess. No special reason, just to talk. Afterwards, she came up to the extra bedroom with the sewing machine and the computer, where I was typing a couple of notes to students on my old Royal, and her red eyes suggested that she had been crying again.

Tess, she told me, thought she was very ill, terminal even, but it's turned out to be OK.

'She said she didn't want to tell me, that she thought I had enough on my plate, that she didn't want to *burden* me with it. That's what she said. "Burden". Can you imagine?'

'That's so crazy,' I said.

'And then she finds out she's actually OK, and felt she could tell me everything, but I just wish she'd told me when she knew, you know? Because she's always been there for me, and no matter what I'm going through, she's always ...' She grabbed a tissue and blew her nose. Finally, she said, 'I can't imagine losing her.'

'I know. Neither can I.'

'When you were so happy, that didn't have anything ...'

'No,' I said. 'Of course not.'

I probably could have told her the truth. I could have afforded to be honest at that moment, but chose not to.

'Oh shit,' she said. 'She asked me to tell you to call her. She probably wants to tell you this herself. Don't tell her I already told you, OK? Please? I just couldn't keep it to myself, you know?'

'Sure,' I said.

I went downstairs and dialed Tess.

'I told her,' Tess said.

'I know,' I said. 'Thank you.'

'He was here.'

'Hmm?'

'The detective. That Mr Abagnall. He's a very nice man.'

'Yes.'

'His wife called while he was here. To tell him what she was making him for dinner.'

'What was it?' I had to know.

'Uh, some sort of roast, I think. Roast beef and Yorkshire pudding.'

'Sounds delicious.'

'Anyway, I told him everything. About the money,

the letter. I gave all of it to him. He was very interested.'

I nodded. 'I would think so.'

'Mr Abagnall wasn't too hopeful about getting fingerprints off those envelopes after all these years.'

'It's been so long, Tess, and you've handled them quite a few times. But I think that was the best thing to do, giving him everything. If you think of anything else, you should give him a call.'

'That's what he asked me to do. He gave me his card. I'm looking at it right now, it's pinned to my board here by the phone, right next to that picture of Grace with Goofy. I don't know which one looks goofier.'

'OK,' I said.

'Give Cynthia a hug for me,' she said.

'I will. I love you, Tess,' I said, and hung up.

'She told you?' Cynthia asked me when I got up to our bedroom.

'She told me.'

Cynthia, now in her nightshirt, lay on the bed, on top of the covers. 'I'd been thinking, all evening, that I would like to make mad, passionate love to you tonight, but I'm so dead tired, I'm not sure I could perform to any reasonable standard.'

'I'm not particular,' I said.

'So how about a rain check?'

'Sure. Maybe what we should do is get Tess to take Grace for a weekend, we could drive up to Mystic. Get a bed and breakfast.'

Cynthia agreed. 'Maybe I'd sleep better up there, too,' she said. 'My dreams have been ... kind of unsettling lately.'

I sat down on the edge of the bed. 'What do you mean?'

'It's like I told Dr Kinzler. I hear them talking. They're talking to me, I think, or I'm talking to them, or we're all talking with each other, but it's like I'm with them but not with them, and I can almost reach out and touch them. But when I do, it's like they're smoke. They just blow away.'

I leaned over, kissed her forehead. 'Have you said goodnight to Grace?'

'While you were talking to Tess.'

'You try to get some sleep. I'll say goodnight to her.'

As usual, Grace's room was in total darkness so as to give her a better view of the stars through her telescope. 'Are we safe tonight?' I asked as I slipped in, closing the door to the hall behind me to keep the light out.

'Looks like it,' Grace said.

'That's good.'

'You wanna see?'

Grace had her telescope set up to her own eye-level, but I didn't want to have to bend over that far. I grabbed the Ikea computer chair from her desk, placed it in front of the telescope, and sat down. I squinted into the end, saw nothing but blackness with a few pinpricks of light. 'OK, what am I looking at?'

'Stars,' Grace said.

I turned and looked at her, grinning impishly in the dim light. 'Thank you, Carl Sagan,' I said. I got my eye back in position, went to adjust the scope a bit, and it slipped partway off its stand. 'Whoa!' I said. Some of the tape Grace had used to secure the telescope had worked free.

'I told you,' she said. 'It's kind of a crappy stand.'

'OK, OK,' I said, and looked back into the scope, but the view had shifted and what I was looking at now was a hugely magnified circle of the sidewalk out front of our house.

And a man, watching it. His face, blurry and indistinct, filled the lens.

I abandoned the telescope, got out of the chair and went to the window. 'Who the hell is that?' I said, more to myself than Grace.

'Who?' she said.

She got to the window in time to see the man run away. 'Who's that, Daddy?' she asked.

'You stay right here,' I said, and bolted out of her room, went down the steps two at a time and nearly flew out the front door. I ran down to the end of the drive, looked up the street in the direction I'd seen the man run. A hundred feet ahead, red brake lights on a car parked at the curb came on as someone turned the ignition, moved it from park to drive, and floored it.

I was too far away, and it was too dark out to catch a license plate, or tell what kind of car it was before it turned the corner and rumbled away. From the sound of it, it was an older model, and dark. Blue, brown, gray, it was impossible to tell. I was tempted to jump in my car, but the keys were in the house, and by the time I had them the man would be halfway to Bridgeport.

When I got back to the front door Grace was standing there. 'I told you to stay in your room,' I said angrily.

'I just wanted to see—'

'Get to bed right now.'

She could tell from my tone that I wasn't interested in an argument, and she tore up the stairs lickety-split.

My heart was pounding and I needed a moment for it to settle down before I went upstairs. When I finally did, I found Cynthia, under the covers, fast asleep. I looked at her and wondered what sorts of conversations she was listening in on or having with the missing or the dead.

Ask them a question for me, I wanted to say. Ask them who's watching our house. Ask them what he wants with us.

EIGHTEEN

Cynthia phoned Pam and arranged to show up for work a bit late the next day. We'd booked a locksmith at nine in the morning, and if he ended up taking longer installing deadbolts than expected, Cynthia was covered.

I told her, over breakfast and before Grace came down to go to school, about the man on the sidewalk. I contemplated not doing so, but only briefly. First of all, Grace would in all likelihood bring it up, and secondly, if there was someone watching the house, whoever he was and for whatever reason, we all needed to be on high alert. For all we knew, this had absolutely nothing to do with Cynthia's particular situation, but was some sort of neighborhood pervert the entire street needed to be alerted to.

'Did you get a good look at him?' Cynthia asked.

'No. I went to chase him down the street, but he got in a car and drove away.'

'Did you get a look at the car?'

'No.'

'Could it have been a brown car?'

'Cyn, I don't know. It was dark, the car was dark.'

'So it could have been brown.'

'Yes, it could have been brown. And it could have been dark blue, or black. I don't know.'

'I'll bet it was the same person. The one who was driving past me and Grace on the way to school.'

'I'm going to talk to the neighbors,' I said.

I managed to catch the people on both sides as they were leaving for work, asked them if they'd noticed anyone hanging around last night, or any other night for that matter, whether they'd seen anything they'd consider suspicious. No one had seen a thing.

But I put in a call to the police anyway, just in case someone else on the street had reported anything out of the ordinary in the last few days, and they transferred me to someone who kept track of these things, and he said, 'Nothing much, although, hang on, there was a report the other day, something quite bizarre, really.'

'What?' I asked. 'What was it?'

'Someone called about a strange hat in their house.' The man laughed. 'At first, I thought maybe this was a typo, that someone got a bat in their house, but nope, it's hat.'

'Never mind,' I said.

Before I left for school, Cynthia said, 'I'd like to go out and see Tess. I mean, I know we were just there, but considering what she's been through lately, I was thinking that ...'

'Say no more,' I said. 'I think that's a great idea. Why don't we go over tomorrow night? Maybe take her out for ice cream or something?'

'I'm going to call her,' Cynthia said.

At school, I found Rolly rinsing out a mug in the school staff room so he could pour himself some of the incredibly horrible coffee they provided. 'How're things?' I asked, coming up behind him.

He jumped. 'Jesus,' he said.

'Sorry,' I said. 'I work here.' I got myself a mug, filled it, added a few extra sugars to mask the taste.

'How's it going?' I tried again.

Rolly shrugged. He seemed distracted. 'Same old. You?'

I let out a sigh. 'Someone was standing in the dark staring at our house last night, and when I tried to find out who it was he ran away.' I took a sip of the coffee I had poured. It tasted bad, but it was so cold you hardly noticed. 'Who's responsible for this? Is the coffee thing contracted out to a sewage disposal company?'

'Someone was watching your house?' Rolly said. 'What do you think he was doing there?'

I shrugged. 'I don't know, but they're putting dead-bolts on the doors this morning and just in time, it seems.'

'That's pretty creepy,' Rolly said. 'Maybe some guy trolling your street, looking for people who've left their garage doors open or something. Just wants to steal some stuff.'

'Maybe,' I said. 'Either way, new locks aren't a bad idea.'

'True,' Rolly said, nodded. He paused, then, 'I'm thinking of taking early retirement.'

So we were done talking about me. 'I thought you had to stay at least until the end of the school year.'

'Yeah, well, what if I dropped dead? They'd have to find someone fast then, wouldn't they? It only means a few bucks less per month on my pension. I'm ready to move on, Terry. Running a school, working in a school, it's not like it used to be, you know? I mean, you always had tough kids, but it's worse now. They're armed. Their parents don't give a shit. I gave the system forty years and now I want out. Millicent and I, we sell the house, sock some money into the bank, head to

Bradenton, maybe my blood pressure will start to go down a little bit.'

'You do look a bit tense today. Maybe you should go home.'

'I'm alright.' He paused. Rolly didn't smoke, but he looked like a smoker who desperately needed to light up. 'Millicent's already retired. There's nothing to stop me. None of us are getting any younger, right? You never know how much longer you've got. You're here one minute, gone the next.'

'Oh,' I said. 'That reminds me.'

'What?'

'About Tess.'

Rolly blinked. 'What about Tess?'

'It turns out, she's going to be OK.'

'What?'

'They did another test, turns out the initial diagnosis was wrong. She's not dying. She's going to be fine.'

Rolly looked stupefied. 'What are you talking about?'

'I'm telling you she's going to be OK.'

'But,' he said slowly, as if unable to take it all in, 'those doctors, they told her she was dying. And now, what, they say they were wrong?'

'You know,' I said. 'This is not what I'd call *bad* news.'

Rolly blinked. 'No, of course not. It's wonderful news. Better than getting good news and then getting bad, I suppose.'

'True.'

Rolly glanced at his watch. 'Listen, I've got to go.'

So did I. My creative writing class started in one minute. The last assignment I'd given them was to write a letter to someone they didn't know, and to tell this person – real or imaginary – something they didn't feel they could tell anyone else. 'Sometimes,' I'd said, 'it's easier to tell a stranger something very personal. It's like there's less risk, opening yourself up to someone who doesn't know you.'

When I asked for a volunteer to kick things off, to my amazement, Bruno, the class wise-ass, put up his hand.

'Bruno?'

'Yes, sir, I'm ready.'

It was unlike Bruno to volunteer, or have completed an assignment. I was wary, but at the same time, intrigued. 'OK, Bruno, let's have it.'

He opened his notebook and began, 'Dear Penthouse . . .'

'Hold it,' I said. The class was already laughing. 'This is supposed to be a letter to someone you don't know.'

'I don't know no one at Penthouse,' Bruno said. 'And I did just like you said. I wrote them about something I wouldn't tell nobody else. Well, not my mama, anyhow.'

'Your mama's the one got a staple through her belly,' someone quipped.

'You wish your mama looked like that,' Bruno said. 'Stead of like somebody's photocopied butt.'

'Anyone else?' I asked.

'No, wait,' Bruno said. 'Dear Penthouse: I'd like to tell you about an experience involving a very close personal friend of mine, whom I shall henceforth call Mr Johnson.'

A kid named Ryan nearly fell off his chair from laughing.

As usual, Jane Scavullo sat at the back of the room, gazing at the window, bored, acting as though everything that was happening in this class was beneath her. Today, perhaps she was right. She looked as though she'd rather be any place but here, and if I could have looked in a mirror right then I might have found myself wearing the same expression.

A girl who sat ahead of her, Valerie Swindon, a pleaser if there ever was one, had her hand up.

'Dear President Lincoln: I think you were one of the greatest presidents because you fought to free slaves and make everyone equal.'

It went on from there. Kids yawned, rolled their eyes and I thought it was a terrible state of affairs when you couldn't be earnest about Abraham Lincoln without seeming like a dweeb. But even as she read her letter, I found my mind wandering to the Bob Newhart routine, the phone conversation between the savvy Madison Avenue type and the president, how he tells Abe maybe he should unwind, take in a play.

I asked a couple of other kids to share, and then tried Jane.

'I'll pass,' she said.

At the end of class, on her way out, she dropped a sheet of paper on my desk.

Dear Anyone: This is a letter from one anyone to another anyone, no names required, because nobody really knows anybody anyway. Names don't make a hell of a lot of difference. The world is made up entirely of strangers. Millions and millions of them. Everyone is a stranger to everyone else. Sometimes we think we know other people, especially those we supposedly are close to, but if we really knew them, why are we so often surprised by the shit they do? Like, parents are always surprised by what their kids will do. They raise them from the time they are babies, spend each and every day with them, think they're these goddamn fucking angels, and then one day the cops come to the door and say hey, guess what parents? Your kid just bashed some other kid's head in with a baseball bat. Or you're the kid, and you think things are pretty fucking OK, and then one day this guy who's supposed to be your dad says so long, have a nice life. And you think, what the fuck is this? So years later, your mom ends up living with another guy, and he seems OK, but you think, when's it coming? That's what life is. Life is always asking yourself, when's it coming? Because if it hasn't come for a long, long time, you know you're fucking due. All the best, Anyone.

I read it a couple of times, and then at the top, with my red pen, I printed an 'A'.

I wanted to drop by Pamela's at lunch again to see Cynthia, and as I was walking to my car in the staff parking lot, Lauren Wells was pulling into the empty spot next to mine, steering with one hand, a cell phone pressed up against her head with the other.

I had managed not to run into her the last couple of days, and didn't want to talk to her now, but she was powering her window down and raising her chin at me while she kept talking on the cell, signaling me to hold on. She stopped the car, said, 'Hang on a sec,' into the phone then turned to me.

'Hey,' she said. 'I haven't seen you since you went back to see Paula. Are you going to be on the show again?'

'No,' I said.

Her face flashed disappointment. 'That's too bad,' she said. 'It might have helped, right? Did Paula say no?'

'Nothing like that,' I said.

'Listen,' Lauren said. 'Can you do me a favor? Just for a second? Can you say hi to my friend?'

'What?'

She held up the cell. 'Her name's Rachel. Just say hi to her. Say, "Hi Rachel". She'll die when I tell her you're the one whose wife was on that show.'

I opened the door to my car and before I got in said, 'Get a life, Lauren.'

She stared at me open-mouthed, then shouted, loud enough for me to hear through the glass, 'You think you're hot shit but you're not!'

When I got to Pamela's, Cynthia was not there.

'She called in, said the locksmith was coming,' Pamela said. I glanced at my watch. It was nearly one. I figured that if the locksmith showed up on time, he'd have been gone by ten, eleven at the latest.

I reached into my pocket for my cell, but Pam offered me the phone on the counter.

'Hi Pam,' Cynthia said when she answered. Caller ID. 'I'm so sorry. I'm on my way.'

'It's me,' I said.

'Oh!'

'I dropped by, figured you'd be here.'

'The guy was late, left only a little while ago. I was just heading over.'

Pam said to me, 'Tell her not to worry, it's quiet. Take the day.'

'You hear that?' I said.

'Yeah. Maybe it's just as well. I can't keep my mind on anything. Mr Abagnall phoned. He wants to see us. He's coming by at 4.30. Can you be home by then?'

'Of course. What did he say? Has he found out anything?'

Pamela's eyebrows went up.

'He wouldn't say. He said he'd discuss everything with us when he gets here.'

'You OK?'

'I feel kind of weird.'

'Yeah, me too. He might be telling us that he hasn't found a thing.'

'I know.'

'We seeing Tess tomorrow?'

'I left a message. Don't be late, OK?'

When I hung up, Pam said, 'What's going on?'

'Cynthia hired – *we* hired someone to look into her family's disappearance.'

'Oh,' she said. 'Well, it's none of my business, but you ask me, it happened so long ago, you're just throwing your money away. No one's ever going to know what happened that night.'

'See you later, Pam,' I said. 'Thanks for the use of the phone.'

'Would you like some coffee?' Cynthia asked as Denton Abagnall came into our house.

'Oh, I'd like that,' he said. 'I'd like that very much.'

He got settled on the couch and Cynthia brought out coffee and cups and sugar and cream on a tray, as well as some chocolate-chip cookies, and then she poured coffee into three cups and held the plate of cookies for Abagnall and he took one, and inside our heads both Cynthia and I were screaming: 'For God's sake, tell us what you know – we can't stand it another minute!'

Cynthia glanced down at the tray and said to me, 'I only got two spoons, Terry. Could you grab another one?'

I went back into the kitchen, opened the cutlery drawer for a spoon, and something caught my eye down in that space between the edge of the Rubbermaid cutlery holder and the wall of the drawer, where all sorts of odds and ends collect, from pencils and pens to those little plastic clips from the ends of bread bags.

A key.

I dug it out. It was the spare back door key that normally hung on the hook.

I went back into the living room with the spoon, and sat down as Abagnall got out his notebook. He opened it up, leafed through a few pages, said, 'Let me just see what I've got here.'

Cynthia and I smiled patiently.

'OK, here we are,' he said. He looked at Cynthia. 'Mrs Archer, what can you tell me about Vince Fleming?'

'Vince Fleming?'

'That's right. He was the boy you were with that night. You and he, you were parked in a car . . .' He stopped himself. 'I'm sorry,' he said, looking at Cynthia and then at me and then back at Cynthia again. 'Are you comfortable with me talking about this in front of your husband?'

'It's fine,' she said.

'You were parked in his car, out at the mall, I believe.

That was where your father found you and brought you home.'

'Yes.'

'I've had a chance to go over the police files on this case, and the producer at that TV show, she showed me a tape of the program – I'm sorry, I never saw it when it originally ran, I don't much care for crime shows – but most of the information they got was from the police. And this Vince Fleming fellow, he has a bit of checkered history, if you get my drift.'

'I'm afraid I didn't really keep in touch with him after that night,' Cynthia said.

'He's been in and out of trouble with the law his whole life,' Abagnall said. 'And his father was no different. Anthony Fleming, he ran a rather significant criminal organization back around that time.'

'Like the Mafia?' I said.

'Not quite that extensive. But he had his hand in a significant portion of the illegal drug market between New Haven and Bridgeport. Prostitution, truck hijackings, that kind of thing.'

'My God,' Cynthia said. 'I had no idea. I mean, I knew Vince was a bit of a bad boy, but I had no idea what his father was involved in. Is his father still alive?'

'No. He was shot in 1992. Some aspiring hoodlums killed him in a deal that went very badly wrong.'

Cynthia was shaking her head, unable to believe it all. 'Did the police catch them?'

'Didn't have to,' Abagnall said. 'Anthony Fleming's people took care of them. Massacred a houseful of them – those who were responsible, and a few who were not but happened to be in the wrong place at the wrong time – in retaliation. They figure Vince Fleming was in charge of that operation, but he was never convicted, never even charged.'

Abagnall reached for another cookie. 'I really shouldn't,' he said. 'I know my wife will be making me something nice for dinner.'

I spoke up. 'But what does all this have to do with Cynthia and her family?'

'Nothing, exactly,' the detective said. 'But I'm learning about the kind of person Vince turned out to be, and I'm wondering about the kind of person he might have been, that night when your wife's family disappeared.'

'You think he had something to do with it?' Cynthia said.

'I simply don't know. But he would have had reason to be angry. Your father had dragged you away from a date with him. That must have been humiliating, not just for you, but for him as well. And if he did have anything to do with your parents' disappearance, and that of your brother, if he ...' His voice softened. 'If he murdered them, then he had a father with the means, and the experience, to help him cover his tracks.'

'But surely the police must have looked into this at the time,' I said. 'You can't be the first person this has occurred to.'

'You're right. The police looked into it. But they never came up with anything concrete. There were only some suspicions. And Vince and his family were each other's alibis. He said he went home after Clayton Bigge took his daughter home.'

'It would explain one thing,' Cynthia said.

'What's that?' I asked.

Abagnall was smiling. He must have known what

Cynthia was going to say, which was, 'It would explain why I'm alive.'

Abagnall nodded.

'Because he liked me.'

'But your brother,' I said. 'He had nothing against your brother.' I turned to Abagnall. 'How do you explain that?'

'Todd may simply have been a witness. Someone who was there, who had to be eliminated.'

We were all quiet for a moment. Then, Cynthia said, 'He had a knife.'

'Who?' Abagnall asked. 'Vince?'

'In the car that night. He was showing it off to me. It was a, what do you call it? One of those knives that springs open.'

'A switchblade,' Abagnall said.

'That's it,' Cynthia said. 'I remember . . . I can remember holding it . . .' Her voice trailed off and her eyes were starting to roll up under her eyelids. 'I feel faint.'

I quickly slipped my arm around her. 'What can I get you?'

'I just, I just need to go . . . freshen up . . . for a minute,' she said, attempting to stand. I waited a moment to see that she was steady on her feet, then watched worriedly as she made her way up the stairs.

Abagnall was watching, too, and when he heard the bathroom door close, he leaned closer to me and said quietly, 'What do you make of that?'

'I don't know,' I said. 'I think she's exhausted.'

Abagnall nodded, didn't speak for a moment. Then said, 'This Vince Fleming, his father made a very good living from his illegal activities. If he felt some sense of responsibility for what his son did, it would have been financially possible for him to leave sums of cash for your wife's aunt to assist her in sending her niece to school.'

'You saw the letter,' I said. 'Tess gave it to you.'

'Yes. In addition to the envelopes. I take it you still haven't told your wife about that?'

'Not yet. I think Tess is ready to, though. Cynthia's decision to hire you, I think Tess sees that as a sign that she's ready to know everything.'

Abagnall nodded thoughtfully. 'It's best to get everything out into the open now, since we're trying to get some answers.'

'We're planning to see Tess tomorrow night. Actually, it might be worth seeing her tonight.' I was, to be honest, thinking about Abagnall's daily rate.

'That's a good ...' Inside his jacket, Abagnall's phone rang. 'A dinner report, no doubt,' he said, taking out the phone. But he looked puzzled when he saw the number, tossed the phone back into his jacket, and said, 'They can leave a message.'

Cynthia was making her way back down the stairs.

'Mrs Archer, are you feeling alright?' Abagnall asked. She nodded and sat back down. He cleared his throat. 'Are you sure? Because I'd like to bring up another matter.'

Cynthia said, 'Yes. Please go ahead.'

'Now, there may be a very simple explanation for this. It might just be some sort of clerical error, you never know. The state bureaucracy has been known to make its share of mistakes.'

'Yes?'

'Well, when you were unable to produce a photograph of your father, as I said I would, I checked with the Department of Motor Vehicles. I thought they would be able to assist me in this regard, but as it turns out, they weren't much help to me.'

'They didn't have his picture? Was that before they put pictures on drivers' licenses?' she asked.

'That's really something of a moot point,' Abagnall said. 'The thing is, they have no record of your father ever having a license at all.'

'What do you mean?'

'There's no record of him, Mrs Archer. As far as the DMV is concerned, he never existed.'

NINETEEN

'But that could just be what you said,' Cynthia said. 'People go missing from computer files all the time.'

Denton Abagnall nodded agreeably. 'That's very true. The fact that Clayton Bigge didn't show up in the DMV files is not, in itself, particularly conclusive of anything. But then I checked past records for his Social Security Number.'

'Yes?' Cynthia said.

'And nothing came up there, either. It's hard to find any record of your father anywhere, Mrs Archer. We have no picture of him. I looked through your shoeboxes and I couldn't find so much as a pay stub from a place of employment. Do you happen to know the name of the actual company he worked for that sent him out on the road all the time?'

Cynthia thought. 'No,' she said.

'There's no record of him with the IRS. Far as I can tell, he never paid any taxes. Not under the name of Clayton Bigge, at any rate.'

'What are you saying?' she asked. 'Are you saying he was a spy or something? Some kind of secret agent?'

Abagnall grinned. 'Well, not necessarily. Nothing quite so exotic.'

'Because he was away a lot,' she said. She looked at me. 'What do you think? Could he have been a government agent, being sent away on missions?'

'It seems kind of out there,' I said hesitantly. 'I mean,

next we'll start wondering whether he was an alien from another planet. Maybe he was sent here to study us and then went back to his home world, took your mother and brother with him.'

Cynthia just looked at me. She was still looking a bit woozy.

'It was supposed to be a joke,' I said apologetically.

Abagnall brought us – me in particular – back to reality. 'That's not one of my working theories.'

'Then, what are your theories?' I asked.

He took a sip of coffee. 'I could probably come up with half a dozen, based on what little I know at the moment,' he said. 'Was your father living under a name that was not his own? Was he escaping some strange past? A criminal one, perhaps? Did Vince Fleming bring harm to your family that evening? Was his father's criminal network somehow linked to something in your father's past that he'd been successfully covering up until that time?'

'We don't really know anything, do we?' Cynthia asked.

Abagnall leaned back tiredly into the couch cushions. 'What I know is that in a couple of days, the unanswered questions in this case seem to be expanding exponentially. And I have to ask you whether you want me to continue. You've already spent several hundred dollars on my efforts, and it could run into the thousands. If you'd like me to stop now, that's fine. I can walk away from this, give you a report on what I've learned so far. Or I can keep digging. It's entirely up to you.'

Cynthia started to open her mouth, but before she could speak, I said, 'We'd like you to continue.'

'Alright,' he said. 'Why don't I stay on this for another

couple of days? I don't need another check at this time. I think another forty-eight hours will really determine whether I can make significant progress.'

'Of course,' I said.

'I think I want to look further into this Vince Fleming character. Mrs Archer, what do you think? Could this man – well, he would have been a very young man back in 1983 – have been capable of bringing harm to your family?'

She thought about that for a moment. 'After all this time, I guess I have to consider that anything is possible.'

'Yes, it's good to keep an open mind. Thank you for the coffee.'

Before leaving, Abagnall returned Cynthia's shoebox of mementoes. Cynthia closed the door as he left, then turned to me and asked, 'Who was my father? Who the hell was my father?'

And I thought of Jane Scavullo's creative writing assignment. How we're all strangers to each other, how we often know the least about those we're closest to.

For twenty-five years, Cynthia had endured the pain and anxiety associated with her family's disappearance without a hint of what might have happened to them. And while we still didn't have the answer to that question, strands of information were floating to the surface, like bits of planking from a ship sunk long ago. These revelations that Cynthia's father might be living under an assumed name, that Vince Fleming's past might be much darker than originally thought. The strange phone call, the mysterious appearance of what was purported to be Clayton Bigge's hat. The man watching our house late at night. The news from Tess that for a period of time envelopes stuffed with cash from an anonymous source had been entrusted to her to look after Cynthia.

It was this last one I felt Cynthia was now entitled to know about. And I thought it would be better for her to learn about it from Tess herself.

We struggled through dinner not to discuss the questions that Abagnall's visit raised. We were both feeling that we'd already exposed Grace to too much of this. She had her radar out all the time, picking up one bit of information one day, matching it up with something else she might hear the next. We were worried that discussing Cynthia's history, the opportunistic psychic, Abagnall's investigation, all of those things, might be contributing to Grace's anxiety, her fear that one night, we'd all be wiped out by an object from outer space.

But try as we might to avoid the subject, it was often Grace who brought it up.

'Where's the hat?' she asked after a spoonful of mashed potatoes.

'What?' Cynthia said.

'The hat. Your dad's hat. The one that got left here. Where is it?'

'I put it up in the closet,' she said.

'Can I see it?'

'No,' Cynthia said. 'It's not to be played with.'

'I wasn't going to *play* with it. I just wanted to *look* at it.'

'I don't want you playing with it or looking at it or touching it!' Cynthia snapped.

Grace retreated, went back to her mashed potatoes.

Cynthia was preoccupied and on edge. Who wouldn't be, having learned only an hour earlier that the man she'd known her entire life as Clayton Bigge might not be Clayton Bigge at all?

'I think,' I said, 'that we should go visit Tess tonight.'

'Yeah,' said Grace. 'Let's see Aunt Tess.'

Cynthia, as though coming out of a dream, said, 'Tomorrow. I thought you said we should go see her tomorrow.'

'I know. But I think it might be good to see her tonight. There's a lot to talk about. I think you should tell her what Mr Abagnall said.'

'What did he say?' Grace asked.

I gave her a look that silenced her.

'I called earlier,' Cynthia said. 'I left her a message. She must be out doing something. She'll call us when she gets the message.'

'Let me make a call,' I said, and reached for the phone. I let it ring half a dozen times before her voicemail cut in. Given that Cynthia had already left a message, I couldn't see the point in leaving another.

'I told you,' Cynthia said.

I looked at the wall clock. It was nearly seven. Whatever Tess might be out doing, chances were she wouldn't be out doing it much longer. 'Why don't we go for a drive, head up to her place, maybe she'll be there by the time we arrive, or we can wait around for a little while until she shows up. You still have a key, right?'

Cynthia nodded.

'You don't think this can all wait till tomorrow?' she asked.

'I think, not only would she want to hear about what Mr Abagnall found out, there might be some things she might want to share with you.'

'What do you mean, she might have something to share with me?' Cynthia asked. Grace was eyeing me pretty curiously too, but had the sense not to say anything this time.

'I don't know. This new information, it might trigger something with her, prompt her to remember things she hasn't thought about in years. You know, if we tell her your father might have had some other, I don't know, identity, then she might go, oh yeah, that explains such and such.'

'You're acting like you already know what it is she's going to tell me.'

My mouth was dry. I got up, ran some water from the tap until it was cold, filled a glass, drank it down, turned around and leaned against the counter.

'OK,' I said. 'Grace, your mother and I need some privacy here.'

'I haven't finished my dinner.'

'Take your plate with you and go watch some TV.'

She took her plate and left the room, a sour expression on her face. I knew she was thinking that she missed all the good stuff.

To Cynthia, I said, 'Before she got those last test results, Tess thought she was dying.'

Cynthia was very still. 'You knew this.'

'Yes. She told me she thought she only had a limited amount of time left.'

'You kept this from me?'

'Please. Just let me tell you this. You can get mad later.' I felt Cynthia's eyes go into me like icicles. 'But you were under a lot of stress at the time, and Tess told me because she wasn't sure you'd be able to deal with that kind of news at the time. And just as well she didn't tell you, because as it turned out, she's OK. That's the thing we can't lose sight of.'

Cynthia said nothing.

'Anyway, at the time, when she thought she was terminal, there was something else she felt she had to tell me, something that she felt you needed to know when the time was right. She wasn't sure she'd get the chance again.'

And so I told Cynthia. Everything. The anonymous note, the cash, how it could show up anywhere, any time. How it helped get her through school. How Tess, taking the author of the note at his or her word, kept this to herself all these years.

She listened, only interrupting me a couple of times with questions, let me spell it all out for her.

When I was done, she looked numb. She said something I didn't hear very often from her. 'I could use a drink,' she said.

I got down a bottle of Scotch from a shelf high in the pantry, poured her a small glass. She drank it down in one long gulp, and I poured her about half as much again. She drank that down too.

'Alright,' she said. 'Let's go and see Tess.'

We would have preferred to go see Tess without bringing Grace along, but it would have been a scramble to find a sitter with no notice. And not only that, knowing that someone had been watching the house made us uneasy about putting Grace in anyone else's care at the moment.

So we told her to bring some things to entertain herself – she grabbed her *Cosmos* book again and a DVD of that Jodie Foster movie, *Contact* – so that the rest of us could talk privately.

Grace wasn't her usual chatty self on the way up. I think she was picking up the tension in the car, and decided, wisely, to lay low.

'Maybe we'll get some ice cream on the way back,' I said, breaking the silence. 'Or have some of Tess's. She probably still has some left from her birthday.'

When we pulled off the main road between Milford and Derby and drove down Tess's street, Cynthia pointed. 'Her car's home.'

Tess drove a four-wheel-drive Subaru wagon. She always said she didn't want to be stranded in a snowstorm if she needed provisions.

Grace was out of the car first and ran up to the front door. 'Hold on, pal,' I said. 'Wait up. You can't just go bursting in.'

We got to the door and I knocked. After a few seconds, I knocked again, only louder.

'Maybe she's around the back,' Cynthia said. 'Working on her garden.'

So we walked around the house, Grace, as usual, charging on ahead, skipping, leaping into the air. Before we'd rounded the house, she was already running back, saying, 'She's not there.' We had to see for ourselves, of course, but Grace was correct. Tess was not in her backyard, working in the garden as twilight slowly turned to darkness.

Cynthia rapped on the back door, which led directly into Tess's kitchen.

There was still no answer.

'That's weird,' she said. It also seemed strange that,

as night was falling, there were no lights on inside the house.

I crowded Cynthia on the back step and peered through the tiny window in the door.

I couldn't be certain about this, but I thought I saw something on the floor of the kitchen, obscuring the black and white checkerboarded tiles.

A person.

'Cynthia,' I said. 'Take Grace back to the car.'

'What is it?'

'Don't let her come into the house.'

'Jesus, Terry,' she whispered. 'What is it?'

I grasped the knob, turned it slowly and pushed, testing to see whether the door was locked. It was not.

I stepped in, Cynthia looking over my shoulder, and felt along the wall for the light switch, flipped it up.

Aunt Tess lay on the kitchen floor, face down, her head twisted at an odd angle, one arm stretched out ahead of her, the other hanging back.

'Oh my God,' Cynthia said. 'She's had a stroke or something!'

I didn't exactly have a medical degree, but there seemed to be an awful lot of blood on the floor for a stroke.

TWENTY

Maybe, if Grace hadn't been there, Cynthia would have lost it completely. But when she heard our daughter running up behind us, preparing to leap right over the step and into the kitchen, Cynthia turned, blocked her, and started moving her around to the front yard.

'What's wrong?' Grace shouted. 'Aunt Tess?'

I knelt next to Cynthia's aunt, tentatively touched her back. It felt very cold. 'Tess,' I whispered. There was so much blood pooled under her that I didn't want to turn her over, and there were these voices in my head telling me not to touch anything. So I shifted around, knelt even closer to the floor, to see her face. The sight of her open, unblinking eyes staring straight ahead left me chilled.

The blood, as best I could tell with my untrained eye, was dry and congealed, as though Tess had been this way for a very long time. And there was a terrible stench in the room that I'd only just now begun to notice.

I stood up and reached for the wall-mounted phone next to the bulletin board, then stopped myself. That voice again, telling me not to touch anything. I dug out my cell and made the call.

'Yes, I'll wait here,' I told the 911 operator. 'I'm not going anywhere.'

But I did leave the house by the back door and walk around to the front, where I found Cynthia sitting, with Grace in her lap, in the front seat of our car with the door open. Grace had her arms around her mother's neck and appeared to have been crying. Cynthia seemed, at the moment, too shocked to weep.

Cynthia looked at me, her eyes sending a question, and I answered by shaking my head back and forth a couple of times, very slowly.

'What is it?' she asked me. 'Do you think it was a heart attack?'

'A heart attack?' said Grace. 'Is she OK? Is Aunt Tess OK?'

'No,' I said to Cynthia. 'It wasn't a heart attack.'

The police agreed.

There must have been ten cars there within the hour, including half a dozen cop cars, an ambulance that sat around for a while, and a couple of TV news vans that were held back at the main road.

A couple of detectives spoke to me and Cynthia separately while another officer stayed with Grace, who was overwhelmed with questions. All we'd told her was that Tess was sick, that something had happened to her. Something very bad.

That was an understatement.

She'd been stabbed. Someone had taken one of her own kitchen knives and driven it into her. At one point, while I was in the kitchen and Cynthia out in one of the patrol cars, answering another officer's questions, I overheard a woman from the coroner's office telling a detective that she couldn't be certain at this point, but there was a good chance the knife got her right in the heart.

Jesus.

They had a lot of questions for me. Why had we come up? For a visit, I said. And to have a bit of a celebration. Tess had just received some good news from the doctor, I said.

She was going to be OK, I said.

The detective made a little snorting noise, but he was good enough not to laugh.

'Do you have any idea who might have done this?' he asked.

'No.' I said. And that was the truth.

'It may have been some kind of break-in,' he said. 'Kids looking for money to buy drugs, something like that.'

'Does it look to you like that's what happened?' I asked.

The detective paused. 'Not really.' He ran his tongue over his teeth, thinking. 'Doesn't look like much was taken, if anything. They could have grabbed her keys, taken her car, but they didn't.'

'They?'

The detective smiled. 'It's easier than saying he or she. It might have been one person, might have been more. We just don't know at this point.'

'This might,' I said hesitantly, 'be related to something that happened to my wife.'

'Hmm?'

'Twenty-five years ago.'

I told him as condensed a version as possible of Cynthia's story. About how there had been some strange developments of late, particularly since the TV item.

'Oh yeah,' said the detective. 'I think I might have seen that. That's the show with what's her name? Paula something?'

'Yeah.' And I told him that we had engaged a private detective in the last few days to look into it.

'Denton Abagnall,' I said.

'Oh, I know him. Good guy. I know where to reach him.'

He let me go, with the proviso that I must not yet go back to Milford, that I hang around a while longer in case he had any last-minute questions, and I went back out to find Cynthia. No one was asking her anything when I found her where she'd been before, in the front of the car with Grace in her lap. Grace looked so vulnerable and afraid.

When she saw me, she asked, 'Is Aunt Tess dead, Dad?'

I glanced at Cynthia, waiting for a signal. Tell her the truth, don't tell her the truth. Something. But there was nothing, so I said, 'Yes, honey. She is.'

Grace's lip started trembling. Cynthia said, so evenly that I could tell she was actually holding back, 'You could have told me.'

'What?'

'You could have told me what you knew. What Tess had told you. You could have told me.'

'Yes,' I said. 'I could have. I should have.'

She paused, choosing her words carefully. 'And then maybe this wouldn't have happened.'

'Cyn, I don't see how, I mean, there's no way to know ...'

'That's right. There's no way to know. But I know this. If you'd told me sooner what Tess had told you, about the money, the envelopes, I'd have been up here talking to her about it, we'd have been putting our heads together trying to figure out what it all meant, and if I'd been doing that, maybe I'd have been here, or maybe we'd have figured something out, before someone had a chance to do this.'

'Cyn, I just don't—'

'What else haven't you told me, Terry? What other things are you holding back, supposedly to protect me? To spare me? What else did she tell you, what else do you know that I'm not able to handle?'

Grace started to cry and buried her face into Cynthia's chest. It appeared that we had given up completely now on trying to shield her from all of this.

'Honey, honest to God,' I said. 'Anything I kept from you, I did it with your best interests in mind.'

She wrapped her arms tighter around Grace. 'What else, Terry? What else?'

'Nothing,' I said.

But there was one thing. Something I'd only just noticed and hadn't mentioned to anyone yet, because I didn't know whether it was significant.

I'd been brought back into the kitchen by the investigating officers, asked to describe all of my movements, where I'd stood, what I'd done, what I'd touched.

As I was leaving the room I happened to look at the small bulletin board next to the phone. There was the picture of Grace that I had taken on our trip to Disney World.

What was it Tess had said on the phone to me? After Denton Abagnall had been out to visit her?

I'd said something along the lines of, 'If you think of anything else, you should give him a call.'

And Tess had said, 'That's what he asked me to do. He gave me his card. I'm looking at it right now, it's pinned to my board here by the phone, right next to that picture of Grace with Goofy.'

There was no card on the board now.

TWENTY-ONE

'You don't say,' she said. This was quite the development.

'Oh, it's true,' he said.

'Well well well,' she said. 'And to think we were just talking about her.'

'I know.'

'That's quite the coinky-dink,' she said slyly. 'You being down there and all.'

'Yeah.'

'She had it coming, you know,' she said

'I knew you wouldn't be upset when I told you. But I think it means we have to hold off for a couple of days on the next part.'

'Really?' she said. She knew she'd preached to him on the virtues of taking his time, but she was feeling impatient all of a sudden.

'There's going to be a funeral here tomorrow,' he said. 'And I guess there's a whole lot of planning for something like that, and she didn't even have any other family to make arrangements, right?'

'That's my understanding,' she said.

'So, my sister, she's going to be pretty busy making all those arrangements, right? So maybe we should wait for that to be over.'

'I see your point. But there's something I'd like you to do for me.'

'Yes?' he said

'It's just a little thing.'

'What?'

'Don't call her your sister.' She was very firm.

'Sorry.'

'You know how I feel.'

'OK. It's just, well, you know, she is—'

'I don't care,' she said.

'OK, Mom,' he said. 'I won't do it again.'

TWENTY-TWO

There weren't many people to call.

Patricia Bigge, Cynthia's mother, had been Tess's only sibling. Their own parents, of course, were long gone. Tess, although she had been married briefly, had never had any children of her own, and there was no point in trying to track down her ex-husband. He wouldn't have come back for the funeral anyway, and Tess wouldn't have wanted the son of a bitch there.

Tess had not kept up any of her friendships with the people at the roads department office where she'd worked before retiring. From what Tess used to say, she didn't have many friends there anyway. They didn't care much for her liberal notions. She belonged to a bridge club, but Cynthia had no idea who any of the members were, so there were no calls to make there.

It wasn't as though we had to alert everyone to the funeral. Tess Berman's death had made the news.

There were interviews with other people who lived on her heavily wooded street, none of whom, by the way, had noticed anything unusual going on in the neighborhood in the hours leading up to Tess's death.

'It really makes you wonder,' said one for the TV cameras.

'Things like that don't happen around here,' said another.

'We're being extra careful to lock our doors and windows at night,' said someone else.

Maybe, if Tess had been fatally stabbed by an ex-husband or a jilted lover, the neighbors could have felt more at ease. But the word from the police was that they had no idea who had done this, no idea as to motive. And no suspects.

There was no sign of forced entry. No signs of a struggle, aside from a kitchen table that was slightly askew and a single chair that had been knocked over. It appeared that Tess's killer had struck quickly. Tess had resisted for only a moment or so, just long enough to make her attacker stumble into the table, knock the chair over. But then the knife was driven home, and she was dead.

Her body, police said, had been on the floor there for as long as twenty-four hours.

I thought of all the things we'd done while Tess lay dead in a pool of her own blood. We'd readied ourselves for bed, slept, gotten up, brushed our teeth, listened to the morning news on the radio, gone to work, had dinner, lived an entire day of our lives that Tess had not.

It was too much to think about.

When I forced myself to stop, my mind went to equally troubling topics. Who had done this? Why? Was Tess the victim of some random attacker, or did this have something to do with Cynthia and the threat in the letter written all those years ago?

Where was Denton Abagnall's business card? Had Tess not pinned it to the board as she'd told me? Had she decided she'd never be calling him with any more information, taken it down and tossed it into the trash?

The next morning, consumed with these and other questions, I found the card Abagnall had left with us and called his cell phone number.

The provider cut in immediately and invited me to leave a message, suggesting that Abagnall's phone was off.

So I tried his home number. A woman answered.

'Is Mr Abagnall there please?'

'Who's calling?'

'Is this Mrs Abagnall?'

'Who is this, please?'

'This is Terry Archer.'

'Mr Archer!' she said, sounding a bit frantic. 'I was just going to call you!'

'Mrs Abagnall, I really need to speak to your husband. It's possible the police have already been in touch. I gave them your husband's name last night and—'

'Have you heard from him?'

'Sorry?'

'Have you heard from Denton? Do you know where he is?'

'No, I don't.'

'This isn't like him at all. Sometimes, he has to work overnight, on surveillance, but he always gets in touch at some point.'

I had a bad feeling in the pit of my stomach. I said, 'He was at our house yesterday afternoon. Late afternoon. He was bringing us up to date.'

'I know,' she said. 'I phoned him just after he left your place. He said he'd had another call, that someone had left him a message, that they'd call back.'

I remembered Abagnall's phone ringing as he sat in our living room, how I had assumed it was his wife calling to tell him what she was cooking for supper, how he'd looked at it, surprised it wasn't a call from home, how he'd let it go to voicemail.

'Did they call back?'

'I don't know. That was the last I spoke to him.'

'Have you heard from the police?'

'Yes. I nearly had a heart attack when they came to the door this morning. But it was about a woman, up near Derby, who'd been murdered in her home.'

'My wife's aunt,' I said. 'We went up to visit her, and found her.'

'My God,' Mrs Abagnall said. 'I'm so sorry.'

I thought about what I was going to say next before I said it, given that I'd developed a habit lately of keeping things from people for fears of worrying them needlessly. But that was a policy that didn't appear to be paying off. So I said, 'Mrs Abagnall, I don't want to alarm you, and I'm sure there's a perfectly good reason your husband hasn't gotten in touch with you, but I think you need to call the police.'

'Oh,' she said quietly.

'I think you should tell them your husband is missing. Even though it hasn't been for very long.'

'I see,' Mrs Abagnall said. 'I'm going to do that.'

'And you can call me if anything happens. Let me give you my home number, if you don't already have it, and my cell too.'

She didn't have to ask to get a pencil. My guess was, being married to a detective, there was a notepad and pen next to the phone at all times.

Cynthia came into the kitchen. She was on her way back down to the funeral home. Tess, bless her heart, had planned ahead to make things as simple as possible for her loved ones. She'd finished paying for her funeral, in small monthly instalments, years ago. Her ashes were to be scattered over Long Island Sound.

'Cyn,' I said.

She didn't respond. She'd frozen me out. Regardless of whether I thought it was rational, she was holding me, at least in part, responsible for Tess's death. Even I was wondering whether things might have gone differently if I had told Cynthia everything I'd known at the time I'd known it. Would Tess have been in her home when her killer came to call, if Cynthia had known how Tess was able to put her through school? Or would the two of them have been some place else entirely, working as a team, maybe helping Abagnall with his investigation?

I couldn't know. And the not knowing was something I was going to have to live with.

We were both home from work, of course. She'd taken time off indefinitely from the dress shop, and I called the school to tell them that I'd be off for the next few days and that they'd better get a substitute teacher who had a clear calendar. Whoever it was, good luck with my crew, I thought.

'I'm not going to keep anything from you from now on,' I told Cynthia. 'And something else has happened that you should know about.'

She stopped before leaving the kitchen, but didn't turn around to look at me.

'I just spoke with Denton Abagnall's wife,' I said. 'He's missing.'

She seemed to list a bit to one side, as if some of the air had been let out of her. 'What did she say?' Cynthia managed to ask.

I told her.

She stood there for another moment, put one hand up to the wall to steady herself, and then said, 'I have to go to the funeral home, make some last-minute decisions.'

'Of course,' I said. 'Do you want me to come with you?'

'No,' she said, and left.

For a while, I didn't quite know what to do with myself, besides worry. I tidied up the kitchen, picked up around the house, attempted, without success, to attach Grace's telescope more securely to its tripod-like stand.

Back downstairs my eyes landed on the two shoe-boxes on the coffee table that Abagnall had returned to us the day before. I picked them up, took them back into the kitchen, and set them on the table.

I started taking things out one at a time. Much the way Abagnall must have, I suspected.

When Cynthia had cleared things out of her house as a teenager, she'd basically dumped the contents of drawers into these boxes, including those from the bed-side tables of her parents. Like most small drawers, they became a repository for things important and not, spare change, keys you no longer knew the use for, receipts, coupons, newspaper clippings, buttons, old pens.

Clayton Bigge wasn't much of a sentimentalist, but he saved the odd thing, like newspaper clippings. There was that one clipping of the basketball team Todd was part of, for example. But if it had anything to do with fishing, it was even more likely Clayton would hang on to it. Cynthia had told me that he read through the newspapers' sports sections for fishing tournament news, through the travel sections for stories about out-of-the-way lakes where there were so many fish, they practically jumped into the boat.

In the box, there were probably half a dozen such clippings that Cynthia must have dug out of Clayton's bedside table years ago before the household furniture, and the house itself, were disposed of and sold off, and I wondered when she would realize that there wasn't much value in saving them any longer. I unfolded each yellowed clipping, careful not to tear them, to make sure what it was.

There was something about one of them that caught my eye.

It had been saved from the pages of the *Hartford Courant*. A piece about fly-fishing on the Housatonic River. Whoever had cut the clipping from the paper – Clayton, presumably – had been meticulous about it, taking the scissors carefully down the gutters between the first column of this story and the last of one that had been discarded. The story had been placed above some unseen ads, or other stories, that had been stacked like steps in the bottom left corner.

That's why it seemed odd to me that a news story, unrelated to fly-fishing but tucked into the bottom right leg of the story, remained.

It was only a couple of inches long.

> Police still have no leads in the hit-run death of Connie Gormley, 27, of Sharon, whose body was found dumped into the ditch alongside U.S. 7 Saturday morning. Investigators believe Gormley, a single woman who worked at a Dunkin' Donuts in Torrington, was walking alongside the highway near the Cornwall Bridge when she was struck by a southbound car late Friday night. Police say it appears that Gormley's body was moved into the ditch after it had been struck by the car.
>
> Police theorize that the driver of the car may have

moved the body off the road and into the ditch, presumably so that she would not be noticed until some time later.

Why, I wondered, had everything else around that article been so neatly trimmed away, but this story left intact? The date on the top of the newspaper page was 15 October, 1982.

I was pondering that when I heard a knock at the door. I set the clipping to one side, got up from my chair and went to answer it.

Keisha Ceylon. The psychic. That woman the TV show had set us up with, who inexplicably lost her ability to pick up supernatural vibrations once she realized the producers weren't cutting her a fat check.

'Mr Archer?' she said. She was still dressed against type, in a professional-looking business suit, no kerchief, no huge hoop earrings.

I nodded, wary.

'I'm Keisha Ceylon? We met at the TV station?'

'I remember,' I said.

'First of all, I'd like to apologize for what transpired there. They had promised to pay me for my trouble, and that did lead to a disagreement, but it should never have happened in front of your wife, in front of Mrs Archer.'

I said nothing.

'Anyway,' she said, filling the gap, evidently not expecting to have to carry both sides of the conversation. 'The fact remains that I did have some things that I wanted to share with you and your wife that might be helpful with regard to her missing family.'

I still wasn't saying anything.

'May I come in?' she asked.

I wanted to close the door in her face, but then I thought about what Cynthia had said before we'd gone to see her the first time, how you have to be willing to look like a fool if there's a chance, even a one in a million chance, that somebody might have something useful to tell you.

Of course, we'd already been burned by Keisha Ceylon, but the fact that she was willing to face us a second time made me wonder whether I should hear her out.

So, after hesitating a moment, I opened the door wide to admit her. I steered her toward the living room couch where Abagnall had sat hours earlier. I plunked down across from her and crossed my legs.

'I can certainly understand that you might be skeptical,' she said. 'But there are a great many mysterious forces around us all the time, and only a few of us are able to harness them.'

'Uh huh,' I said.

'When I come into possession of information that would be important to a person going through troublesome times, I feel an obligation to share that knowledge. It's the only responsible thing to do when you are blessed with such a gift.'

'Of course.'

'The financial reward is secondary.'

'I can well imagine.' Even though I was almost well-intentioned when I allowed Keisha Ceylon into the house, I was already beginning to think I'd made a mistake.

'I can tell you are mocking me, but I do see things.'

Shouldn't she have said, 'I see dead people.' Wasn't that the line?

'And I am prepared to share these things with you and your wife if you like,' she said. 'I would ask, however, that you consider some sort of compensation for me. Seeing as how the television network was unwilling to make that sort of commitment on your behalf.'

'Ahhh,' I said. 'What sort of compensation did you have in mind?'

Ceylon's eyebrows shot up, as though she'd given no consideration to any actual amount before knocking on our door. 'Well, you've put me on the spot,' she said. 'I was thinking perhaps in the area of a thousand dollars. That was what I had understood the TV show would be paying me before they reneged.'

'I see,' I said. 'Perhaps if you were able to give me a hint of what this information is first, then I'd be able to decide whether it was worth a thousand dollars to get more.'

Ceylon nodded. 'That seems reasonable,' she said. 'Just give me a moment.' She sat back against the cushions, raised her head up and closed her eyes. For about thirty seconds she didn't move, didn't make a sound. It looked like she was falling into some sort of trance, getting ready to hook up with the spirit world.

Then: 'I see a house.'

'A house,' I said. Now we were getting somewhere.

'On a street, with children playing, and there are lots of trees, and I see an old lady walking past this house, and an old man, and there's a man walking along with them, although he's not as old. He could be their son. I believe he could be Todd ... I'm trying to get a good look at the house, to focus in on it ...'

'This house,' I said, leaning closer. 'Is it a pale yellow house?'

Ceylon seemed to close her eyes more tightly. 'Yes, yes it is.'

'My God,' I said. 'And the shutters ... are they green? A dark green?'

She cocked her head slightly to one side, as if checking. 'Yes, they are.'

'And under the windows, are there window boxes?' I asked. 'For flowers? And are the flowers petunias? Are you able to tell that? It's very important.'

She nodded very slowly. 'Yes, you're exactly right. The window boxes are full of petunias. This house. You know this house?'

'No,' I said, shrugging. 'I'm just making this up as I go along.'

Ceylon's eyes flashed open in anger. 'You son of a bitch motherfucker.'

'I think we're done here,' I said.

'You owe me a thousand dollars.'

Fool me once, shame on you. Fool me twice ...

'I don't think so,' I said.

'You pay me a thousand dollars, because ...' She was trying to think of something. 'I know something else. I've had another vision. About your daughter, your little girl. She's going to be in great danger.'

'Great danger?' I said.

'That is right. She's in a car. Up high. You pay me, and I can tell you more so you can save her.'

I heard a car door slam shut outside. 'I'm having a vision of my own,' I said to her, touching my fingers to my temples. 'I see my wife, coming through that door, any second now.'

And so she did. Cynthia surveyed the living room without saying a word.

'Hi honey,' I said, very offhand. 'You remember Keisha Ceylon, world's greatest psychic? She was having a tough sell here on the conjuring-up-the-past thing, so now, in a last ditch attempt to get a thousand bucks out of us, she's concocted a vision involving Grace's future. Trying to exploit our most basic fears, if you will, when we're at our lowest point.' I looked at Keisha. 'That about right?'

Keisha Ceylon said nothing.

To Cynthia, I said, 'How'd things go down at the funeral home?' I glanced at Keisha. 'Her aunt just died. Your timing couldn't be better.'

It all happened so fast.

Cynthia grabbed the woman by the hair and yanked her right off the couch, dragged her screaming to the front door.

Cynthia's face was red with fury. Keisha was a big woman, but Cynthia whipped her across the floor like she was stuffed with straw. She ignored the woman's screams, the stream of obscenities coming out of her mouth.

Cynthia got her to the door, opened it with her free hand, and pitched the con artist out onto the front step. But the woman couldn't regain her footing, and stumbled down the stairs, going headfirst into the lawn.

Before Cynthia slammed the door she shouted, 'Leave us alone, you opportunistic, bloodsucking bitch.' Her eyes were still wild as she looked at me, catching her breath.

I felt as though the wind had been knocked out of me as well.

TWENTY-THREE

After the service, the funeral home director took me and Cynthia and Grace in his Cadillac down to Milford Harbor, where he kept a small cabin cruiser. Rolly Carruthers and his wife Millicent followed, having offered to give Pamela a ride with them in their car, and the three of them joined our family on the boat.

Once we had left the sheltered harbor we put out into Long Island Sound, only about a mile, out front of the beach houses along East Broadway. I'd always thought it would be great to have one of those places, certainly as a kid, but when Hurricane Gloria swept through in 1985, I started to have second thoughts. It was hard to keep all the hurricanes straight if you lived in Florida, but the ones that hit Connecticut you tended to remember.

Fortunately, given the nature of our task out there on the water that day, the winds were light. The funeral director, a man whose charm seemed genuine rather than forced, had brought along the urn containing Tess's ashes.

There wasn't a lot of conversation on the boat, although Millicent made an attempt. She put her arm around Cynthia and said, 'Tess couldn't have had a more beautiful day to see her final request carried out.'

Maybe, if Tess had actually died from an illness, there might have been some comfort in this, but when someone dies by violence, it's hard to find consolation anywhere.

But Cynthia attempted to take the comment in the spirit it was offered. Millicent and Rolly had been friends to her long before I'd even met her. They were an unofficial aunt and uncle, and had always looked in on her over the years. Going way back, Millicent had grown up on the same street as Cynthia's mother and even though Patricia had been a few years older, they had become friends. When Millicent met and married Rolly, and Patricia met and married Clayton, the couples saw each other socially, and that was how Millicent and Rolly had the opportunity to watch Cynthia grow up, and take an interest in her life after her family had disappeared. Although it was Rolly, more than Millicent, who was most there for Cynthia.

'It is a beautiful day,' Rolly said, echoing his wife. He approached Cynthia, his eyes looking down at the deck, perhaps figuring this would help him keep his footing as the boat went over the choppy water. 'But I know that doesn't make any of this any easier to bear.'

Pam came up to Cynthia, teetered a bit, probably realizing that heels weren't that great a thing to wear on a boat, and gave her a hug. 'Who would do this?' Cynthia asked her. 'Tess never meant any harm to anyone.' She sniffed. 'The last person from that part of my family. Gone.'

Pam pulled her closer. 'I know, love. She was so good to you, so good to everyone. It had to be some sort of a crazy person.'

Rolly shook his head in disgust, a kind of 'what's-the-world-coming-to' gesture, and walked down to the stern to watch the boat's wake. I came up alongside him. 'Thanks for coming today,' I said. 'It means a lot to Cynthia.'

He looked surprised. 'You kidding? You know we've always been there for both of you.' He shook his head again. 'You think that's what it was? Some sort of crazy person?'

'No,' I said. 'I don't. At least not in the sense of it being a total stranger. I think Tess was killed by someone for a specific reason.'

'What?' he asked. 'What do the police think?'

'They haven't got a clue, far as I can tell,' I said. 'I start telling them all this stuff that happened years ago, you see their eyes start to cloud over, like it's too much for them to take in.'

'Yeah, well, what do you expect?' Rolly asked. 'They got their hands full trying to maintain peace in the here and now.'

The boat slowed to a stop, and the funeral director approached. 'Mr Archer? I think we're ready.'

We gathered tightly together on the deck, as the urn was placed formally in Cynthia's hands. I helped her open it, both of us acting as though we were handling dynamite, afraid that we might drop Tess at the wrong moment. Grabbing it firmly between both hands, Cynthia moved to the side of the boat and upended the urn while Grace and I, Rolly and Millicent, and Pam watched.

The ashes fell out and settled on the water, dissolved and dispersed. In a few seconds, what physically remained of Tess was gone. Cynthia handed the urn back to me, and for a moment appeared light-headed. Rolly went to support her, but then she held out her hand to indicate she was OK.

Grace had brought a rose – her own idea – which she cast upon the water. 'Goodbye, Aunt Tess,' she said. 'Thank you for the book.'

Cynthia had said that morning that she wanted to say a few words, but when the time came, she didn't have the strength. And I could find no words that I thought were any more meaningful, or heartfelt, than Grace's simple farewell.

Coming back into the harbor, I saw a short, black woman in a pair of jeans and tan leather jacket standing at the end of the dock as we came back into the harbor. She was nearly as round as she was short, but she showed grace and agility as she grabbed on to the boat as it drew close, and assisted in securing it. She said to me, 'Terrence Archer?' There was a hint of Boston in her voice.

I said yes.

She flashed me a badge that identified herself as Rona Wedmore, a police detective. And not from Boston, but from Milford. She held out a hand to assist Cynthia onto the dock while I lifted Grace onto the weathered planking.

'I'd like to speak with you a moment,' she said, not asking.

Cynthia, who had Pam at her side, said she would watch Grace. Rolly stayed back with Millicent. Wedmore and I walked slowly along the dock toward a black unmarked cruiser.

'Is this about Tess?' I asked. 'Has there been an arrest?'

'No sir, there has not,' she said. 'I'm sure every effort is being made to do just that, but that's another detective's case. I'm aware, one way or another, what progress is being made in that regard.' She spoke rapid fire, the words coming at me like bullets. 'I'm here to ask you about Denton Abagnall.'

I underwent a bit of mental whiplash. 'Yes?'

'He's missing. Two days now,' she said.

'I spoke to his wife the morning after he'd been to our home. I told her to call the police.'

'You haven't seen him since then?'

'No.'

'Heard from him?' Ping, ping, ping.

'No,' I said. 'I can't help but think it might have something to do with the murder of my wife's aunt. He'd been to see her not long before her death. He'd left her a business card, which she told me was pinned to the bulletin board by the phone. But it wasn't there after she died.'

Wedmore wrote something down in her notebook. 'He was working for you.'

'Yes.'

'At the time of his disappearance.' It wasn't a question, so I simply nodded. 'What do you think?'

'About?'

'What happened to him?' A glimpse of impatience. Like, what else do you think I mean?

I paused and looked up at the cloudless blue sky. 'I hate to let my mind go there,' I said. 'But I think he's dead. I think he may even have gotten a phone call from his killer while he was in our home, reviewing our case with us.'

'What time was that?'

'It was around five in the afternoon, something like that.'

'So was it before five, or after five, or five?'

'I'd say five.'

'Because we got in touch with his cell phone provider, had them check all his incoming and outgoing calls. There was a call at five, made from a pay phone up in Milford. There was another one later, from another Milford pay phone, that went through, then later in the day, some calls from his wife that went unanswered.'

I had no idea what to make of that.

Cynthia and Grace were getting into the back of the funeral director's Caddy.

Wedmore leaned toward me aggressively, and even though she was probably five inches shorter, she had presence. 'Who'd want to kill your aunt, and Abagnall?' she asked.

'Someone who's trying to make sure that the past stays in the past,' I said.

Millicent wanted to take us all for lunch, but Cynthia said she'd prefer to go straight home, and that was where I took her. Grace had clearly been moved by the service and the entire morning had been an eye-opener for her – her first funeral – but I was actually glad to see she still had an appetite. The moment we came through the door she said she was starving and that if she didn't get something to eat immediately, she would die. Then, 'Oh, sorry.'

Cynthia smiled at our girl. 'How about a tuna sandwich?'

'With celery?'

'If we have any,' Cynthia said.

Grace went into the fridge, opened up the crisper. 'There's some celery, but it's kind of soft?'

'Bring it out,' Cynthia said. 'We'll have a look.'

I hung my suit jacket on the back of a kitchen chair, loosened my tie. I didn't have to dress this well to teach high school, and the formal attire made me feel constricted and awkward. I sat down, put everything that had happened so far that day on the back burner for a moment, and watched my two girls. Cynthia hunted up a tin of tuna and a can opener while Grace put the celery on the counter.

Cynthia drained the oil from the tuna can, dumped it into a bowl, and asked Grace to get the Miracle Whip. She went back to the fridge, brought out the jar, got the lid off and put it on the counter. She broke off a celery stalk, waved it in the air. It was a piece of rubber.

Playfully, she hit her mother on the arm with it.

Cynthia turned and looked at her, reached over very deliberately and broke off a rubbery stalk of her own, and hit Grace back. Then they used the stalks as swords. 'Take that!' said Cynthia. Then they both started to laugh and slipped their arms around each other.

And I thought, I've always wondered what sort of mother Patricia was like, and the answer's always been here right in front of me.

Later, after Grace had eaten and gone upstairs to get back into some regular clothes, Cynthia said to me, 'You looked nice today.'

'You too,' I said.

'I'm sorry,' she said.

'Hmm?'

'I'm sorry. I don't blame you. For Tess. I was wrong to say what I said.'

'It's OK. I should have told you everything. Earlier.'

She looked at the floor.

'Can I ask you something?' I said, and she nodded. 'Why do you think your father would have saved a clipping about a hit-and-run accident?'

'What are you talking about?' she said.

'He saved a clipping about a hit-and-run accident.'

The shoeboxes were still on the kitchen table, the clipping about fly-fishing, which included the one about the woman from Sharon whose body was found in a ditch, sitting on top.

'Let me see,' Cynthia said, rinsing her hands and drying them off. I handed her the clipping and she accepted it delicately, like parchment. She read it. 'I can't believe I've never noticed it before.'

'You thought your dad saved the clipping because of the fly-fishing piece.'

'Maybe he did save it because of the fly-fishing piece.'

'I think, in part, he did,' I said. 'But what I'm wondering is which came first. Did he see the story about the accident and go to clip it out, but then given his interests, he clipped the fly-fishing story with it. Or did he see the fly-fishing story, then spotted the other one, and, for some reason, clipped it, too. Or . . .' I paused for a moment. 'Did he want to clip the hit-and-run story, but worried that clipping it alone would lead to questions should someone, like your mother, find it, whereas clipping it with the other story, well, that was like camouflaging it?'

Cynthia had handed the clipping back to me and said, 'What in the hell are you talking about?'

'God, I don't know,' I said.

'Every time I look through those boxes,' Cynthia said, 'I keep hoping I'll find something I've never noticed before. It's frustrating, I know. You want to find an answer but it's not there. And yet,' she said, 'I keep thinking I'll find it. Some tiny clue. Like that one piece in a jigsaw puzzle, the one that helps you place all the others.'

'I know,' I said. 'I know.'

'This accident, this woman who got killed – what was her name again?'

'Connie Gormley,' I said. 'She was twenty-seven.'

'I've never heard that name in my life. It doesn't mean a thing. And what if that's it? What if that's the piece?'

'Do you think it is?' I asked.

She shook her head slowly. 'No.'

Neither did I.

But it didn't stop me from going upstairs with the clipping and sitting in front of the computer and looking for any information about a 26-year-old hit-and-run accident that left Connie Gormley dead.

I came up with nothing.

So then I started looking up Gormleys in that part of Connecticut, using the online phone listings, wrote down names and numbers onto a scratch pad, stopped when I had half a dozen, and was about to start calling them when Cynthia poked her head into the room. 'What are you doing?' she asked.

I told her.

I don't know whether I was expecting her to protest, or offer encouragement, to grasp onto any thread no matter how slender. Instead, she said, 'I'm going to go lie down for a while.'

When someone actually answered, I identified myself as Terrence Archer from Milford, said that I probably had the wrong number, but I was trying to track down anyone who might have information about the death of Connie Gormley.

'Sorry, never heard of her,' said the person at the first number.

'Who?' said an elderly woman at the second. 'I never knew no Connie Gormley, but I have a niece goes by Constance Gormley, and she's a real estate agent in Stratford. She's terrific and if you're looking for a house she could find you a good one. I've got her number right here if you'll hold on a second.' I didn't want to be rude, but after I'd held for five minutes, I hung up.

The third person I reached said, 'Oh, God, Connie? It was so long ago.'

It turned out that I had managed to reach Howard Gormley, her 65-year-old brother.

'Why would anyone want to know about that, after all these years?' he asked, his voice hoarse and tired.

'Honestly, Mr Gormley, I don't quite know what to tell you,' I said. 'My wife's family had some trouble a few months after your sister's accident, stuff that we've still been trying to sort out, and an article about Connie was found among some mementoes.'

'That's kind of strange, isn't it?' Howard Gormley said.

'Yes, it is. If you wouldn't mind answering a few questions, it might clear things up, at least allow me to eliminate any connection between your family's tragedy and ours.'

'I suppose.'

'First of all, did they ever find out who ran your sister down? I don't have any other information. Was someone finally charged?'

'Nope, never. Cops never found out a thing, never put anyone in jail for it. After a while, they just gave up, I guess.'

'I'm sorry.'

'Yeah, well, it just about killed our parents. Grief ate away at them. Our mother died a couple years after that, and our dad went a year later. Cancer, both of them, but you ask me, it was the sorrow that overtook them.'

'Did the police ever have any leads? Did they ever find out who was driving?'

'Just how up to date was that article you found?'

I had it next to the computer, and read it to him.

'That was pretty early on,' he said. 'That was before they found out the whole thing had kind of been staged.'

'Staged?'

'Well, at first, they figured it was a hit and run, plain and simple. Maybe a drunk, or just a bad driver. But when they did the autopsy, they noticed something kind of funny.'

'What do you mean, funny?'

'I'm no expert, you know? I've been a roofer all my life. But what they told us was, a lot of what happened to Connie, the damage done to her from the car? That happened after she was already dead.'

'Wait a sec,' I said. 'Your sister was already dead when the car hit her?'

'That's what I just said. And ...'

'Mr Gormley?'

'It's just, this is hard to talk about, even after all this time. I don't like to say things that reflect badly on Connie, even after all these years, if you understand.'

'I do.'

'But they said, well, that she might have been with someone shortly before she got left in that ditch.'

'You mean ...'

'They're not saying she was raped, exactly, although that might have happened, I suppose. But my sister, she kind of got around, if you understand, and they say she met up with someone that evening, most likely. And I've always wondered if that's who it was, who set it up to look like she got hit by a car, dumped her into that ditch.'

I didn't know what to say.

'Connie and me was close. I didn't approve of the way she lived her life, but then, I was never no angel myself and was never in any position to point a finger. After all these years, I'm still angry, and wish they'd find the bastard who did it, but the thing is, it was so long ago, there's a pretty good chance that son of a bitch may be dead himself by now.'

'Yes,' I said. 'That's very possible.'

When I was done talking to Howard Gormley, I just sat there at my desk for a while, staring off into space, trying to figure out whether it meant anything.

Then, reflexively as I often do, I hit the 'mail' button on the computer keypad to see whether we had any messages. As usual, there were a bunch, most of them offering deals on Viagra or stock tips or places to get a cheap Rolex or solicitations from widows of wealthy Nigerian gold mine owners looking for assistance transferring their millions to a North American account. Our anti-spam filter caught only a fraction of these annoyances.

But there was one e-mail, from a Hotmail address that was nothing but numbers – 05121983 – with the words 'It won't be much longer' in the Subject line.

I clicked on it.

The message was short. It read: 'Dear Cynthia: As per our earlier conversation, your family really does forgive you. But they can't ever stop asking themselves: Why?'

I must have read it five times, then went back up to the Subject line. It wouldn't be much longer till what?

TWENTY-FOUR

'How could someone get our e-mail address?' I asked Cynthia. She was sitting in front of the computer, staring at the screen. At one point, she reached toward the monitor, as if touching the message might somehow reveal more about it.

'My father,' she said.

'What about your father?'

'When he got in here, when he left the hat,' Cynthia said. 'He could have come up here and looked around, got on the computer, figured out our e-mail address.'

'Cyn,' I said cautiously. 'We still don't know that your father left that hat. We don't know who left that hat.'

I thought back to Rolly's theory, and my own briefly held suspicion, that Cynthia could have placed the hat there herself. And for an instant, no longer, I thought about how easy it would be to set up a Hotmail address and send an e-mail to yourself.

Knock it off, I told myself.

I could sense Cynthia bristling at my comment of a moment ago, so I added, 'But you're right. Whoever got in here, they could have come upstairs and nosed around, turned on the computer, gotten our e-mail address.'

'So it's the same person,' Cynthia said. 'The person who phoned me, the one you said was just a crank, is the same person who sent this e-mail, and the same person who snuck into our house and left the hat. My father's hat.'

That made sense to me. The part I was having trouble with was, who was that person? Was it the same person who'd murdered Tess? Was it the man I'd spotted through Grace's telescope the other night, watching our house?

'And he's still talking about forgiveness,' Cynthia said. 'That they forgive me. Why does he say that? And what does it mean, that it won't be much longer?'

I shook my head. 'And the address,' I said, pointing to the e-mail box on the screen. 'Just a jumble of numbers.'

'That's not a jumble of numbers,' Cynthia said. 'It's a date. 12 May 1983. The night my family disappeared.'

'We're not safe,' Cynthia said later that night.

She was sitting up in bed, the covers pulled up to her waist. I happened to be looking out the bedroom window, taking one last peek at the street before I got under the covers with her. This was a habit I'd developed in the last week.

'We're not,' she repeated. 'And I know you feel the same way, but you don't want to talk about it. You're worried you're going to upset me, send me over the edge or something.'

'I'm not afraid you're going to go over the edge,' I said.

'But you're not willing to say we're safe,' Cynthia said. 'You're not safe, I'm not safe, Grace is not safe.'

I knew that very well. She did not need to remind me. It was never out of my thoughts.

'My aunt has been murdered,' Cynthia said. 'The

man I – we – hired to find out what happened to my family is missing. You and Grace saw a man watching our house a few nights ago. Someone was in our house, Terry. If not my father, then somebody. Somebody who left that hat, sat at our computer.'

'It wasn't your father,' I said.

'Are you saying that because you really know who left it there, or are you saying that because you think my father's dead?'

I had nothing to say.

'Why do you think the DMV has no record of my father's license?' she asked. 'Why's there no record of him with social security?'

'I don't know,' I said tiredly.

'Do you think Mr Abagnall found out something about Vince? Vince Fleming? Didn't he say he wanted to find out some more about him? Maybe that's what he was doing when he disappeared. Maybe Mr Abagnall's OK, but he's following Vince, hasn't been able to call his wife.'

'Look,' I said. 'It's been a long day. Let's try and get some sleep.'

'Please tell me you're not keeping anything else from me,' Cynthia said. 'Like you did about Tess's illness. Like you did about the payments she received.'

'I'm not keeping anything from you,' I said. 'Didn't I just show you that e-mail? I could have just deleted it, not even told you about it. But I agree with you, we have to be careful. We've got new locks on the doors. No one's breaking in now. And I'm not going to give you a hard time about walking Grace to school.'

'What *do* you think's going on?' Cynthia said. There was something in the way she asked the question, something almost accusatory, that suggested to me she still suspected I was holding something back.

'Jesus Christ,' I snapped. 'I don't know. It wasn't my fucking family that vanished off the face of the fucking earth.'

It stunned Cynthia into silence. I'd stunned myself. 'I'm sorry,' I said. 'I'm sorry. I didn't mean that. It's just, this is taking a toll on all of us.'

'*My* problems are taking a toll on *you*,' Cynthia said.

'That's not it,' I said. 'Look, remember I said we should go away for a while? The three of us. We'll pull Grace out of school. I can wangle a few days from Rolly, he'll cover for me, keep my substitute in, they'll understand if you take some time away ...'

She threw the covers off her legs and got up. 'I'm going to sleep with Grace,' she said. 'I want to be sure she's OK. Somebody has to do something.'

I said nothing as she tucked her pillows under her arm and left the room.

I had a headache and was headed for the bathroom to find some Tylenols in the medicine cabinet, when I heard running in the hall.

Before Cynthia actually appeared at the bedroom door, she was screaming, 'Terry! Terry!'

'What?' I said.

'She's gone. Grace isn't in her room. She's gone!'

I followed her down the hall, back to Grace's room, flipping on lights as I went. I passed Cynthia, went into Grace's room ahead of her.

'I looked!' Cynthia said. 'She's not in here!'

'Grace!' I said, opening her closet door, glancing under her bed. The clothes she'd been wearing that day were balled up and left sitting on her desk chair. I ran back out and into the bathroom, pulled back the curtain on the bathtub, found it empty. Cynthia had gone into the room where we kept the computer. We met back in the hall.

No sign of her.

'Grace!' Cynthia shouted.

We threw on more lights, as we came running down the stairs. This couldn't be happening, I told myself. This simply could not be happening.

Cynthia swung open the basement door, shouted our daughter's name down into the darkness. No response.

As I entered the kitchen I noticed the back door, with its new deadbolt installed, was just barely ajar.

I felt my heart stop.

'Call the police,' I said to Cynthia.

'Oh my God,' she said.

I turned on the outside light over the door as I swung it open and ran out, in my bare feet, into the yard.

'Grace!' I shouted.

And then a voice. Annoyed. 'Dad, turn off that light!'

I glanced to my right, and there was Grace, standing in the yard in her pajamas, her telescope set up on the lawn, pointed at the night sky.

'What?' she said.

We both could, and probably should, have taken more time off work, especially after the night we'd put in, but we both returned to our jobs the following morning.

'I'm really sorry,' Grace said, for about the hundredth time, as she ate her Cheerios.

'Don't you *ever* pull a stunt like that again,' Cynthia said.

'I said I'm *sorry*.'

Cynthia still ended up sleeping with her for the night. She wasn't about to let Grace out of her sight for a while.

'You snore, you know,' Grace told her.

It was the first time I'd felt inclined to laugh in a while, but I managed to hold it in.

I left first for work, as usual. Cynthia did not say goodbye or walk me to the door. She still hadn't forgotten our fight before the false alarm with Grace. Just when we needed to pull together, there was this invisible wedge being driven between us. Cynthia remained suspicious of me that I was still keeping things from her. And I was feeling uneasy about Cynthia in ways I was finding it hard to articulate, even to myself.

Cynthia thought I was blaming her for all our current troubles. It was undeniable that her history, her proverbial baggage, was currently haunting our days and nights. And at some level, maybe I *was* blaming her, even though it wasn't her fault that her family had disappeared.

The one concern we had in common, of course, was how all this was affecting Grace. And the way our daughter had chosen to cope with the household angst – so troubling to her that thoughts of a destructive asteroid actually provided some sort of an escape – had itself become the catalyst for another blow-up.

My students were amazingly well behaved. Word must have gotten around about why I'd been away the last couple of days. A death in the family. High-school kids, like most natural predators, will typically seize on a prey's weakness, use it to their advantage. From all reports, they had certainly done this with the woman who'd been called in to cover my classes. She had the tiniest trace of a stutter, usually no more than a hesitation with the first word in any given sentence, but it was noticeable enough for the kids to all start mimicking it. She'd evidently gone home the first day in tears, other staff members told me over lunch without a hint of sympathy in their voices. It was a jungle down that hallway, and you either made it or you didn't.

But they cut me some slack. Not just my creative writing group, but my two other English classes as well. I think they were behaving not just out of respect for my feelings, in fact, that was probably a very small part of it. They didn't act up because they were watching for signs that maybe I'd behave differently, shed a tear, get impatient with someone, slam a door, anything.

But I did not. So I could expect no special considerations the next day.

Jane Scavullo hung back as my morning class filed out of the room. 'Sorry about your aunt,' she said.

'Thank you,' I said. 'She was my wife's aunt, actually, although I felt every bit as close to her.'

'Whatever,' she said, and caught up with the others.

About mid-afternoon, I was walking down the hall near the office when one of the secretaries charged out, saw me, and stopped dead. 'I was just going to go looking for you,' she said. 'I paged your office, you weren't there.'

'That's because I'm here,' I said.

'Phone call for you,' she said. 'I think it's your wife.'

'OK.'

'You can take it in the office.'

'OK.'

I followed her in and she pointed to the phone on her desk. One of the lights was flashing. 'Just press that one,' she said.

I grabbed the receiver, hit the button. 'Cynthia?'

'Terry, I—'

'Listen, I was going to call you. I'm sorry about last night. What I said.'

The secretary sat back down at her desk, pretended not to be listening.

'Terry, something—'

'Maybe we need to hire another guy. I mean, I don't know what's happened to Abagnall, but—'

'Terry, shut up,' Cynthia said.

I shut up.

'Something's happened,' Cynthia said, her voice low, almost breathless. 'I know where they are.'

TWENTY-FIVE

‘Sometimes, when you don’t call when I’m expecting you to,’ she said, ‘I think I’m *the one being driven crazy.’*

‘Sorry,’ he said. ‘But I’ve got good news. I think it’s happening.’

‘Oh, that’s lovely. What was it Sherlock Holmes used to say? The game is afoot? Or was it Shakespeare?’

‘I’m not really sure,’ he said.

‘So, you delivered it?’

‘Yes.’

‘But you need to stay a little longer to see what happens.’

‘Oh, I know,’ he said. ‘I’m sure it will end up on the news.’

‘I wish I could tape it here.’

‘I’ll bring home the newspapers.’

‘Oh, I’d love that,’ she said.

‘There haven’t been any more stories about Tess. I guess that means they haven’t found out anything.’

‘I guess we should just be grateful for whatever good fortune comes our way, shouldn’t we?’

‘And there was something else on the news, about this missing detective. The one my . . . you know . . . hired.’

‘Do you think they’ll find him?’ she asked.

‘Hard to say.’

‘Well, we can’t worry about that,’ she said. ‘You sound a bit nervous.’

‘I guess.’

‘This is the hard part, the risky part, but when you add it

all together, it's going to pay off. And when it's time, you can come back and get me.'

'I know. Won't he wonder where you are, why you're not going to see him?'

'He hardly gives me the time of day,' she said. 'He's winding down. Maybe a month left. Long enough.'

'You think he's ever really loved us?' he asked.

'The only one he's ever loved is her,' she said, making no attempt to hide her bitterness. 'And has she ever been there for him? Looked after him? Cleaned up after him? And who solved his biggest problem? He's never been grateful for what I've done. We're the ones who've been wronged here. We were robbed of having a real family. What we're doing now, this is justice.'

'I know,' he said.

'What do you want me to make for you when you get home?'

'A carrot cake?'

'Of course. It's the least a mother can do.'

TWENTY-SIX

I phoned the police and left a message for Detective Rona Wedmore, who'd given me her card when she'd asked me questions after we'd scattered Tess's ashes on the sound. I asked if she could meet me and Cynthia at our home, that we'd both be there shortly. Gave her the address in case she didn't already know it, but I was betting she did. In my message I said that what I was calling about didn't have to do, specifically, with the disappearance of Denton Abagnall, but it might, in some way, be related.

I said it was urgent.

I asked Cynthia on the phone whether she wanted me to pick her up at work, but she said she was OK to drive home. I left the school without explaining to anyone why, but they were, I guess, becoming accustomed to my erratic behavior. Rolly had just come out of his office, seen me on the phone, and watched as I'd run out of the building.

Cynthia beat me home by a couple of minutes. She was standing in the door, the envelope in her hand.

I came inside and she handed it to me. There was one word – 'Cynthia' – printed on the front. No stamp. It had not gone through the mail.

'Now we've both touched it,' I said, suddenly realizing we were probably making all kinds of mistakes the police would give us shit for later.

'I don't care,' she said. 'Read it.'

I took the sheet of plain business paper out of the envelope. It had been folded perfectly in thirds, like a proper letter. The back side of the sheet was a map, crudely drawn in pencil, some intersecting lines representing roads, a small town labeled 'Otis', a rough egg shape labeled 'quarry lake', and an 'X' in one corner of it. There were some other notations, but I wasn't sure what they meant.

Cynthia, speechless, watched me take it all in.

I flipped the sheet over and the moment I saw the typed message, I noticed something about it, something that jumped out at me, something that disturbed me very much. Even before I'd read the contents of the note, I wondered about the implications of what had caught my eye.

But for the moment, I held my tongue, and read what it said.

> Cynthia: It's time you knew where they were. Where they still ARE, most likely. There's an abandoned quarry a couple of hours north of where you live, just past the Connecticut border. It's like a lake, but not a real lake because it's where they took out gravel and stuff. It's real deep. Probably too deep for any kids swimming there to have found all these years. You take 8 north, cross into Mass., keep going till you get to Otis, then go east. See the map on the other side. There's a small lane behind a row of trees that leads to the top of the quarry. You have to be careful when you get up there, because it's really steep. Down into the quarry there. Right down there, at the bottom of that lake, that's where you'll find your answer.

I flipped the sheet over again. The map showed all the details that were set out in the note.

'That's where they are,' Cynthia whispered, pointing to the paper in my hand. 'They're in the water.' She took in a breath. 'So ... they're dead.'

Things seemed almost blurry before my eyes. I blinked a couple of times, refocused. I turned the sheet over again, reread the note, then looked at it not for what it said, but from a more technical point of view.

It had been composed on a standard typewriter. Not on a computer. Not printed off.

'Where did you get this?' I asked, trying very hard to keep my voice controlled.

'It was in the mail at Pamela's,' Cynthia said. 'In the mailbox. Someone left it there. The mailman didn't bring it. It doesn't have a stamp on it or anything.'

'No,' I said. 'Someone put it there.'

'Who?' she asked.

'I don't know.'

'We have to go up there,' she said. 'Today, now, we have to find out what's there, what's under the water.'

'The detective, the woman who met us at the dock, Wedmore, she's coming. We'll talk to her about that. They'll have police divers. But there's something else I want to ask you about. It's about this note. Look at it. Look at the typing—'

'They have to get up there immediately,' Cynthia said. It was as if she thought whoever was at the bottom of that quarry might still be alive, that they might still have a bit of air left.

I heard a car stop out front, looked out the window

and saw Rona Wedmore striding up the driveway, her short, stocky frame looking capable of walking straight through the door.

I felt a sense of panic.

'Honey,' I said. 'Is there anything else you want to tell me about this note? Before the police get here? You have to be totally honest with me here.'

'What are you talking about?' she said.

'Don't you see something odd about this?' I said, holding the letter in front of her. I pointed, very specifically, to one of the words in the letter. 'Right here, at the beginning,' I said, pointing to 'time'.

'What?'

The horizontal line in the 'e' was faded, making it almost look like a 'c'. The word almost appeared to be 'timc.'

'I don't know what you're talking about,' Cynthia said. 'What do you mean, be honest with you? Of course I'm being honest with you.'

Wedmore was mounting the front step, fist ready to knock.

'I have to go upstairs for a moment,' I said. 'Answer that, tell her I'll be right down.'

Before Cynthia could say another thing, I bolted up the stairs. Behind me, I heard Wedmore knock, two sharp knocks, then Cynthia open the door, the two of them exchange greetings. By then I was in the small room I use to mark papers, prepare lessons.

My old Royal typewriter sat on the desk, beside the computer.

I had to decide what to do with it.

It was obvious to me that the note Cynthia was, at that moment, showing to Detective Wedmore had been written on this typewriter. The faded 'e' was instantly recognizable.

I knew that I had not typed that letter.

I knew Grace could not have done it.

That left only two other possibilities. The stranger we had reason to believe had entered our home had used my typewriter to write that note, or Cynthia had typed it herself.

But we'd had the locks changed. I was as sure as I could be that no one had been in this house in the last few days who wasn't supposed to be here.

It seemed unthinkable that Cynthia had done this. But what if . . . what if, under what could only be described as unimaginable stress, Cynthia had written this note, directing us to a remote location where supposedly we would learn the fate of her family?

What if Cynthia had typed it up, and what happened if it turned out to be right?

'Terry!' Cynthia shouted. 'Detective Wedmore is here!'

'In a minute!' I said.

What would that mean? What would it mean if Cynthia somehow actually knew, all these years, where her family could be found?

I was breaking into a sweat.

Maybe, I told myself, she'd repressed the memory. Maybe she knew more than she was aware. Yes, that could be it. She saw what happened, but had forgotten it. Didn't that happen? Didn't the brain sometimes decide, hey, what you're seeing is so horrible, you have to forget it, otherwise you'll never be able to get on with your life. Wasn't there an actual syndrome they talked about that covered this sort of thing?

And then again, what if it wasn't a repressed memory? What if she'd always known …

No.

No, it had to be another explanation altogether. Someone else used our typewriter. Days ago. Planning ahead. That stranger who'd come into the house and left the hat.

If it was a stranger.

'Terry!'

'Right there!'

'Mr Archer!' Detective Wedmore shouted. 'Haul it down here, please.'

I acted on impulse. I opened the closet, picked up the typewriter – God those old machines were heavy – and put it inside, on the floor. Then I draped some other things over it, an old pair of pants I'd used to paint in, a stack of old newspapers.

As I came down the stairs, I saw that Wedmore was now with Cynthia in the living room. The letter was on the coffee table, open, Wedmore leaning over it, reading it.

'You touched this,' she scolded me.

'Yes.'

'You've both touched it. Your wife, that I could understand, she didn't know what it was when she took it out. What's your excuse?'

'I'm sorry,' I said. I ran my hand over my mouth and chin, tried to wipe away the sweat I was sure would betray my nervousness.

'You can get divers, right?' Cynthia said. 'You can get divers to go into the quarry, see what's there?'

'This could be a crank,' Wedmore said, taking a strand

of hair that had fallen in front of her eye and tucking it behind her ear. 'Could be nothing.'

'That's true,' I offered.

'But then again,' the detective said. 'We don't know.'

'If you don't send in divers, I'll go in myself,' Cynthia said.

'Cyn,' I said. 'Don't be ridiculous. You don't even swim.'

'I don't care.'

'Mrs Archer,' Wedmore said. 'Calm down.' It was an order. Wedmore had a kind of football coach thing going on.

'Calm down?' said Cynthia, unintimidated. 'You know what this person, who wrote this letter, is saying? They're down there. Their bodies are down there.'

'I'm afraid,' Wedmore said, shaking her head skeptically, 'that there might be a lot down there after all these years.'

'Maybe they're in a car,' Cynthia said. 'My mother's car, my father's car, they were never found.'

Wedmore took a corner of the letter between two brilliant red-polished fingernails and turned it over. She stared at the map.

'We'll have to get the Mass state police in on this,' she said. 'I'll make a call.' She reached into her jacket for her cell phone, opened it up, prepared to put in a number.

'You're going to get some divers?' Cynthia said.

'I'm making a call. And we're going to have to get that letter to our lab, see if they can get anything off it, if it hasn't already been made pretty useless.'

'I'm sorry,' Cynthia said.

'Interesting,' Wedmore said, 'that it was written on a typewriter. Hardly anyone uses typewriters.'

I felt my heart in my mouth. And then Cynthia said something I couldn't believe I was hearing.

'We have a typewriter,' she said.

'You do?' Wedmore said, holding off before entering the last number.

'Terry still likes to use one, right, honey? For short notes, that kind of thing. It's a Royal, isn't it, Terry?' To Wedmore, she said, 'He's had it since his college days.'

'Show it to me,' Wedmore said, slipping the phone back into her jacket.

'I could go get it,' I said. 'Bring it down.'

'Just show me where it is.'

'It's upstairs,' Cynthia said. 'Come, I'll show you.'

'Cyn,' I said, standing at the bottom of the stairs, trying to act as a barrier. 'It's a bit of a mess up there.'

'Let's go,' Wedmore said, moving past me and up the stairs.

'First door on the left,' Cynthia said. To me, she whispered, 'Why do you think she wants to see our typewriter?'

Wedmore disappeared into the room. 'I don't see it,' she said.

Cynthia was up the stairs before me, turned into the room, said, 'It's usually right there. Terry, isn't it usually right there?'

She was pointing to my desk as I came into the room. She and Wedmore were both looking at me.

'Uh,' I said. 'It was in my way, so I tucked it into the closet.'

I opened the closet door, knelt down. Wedmore was peering in, over my shoulder. 'Where?' she said.

I pulled away the newspapers and the paint-splattered

pants to reveal the old black Royal. I lifted it out, set it back on the desk.

'When did you put it in there?' Cynthia said.

'Just a while ago,' I said.

'Got covered up awful fast,' Wedmore said. 'How do you explain that?'

I shrugged. I had nothing.

'Don't touch it,' she said, and got her phone back out of her jacket.

Cynthia looked at me with a puzzled expression. 'What's with you? What the hell is going on?'

I wanted to ask her the same thing.

TWENTY-SEVEN

Rona Wedmore made several calls on her cell, most of them from out on the driveway where we wouldn't be able to hear what she had to say.

That left Cynthia and me, and Grace – Cynthia had been permitted by Wedmore to drive over to the school quickly to pick her up – in the house to mull over these latest developments. Grace was in the kitchen, asking who the big woman making phone calls was while she made herself an after-school snack of peanut butter on toast.

'She's with the police,' I said. 'And I don't think she'll take kindly to you calling her big.'

'I won't say it to her *face*,' Grace said. 'Why is she here? What's going on?'

'Not now,' Cynthia told her. 'Take your snack and go to your room, please.'

Once Grace had left, grumbling the whole way, Cynthia asked, 'Why did you hide the typewriter? That note, it was written on your typewriter, wasn't it?'

'Yes,' I said.

She studied me a moment. 'Did you write that note? Is that why you hid the typewriter?'

'Jesus, Cyn,' I said. 'I hid it because I wondered whether *you'd* written it.'

Her eyes went wide in shock. 'Me?'

'Is that any more shocking than thinking I'd written it?'

'I didn't try to hide the typewriter, you did.'

'I was doing it to protect you.'

'What?'

'In case you had written it. I didn't want the police to know.'

Cynthia said nothing for a moment, slowly paced the room a couple of times. 'I'm trying to get my head around this, Terry. So what are you saying? Are you saying you think I wrote that note? And if I did, that I've always known where they were? My family? I've always known they're in this quarry?'

'Not … necessarily,' I said.

'Not necessarily? Then what are you thinking, exactly?'

'Honest to God, Cyn, I don't know. I don't know what to think any more. But the moment I saw that letter, I knew it had come from my typewriter. And I knew I hadn't written it. That left you, unless someone else came in here and wrote it on that typewriter to, to, I don't know, to make it look like one of us had done it.'

'We already know someone else was in here,' Cynthia said. 'The hat, the e-mail. But despite that, you'd rather think I did it?'

'I'd rather not think that at all,' I said.

She looked right into my eyes, adopted a deadly serious expression. 'Do you think I killed my family?' she asked.

'Oh, for Christ's sake.'

'That's not an answer.'

'No, I don't.'

'But it's crossed your mind, hasn't it? You've wondered, every once in a while, whether it's possible.'

'No,' I said. 'I have not. But I have wondered, lately, whether the stress of what you've been through, what you've had to carry all these years, has made you ...' I could feel the eggshells cracking under my shoes, '... think, or perceive things, or maybe even do things, in a way that's not been, I don't know, totally rational.'

'Oh,' Cynthia said.

'Like when I saw that the letter had been done on my typewriter, I thought, could you have done this as a way to get the police interested in the case again, to do something, to try to solve it once and for all?'

'So I'd send them on a wild goose chase? Why would I pick that spot, that particular place?'

'I don't know.'

Someone rapped on the wall outside our room and Detective Rona Wedmore stepped through the doorway. I had no idea how long she had been standing there, how long she might have been listening.

'It's a go,' she said. 'We're sending in divers.'

It was set up for the following day. A police diving squad was to be on site for 10 a.m. Cynthia walked Grace to school and arranged for one of the neighbors to meet her at the end of the day and take her back to her house in the event we weren't home in time.

I called the school again, got Rolly, said I would not be in.

'Jesus, what now?' he asked.

I told him where we were off to, that divers were going into the quarry.

'God, my heart goes out to you guys,' he said. 'It never ends. Why don't I get someone to cover your classes for the next week? I know a couple recently retired teachers who could come in, do a short-term thing.'

'Not the one who stammers. The kids ate her alive.' I paused. 'Hey, this is kind of out of the blue, but let me bounce something off you.'

'Shoot.'

'Does the name Connie Gormley mean anything to you?'

'Who?'

'She was killed a few months before Clayton and Patricia and Todd vanished. Upstate. Looked like a hit-and-run, but wasn't, exactly.'

'I don't know what you're talking about,' Rolly said. 'What do you mean, it looked like a hit-and-run but wasn't? And what could that possibly have to do with Cynthia's family?'

He almost sounded annoyed. My problems, and the conspiracies whirling around them, were starting to wear him down just as they had me.

'I don't know that it does. I'm just asking. You knew Clayton. Did he ever mention anything about an accident or anything?'

'No. Not that I can remember. And I'm pretty sure I'd remember something like that.'

'OK. Look, thanks for getting someone for my classes. I owe you.'

Cynthia and I hit the road shortly after that. It was more than a two-hour drive north. Before the police took away the anonymous letter in a plastic evidence bag, we copied the map onto another piece of paper so we'd know where we were going. Once we were on our way, we didn't want to stop for coffee or anything else. We just wanted to get there.

You might have thought that we'd have been talking non-stop all the way up, speculating about what the divers might find, what it might mean, but in fact we hardly said anything at all. But I imagined we were both doing a lot of thinking. What Cynthia was thinking, I could only guess. But my mind was all over the place. What would they find in the quarry? If there actually were bodies down there, would they be Cynthia's family? Would there be anything to indicate who'd put them there?

And was that person, or persons, still walking around?

We headed east once we passed Otis, which really isn't a town, but a few houses and businesses spaced out along the meandering two-lane road that eventually winds its way up to Lee and the Massachusetts Turnpike. We were hunting for Fell's Quarry Road, which was supposed to run off to the north, but we didn't have to look that hard for it. There were two cars with Massachusetts state troopers marking the turnoff for us.

I put down the window and explained to an officer in a trooper hat who we were, and he went back to his car and talked to someone on a radio, then came back and said Detective Wedmore was already at the scene, expecting us. He pointed up the road, told us of a narrow grassy laneway about one mile up that led to the left and climbed, and that we'd find her there.

We drove in slowly. It wasn't much of a road, just gravel and dirt, and when we reached the laneway it got even narrower. I turned in, heard tall grass brushing the underside of the car. We were driving uphill now, thick trees on either side, and after about a quarter of a mile the ground leveled off and the trees gave way to an open area that nearly took our breath away.

We were looking out over what appeared to be a vast

canyon. About four car lengths ahead of us the ground dropped away sharply. If there was a lake down there, we couldn't yet see it from where we sat in the car.

There were two other vehicles already there. Another Mass state police car, and an unmarked sedan that I recognized as Wedmore's. She was leaning up against the fender, talking to the officer from the other car.

When she saw us she approached.

'Don't get close,' she said to me through the open window. 'It's a hell of a drop.'

We got out of the car slowly, as if jumping out would cause the ground to give way. But it felt pretty solid.

'This way,' Wedmore said. 'Either of you have trouble with heights?'

'A bit,' I said. I was speaking more for Cynthia than myself, but she said she was fine.

We took a few steps closer to the edge, and now we could see the water. A mini-lake, maybe eight or nine acres in size, at the bottom of a chasm. Years ago, this area had been carved out for rock and gravel, the pit left to fill with rain and springs once the aggregate company had moved on. On an overcast day like this one, it was difficult to tell what color the water might normally be. Today it was gray and lifeless.

'The map and the letter indicated that if we're to find anything,' Wedmore said, 'it'll be right down here.' She pointed straight down the cliff we were standing atop. I felt a brief wave of vertigo.

Down below, crossing the body of water, was a yellow inflatable boat, maybe fifteen feet long with a small outboard attached to the back. In the boat were three men, two dressed in black wetsuits, diving masks, tanks on their backs.

'They had to come in from another direction,' Wedmore explained. She pointed to the far side of the quarry. 'There's another road that comes in from the north that comes up to the water's edge, so they were able to launch their boat there. They're looking for us.' At which point Wedmore waved to the men in the boat – not friendly, just a signal – and they waved back. 'They'll start searching below this point.'

Cynthia nodded. 'What will they be looking for?' she asked.

Wedmore gave her a look that seemed to say 'duh', but she was at least sensitive enough to realize she was dealing with a woman who'd been through a lot. 'I'd say a car. If it's there, they'll find it.'

The lake was too small for the wind to whip up much in the way of waves, but the men in the boat dropped a small anchor just the same to keep from drifting away from their spot. The two men in wetsuits dropped backwards out of the boat and in another moment disappeared from view, a few bubbles on the surface the only evidence that they'd once been there.

A cool wind blew over the top of the cliff. I moved closer to Cynthia and slipped my arm around her. To my surprise, and relief, she did not push me away.

'How long can they stay down there?' I asked.

Wedmore shrugged. 'I don't know. I'm sure they have way more air than they need.'

'If they do find something, what then? Can they bring it up?'

'Depends. We might need more equipment.'

Wedmore had a radio that connected her to the man left in the boat. 'What's happening?' she asked.

In the boat, the man spoke into a small black box.

'Not much so far,' a voice crackled through Wedmore's radio. 'It's about thirty to forty feet here. Some spots, further off, even deeper.'

'OK.'

We stood and watched. Maybe for ten, fifteen minutes. Seemed like hours.

And then two heads emerged. The divers swam over to the boat, hung their arms over the inflated rubber-tube edges for support, lifted up their masks and removed from their mouths the gear that allowed them to breathe underwater. They were telling the man something.

'What are they saying?' Cynthia asked.

'Hang on,' Wedmore said, but then we saw the man pick up his radio and Wedmore grabbed hers.

'Got something,' the radio crackled.

'What?' Wedmore asked.

'Car. Been there a long time. Half buried in silt and shit.'

'Anything inside it?'

'They're not sure. We're going to have to get it out.'

'What kind of car?' Cynthia asked. 'What does it look like?'

Wedmore relayed the question, and down in the lake, we could see the man asking the divers some questions.

'Looks sort of yellow,' the man said. 'A little compact car. Can't see the plates, though. The bumpers are buried.'

Cynthia said. 'My mother's car. It was yellow. A Ford Escort. A small car.' She turned in to me, held me. 'It's them,' she said. 'It's them.'

Wedmore said, 'We won't know that for a while. We don't even know if there's anyone in that car.' Back into the radio, she said, 'Let's do what we have to do.'

*

That meant bringing in more equipment. They thought that if they brought in an oversized tow truck from the north, got it right up to the edge of the lake, they could run a cable out into the water, have the divers attach it to the submerged car, and slowly pull it out of the muck at the bottom of the lake and to the surface.

If that didn't work, they'd have to bring in some sort of barge affair, take it out onto the water, position it over the car and lift it up directly from the bottom.

'Nothing's going to happen for a few hours,' Wedmore told us. 'We've got to get some people up here, they've got to figure out how they're going to do this. Why don't you go some place, head back to the highway, maybe go up to Lee, get some lunch? I'll call your cell when it looks like something's about to happen.'

'No,' Cynthia said. 'We should stay.'

'Honey,' I said. 'There's nothing we can do now. Let's go eat. We both need our strength, we need to be able to handle what may come next.'

'What do you figure happened?' Cynthia asked.

Wedmore said, 'I guess someone drove that car right up here, where we're standing, then ran it right off the edge of this cliff.'

'Come on,' I said again to Cynthia. To Wedmore, 'Please keep us posted.'

We drove back down to the main road, back to Otis, then north to Lee, where we found a diner and ordered coffee. I hadn't had much of an appetite first thing in the morning, so I ordered a midday breakfast of eggs and sausage. All Cynthia could manage was some toast.

'So, whoever wrote that note,' Cynthia said, 'knew what he was talking about.'

'Yeah,' I said, blowing on my coffee to cool it down.

'But we don't even know if there's anyone in the car. Maybe the car was ditched there, to hide it. But it doesn't mean anyone died in that accident.'

'Let's wait and see,' I said.

We ended up waiting a couple of hours. I was on my fourth coffee when my cell phone rang.

It was Wedmore. She gave me some directions that would get me to the lake from the north side.

'What's happened?' I asked.

'It's gone faster than we thought,' she said, bordering on amiable. 'It's out. The car's out.'

The yellow Escort was already sitting on the back of a flatbed truck by the time we arrived at the site. Cynthia was out of the car before I'd come to a full stop, running toward the truck, shouting, 'That's the car! My mother's car!'

Wedmore grabbed hold of her before she could get close.

'Let me go,' Cynthia said, struggling.

'You can't go near it,' the detective told her.

The car was covered in mud and slime and water was seeping out around the cracks of the closed doors, enough so that the interior, at least above the window line, was clear of water. But there was nothing to be seen but a couple of waterlogged headrests.

'It's going to the lab,' Wedmore said.

'What did they find?' she asked. 'Was there anything inside?'

'What do you think they found?' Wedmore asked. I didn't feel good about the way she'd asked. It was as though she thought Cynthia already knew the answer.

'I don't know,' Cynthia said. 'I'm scared to say.'

'There appear to be the remains of two people in there,' she said. 'But as you can understand, after twenty-five years . . .'

One could only imagine.

'Two?' Cynthia said. 'Not three?'

'It's early yet,' Wedmore said. 'Like I said, we have a lot of work before us.' She paused. 'And we'd like to take a buccal swab from you.'

Cynthia did a kind of double take. 'A what?'

'I'm sorry. It's Latin, for cheek. We'd like to get a DNA sample from you. We take a sample from your mouth. It doesn't hurt or anything.'

'Because?'

'If we're fortunate enough to be able to recover any DNA from . . . what we find in the car, we'll be able to compare it to yours. If, for example, one of those bodies is your mother, they can do a kind of reverse maternity test. It'll confirm if she is, in fact, your mother. Same for the other members of your family.'

Cynthia looked at me, tears forming in her eyes. 'For twenty-five years I've waited for some answers, and now that I'm about to get some, I'm terrified.'

I held her. 'How long?' I asked Wedmore.

'Normally, weeks. But this is a more high-profile case, especially since there was the TV show about it. A few days, maybe just a couple. You might as well go home. I'll have someone come by later today for the sample.'

Heading back seemed the only logical thing to do. As we turned to walk back to our car, Wedmore called out, 'And you'll need to be available in the meantime, even before the test results come back. I'm going to have more questions.'

There was something ominous about the way she said it.

TWENTY-EIGHT

As promised, Rona Wedmore showed up to ask questions. There were things about this case she did not like.

That was certainly something we all had in common, although Cynthia and I didn't feel that Wedmore was an ally.

She did confirm one thing I already knew, however. The letter that had directed us to the quarry had been written on my typewriter. Cynthia and I had both been requested – as if there were any option – to come down to headquarters and be fingerprinted. Cynthia's fingerprints apparently were on file. She'd provided them twenty-five years ago when police were combing her house, looking for clues to her family's disappearance. But the police wanted them again, and I'd never been asked to provide mine before.

They compared our prints against those on the typewriter. They found a few of Cynthia's on the body of the machine. But the actual keys were covered with mine.

Of course, there wasn't much to make of that. But it didn't support our contention that someone had broken into our house and written the letter on my typewriter, someone who could have been wearing gloves and left no prints behind.

'And why would someone do that?' asked Wedmore, her hands made into fists and resting on her considerable hips. 'Come into your house and use your typewriter to write that note?'

That was a good question.

'Maybe,' Cynthia said, very slowly, kind of thinking out loud, 'whoever did it knew the note would most likely be traced back to Terry's typewriter. They wanted it traced back to him, they wanted you to think he'd written it.'

I thought Cynthia was on to something, with one small change. 'Or you,' I said to her.

She looked at me for a moment, not accusingly, but thoughtful. 'Or me,' she said.

'Again, why would anyone do that?' Wedmore asked, still unconvinced.

'I have no idea,' Cynthia said. 'It doesn't make any sense at all. But you know someone was here. You must have a record of it. We called the police and they came out here, they must have made a report.'

'The hat,' Wedmore said, unable to keep the skepticism out of her voice.

'That's right. I can get it for you if you'd like,' Cynthia offered. 'Would you like to see it?'

'No,' Wedmore said. 'I've seen hats before.'

'The police thought we were nuts,' Cynthia said.

Wedmore let that one go. It must have taken some effort on her part.

'Mrs Archer,' she said. 'Have you ever been up to the Fell's Quarry before?'

'No, never.'

'Not as a girl? Not even when you were a teenager?'

'No.'

'Maybe you were up there, and didn't even realize it was that location. Driving around with someone, you might have gone up there to, well, to park, that kind of thing.'

'No. I have never been up there. It's a two-hour drive up there, for Christ's sake. Even if some boy and I were going to go parking, we'd hardly drive two hours to get there.'

'What about you, Mr Archer?'

'Me? No. And twenty-five years ago, I never even knew anyone in the Bigge family. I'm not from the Milford area. It wasn't until university that I met Cynthia and learned about what had happened to her, to her family.'

'OK, look,' Wedmore said, shaking her head. 'I'm having a bit of trouble with this. A note, written in this home, on your typewriter,' she looked at me, 'leads us to the very spot where your mother's car,' she looked at Cynthia, 'was found, some twenty-five years after it disappeared.'

'I told you,' Cynthia said. 'Someone was here.'

'Well, whoever that someone was, he didn't try to hide that typewriter. Your husband's the one who did that.'

I said, 'Should we have a lawyer here when you're asking these questions?'

Wedmore pushed her tongue around the inside of her cheek. 'I suppose you'd have to ask yourself whether you believe you need one.'

'We're the victims here,' Cynthia said. 'My aunt has been murdered, you've found my mother's car in a lake. And you're talking to us – talking to me – like we're the criminals. Well, we're not the criminals.' She shook her head in exasperation. 'It's like, it's like someone else has planned this all out, planned it to make it look like I'm going crazy or something. That phone call, someone putting my father's hat in the house, that letter being written on our typewriter. Don't you see? It's like someone wants you to think that maybe I'm losing it, that all these things that happened in the past are making me do these things, imagine these things now.'

That tongue moved from the inside of one cheek to the other. Finally, Wedmore said, 'Mrs Archer, have you ever thought about talking to someone? About this conspiracy that seems to be swirling around you?'

'I am seeing a psy—' Cynthia stopped herself.

Wedmore smiled. 'Well, there's a shocker.'

'I think we've had enough for now,' I said.

'I'm sure we'll be talking again,' Wedmore said.

Very soon, as it turned out. Right after they found the body of Denton Abagnall.

I guess I'd thought, if there were any developments in the hunt for the man we'd hired to find Cynthia's family, we would have heard about them first from the police. But I was listening to the radio in our sewing room/study, not paying that much attention, until the words 'private detective' came out of the speaker. I reached over and turned up the volume.

'Police found the man's car in a parking garage near the Stamford Town Center,' the news reader said. 'Management noticed the car had been there for several days, and when they notified police they said its registration matched that of a man police had been searching for, for about as long as the car had been there. When the trunk was forced open, the body of Denton Abagnall, who was fifty-one years old, was found inside. He died of blunt trauma to the head. Police are reviewing security video as part of their investigation. Police refused to speculate as to motive, or whether the slaying might be in any way gang related.'

Gang related. If only.

I found Cynthia at the far end of the backyard, just standing there, hands tucked into the pockets of her windbreaker, looking back at the house.

'I just needed to get out,' she said as I approached. 'Is everything OK?'

I told her what I'd heard on the radio.

I didn't know what sort of reaction to expect, and wasn't all that surprised when Cynthia didn't have much of one. She said nothing for a moment, then, 'I'm starting to feel numb, Terry. I don't know what to feel any more. Why's all this happening to us? When's all of this going to stop? When are we going to get our normal lives back?'

'I know,' I said, putting my arms around her. 'I know.'

The thing was, Cynthia hadn't really had a normal life since she was fourteen.

When Rona Wedmore showed up again, she was direct and to the point. 'Where were you the night Denton Abagnall went missing? The night he left here, the last night anyone ever heard from him. Say around eight?'

'We had dinner,' I said. 'And then we went to visit Cynthia's aunt. She was dead. We called the police. We were with the police pretty much the entire evening. So I guess the police would be our alibi, Detective Wedmore.'

For the first time, Wedmore appeared embarrassed, and off her game. 'Of course,' she said. 'I should have realized that. Mr Abagnall drove into that parking garage at 8.03 according to the ticket that was sitting on the dash.'

'So,' Cynthia said coldly. 'I guess at least we're off the hook for that one.'

Heading out the door, I asked Wedmore, 'Did they find any papers with Mr Abagnall? A note, some empty envelopes.'

'Far as I know,' Wedmore said, 'there was nothing. Why?'

'Just wondering,' I said. 'You know, one of the last things Mr Abagnall told us was that he was going to be checking out Vince Fleming, who was with my wife the night her family disappeared. You know about Vince Fleming?'

'I know the name,' she said.

Wedmore showed up again, the following day.

When I saw her walking up the drive, I said to Cynthia, 'Maybe she's tied us in to the Lindbergh kidnapping.'

I opened the door before she knocked. 'Yes?' I said. 'What now?'

'I have news,' she said. 'May I come in?' Her tone was less abrasive today. I didn't know whether that was good news, or meant she was setting us up for something.

I showed Wedmore into the living room and invited her to take a seat. Cynthia and I both sat down.

'First of all,' she said, 'you need to know I'm no scientist. But I understand the basic principles, and will do my best to explain them to you.'

I looked at Cynthia. She nodded for Wedmore to continue.

'The chances of being able to extract any DNA from the remains in your mother's car – and there were just two bodies, not three – were always slim, but not non-existent. Over the years, the natural process of decay had eaten away all of the ...' She stopped herself. 'Mrs Archer, may I be straightforward here? It's not pleasant to listen to, I understand.'

'Go ahead,' Cynthia said.

Wedmore nodded. 'As you might guess, the decay over the years – enzymes being released from human cells as they die, human bacteria, environmental and in this case aquatic micro-organisms – had pretty much destroyed all the flesh on the bodies. The bone decomposition would have been even worse had this been salt water, but it wasn't, so we caught a bit of a break there.' She cleared her throat. 'Anyway, we had bones, and we had teeth, so we attempted to get dental records for your family, but struck out. Your father, from what we could tell, had no dentist, although the coroner determined pretty quickly, based on the bone structure of the two people in the car, that neither was an adult male.'

Cynthia blinked. So Clayton Bigge's body was not one of the two in that car.

'As for the dentist your brother and mother went to, he passed away many years ago, the practice closed down and all the records were destroyed.'

I glanced at Cynthia. She seemed to be steeling herself for disappointment. Maybe we weren't going to learn anything definitive.

'But the thing was, even if we didn't have dental records, we still had teeth,' Wedmore said. 'From each of the two bodies. The enamel on the outside, there's no DNA there, nothing to test, but deep in the center of the tooth, in the root, it's so protected in there, they can find nucleated cells.'

Cynthia and I must have both looked lost, so Wedmore said, 'Well, the bottom line is, if our forensic people can get in there, and get to those cells, and extract sufficient DNA, the results will show a unique profile for each individual, including sex.'

'And?' Cynthia asked, holding her breath.

'It was a male and a female,' Wedmore said. 'The coroner's analysis, even before DNA testing, suggests a male in his mid-teens, most likely, and a woman probably in her late thirties, maybe early forties.'

Cynthia glanced at me, then back to Wedmore.

Wedmore continued. 'So, a very young man and a woman were in that car. Now the question becomes whether there's a connection between them.'

Cynthia waited.

'The two DNA profiles suggest a close relatedness, possibly parent-child. The forensic results, coupled with the coroner's findings, do suggest a mother and son relationship.'

'My mother,' Cynthia whispered. 'Todd.'

'Well, here's the thing,' Wedmore said. 'While a relationship between the two deceased has been more or less determined, we don't know beyond a shadow of a doubt that it is in fact Todd Bigge and Patricia Bigge. If you still had anything of your mother's that might provide a sample, an old hairbrush for example, with some hairs still caught in the bristles ...'

'No,' said Cynthia. 'I don't have anything like that.'

'Well, we do have your DNA sample, and additional reports are pending with regard to any possible relationship you may have to the remains we took from the car. Once your sample is typed, and they're working on that now, they'll be able to determine the probability of maternity regarding the female deceased, and the probability of a sibling relationship to the male deceased.'

Wedmore paused. 'But based on what we know now, that these two bodies are related, that it's a mother and son, that the car is in fact your mother's, the working assumption is that we've found your mother and your brother.'

Cynthia looked dizzy.

'But not,' Wedmore pointed out, 'your father. I'd like to ask you a few more questions about him, what he was like, what kind of person he was.'

'Why?' Cynthia asked. 'What are you implying?'

'I think we have to consider the possibility he murdered both of them.'

TWENTY-NINE

'Hello?'

'It's me,' he said.

'I was just thinking about you,' she said. 'I haven't heard from you for a while. I hope everything's OK.'

'I wanted to wait to see what would happen,' he said. 'How much they might find out. There's been stuff on the news. They showed the car. On TV.'

'Oh my . . .'

'They had a picture of it being taken away from the quarry. And they had a story today, in the newspapers, about the DNA tests.'

'Oh, this is so exciting,' she said. 'I wish I was there with you. What did it say?'

'Well, it said some stuff but not others, of course. I've got the paper right here. It said, "DNA tests indicate a genetic link between the two bodies in the car, that they are a mother and son."'

'Interesting.'

'"Forensic tests have yet to determine whether the bodies are genetically linked to Cynthia Archer. Police are operating on the assumption, however, that the recovered bodies are Patricia Bigge and Todd Bigge, missing for 25 years."'

'So the story doesn't actually say that's who was in the car?' she said.

'Not quite.'

'You know what they say about "assume". It makes an ass out of you and—'

'I know, but . . .'

'But still, it's amazing what they can do these days, isn't it?' She sounded almost cheerful.

'Yeah.'

'I mean, back then, when your father and I got rid of that car, who'd even heard of DNA tests? It boggles the mind, that's what it does. You still feeling nervous?'

'A little, maybe.' He did sound subdued to her.

'Even as a boy, you were a worrier, you know that? Me, I just take hold of a situation and deal with it.'

'Well, you're the strong one, I guess.'

'I think you've done a wonderful job, lots to be proud of. Soon you'll be home and you can take me back. I wouldn't want to miss this for the world. When the moment comes, I can't wait to see the expression on her face.'

THIRTY

'So, how are you dealing with this?' Dr Kinzler asked Cynthia. 'The apparent discovery of your mother and your brother?'

'I'm not sure,' Cynthia said. 'It's not relief.'

'No, I can see why it wouldn't be.'

'And the fact that my father was not there with them. This detective, Wedmore, she thinks maybe he killed them.'

'If that turns out to be true,' Dr Kinzler said, 'are you going to be able to deal with that?'

Cynthia bit her lip, looked at the blinds, as though she had x-ray vision and could see out to the highway. This was our regular session, and I'd talked Cynthia into keeping it, even though she'd been talking about canceling. But now that Dr Kinzler was asking such probing questions, that to my mind just opened wounds as opposed to healing them, I was questioning myself.

'I'm already having to come to terms with the idea that my father may have been something other than the man I knew,' Cynthia said. 'The fact that there's no record of him, no social security number, no driver's license.' She paused. 'But the idea that he could have killed them, that he could have killed my mother and Todd, I can't believe it.'

'You think he left the hat?' Dr Kinzler said.

'It's a possibility,' Cynthia said.

'Why would your father break into your house, leave

you a message like that, write a letter on your own typewriter with a map leading you to the others?'

'Is he ... is he trying to settle things?'

Dr Kinzler shrugged. 'I'm asking you what you think.'

Standard shrink procedure, I thought.

'I don't know what to think,' Cynthia said. 'If I thought he'd done it, then the notes, everything, it might be him trying to set the record straight, to confess. I mean, whoever left that note had to be involved somehow in their deaths. To know those kinds of details.'

'True,' Dr Kinzler said.

'And Detective Wedmore, even though she talks like my father killed them years ago, I think she thinks I wrote the note,' Cynthia said.

'Maybe,' Dr Kinzler speculated, 'she thinks you and your father are in this together. Because his body wasn't found. Because you weren't in that car with your mother and your brother.'

Cynthia paused before nodding. 'I know, years ago, the police must have wondered about me. I mean, when they weren't able to turn up anything, I guess they would have considered everything, wouldn't they? They probably wondered whether I might have done it with Vince. Whether we'd done it together. Because of the fight I'd had that night with my parents.'

'You've told me you don't remember a lot about that night,' Dr Kinzler said. 'Do you think it's possible there are things you know that you've blocked out? I have occasionally referred people to someone I trust very much who does hypnosis therapy.'

'I'm not blocking things out. I *blacked* out. I came home drunk. I was a kid. I was stupid. I came home,

I passed out. I woke up the next morning.' She raised her hands, dropped them in her lap. 'I couldn't have committed a crime if I'd wanted to. I was out of it.' She sighed. 'Don't you believe me?'

'Of course,' Dr Kinzler said. Gently, she asked, 'Tell me more about your relationship with your father.'

'Normal, I guess. I mean, we had fights, but we more or less got along. I think ...' she paused again, 'that he loved me. I think he loved me very much.'

'More than the other members of your family?'

'What do you mean?'

'Well, if he was in a state of mind that led him to kill your mother and your brother, why wouldn't he have killed you, too?'

'I don't know. And I've told you, I don't believe he did it. I ... I can't explain any of this, OK? But my father wouldn't do something like that. He couldn't have killed my mother. He'd never have killed his own son, my brother. You know why? Not just because he loved us. He wouldn't have been able to do anything like that because he was too weak.'

That caught my attention.

'He was a sweet man, but – this is hard to say about a parent – but he just wouldn't have had it in him to do something like that.'

I said, 'I don't see where any of this is getting us.'

'We know that your wife is deeply troubled by the questions raised by this discovery,' the psychiatrist said. 'I'm trying to help her with that.'

'What if they arrest me?' Cynthia said.

'Pardon?' said Dr Kinzler.

'What?' I said.

'What if Detective Wedmore arrests me?' she asked.

'What if she becomes convinced I had something to do with it? What if she thinks I'm the only person who could possibly have known what was in that quarry? If she arrests me, how will I explain this to Grace? Who'll look after her if they take me away? She needs her mother.'

'Honey,' I said. I almost blurted out that I would look after Grace, but that would have suggested I believed that the scenario she was laying out for us was likely, and imminent.

'If she arrests me, she'll stop trying to find the truth,' Cynthia said.

'That's not going to happen,' I said. 'If she arrested you, she'd have to believe that you had something to do with everything else, with Tess's death, maybe even Abagnall's death. Because all these things, they must be connected somehow. These things are all part of the same puzzle. They're all related. We just don't know how.'

'I wonder if Vince knows,' Cynthia said. 'I wonder if anyone has talked to him lately.'

'Abagnall said he was looking into him,' I said. 'Didn't he say something, the last time we saw him, about checking into his background a bit more?'

Dr Kinzler, attempting to get us back on track, said, 'I don't think we should wait for two more weeks before your next appointment.' She was looking at Cynthia when she said it, not me.

'Sure,' she said, her voice soft and distant. 'Sure.' She excused herself and left the office to use the washroom.

I said to Dr Kinzler, 'Her aunt, Tess Berman, came to see you a couple of times.'

The eyebrows went up. 'Yes.'

'What did she have to say?'

'I wouldn't normally discuss another patient with you, but in Tess Berman's case, there isn't anything to discuss. She came a couple of times, but never opened up to me. I think she had contempt for the process.'

I loved Tess.

There were ten calls on our answering machine when we got home, all from different media outlets. There was a long, impassioned message from Paula, from *Deadline*. She said Cynthia owed their viewers a chance to revisit this case in light of recent developments. Just name the time and place, and she'd be there with a film crew, Paula said.

I watched as Cynthia hit the button to delete the message. Not flustered. No confusion. One quick motion with a steady index finger.

'Didn't have any trouble that time,' I said. God forgive me, it just slipped out.

'What?' she said, looking at me.

'Nothing,' I said.

'What did you mean? That I didn't have any trouble that time?'

'Forget it,' I said. 'I didn't mean anything.'

'You mean when I deleted that message?'

'I said it was nothing.'

'You're thinking about that morning. When I got the call. When I accidentally erased the call history. I told you what happened. I was shook up.'

'Of course you were.'

'You don't even believe I got that call, do you?'

'Of course I do.'

'And if I didn't get that call, then that e-mail, I must have written that, too? Maybe at the same time I was typing up that note on your typewriter?'

'I didn't say that.'

Cynthia moved closer to me, raised her hand and pointed at me. 'How can I stay here under this roof, if I can't be a hundred per cent certain that I have your support? Your trust? I don't need you looking at me sideways, second-guessing everything I do.'

'I'm not doing that.'

'So say it. Tell me right now. Look me in the eye and tell me you believe in me, that you know I haven't had a hand in any of this.'

I swear I was going to say it. But my tenth-of-a-second hesitation was all it took for Cynthia to turn and walk away.

When I went into Grace's room that night, and found the lights all turned off, I expected to find her peering through her telescope, but she was already under the covers. She was wide awake.

'I'm surprised to find you here,' I said, sitting on the edge of the bed and touching the side of her head.

Grace didn't say anything.

'I thought you'd be looking for asteroids. Or did you already look?'

'I didn't bother,' she said so softly I almost couldn't hear.

'Are you not worried about asteroids any more?' I asked.

'No,' she said.

'So, there aren't any coming to hit the earth any time

soon?' I said, brightening. 'Well, that has to be a good thing.'

'They might still be coming,' Grace said, turning her head into the pillow. 'But it doesn't matter.'

'What do you mean by that, honey?'

'Everyone around here is so sad all the time.'

'Oh, honey. I know. These have been a tough few weeks.'

'It didn't matter whether an asteroid was coming or not. Aunt Tess still died. I heard you guys talking about them finding the car. People die all the time from all sorts of things. They get hit by cars. They can drown. And sometimes people kill them.'

'I know.'

'And Mom's acting like we're not safe, and she hasn't looked in my telescope even once. She thinks something's coming to get us, but it's not something from outer space.'

'We would never let anything happen to you,' I said. 'Your mother and I love you very much.'

Grace said nothing.

'I still think it would be worth checking just once,' I said, shifting off the bed and kneeling in front of the telescope. 'You mind if I have a look?' I asked.

'Knock yourself out,' Grace said. If the lights had been on, she might have seen me react to that.

'OK,' I said, settling into position, but glancing first out the window to make sure the house wasn't being watched, then put my eye up to the lens, took hold of the telescope.

I pointed it up into the night sky, saw stars fly past the end like a pan shot from *Star Trek*.

'Let's have a look here,' I said, and then the scope

broke free of its stand, hit the floor, and rolled under Grace's desk.

'I told you, Dad,' she said. 'It's just a piece of junk.'

I found Cynthia under the covers, too. They were pulled up right to her neck, as though she were cocooned. Her eyes were closed, although I had a feeling she was not asleep. She just didn't want to engage in conversation.

I stripped down to my boxers, brushed my teeth, threw back the covers and got into bed next to her. There was an old *Harper's* next to the bed, and I flipped through the pages briefly, tried to read the index, but couldn't concentrate.

I reached over and turned the bedside lamp off. I settled in on my side, my back to Cynthia.

'I'm going to go lie with Grace,' Cynthia said.

'Sure,' I said into my pillow. Without looking at her, I said, 'Cynthia, I love you. We love each other. What's happening now, it's tearing us up, tearing us apart. We need to come up with some plan, some way to take this on together.'

But she slipped out of bed without responding. A sliver of light from the hallway cut across the ceiling like a knife as she opened the door, then vanished as she closed it. Fine, I thought. I was too tired to fight, too tired to try to make up. Soon, I fell asleep.

In the morning, when I got up, Cynthia and Grace were gone.

THIRTY-ONE

Even if we hadn't fought, I wouldn't have been surprised to find Cynthia missing from our bed the next morning. When I woke up at 6.30 I figured she'd fallen asleep on Grace's bed and spent the night there. So I didn't immediately trudge down the hall to check on them.

I got up, pulled on my jeans, wandered into the adjoining bathroom and splashed some water on my face. I had looked better. The stress of the last few weeks was taking its toll. There were dark circles under my eyes, and I think I'd actually lost a few pounds. That was something I could stand to do, but I would have preferred to do it following a plan that did not consist entirely of stress. There was red in the corner of my eyes, and I looked as though I could use a haircut.

The towel bar is right next to the window that looks down over the driveway. As I reached for a towel there was something different about how the world beyond looked through the blinds. The cracks between the blinds are usually filled with white and silver, the colors of our two cars. But this time there was silver and asphalt.

I pried apart the blinds. Cynthia's car was not in the driveway.

I muttered something along the lines of 'What the fuck?'

Then I padded down the hall, barefoot and shirtless, and eased open the door to Grace's room. Grace was never up this early, and I had every reason to expect to find her in bed.

The covers were turned back, the bed empty.

I could have just shouted out my wife's name, or my daughter's, standing up there at the top of the stairs, but it was still very early in the morning, and if there was a chance that there were still others in this house with me, and they were asleep, I didn't want to wake them.

I popped my head into the study, found it empty, went down to the kitchen.

It looked as it had the night before. Everything cleaned up and put away. No one had had an early breakfast before departing.

I opened the door to the basement, and this time I felt comfortable shouting. 'Cyn!' It was dumb, I know, given that her car was not in the driveway, but because that didn't make sense, at some level I must have been operating on the theory that it had been stolen. 'You down there?' I waited a beat, then, 'Grace!'

When I opened the front door, the morning newspaper was there waiting for me.

It was hard, at that moment, not to shake the feeling that I was living out an episode from Cynthia's life.

But this time, unlike that morning twenty-five years ago, there was a note.

It was folded and standing on its side, on the kitchen table, tucked in between the salt and pepper shakers. I reached for it, unfolded it. It was handwritten, and the writing was unmistakably Cynthia's. It read:

Terry:

I'm going away.

I don't know where, or for how long. I just know

I can't stay here another minute.

I don't hate you. But when I see the doubt in your eyes, it tears me apart. I feel like I'm losing my mind, that no one believes me. I know Wedmore still doesn't know what to think.

What's going to happen next? Who will break into our house? Who will be watching it from the street? Who will be next to die?

I don't want it to be Grace. So I'm taking her with me. I figure you have the smarts to look after yourself. Who knows. Maybe with me out of the house, you'll actually feel safer.

I want to look for my father, but I don't have any idea where to start. I believe he's alive. Maybe that's what Mr Abagnall discovered after he went to see Vince. I just don't know.

All I do know is I need some space. Grace and I need to be a mother and daughter, who don't have to worry about anything else except being a mother and daughter.

I won't have my cell on very often. I know they can do that thing, triangulate, to find people. But I'll check it once in a while for messages. Maybe, at some point, I'll feel like talking to you. Just not right now.

Call the school, tell them Grace will be gone for a while. I'm not calling the shop. Let Pamela think what she wants.

Don't look for me.

I still love you, but I don't need you to find me right now.

L, Cyn

I read it three, maybe four times. Then I picked up the phone and called her cell, despite what she'd written. It went straight to message, and I left one. 'Cyn. Jesus. Call me.'

And then I slammed the phone down. 'Shit!' I shouted. 'Shit!'

I paced the kitchen a few times, unsure what to do. I opened the door, walked down to the end of the drive, still in nothing but my jeans, and looked up and down the street, as if somehow I could magically divine which way Cynthia and Grace had gone. I went back into the house, grabbed the phone again, and, as if in a trance, dialed the number I always did when I needed to talk to someone who loved Cynthia as much as I did.

I had dialed Tess.

And when the phone rang a third time and no one picked up, I realized what I'd done, the incredible mistake I had made. I hung up and sat at the kitchen table and began to cry. With my elbows on the table, I put my head in my hands and let it all come out.

I don't know quite how long I sat there, alone, at my kitchen table, letting the tears run down my cheeks. Long enough until there weren't any left, I guess. Once I'd exhausted the supply, I had no choice but to come up with another course of action.

I went back upstairs, finished dressing. I had to keep telling myself a few things.

The first was that Cynthia and Grace were OK. It wasn't as though they'd been kidnapped or anything. And second, I couldn't imagine that Cynthia would let anything bad happen to Grace, no matter how upset she was.

She loved Grace.

But what was my daughter to think? Her mother getting her up in the middle of the night, making her pack a bag, sneaking out of the house together so her father wouldn't hear?

Cynthia had to have believed, in her heart, that this was the right thing to do, but it wasn't. It was wrong, and it was wrong to put Grace through something like this.

And that was why I had no problem ignoring Cynthia's orders not to look for them.

Grace was my daughter. She was missing. And I was bloody well going to look for her. And try to work out things with my wife.

I dug around in the bookcase and got out a map of New England and New York State, opened it up on the kitchen table. I let my eyes wander, from Portland south to Providence, Boston west to Buffalo, asking myself where Cynthia might go. I looked at the Connecticut-Massachusetts line, the town of Otis, the vicinity of the quarry. I couldn't see her going there. Not with Grace in tow. What would be the point? What was to be learned from a return trip?

There was the village of Sharon, where Connie Gormley, the woman who was killed in some sort of staged hit-and-run accident, had been from, but that didn't make any sense either. Cynthia had never really grabbed on to that story in the newspaper clipping as meaning anything, not the way I had. I couldn't see her heading up that way.

Maybe the answer wasn't to be found in looking at a map. Maybe I needed to be thinking about names. People from her past. People Cynthia might turn to, in these very desperate times, for answers.

I went into the living room, where I found the two shoeboxes of mementoes from Cynthia's childhood. Given what the last few weeks had been like, the boxes had never found their way back to their usual hiding place, in the bottom of our closet.

I started riffling through the contents randomly, tossing old receipts and clippings onto the coffee table, but they held no meaning for me. They seemed to coalesce into one huge puzzle with no discernible pattern.

I went back into the kitchen, phoned Rolly at home. It was too early for him to have left for school yet. Millicent answered.

'Hi, Terry,' she said. 'What's going on? Are you not going in today?'

'Rolly already has me off,' I said. 'Millie, you haven't heard from Cynthia by any chance?'

'Cynthia? No. Terry, what's going on? Isn't Cynthia home?'

'She's gone. She took Grace with her.'

'Let me get Rolly.'

I heard her set the phone down and a few seconds later Rolly said, 'Cynthia's gone?'

'Yeah. I don't know what to do.'

'Shit. And I was going to call her today, see how she's doing, if she wanted to talk. She didn't tell you where she was going?'

'Rolly, if I knew where she was going I wouldn't be calling you so fucking early in the morning.'

'OK, OK. Jesus, I don't know what to say. Why did she go? Did you guys have a fight or something?'

'Yeah, kind of. I fucked up. And I think everything's just gotten to her. She wasn't feeling safe here, she wanted to protect Grace. But this was the wrong way to go about it. Look, if you hear from her, if you see her, let me know, OK?'

'I will,' Rolly said. 'And if you find her, call.'

Next, I called Dr Kinzler's office. It hadn't opened yet, so I left a message, said Cynthia was missing, asked her to please call me, left my home and cell numbers.

The only other person I could think to call was Rona Wedmore. I considered it, then decided not to. She wasn't, as far as I could tell, solidly in our corner.

I think I understood Cynthia's motivations for disappearing, but I was less sure Wedmore would.

And then a name popped into my head. Someone I'd never met, never spoken to, never even seen across a room. But his name kept coming up.

Maybe it was time to have a chat with Vince Fleming.

THIRTY-TWO

If I could have brought myself to call Detective Wedmore I could have asked her outright where I might find Vince Fleming and saved myself some time. She'd already said she knew the name. Abagnall had told us he had a record for a variety of offences. He was even believed to have participated in a revenge killing after the murder of his father back in the early nineties. There was a pretty good chance that a police detective would know where someone like that might hang out.

But I didn't want to talk to Wedmore.

I went up to the computer and started doing some searches on Vince Fleming and Milford. There were a couple of news stories from a New Haven paper over the last few years, one that detailed how he had been charged with assault. He'd used someone's face to open a beer bottle. That one got dismissed when the victim decided to drop charges. I was willing to bet there was more to that story, but the online edition of this newspaper certainly didn't have it.

There was another story where Vince Fleming got a passing reference as someone rumored to be behind a rash of auto thefts in southern Connecticut. He owned a body shop in an industrial district somewhere in town, and there was a photo of him, one of those slightly grainy ones taken by a photographer who doesn't want his subject to know he's there, going into a bar called Mike's.

I'd never been in, but I'd driven past the place.

I got out the Yellow Pages, found several pages listing businesses that would fix a dented automobile. From the listings, it wasn't immediately obvious which one might belong to Vince Fleming – there was no Vince's Auto Body, no Fleming's Fender Repair.

I could start phoning every body shop in the Milford area, or I could try asking around for Vince Fleming at Mike's. Maybe there I might find someone who could point me in the right direction, at least give me the name of the body shop he owned, and where, if the papers were to believed, he chopped up the occasional stolen car for parts.

Although not particularly hungry, I felt I needed some food in my stomach and put a couple of slices of bread into the toaster, slathered peanut butter over them. I threw on a jacket, made sure I had my cell phone with me, and went to the front door.

When I opened it, Rona Wedmore was standing there.

'Whoa,' she said, her fist suspended in mid-air, ready to knock.

I jumped back. 'Jesus,' I said. 'You scared the shit out of me.'

'Mr Archer,' she said, maintaining her composure. Evidently my sudden opening of the door scared me more than it did her.

'Hello,' I said. 'I was just on my way out.'

'Is Mrs Archer here? I don't see her car.'

'She's out. Is there something I can help you with? Have you any new information?'

'No,' she said. 'When will she back?'

'I can't say, exactly. What did you want her for?'

Wedmore ignored my question. 'Is she at work?'

'Perhaps.'

'You know what? I'll just give her a call. I think I made a note here of her cell phone number.' She had her notebook out.

'She's not answer—' I stopped myself.

'She's not answering her phone?' Wedmore said. 'Let's see if you're right about that.' She punched in the number, put the phone to her ear, waited, closed the phone. 'You're right. Does she not like to answer her phone?'

'Sometimes,' I said.

'When did Mrs Archer leave?' she asked.

'This morning,' I said.

'Because I drove by here around one in the morning, getting off shift late and all, and her car wasn't here then, either.'

Shit. Cynthia had hit the road with Grace even earlier than I'd imagined.

'Really?' I said. 'You should have dropped in and said hello.'

'Where is she, Mr Archer?'

'I don't know. Check back in the afternoon. Maybe she'll be here then.' Part of me wanted to ask for Wedmore's help, but I was afraid of making Cynthia seem guiltier than I feared Wedmore already viewed her.

That tongue was poking around inside her mouth again. It took a break so she could ask, 'Has she taken Grace, too?'

I found myself unable to say anything for a moment, then, 'I really have things to do.'

'You look worried, Mr Archer. And you know what?

You should be. Your wife has been under one hell of a strain. I want you to get in touch with me the moment she shows up.'

'I don't know what it is you think she's done,' I said. 'My wife's the victim here. She's the one who was robbed of her family. Her parents and brother first, now her aunt.'

Wedmore tapped me on the chest with an index finger. 'Call me.' She handed me another one of her business cards before heading back to her car.

Seconds later, I was in mine, driving west on Bridgeport Ave. into the Milford neighborhood of Devon. Mike's was a small brick building next to a 7-Eleven, its five-letter neon sign running vertically down the second storey, ending above the entrance. The front windows were decorated with signs advertising Schlitz and Coors and Budweiser.

I parked around the corner and walked back, not sure whether Mike's would even be open in the morning for business, but once inside I realized that for many, it was never too early to drink.

There were about a dozen customers in the dimly lit bar, two perched on stools up at the counter having a conversation, the rest scattered about the tables. I approached the bar just down from the two guys, leaned against it until I had caught the attention of the short, heavyset man in a check shirt working behind it.

'Help ya?' he asked, a damp mug in one hand, a towel in the other. He worked the towel into the mug, twisted it around.

'Hi,' I said. 'I'm looking for a guy, I think he comes in here a lot.'

'We get a lot of people,' he said. 'Got a name?'

'Vince Fleming.'

The bartender had a pretty good poker face. Didn't flinch, raise an eyebrow. But he didn't say anything right away, either.

'Fleming, Fleming,' he said. 'Not sure.'

'He's got a body shop in town here,' I said. 'He's the kind of guy, I think, if he does come in here, you'd know him.'

I became aware that the two guys at the bar were no longer talking.

'What sort of business you got with him?' the bartender asked.

I smiled, trying to be polite. 'It's sort of a personal matter,' I said. 'But I'd be most grateful if you could tell me where I could find him. Wait, hang on.' I dug out my wallet, struggling for a second to get it out of the back pocket of my jeans. It was a clumsy, awkward maneuver. I made Columbo look smooth. I laid a ten on the counter. 'It's a bit early for me for a beer, but I'd be happy to pay you for your trouble.'

One of the guys at the bar had slipped away. Maybe to use the can.

'You can keep your money,' the bartender said. 'If you want to leave your name, next time he's in, I could pass it on to him.'

'Maybe, if you could just tell me where he works. Look, I don't mean him any trouble. I'm just wondering if maybe, someone I'm looking for might have been to see him.'

The bartender weighed his options, must have decided Fleming's place of business was probably pretty common knowledge, so he said, 'Dirksen Garage. You know where that is?'

I shook my head.

'Across the bridge over into Stratford,' he said. He drew me a small map on a cocktail napkin.

I went back outside, took a second to let my eyes adjust to the sunlight and got back in my car. Dirksen Garage was only a couple of miles away, and I was there in under five minutes. I kept glancing in my rear-view mirror, wondering whether Rona Wedmore might be following me, but I didn't spot any obvious unmarked cars.

Dirksen Garage was a single-storey cinder-block building with a paved front yard and a black tow truck out front. I parked, walked past a Beetle with its nose smashed in and a Ford Explorer with the two driver's side doors caved in, and entered the garage through the business entrance.

I'd come into a small, windowed office that looked out onto a large bay with half a dozen cars in various stages of repair. Some were brown with primer, others masked with paper in preparation for painting, a couple with fenders removed. A strong chemical smell traveled up my nostrils and bore straight into my brain.

There was a young woman at the desk in front of me who asked what I wanted.

'I'm here to see Vince,' I said.

'Not in,' she said.

'It's important,' I said. 'My name's Terry Archer.'

'What's it about?'

I could have said that it was about my wife, but that was going to raise a whole bunch of red flags. When one guy goes looking for another guy, and says it's about his wife, it's hard to believe anything good can come of that.

So I said, 'I need to speak with him.'

And what, exactly, was I going to speak with him about? Had I figured that part out yet? I could start with, 'Have you seen my wife? Remember her? You knew her as Cynthia Bigge. You were on a date with her the night her family vanished?'

And once I'd broken the ice, I could try something like, 'Did you, by the way, have anything to do with that? Did you happen to put her mother and brother in a car and dump them off a cliff into an abandoned quarry?'

It would have been better if I had a plan. But the only thing that was driving me now was that my wife had left me, and this was my first stop as I went beating about the bushes.

'Like I said, Mr Fleming is not here right now,' the woman said. 'But I'll take a message.'

'The name,' I said again, 'is Terry Archer.' I gave her my home and cell numbers. 'I'd really like to talk to him.'

'Yeah, well, you and plenty of others,' she said.

So I left the Dirksen Garage, stood out front in the sun and said to myself, 'What now, asshole?'

All I really knew for sure was that I needed a coffee. Maybe, drinking a coffee, some intelligent course of action would come to me. There was a doughnut place about half a block down, so I walked over to it. I bought a medium with cream and sugar and sat down at a table littered with doughnut wrappers. I brushed them out of my way, careful not to get any icing or sprinkles on me, and got out my cell phone.

I tried Cynthia again, and again it went straight to voice mail. 'Honey, call me. Please.'

I was slipping the phone back into my jacket when it rang. 'Hello? Cyn?'

'Mr Archer?'

'Yes.'

'Dr Kinzler here.'

'Oh, it's you. I thought it might be Cynthia. But thanks for returning my call.'

'Your message said your wife is missing?'

'She left in the middle of the night,' I said. 'With Grace.' Dr Kinzler said nothing. I thought I'd lost my call. 'Hello?'

'I'm here. She hasn't been in touch with me. I think you should find her, Mr Archer.'

'Well, thanks. That's very helpful. That's kind of what I'm trying to do right now.'

'I'm just saying, your wife has been under a great deal of stress. Tremendous strain. I'm not sure that she's entirely ... stable. I don't think it's a very good environment for your daughter.'

'What are you saying?'

'I'm not saying anything. I just think it would be best to find her as soon as you can. And if she does get in touch with me, I will recommend to her that she return home.'

'I don't think she feels safe there.'

'Then you need to make it safe,' Dr Kinzler said. 'I have another call.'

And she was gone. As helpful as always, I thought.

I'd downed half my coffee before I realized it was bitter to the point of being undrinkable, tossed the rest, and walked out the front of the shop.

A red SUV bounced up and over the curb and stopped abruptly in front of me. The back and front doors on the passenger side opened and two rumpled looking, slightly pot-bellied men in oil-stained jeans, denim jackets and dirty T-shirts jumped out – one was bald and the other had dirty blond hair.

'Get in,' Baldy said.

'Excuse me?' I said.

'You heard him,' said Blondie. 'Get in the fucking car.'

'I don't think so,' I said, taking a step back toward the doughnut shop.

They lunged forward together, each grabbing an arm. 'Hey,' I said as they dragged me toward the SUV's back door. 'You can't do this. Let go of me! You can't just grab people off the street!'

They heaved me in. I went sprawling onto the floor of the back seat. Blondie got in front, Baldy got in the back, rested his work-booted foot on my back to keep me there. As I was going down I caught a glimpse of a third man behind the wheel.

'You know what I thought he was going to say for a second there?' Baldy asked his buddy.

'What?'

'I thought he was going to say "unhand me".' They both started pissing themselves laughing.

The thing was, it had been the next thing I was going to say.

THIRTY-THREE

As a high-school English teacher, I didn't have a lot of experience in how to handle being grabbed by a couple of thugs out front of a doughnut shop and tossed into the back of an SUV.

I was learning, very quickly, that no one was particularly interested in what I had to say.

'Look,' I said from my position on the floor of the back seat. 'You guys have made some kind of mistake.' I tried twisting around a bit, onto my side, so I could at least get a glimpse of the bald man who was pressing down on my back with his boot.

'Shut the fuck up,' he said, looking at me.

'I'm just saying,' I said. 'I'm not the kind of guy anyone would be interested in. I don't mean you guys any harm. Who do you think I am? Some gang guy? A cop? I'm a *teacher*.'

From the front seat, Blondie said, 'I fucking hated all my teachers. That's enough right there to get you capped.'

'I'm sorry, I know there are a lot of shitty teachers out there, but what I'm trying to tell you is I don't have anything to do ...'

Baldy sighed, opened up his jacket, and produced a gun that was probably not the biggest handgun in the world, but from my position below him, it looked like a cannon. He pointed it at my head.

'If I have to shoot you in this car, my boss is going to be pissed that there'll be blood and bone and brain matter all over the fucking upholstery, but when I explain to him that you wouldn't shut the fuck up like you were told to do, I think he'll understand.'

I shut up.

It didn't take Sherlock Holmes to figure out that this had something to do with my asking questions about where to find Vince Fleming. Maybe one of those two guys at the bar at Mike's had made a call. Maybe the bartender had phoned the auto body shop before I'd even got there. Then somebody'd put in a call to these two goons to find out why it was I wanted to see Vince Fleming.

Except nobody was asking that question.

Maybe they didn't care. Maybe it was enough that I was asking. You ask around about Vince, you end up in the back of an SUV and nobody ever sees you again.

I started thinking about a way out. It was me against three big guys. Judging by the extra fat they were carrying around their middles, maybe not the fittest thugs in Milford, but how in shape did you have to be when you were armed? If one of them had a gun, it seemed reasonable to assume the other two did as well. Could I get Baldy's gun from him, shoot him, open the door and jump from a moving car?

Not in a million years.

The gun was still in Baldy's hand, resting on top of his knee. The other leg remained propped on top of me. Blondie and the driver were talking, nothing to do with me, but about a ball game from the night before. Then Blondie said, 'What the fuck is that?'

The driver said, 'It's a CD.'

'I can see it's a CD. It's what CD it is that's got me worried. You are not putting that in the player.'

'Yeah, I am.'

I heard the distinctive whir of a CD being loaded into a dashboard player.

'I don't fucking believe you,' Blondie said.

'What?' Baldy asked from the back seat.

Before anyone else could say anything, the music started. An instrumental intro, and then: 'Why do birds suddenly appear ... every time ... you are near?'

'Fuck me,' said Baldy. 'The fucking Carpenters?'

'Hey,' said the driver. 'Knock it off. I grew up with this.'

'Jesus,' said Blondie. 'This chick singing, isn't she the one who wouldn't eat anything?'

'Yeah,' the driver said. 'She had anorexia.'

'People like that,' said Baldy. 'They should have a fucking hamburger or something.'

Could three guys debating the merits of a seventies singing group really be planning to take me some place and execute me? Wouldn't the mood in the car have to be a bit more grim? For a moment, I felt encouraged. And then I thought of the scene in *Pulp Fiction*, where Samuel L. Jackson and John Travolta are arguing over what a Big Mac is called in Paris, moments before they go up to an apartment and commit murder. These guys didn't even have that kind of style. In fact, there was an unmistakable whiff of body odor coming off one or more of them.

Is this how it ends? In the back seat of an SUV? One minute you're having coffee in a doughnut shop, trying to find your missing wife and daughter, and the next you're looking down the barrel of a stranger's gun, wondering if the last words you hear will be: 'They long to be ... close to you.'

We took a couple of turns, went over some railroad tracks, and then it felt as though the SUV was descending, ever so slightly, as though we were heading toward the shore. Down toward the sound.

Then, the truck slowed, did an abrupt right, bounced up over a curb and came to a stop. Looking up through the windows, I saw mostly sky, but also the side of a house. When the driver killed the engine, I heard seagulls.

'OK,' said Baldy, looking down at me. 'I want you to be nice. We're getting out and going up some stairs and into a house, and if you try to run away, or if you try shouting for help, or try doing any other kind of retarded thing, I'm going to hurt you. You understand?'

'Yes,' I said.

Blondie and the driver were already out. Baldy opened his door, got out, and I pulled myself up first onto the back seat, then scooted over until I was out the side.

We were parked in a driveway between two beach houses. I had a pretty good idea we were on East Broadway. The houses are packed in pretty tight together along there, and glancing south between the houses I could see beach and beyond that, Long Island Sound. When I saw Charles Island out there I was even more sure where we were.

Baldy motioned for me to climb up a set of open-back stairs that went up the side of a pale yellow house to the second floor. The first floor was mostly garage. Blondie and the driver went ahead, then me, then Baldy. The steps were gritty with beach sand and made soft, scratching noises under our shoes.

At the top of the stairs the driver held open a screen door, and the rest of us walked in ahead of him. We entered into a large room with sliding glass doors facing the water, and a deck that was suspended over the beach. There were some chairs and a couch just inside the door, a shelf weighed down with paperback novels, then as you moved back into the room there was a table and a kitchen along the back wall.

Another heavyset man with his back to me was standing at the stove, steadying a frying pan with one hand, a spatula in the other.

'Here he is,' Blondie said.

The man nodded without saying anything.

'We'll be down in the truck,' Baldy said, and motioned for Blondie and the driver to follow him out. The three of them walked out and I could hear their boots receding on the steps.

I stood there in the center of the room. Normally, I would have turned to take in the view out the glass doors, maybe even walked out onto the deck and taken in a whiff of sea air. But instead, I stared at the man's back.

'You want some eggs?' he asked.

'No thanks,' I said.

'It's no trouble,' he said. 'Fried, scrambled, over easy, whatever.'

'No, but thanks just the same,' I said.

'I get up a little later, sometimes it's nearly lunchtime before I make breakfast,' he said. He reached up into a cupboard and brought down a plate, transferred some scrambled eggs to it, added some sausages he must have cooked earlier that had been sitting on a paper towel, then reached into a cutlery drawer for a fork and what appeared to be a steak knife.

He turned around and walked over to the table, pulled out a chair and sat down.

He was about my age, although I think I can say, objectively, that he looked a bit worse for wear. His face was pockmarked, he had an inch-long scar above his right eye, and his once black hair was now heavily peppered with grey. He was in a black T-shirt, tucked into some black jeans, and I could see the bottom edge of a tattoo on his upper right arm, but not enough to discern what it was of. His stomach strained against his shirt, and he sighed at the effort of plopping down into his chair.

He motioned to the chair opposite him. I approached, cautiously, and sat down. He upended a bottle of ketchup, waited for a huge dollop to land on the plate by his eggs and sausage. He had a mug of coffee in front of him, and when he reached for it, said, 'Coffee?'

'No,' I replied. 'I just had some at the doughnut shop.'

'The one by my business?' he said.

'Yes.'

'It's not very good there,' he said.

'No, it's not. I threw out half of it,' I said.

'Do I know you?' he asked, shoving some eggs into his mouth.

'No,' I said.

'But you're asking around for me. First at Mike's, then at my place of business.'

'Yes,' I said. 'It wasn't my intention to alarm you.'

'"Wasn't my intention,"' he parroted. The man I now knew to be Vince Fleming speared a sausage with his fork, held it in place, then picked up the steak knife and cut off a piece. He shoved it into his mouth. 'Well, when people I don't know start asking around for me, that can be a cause for concern.'

'I guess I didn't fully appreciate that.'

'Given the kind of business I do, sometimes I run into people with unorthodox business practices.'

'Sure,' I said.

'So when people I don't know start asking around for me, I like to arrange a meeting where I feel I have the advantage.'

'I think you do,' I said.

'So who the fuck are you?'

'Terry Archer. You know my wife.'

'I know your wife,' he said, as if to say, 'So?'

'Not any more. But a long time ago.'

Fleming scowled at me as he took another bite of sausage. 'What is this? Did I fool around with your old lady or something? Look, it's not my fault if you can't keep your woman happy and she needs to come to me for what she wants.'

'It's not that kind of thing,' I said. 'My wife's name is Cynthia. You would have known her when she was Cynthia Bigge.'

He stopped in mid-chew. 'Oh. Shit. Man, that was a fucking long time ago.'

'Twenty-five years,' I said.

'You've taken a long time to drop by,' Vince Fleming said.

'There have been some recent developments,' I said. 'I take it you remember what happened that night?'

'Yeah. Her whole fucking family vanished.'

'That's right. They've just found the bodies of Cynthia's mother, and her brother.'

'Todd?'

'That's right.'

'I knew Todd.'

'You did?'

Vince Fleming shrugged. 'A bit. I mean, we went to the same school. He was an OK guy.' He shoveled in some more ketchup-covered eggs.

'You're not curious about where they found them?' I asked.

'I figure you're going to tell me,' he said.

'They were in Cynthia's mother's car, a yellow Ford Escort, at the bottom of a lake in a quarry, up in Massachusetts.'

'No shit.'

'No shit.'

'They must have been there a while,' Vince said. 'And they were still able to tell who they were?'

'DNA,' I said.

Vince shook his head in admiration. 'Fucking DNA. What did we ever do without it?' He finished off a sausage.

'And Cynthia's aunt was murdered,' I said.

Vince's eyes narrowed. 'I think Cynthia talked about her. Bess?'

'Tess,' I said.

'Yeah. She bought it?'

'Someone stabbed her to death in her kitchen.'

'Hmm,' Vince said. 'Is there some reason why you're telling me all this?'

'Cynthia's missing,' I said. 'She's ... run off. With our daughter. We have a daughter named Grace. She's eight.'

'That's too bad.'

'I thought there was a chance Cynthia might have

come looking for you. She's trying to find the answers to what happened that night, and it's possible you might have some of them.'

'What would I know?'

'I don't know. But you were probably the last person to see Cynthia that night, other than her family. And you had a run-in with her father before he brought Cynthia home.'

I never saw it coming.

Vince Fleming reached across the table with one hand, grabbed my right wrist with his left, yanked it across the table toward him, while his other hand grabbed the steak knife he'd been using to cut his sausage. He swung it down toward the table in a long, swift arc, and the blade buried into the wood table between my middle and fourth finger.

I screamed. 'Jesus!'

Vince's hand was a vice on my wrist, pinning it to the table. 'I don't like the sound of what you're suggesting,' he said.

I was panting too hard to respond. I kept looking at the knife, desperate to reassure myself that it had not actually gone through my hand.

'I have a question for you,' Vince said very quietly, still holding my wrist, leaving the knife standing straight up. 'There's been a guy, another guy, asking around about me. You know anything about that?'

'What guy?' I said.

'In his fifties, short guy, might have been private. Asked around without being quite so obvious as you.'

'It might have been a man named Abagnall,' I said. 'Denton Abagnall.'

'And how would you know that?'

'Cynthia hired him. We both hired him.'

'To check up on me?'

'No. I mean, not specifically. We hired him to try and find Cynthia's family. Or at least, what happened to them.'

'And that meant asking about me?'

I swallowed. 'He mentioned that he thought you were worth taking a look at.'

'Really? And what's he found out about me?'

'Nothing,' I said. 'I mean, if he did find out anything, we don't know what it was. And we're not likely to find out, either.'

'Why's that?' Vince Fleming asked.

He either didn't know, or was very good with the poker face.

'He's dead,' I said. 'He was murdered, too. In a parking garage in Stamford. We think it might have something to do with Tess's murder.'

'And the boys also said some cop was nosing around asking for me. Black chick, short and fat.'

'Wedmore,' I said. 'She's been looking into all of it.'

'Well,' said Vince, letting go of my wrist and working the knife out of the table. 'That's all very interesting, but I don't particularly give a fuck.'

'So, you haven't seen my wife?' I said. 'She hasn't been by here, or your work, to talk to you?'

Very evenly, he said, 'No.' And he stared into my eyes, as though daring me to contradict him.

I held his gaze. 'I hope you're telling me the truth, Mr Fleming. Because I'll do anything to make sure she and my daughter get home safely.'

He got up from his chair and walked around to my

side of the table. 'Should I take that as some sort of a threat?'

'I'm just saying that when it comes to family, even people like me, people who don't have nearly as much influence as people like you, will do whatever they have to do.'

He grabbed my hair in his fist, bent down and put his face into mine. His breath smelled of sausage and ketchup.

'Listen, fuckface, do you have any idea who you're talking to? Those guys who brought you here. You have any idea what they can do? You could end up in a wood chipper. You could be chum thrown off a boat in the sound out there. You could—'

Outside, at the base of the stairs, I heard one of the three guys who'd delivered me here shout, 'Hey, don't go up there.'

And a woman, shouting back, 'Go fuck yourself.' Then footsteps on the stairs.

I was staring into Vince's face and couldn't see the screen door, but I heard it swing open, and then a voice I thought I recognized said, 'Hey Vince, you seen my mom, because ...'

Then, seeing Vince Fleming with a man's hair in his fist, she stopped talking.

'I'm kind of busy here,' he told her. 'And I don't know where your mother is. Try the goddamn mall.'

'Jesus, Vince, what the fuck are you doing to my teacher?' the woman said.

Even with Vince's meaty fingers holding on to my scalp, I managed to turn my head far enough to see Jane Scavullo.

THIRTY-FOUR

'Your teacher?' Vince said, not relaxing his grip on my hair. 'What teacher?'

'My fucking creative writing teacher,' Jane said. 'If you're going to beat the shit out of my teachers, there are other ones you could start with first. This is Mr Archer. He's like, the least assholish of any of them.' She approached. 'Hi, Mr Archer.'

'Hi, Jane,' I said.

'When are you coming back?' she asked. 'This guy they got in to teach your class is a complete dweeb. Everybody's skipping. He's worse than that woman who stutters. Nobody gives a shit whether he takes attendance or not. He's always got something stuck in his teeth, and he's got his finger in there, trying to get it out, but he does it quick, like he thinks you won't notice, but he's not fooling anybody.' I noticed that Jane, outside of school, was not nearly so shy about talking to me.

Then, casually, she asked Vince, 'What's the deal?'

'Why don't you run along, Jane, OK?' Vince said.

'Have you seen my mom?'

'I said try the mall. Or maybe she's up at the garage. Why?'

'I need some money.'

'What for?'

'Stuff.'

'What stuff?'

'Stuff stuff.'

'How much you need?'

Jane Scavullo shrugged. 'Forty?'

Vince Fleming let go of my hair and reached into his back pocket for his wallet, pulled out two twenties and handed them to Jane.

He said, 'Is this the guy? The one you were talking about? Who likes your stories?'

Jane nodded. She was so relaxed, I had to assume she'd seen others getting this sort of treatment from Vince. The only thing different this time was that it was one of her teachers. 'Yeah. Why you fucking him over?'

'Look, honey, I can't really get into this with you.'

'I'm trying to find my wife,' I said. 'She's with my daughter, and I'm very worried about them. I thought your fa ... I thought Vince here might be able to help me.'

'He's not my father,' Jane said. 'He and my mom have been together for a while now.' To Vince, she said, 'I don't mean that like an insult, about you not being my father. Because you're OK.' To me, she said, 'Remember that one story I wrote for you, about the guy making me eggs?'

I had to think. 'Yes,' I said. 'I do.'

'That was sort of based on Vince here. He's decent.' She smiled at the irony. 'Well, to me. So if you're just trying to find your wife and kid, why's Vince here getting all pissed with you?'

'Sweetheart,' Vince said.

She walked up to Vince, got right in his face. 'You be nice to him or I'm fucked. His is like the only class where I'm getting any decent grades. If he wants help finding his wife why don't you help him find her because if he's not coming back to school until his wife gets found then I got to look at this guy picking his teeth every day and that's not good for my education. It also makes me want to puke.'

Vince put an arm around her shoulder and walked her to the door. I couldn't hear what he was saying to her, but just before she went back down the stairs, she said to me, 'See ya, Mr Archer.'

'Goodbye, Jane,' I said, barely able to hear her receding steps once the door had closed.

Vince walked back over to the table, much of the menace gone out of his posture, and sat back down at the table. He looked a bit sheepish, and didn't say anything right away.

'She's a good kid,' I said.

Vince nodded. 'Yeah, she is. Her mom, she and I've hooked up, and she's a bit of a flake, but Jane, she's OK. She's been needing some, what you call it, stability in her life. I never raised any kids, and sometimes, I kind of think of her like a daughter.'

'She seems to get on pretty good with you,' I said.

'She fucking wraps me around her finger,' he said, and grinned. 'She's mentioned you. I didn't make the connection when you told me who you were. But it's Mr Archer this, Mr Archer that.'

'Really?' I said.

'She says you've encouraged her,' Vince said. 'About her writing.'

'She's pretty good.'

Vince pointed to the jammed bookshelves. 'I read a lot. I'm not what you'd call a very educated kind of guy, but I like to read books. I especially like history, biography. Some adventure books. I'm kind of amazed by people who can do that, who can sit down and write a whole book. So when Jane said you thought she could be a writer, I thought that was kind of interesting.'

'She has her own voice,' I said.

'Huh?'

'You know how, when you read some writers, you'd know it was them even if their name wasn't on the cover?'

'Sure.'

'That's voice. I think Jane has that.'

Vince nodded. 'Listen,' he said. 'About what happened ...'

'Don't worry about it,' I said, working up some spit in my mouth so I could swallow.

'People start asking questions about you, trying to find you, that can be a bit worrying for someone like me,' he said.

'What does that mean, someone like you?' I asked, running my fingers through my hair, trying to get it looking normal again.

'Well, let me put it this way,' Vince said. 'I'm not a creative writing teacher. I don't imagine, in your line of work, that you might have to do some of the things that I have to do in mine.'

'Like sending out guys in SUVs to grab people off the street?' I said.

'Exactly,' Vince said. 'That kind of thing.' He paused. 'Can I get you some coffee?'

'Thanks,' I said. 'That'd be good.'

He walked over to the counter, poured me a cup from the coffee maker, and came back to the table. 'I'm still concerned that you and that detective and that cop have been asking around for me,' he said.

'May I be frank without having my hair pulled out or

a knife stabbed into the table between my fingers?'

Slowly, Vince nodded, not taking his eyes off me.

'You were with Cynthia that night. Her father found the two of you and dragged her home. Less than twelve hours later, Cynthia wakes up and she's the only one left in her family. As I was trying to say before, you are, presumably, one of the last people to see a member of her family, other than Cynthia herself, alive. And I'm not sure whether you had a fight with her father, Clayton Bigge, but at the very least it must have been an awkward situation, her father finding you, taking her home with him.' I paused. 'But I'm sure the police went over all this with you at the time.'

'Yeah.'

'What did you tell them?'

'I didn't tell them anything.'

'What do you mean?'

'Exactly what I said. I didn't tell them anything. That was one thing I learned from my old man, God rest his soul. You never answer questions from the cops. Even if you're one hundred per cent innocent. Nobody's situation ever improved after talking to the cops.'

'But you might have been able to help them figure out what happened.'

'Wasn't my concern.'

'But didn't that make the police suspect you had something to do with it? Refusing to talk?'

'Maybe. But they can't convict you on suspicion. They need evidence. And they didn't have any of that. If they'd had any evidence, I probably wouldn't be sitting here having a nice chat with you right now.'

I took a sip of my coffee. 'Whoa,' I said. 'This is excellent.' It was.

'Thank you,' Vince said. 'Now, may I be frank with you without you pulling *my* hair out?' He grinned.

'I don't think you have much to worry about there,' I said.

'I felt bad about it. About not being able to help Cynthia. Because she was ... I don't wish to offend you here at all, being her husband.'

'It's OK.'

'She was a very, very nice girl. A bit fucked up like all kids that age, but nothing compared to me. I'd already been in shit with the cops. I guess she went through a period of being attracted to the bad boy. Before she met you.' He said it like I was a bit of a comedown for her. 'No offense intended.'

'None taken.'

'She was a sweet kid, and I felt terrible about what happened to her. Jesus, imagine, you wake up one day, your fucking family's gone. And I wished I could do something for her, you know? But my dad said to me, he said walk away from a chick like that. You don't need those kinds of problems. Cops are going to be looking at you enough already, with your background, with an old man like me involved in the shit I'm involved in, that's all we need, you messed up with a girl whose entire family probably got murdered.'

'I guess I can understand that.' I chose my words carefully. 'Your father, he did OK, am I right?'

'Money?'

'Yeah.

'Yeah. He did alright for himself. While he could. Before he got killed.'

'I heard a bit about that,' I said.

'What else did you hear?'

'I heard that the people who most likely did it got paid back.'

Vince smiled darkly. 'That they did.' He came back to the present and asked, 'So what's your point, about money?'

'Do you think your father, do you think he would have had any sympathy for Cynthia, the situation she found herself in? To the point that he would have helped pay for her education, to go to college?'

'Huh?'

'I'm just asking. Do you think he might have thought you were responsible somehow, that maybe you had something to do with her family going missing, and that he gave money to Cynthia's aunt, Tess Berman, anonymously, to help cover the costs of her schooling?'

Vince looked at me as though I had lost my mind. 'You say you're a teacher? They let people teach in the public schools with minds this fucked up?'

'You could just say no.'

'No.'

'Because,' I said, and I was debating with myself whether I should be sharing this information, but sometimes you just go with your gut, 'someone did that.'

'No shit?' Vince asked. 'Someone was giving her aunt money for school?'

'That's right.'

'And no one ever knew who?'

'That's right.'

'Well, that's weird,' he said. 'And this aunt, you say she's dead?'

'That's right.'

Vince Fleming leaned back in his chair, looked up at

the ceiling a moment, came back forward and put his elbows on the table. He let out a long sigh.

'Well, I'll tell you something,' he said. 'But not if you're going to tell the cops, because if you do, I'll tell them I never said any of this because they might find a way to use it against me, the fuckers.'

'OK.'

'Maybe I could have told them this and it wouldn't have come back to bite me in the ass, but I couldn't afford to take the chance. I couldn't admit to being where I was at the time, even if it might have helped Cynthia out. I guessed it might cross the cops' minds at some point that she had something to do with killing her own family, even though I knew she could never do that. I didn't want to get dragged into it.'

My mouth felt dry. 'Anything you can tell me now, I'd be grateful.'

'That night,' he said, closing his eyes a moment, as though picturing it, 'after her old man found us in the car, took her home, I drove after them. Didn't follow them exactly, but I guess I was wondering just how much shit she was in, thought maybe I could see whether her father was screaming at her, that kind of thing. But I was way back, really couldn't see all that much.'

I waited.

'I saw them pull into the driveway, go into the house together. She was a bit wobbly on her feet, you know? She'd had a bit to drink, we both had, but I'd already built up a pretty good tolerance by that point.' He grinned. 'I was a young starter.'

I felt Vince was moving toward something important and didn't want to slow him down with my own stupid comments.

'Anyway,' he continued. 'I parked down the street, thinking maybe she'd leave again after her parents reamed her out, you know, she'd get all pissed off and storm out, and then I could drive up and pick her up. But that didn't happen. And after a while, this other car drove past me, going slow, like someone was trying to read the house numbers, you know?'

'OK.'

'I didn't really pay much attention, but then when it got down to the end of the street, it turned around, and then parked on the other side of the street, a couple of houses down from Cynthia's place.'

'Could you see who was in it? What kind of car was it?'

'It was some piece of AMC shit, I think. An Ambassador or Rebel or something. Blue, I think. Looked like one person in the car. I couldn't really tell who it was, but it looked to me like it was a woman. Don't ask me why, but that was the sense I got.'

'A woman was parked out front of the house. Watching it?'

'Seemed like it. And I remember, they weren't Connecticut plates on the car. New York State, which were kinda orange, I think, back then. But shit, you see plenty of those around.'

'How long did the car stay there?'

'Well, after a while, not that long really, Mrs Bigge and Todd, the brother?'

I nodded.

'They came out and got in the mother's car, this yellow Ford, and they drove off.'

'Just the two of them? The father, Clayton, he wasn't with them?'

'Nope. Just Mom and Todd. He got in the passenger side, I don't think he had his license yet, but I don't really know. But they went somewhere. I don't know where. As soon as they rounded the corner, this other car's lights came on, and it followed them.'

'What did you do?'

'I just sat there. What else would I do?'

'But this other car, this Ambassador or whatever, it followed Cynthia's mother and brother.'

Vince looked at me. 'Am I going too fast?'

'No, no, it's just, in twenty-five years, I know Cynthia has never heard about this.'

'Well, that's what I saw.'

'Is there anything else?'

'I guess I sat there for another forty-five minutes or so, and was just thinking of fucking off and going home, and suddenly the front door of the house opens, and the father, Clayton, he comes running out of the house like he's got a huge bug up his ass. Gets in his car, backs out at like a hundred miles an hour, drives off fast as can be.'

I let that sink in.

'So anyway, I can do the math, right? Everyone's gone, except Cynthia. So I drive up, I knock on the door, figured I could talk to her. I banged on it half a dozen times, real hard, didn't get any answer, figured she was probably sleeping it off, right? So I fucked off and went back home.' He shrugged.

'Someone had been there,' I said. 'Watching the house.'

'Yup. Not just me.'

'And you've never told anyone this? You didn't tell the cops. You never told Cynthia?'

'No. And like I said, I didn't tell the cops. You think it would have made sense to tell them I was sitting outside that house for any time that night?'

I gazed out the window and into the sound, at Charles Island in the distance, as if the answers I'd been searching for, the answers Cynthia had been searching for, were always beyond the horizon, impossible to reach.

'And why are you telling me this now?' I asked Vince.

He ran his hand over his chin, squeezed his nose. 'Fuck, I don't know. I'm guessing, all these years have been hard on Cyn, am I right?'

I felt that like a slap, to know that Vince might have called Cynthia by the same term of endearment I used. 'Yes,' I said. 'Very hard. Especially lately.'

'And why's she disappeared?'

'We had a fight. And she's scared. All the things that have happened in the last few weeks, the fact that the police don't seem to entirely trust her. She's scared for our daughter. The other night, there was someone standing on the street, looking at our house. Her aunt is dead. The detective we hired has been murdered.'

'Hmm,' Vince said. 'That's a hell of a mess. I wish there was something I could do to help.'

We were both startled at that moment when the door opened. Neither of us had heard anyone coming up the stairs.

It was Jane again.

'Jesus Christ, Vince, are you going to help the poor bastard or not?'

'Where the hell were you?' he said. 'You been listening in this whole time?'

'It's a goddamn screen door,' Jane said. 'You don't

want people to listen maybe you better build yourself a little bank vault up here.'

'Goddamn,' he said.

'So, are you going to help him? It's not like you're really busy or anything. And you got the three stooges to help you if you need them.'

Vince looked tiredly at me. 'So,' he said. 'Is there any way I could be of assistance to you?'

Jane was watching him with her arms folded across her chest.

I didn't know what to say. Not knowing what I was up against, I couldn't predict whether I needed the kinds of services someone like Vince Fleming offered. Even though he'd stopped trying to yank my hair out by the roots, I was still intimidated by him.

'I don't know,' I said.

'Why don't I tag along for a while, see what develops,' he said. When I didn't immediately take him up on it, he said, 'You don't know whether to trust me, do you?'

I figured he'd be able to spot a lie. 'No,' I said.

'That's smart,' he said.

'So, you'll help him?' Jane said. Vince nodded. To me, she said, 'You better get back to school fast.' Then she left, and this time we could hear her going down the stairs.

Vince said, 'She scares the living shit out of me.'

THIRTY-FIVE

I couldn't think of anything cleverer to do at that moment than drive home, check and see whether Cynthia or anyone else might have phoned. If she tried to get me, she'd probably try my cell if she couldn't raise me at home, but I was feeling a bit desperate.

Vince Fleming released his thugs with the SUV, and offered to drive me back to my car in his own vehicle, which turned out to be an aggressive looking Dodge Ram pickup. My house was not far off the route back to the body shop, where I'd left my car before walking over to the doughnut shop, and later been abducted. I asked Vince if he'd mind stopping there briefly so I could check whether, by any chance, Cynthia had come home, or even dropped by and left me a message.

'Sure,' he said as we got into his truck, which was parked alongside the curb on East Broadway.

'I've always wanted to get a place along here, as long as I've lived in Milford,' I said.

'I've always lived around here,' Vince said. 'You?'

'I didn't grow up around here.'

'As kids, sometimes, when the tide was out, we'd walk out to Charles Island. But then, you wouldn't have time to get back before the tide came in again. That was always fun.'

I felt some anxiety about my new friend. Vince was, not to put too fine a point on it, a criminal. He ran a criminal organization. I had no idea how big or small it was. It was certainly big enough to have three guys on the payroll who were on call to grab people off the street who made Vince nervous.

What if Jane Scavullo hadn't walked in? What if she hadn't persuaded Vince I was an OK guy? What if Vince had continued to believe that I presented some sort of a threat to him? How might things have turned out?

Like a fool, I decided to ask.

'Suppose Jane hadn't dropped by when she did,' I said. 'What would have happened to me?'

Vince, right hand on the wheel, left arm resting on the window sill, glanced over. 'You really want an answer to that question?'

I let it go. My mind was already heading in another direction, questioning Vince Fleming's motives. Was he helping me because Jane wanted him to, or was he genuinely concerned about Cynthia? Was it a bit of both? Or had he decided that doing what Jane wanted was a good way to keep an eye on me?

Was his story about what he saw out front of Cynthia's house that night true? And if it wasn't, what possible point would there be in telling it?

I was inclined to believe it.

I gave Vince directions to our street, pointed out the house up ahead. But he kept on driving, didn't even slow down. Went right past the house.

Oh no. I'd been suckered. I was about to have a date with a wood chipper.

'What's going on?' I asked. 'What are you doing?'

'You got cops out front of your house,' he said. 'Unmarked car.' I glanced into the oversized mirror hanging off the driver's door, saw the car spotted across the street from the house receding into the background.

'That's probably Wedmore,' I said.

'We'll drive around the block, come in from the back,' Vince said, like he did this sort of thing all the time.

And that's what we did. We left the truck one street over, walked between a couple of houses, and approached my house through the backyard.

Once inside, I looked for any evidence that Cynthia might have returned, a note, anything.

She had not.

Vince wandered the first floor, looking at the pictures on the walls, the books we had on our shelves. Casing the joint, I thought. His eyes landed on the open shoeboxes of mementoes.

'The hell's this stuff?' he asked.

'It's Cynthia's. From her house when she was a kid. She goes through it all the time, hoping it will offer up some sort of secret. I was kind of doing the same thing today, after she left.'

Vince sat on the couch, ran his hand through the stuff. 'Looks like a lot of useless shit to me,' he said.

'Yeah, well, so far that's exactly what it's been,' I said.

I tried phoning Cynthia's cell on the off chance that it might be on. I was about to hang up after the fourth ring when I heard Cynthia say, 'Hello?'

'Cyn?'

'Hi, Terry.'

'Jesus, are you OK? Where are you?'

'We're fine, Terry.'

'Honey, come home. Please come home.'

'I don't know,' she said. There was a lot of background noise, a kind of humming.

'Where are you?'

'In the car.'

'Hi, Dad!' It was Grace, shouting so she could be heard from the passenger seat.

'Hi, Grace!' I said.

'Dad says hi,' Cynthia said.

'When are you coming back?' I asked.

'I said I don't know,' Cynthia said. 'I just need some time. I told you in my letter.' She didn't want to go over it again, not in front of Grace.

'I'm worried about you, and I miss you,' I said.

'Tell her hi,' Vince shouted from the living room.

'Who's that?' Cynthia asked.

'Vince Fleming,' I said.

'What?'

'Don't run off the road,' I said.

'What's he doing there?'

'I went to see him. I had this crazy idea maybe you'd have gone to visit him.'

'Oh my God,' Cynthia said. 'Tell him ... I said hi.'

'She says hi,' I told Vince. He just grunted from the other room, rooting about in the shoeboxes.

'But he's at the house? Now?'

'Yeah. He was giving me a lift back to my car. It's kind of a long story. I'll tell you about it when you get back. Plus ...' I hesitated. 'He told me a couple of other things, about that night, that he hadn't told anyone about before.'

'Like what?'

'Like he followed you and your dad back home that night, sat out front for a while, waiting for a chance to knock on your door and see how you were doing, and he saw Todd and your mom leave, then later, your dad left. In a hurry. And there was another car out front for a while that left after your mom and Todd did.'

There was nothing but road noise coming through the phone.

'Cynthia?'

'I'm here. I don't know what it means.'

'Me neither.'

'Terry, there's traffic, I have to get off the road. I'm turning off the phone. I forgot to bring a charger and there's not much battery left.'

'Come home soon, Cyn. I love you.'

'Bye,' she said, and ended the call. I replaced the receiver and went into the living room.

Vince Fleming handed me a newspaper clipping, the one of Todd standing with fellow members of a basketball team.

'That looks like Todd in that one,' Vince said. 'I remember him.'

I nodded, not taking the clipping from his hand. I'd seen it a hundred times before. 'Yeah. Did you have classes together or something?'

'Maybe one. Picture's goofy, though.'

'What do you mean?'

'I don't recognize anyone else in it. It's nobody from our school back then.'

I took it from him, although there wasn't much point. I didn't go to school with Todd or Cynthia and wouldn't know any of their classmates. Cynthia had never paid that much attention to this picture, as far as I could tell. I gave it a passing glance.

'And the name is wrong,' Vince said, pointing to the cutline under the picture listing the names of the players from left to right, bottom row, center row, top row.

I shrugged. 'OK. So newspapers get names wrong.' I looked at the cutline, which gave everyone's last name and first initial. Todd was standing two from the left, center row. I scanned the cutline, read the name where his should have been.

The name was J. Sloan.

I stared for a moment at the initial and the word that followed it.

'Vince,' I said. 'Does the name J. Sloan mean anything to you?'

He shook his head. 'No.'

I double-checked that the name was, in fact, referring to the individual in the center row, two from the left.

'Holy fuck,' I said.

Vince looked at me. 'You wanna fill me in?'

'J. Sloan,' I said. 'Jeremy Sloan.'

Vince shook his head. 'I still don't get it.'

'The man in the food court,' I said. 'At the Post Mall. That was the name of this man Cynthia thought was her brother.'

THIRTY-SIX

'What are you talking about?' Vince asked.

'A couple of weeks ago,' I said: 'Cynthia and Grace and I are at the mall, and Cynthia sees this guy, she's convinced he's Todd. Says he looks like what Todd would probably look like all grown up, twenty-five years later.'

'How did you get his name?'

'Cynthia followed him, out to the parking lot. She called out to him, called him Todd, he didn't respond, so she goes right up to him, says she's his sister, that she knows he's her brother.'

'Jesus,' Vince said.

'It was a horrible scene. The guy denied up and down that he was her brother, he acted like she was a crazy person, and she *was* acting like a crazy person. So I took the guy aside, said I was sorry, said maybe if he showed Cynthia his driver's license, if he could prove to her he wasn't who she thought she was, she'd leave him alone.'

'He did that?'

'Yeah. I saw the license. New York State. His name was Jeremy Sloan.'

Vince took the clipping back from me, looked at the name attached to Todd Bigge's face. 'That's pretty fucking curious, isn't it?'

'I can't figure this out,' I said. 'This doesn't make any sense. Why is Todd's picture in an old newspaper clipping with this different name?'

Vince was quiet for a moment. 'This guy,' he said finally. 'The one from the mall. He say anything at all?'

I tried to think. 'He said he thought my wife should get help. But not much other than that.'

'What about the license?' Vince said. 'You remember anything about that?'

'Just that it was New York,' I said.

'It's kind of a fucking big state,' Vince said. 'He might live across the line in Port Chester or White Plains or something, and he might be from fucking Buffalo.'

'I think it was Young something.'

'Young something?'

'I'm not sure. Shit, I only saw the license for a second.'

'There's a Youngstown in Ohio,' Vince said. 'You sure it wasn't an Ohio license?'

'I could tell that much.'

Vince flipped the clipping over. There was text on the back, but the clipping had clearly been saved for the picture. The scissor had gone through the center of a column, cut a headline in half on the back side.

'That's not why he would have saved it,' I said.

'Shut up,' Vince said. He was reading bits and pieces of stories, then looked up. 'You got a computer?'

I nodded.

'Fire it up,' Vince said. He followed me upstairs, stood over me as I pulled up a chair and turned the computer on. 'There's bits of a story here, involving Falkner Park and Niagara County. Throw all that into Google.'

I asked him to spell Falkner, then typed in the words, hit Search. It didn't take long to figure it all out. 'There's a Falkner Park in Youngstown, New York, in Niagara County,' I said.

'Bingo,' Vince said. 'So this is most likely from some paper from that area, because it's just a piss-piddly story about park maintenance.'

I turned around in my chair, looked up at him. 'Why is Todd in a picture in a paper from Youngstown, New York, with a bunch of basketball players from some other school, and he's listed as J. Sloan?'

Vince leaned up against the door frame. 'Maybe it's not a mistake.'

'What do you mean?'

'Maybe it's not a picture of Todd Bigge. Maybe it's a picture of J. Sloan.'

I gave that a second to sink in. 'What are you saying? That there are two people? One named Todd Bigge and one named J. Sloan – Jeremy Sloan – or is there one person with two names?'

'Hey,' said Vince. 'I'm just here because Jane asked me.'

I turned back to the computer, went to the White Pages website where you could look up phone numbers, entered in Jeremy Sloan for Youngstown, New York.

The search came up empty, but suggested I try alternatives, like J. Sloan, or the last name only. I tried the latter, and up came a handful of Sloans in the Youngstown area.

'Jesus,' I said, and pointed to the screen for Vince. 'There's a Clayton Sloan listed here on Niagara View Drive.'

'Clayton?'

'Yeah, Clayton.'

'That was Cynthia's father's first name,' Vince said, just wanting to be sure.

'Yeah,' I said. I grabbed a pencil and paper from the

desk, wrote down the phone number off the computer screen. 'I'm going to give this number a call.'

'Whoa!' Vince said. 'You out of your fucking mind?'

'What?'

'Look, I don't know what you've found here, or whether you've found anything, but what are you going to say when you call? On this phone? If they've got caller ID, they know right away who it is. Now, maybe they know who you are and maybe they don't, but you don't want to be tipping your hand, do you?'

What the hell was he up to? Was this actually good advice, or did Vince have some reason for not wanting me to call? Was he trying to keep me from connecting the dots?

He handed me his cell phone. 'Use this,' he said. 'They won't know who the hell is calling.'

I took the phone, flipped it open, looked at the phone number on the monitor, took a breath, and entered it into Vince's phone. I put it to my ear and waited.

One ring. Two rings. Three rings. Four rings.

'There's nobody there,' I said.

'Give it a little longer,' Vince said.

When it got to be eight rings, I started to pull the phone away when I heard a voice.

'Hello?' It was a woman's voice. Older, I thought, sixties at least.

'Oh, yes, hello,' I said. 'I was just about to hang up.'

'Can I help you?'

'Is Jeremy there?' Even as I said it, I thought, and what if he is? What am I going to say? What on earth am I going to ask him? Or should I just hang up? Find out if he's there, confirm that he actually exists, then end the call?

'I'm afraid not,' the woman said. 'Who's calling?'

'Oh, that's OK,' I said. 'I can try again in a little while.'

'He won't be here later, either.'

'Oh. Do you know when I might be able to reach him?'

'He's out of town,' the woman said. 'I can't say for sure when he'll be back.'

'Oh, of course,' I said. 'He mentioned something to me about going to Connecticut.'

'He did?'

'I think so.'

'Are you sure about this?' She sounded quite perturbed.

'I could be wrong. Listen, I'll just catch him later, it's no big deal. Just a golf thing.'

'Golf? Jeremy doesn't play golf. Who is this? I demand that you tell me.'

The call was already spiraling out of control. Vince, who had been leaning into me as I made the call and could hear both sides, drew a finger across his throat, mouthed the word 'abort'. I folded the phone shut, ending the call, without saying another thing. I handed it back to Vince, who slipped it into his jacket.

'Sounds like you got the right place,' he said. 'You might have played it a bit better, though.'

I ignored his critique. 'So the Jeremy Sloan Cynthia found at the mall is very likely the Jeremy Sloan who lives in Youngstown, New York, at a house where the phone is listed under the name Clayton Sloan. And Cynthia's father had kept a clipping in his drawer, of him with a basketball team.'

Neither of us said anything. We were both trying to get our heads around it.

'I'm going to call Cynthia,' I said. 'Bounce this off her.'

I raced back downstairs to the kitchen, dialed Cynthia's cell. But as she'd promised, her phone was off. 'Shit,' I said as Vince came into the kitchen behind me. 'You got any ideas?' I asked him.

'Well, this Sloan guy, according to that woman – maybe she's his mother, I don't know – is still out of town. Which means he may still be in the Milford area. And unless he has friends or family here, he's probably in some local motel or hotel.' He got the phone back out of his jacket, brought up a number from his recall list, hit one button. He waited a moment, then said, 'Hey, it's me. Yeah, he's still with me. Something I need you to do.'

And then Vince told whoever was on the other end of the line to gather up a couple of the other guys – I suspected this crew consisted of the two guys who had grabbed me and their driver, the ones Jane called the three stooges – and start doing the rounds of the hotels in town.

'No, I *don't* know how many there are,' he said. 'Why don't you count them for me? I want you to find out if there's a guy named Jeremy Sloan, from Youngstown, New York, staying at one of them. And if you find out he is, you let me know. Don't do anything. OK. Maybe start with the Howard Johnson's, the Red Roof, the Super 8, whatever. And Jesus, what the fuck is that horrible noise in the background? Huh? Who listens to the fucking Carpenters?'

Once the instructions were relayed and Vince was

confident that they were fully understood, he put the phone back in his coat. 'If this Sloan guy is in town, they'll find him,' he said.

I opened the fridge, showed Vince a can of Coors. 'Sure,' he said and I tossed it to him, got one out for myself, and took a seat at the kitchen table. Vince sat down opposite me.

He said, 'Do you have any fucking idea what's going on?'

I swallowed some beer. 'I think I might be starting to,' I said. 'That woman who answered the phone. What if she's this Jeremy Sloan's mother? And what if this Jeremy Sloan really is my wife's brother?'

'Yeah?'

'What if I just spoke to my wife's mother?'

If Cynthia's brother and mother were alive, then how did one explain the DNA tests on the two bodies they'd found in that car they'd fished out of the quarry? Except, of course, all Wedmore had been able to confirm for us up to now was that the bodies in the car were related to one another, not that they actually *were* Todd and Patricia Bigge. We were awaiting further tests to determine a genetic link between them and Cynthia's DNA.

I was trying to get my head around this increasingly confusing jumble of information when I realized Vince was talking.

'I just hope those boys of mine don't find him and kill him,' he said, taking another swig. 'It'd be just like them.'

THIRTY-SEVEN

'Someone phoned here for you,' she said.

'Who?'

'He didn't say who it was.'

'Who did it sound like?' he asked. 'Was it one of my friends?'

'I don't know who it sounded like. How would I know that? But he asked for you, and when I said you were away, he said he remembered you saying something about going to Connecticut.'

'What?'

'You shouldn't have told anyone where you were going!'

'I didn't!'

'Then how did he know? You must have told someone. I can't believe you could be that stupid.' She sounded very annoyed with him.

'I'm telling you I didn't!' He felt about six years old when she spoke to him this way.

'Well, if you didn't, how would he know?'

'I don't know. Did it say on the phone where the call was from? Was there a number?'

'No. He said he knew you from golfing.'

'Golfing? I don't golf.'

'That's what I told him,' she said. 'I told him you don't golf.'

'You know what, Mom? It was probably just a wrong number or something.'

'He asked for you. He said Jeremy. Plain as day. Maybe

you just mentioned it to somebody, passing, that you were going.'

'Look, Mom, even if I did, which I didn't, you don't have to make such a big deal about it.'

'It just upset me.'

'Don't be upset. Besides, I'm coming home.'

'You are?' Her whole tone changed.

'Yeah. Today I think. I've done everything I can do here, the only thing left is . . . you know.'

'I don't want to miss that. You don't know how long I've been waiting for this.'

'If I get out of here soon,' he said. 'I guess I'll be home pretty late tonight. It's already after lunch, and sometimes I get kind of tired, so I might stop a while around Utica or something, but I'll still make it in one day.'

'That'll give me time to make you a carrot cake,' she said brightly. 'I'll make it this afternoon.'

'OK.'

'You drive safely. I don't want you falling asleep at the wheel. You've never had the same kind of driving stamina your father had.'

'How is he?'

'I think, if we get things done this week, he'll last at least that long. I'll be glad when this is finally over. You know what it costs to take a taxi down to see him?'

'It won't matter soon, Mom.'

'It's about more than the money, you know,' she said. 'I've been thinking about how it'll be done. We're going to need some rope, you know. Or some of that tape. And I guess it makes sense to do the mother first. The little one'll be no trouble after that. I can help you with her. I'm not completely useless, you know.'

THIRTY-EIGHT

Vince and I finished our beers, then snuck out through the backyard and returned to his truck. He was going to drive me back to get my car, still parked near his body shop.

'So, you know Jane has been having a bit of trouble at school,' he said.

'Yeah,' I said.

'I was thinking, my helping you out and all, maybe you could put in a word for her with the principal,' he said.

'I have already, but I don't mind doing it again,' I said.

'She's a good kid, but she has a bit of a temper at times,' Vince said. 'She doesn't take shit from anyone. Certainly not me. So when she gets in trouble, basically, she's just defending herself.'

'She needs to get a handle on that,' I said. 'You can't solve every problem by beating the shit out of someone.'

He chuckled softly to himself.

'Do you want her to have a life like yours?' I asked. 'No offense intended.'

He slowed for a red light. 'No,' he said. 'But the odds are kind of stacked against her. I'm not the best role model. And her mother, she's bounced Jane around to so many homes, the kid's never had any stability. That's what I've been trying to do for her, you know? Give her something to hold on to for a while. Kids need that. But it takes a long time to build up any kind of trust. She's been burned so many times before.'

'Sure,' I said. 'You could send her to a good school. When she finishes high school, maybe send her to some place for journalism, or an English program, something where she could develop her talents.'

'Her marks aren't too good,' he said. 'Be hard for her to get in somewhere.'

'But you could afford to send her some place, right?'

Vince nodded.

'Maybe help her set some goals. Help her look past where she is now, tell her if she can get some half-decent marks, you're prepared to cover some tuition costs, so she can reach her potential.'

'You help me with that?' He glanced at me from the corner of his eye.

'Yeah,' I said. 'The thing is, will she listen?'

Vince shook his head tiredly. 'Yeah, well, that's the question.'

'I have one,' I said.

'Shoot.'

'Why do you care?'

'Huh?'

'Why do you care? She's just some kid, daughter of a woman you've met. A lot of guys, they wouldn't take an interest.'

'Oh, I get it, you think maybe I'm some sort of perv? I want to get in to her pants, right?'

'I didn't say that.'

'But you're thinking it.'

'No,' I said. 'I think, if that's what you were up to, there'd be some clue in Jane's writing, in how she behaves toward you. I think she wants to trust you. So the question still is, why do you care?'

The light turned green, Vince tromped on the gas. 'I had a daughter,' he said. 'Of my own.'

'Oh,' I said.

'I was pretty young at the time. Twenty. Knocked up this girl from Torrington. Agnes. No shit, Agnes. My dad, he just about beat the shit out of me, asking how I could be so fucking dumb. Hadn't I ever heard of a rubber? he wanted to know. Yeah, well, you know how it is sometimes, right? Tried to talk Agnes into, you know, getting rid of it, but she didn't want to do that, she had the kid, and it was a girl, and she named her Collette.'

'Pretty name,' I said.

'And when I saw this kid, I just fucking loved her, you know? And my old man, he doesn't want to see me stuck with this Agnes just because I couldn't keep it in my pants, but the thing was, she wasn't that bad, this Agnes, and the baby, Collette, she really was the most beautiful thing I'd ever seen. You'd think, twenty years old, it'd be easy to fuck off, not be responsible, but there was something about her.

'So I started thinking maybe I'd marry her, right? And be this kid's father. And I was working up my nerve, to ask her, to tell my old man what I was planning to do, and Agnes, she's pushing Collette in this stroller and they're crossing Naugatuck Ave. and this fucking drunk in a Caddy runs the light and takes them both out.'

Vince's grip on the steering wheel seemed to grow tighter, as if he was trying to strangle it.

'I'm sorry,' I said.

'Yeah, well, so was that fucking drunk,' Vince said.

'Waited six months, didn't want to do anything too soon, you know? This was after they threw out the charges, lawyer was able to make the jury think Agnes walked out against the light, that even if he'd been sober, he'd still have hit them. So, funny thing happens, a few months later, one night, he's coming out of a bar in Bridgeport, it's pretty late, he's drunk again, the bastard hadn't learned a thing. He was going down this alley, and someone shoots him right in the fucking head.'

'Wow,' I said. 'I guess you didn't shed a tear over that when you heard.'

Vince shot me a quick glance.

'The last thing he heard before he died was, "This is for Collette." And the son of a bitch, you know what he said just before the bullet went into his brain?'

I swallowed. 'No.'

'He said, "Collette who?" His wallet got stolen, cops figured it was some kind of robbery.' He glanced over at me again. 'You should close your mouth, a bug'll fly in,' he said.

I closed it.

'There ya go,' Vince said. 'So anyway, to answer your question, maybe that's why I fucking care. Is there anything else you'd like to know?' I shook my head. He looked ahead. 'That your car?'

I nodded.

As he pulled up behind it, his cell rang. 'Yeah?' he said. He listened a moment, then said. 'Wait for me.'

He put the phone away, said to me, 'They found him. He's registered at the HoJo's.'

'Shit,' I said, about to open my door. 'I'll follow you.'

'Forget your car,' Vince said, hitting the gas again,

whipping out around my car. He headed up to I-95. It wasn't the most direct route, but probably the fastest, given that the Howard Johnson hotel was the other side of town, at the end of an I-95 off ramp. He barreled up the ramp and was doing eighty-five by the time he was merging with traffic.

Traffic on the interstate was light and we were on the other side of town in just a few minutes. Vince had to lay on the brakes pretty hard coming down the ramp. He was still doing seventy when I saw the traffic light ahead of us.

He hung a right, then took another right into the HoJo parking lot. The SUV I'd ridden in earlier was parked just beyond the doors to the lobby, and when Blondie saw us he ran over to Vince's window. He powered it down.

Blondie gave Vince a room number, said if you drove up the hill and around back, it was one of the ones you could pull right up to. Vince backed up, stopped, threw the gear into Drive, and headed up a long, winding driveway that went behind the complex. The road swung hard left and leveled out behind a row of rooms with doors that opened onto the curb.

'Here it is,' Vince said, pulling the truck into a spot.

'I want to talk to him,' I said. 'Don't do anything crazy to him.'

Vince, already out of the truck, gave me a dismissive wave without looking back at me. He went up to a door, paused a moment, noticed that it was already open, and rapped on it.

'Mr Sloan?' he said.

A few doors down, a cleaning lady who'd just wheeled her cart up to a door, looked in our direction.

'Mr Sloan!' Vince shouted, opening the door wider. 'It's the manager. We have a bit of a problem. We need to talk to you.'

I stood away from the door and the window, so if he looked out he wouldn't see me. It was possible, if he was the man who'd been standing in front of our house that night, that he knew what I looked like.

'He gone,' the maid said, loud enough for us to hear.

'What?' Vince said.

'He just check out, a few minute ago,' she said. 'I'm cleaning it next.'

'He's gone?' I said. 'For good?'

The woman nodded.

Vince opened the door wide, strode into the room. 'You can not go in there,' the maid called down to us. But even I was inclined to ignore her, and followed Vince in.

The bed was unmade, the bathroom a mess of damp towels, but there were no signs that anyone was still staying in the unit. Toiletries gone, no suitcase.

One of Vince's henchmen, Baldy, appeared in the doorway. 'Is he here?'

Vince whirled around, walked up to Baldy and threw him up against the wall. 'How long ago did you guys find out he was here?'

'We called you soon as we knew.'

'Yeah? Then what? You sat in the fucking car and waited for me when you should have been keeping your eyes open? The guy's left.'

'We didn't know what he looked like! What were we supposed to do?'

Vince tossed Baldy aside, walked out of the room and nearly ran into the maid. 'You're not supposed—'

'How long ago?' Vince asked, taking a twenty out of his wallet and handing it to her.

She slipped it into the pocket of her uniform. 'Ten minute?'

'What kind of car did he have?' I asked.

She shrugged. 'I don't know. Just a car. Brown. Dark window.'

'Did he say anything to you, say if he was heading home, anything like that?' I asked.

'He didn't say anything to me.'

'Thanks,' Vince said to her. He tipped his head in the direction of his pickup, and we both got back in.

'Shit,' Vince said. 'Shit.'

'What now?' I said. I had no idea.

Vince sat there a moment. 'You need to pack?' he asked.

'Pack?'

'I think you're going to Youngstown. You can't get there and back in a day.'

I considered what he'd said. 'If he's checked out,' I said. 'It makes sense he's going home.'

'And even if he isn't, looks to me like that might be the only place at the moment where you might find some answers.'

Vince reached across the car in my direction, and I recoiled for a second, thinking he was going to grab me, but he was just opening the glove box.

'Jesus,' he said. 'Fucking relax.' He grabbed a road map, unfolded it. 'OK, let's have a look here.' He scanned the map, looking into the upper left corner, then said, 'Here it is. North of Buffalo, just north of Lewiston. Youngstown. Tiny little place. Should take us eight hours maybe.'

'Us?'

Vince attempted, briefly, to fold the map back into its original form, then shoved it, a jagged edged paper ball, at me. 'That'll be your job. You get that back together, I might even let you do some of the driving. But don't even think of touching the radio. That's fucking off limits.'

THIRTY-NINE

Looking at the map, it appeared our fastest route was to head straight north, into Massachusetts as far north as Lee, head west from there into New York State, then catch the New York Thruway up to Albany and west to Buffalo.

Our route was going to take us through Otis, which would put us within a couple of miles of the quarry where Patricia Bigge's car had been found.

I told Vince. 'You want to see?' I asked.

We'd been averaging over eighty miles per hour. Vince had a radar detector engaged. 'We're making pretty good time,' he said. 'Yeah, why not?'

Even though there were no police cars marking the entrance this time, I was able to find the narrow road in. The Dodge Ram, with its greater clearance, took it a lot better than my basic sedan, and when we crested the final hill, where the woods opened up at the edge of the cliff, I thought, sitting up high in the passenger seat, that we were going to plunge over the side.

But Vince gently braked, put the truck in park, and engaged the emergency brake, which I'd never observed him do before. He got out and walked to the cliff's edge and looked down.

'They found the car right down there,' I said, coming up alongside him and pointing.

Vince nodded, impressed. 'If I was going to dump a car with a couple people inside,' he said. 'I could do a lot worse than a spot like this.'

I was riding with a cobra.

No, not a cobra. A scorpion. I thought of that old American Indian folk tale about the frog and scorpion, the one where the frog agrees to help the scorpion across the river if it promises not to sting him with its poisonous venom. The scorpion agrees, then halfway across, even though it means he too will perish, he plunges his stinger into the frog. The frog, dying, asks, 'Why did you do this?' And the scorpion replies, 'Because I am a scorpion, and it is my nature.'

At what point, I wondered, might Vince sting me?

If he did, I couldn't imagine he'd suffer the same fate as the scorpion. Vince struck me as much more of a survivor.

Once we neared the Mass Pike, and the little bars on my phone started reappearing, I tried Cynthia once again. When there was no answer on her cell, I tried home, but without any real expectation that she would be there.

She was not.

Maybe it was just as well that I couldn't reach her. I'd rather call her when I had real news, and maybe, after we'd reached Youngstown, I'd have some.

I was about to put the phone away when it rang in my hand. I jumped.

'Hello?' I said.

'Terry.' It was Rolly.

'Hi,' I said.

'Heard anything from Cynthia?'

'I spoke to her before I left, but she didn't tell me where she was. But she and Grace sounded OK.'

'Before you left? Where are you?'

'We're just about to get on the Mass Turnpike, at Lee. We're on our way to Buffalo. Actually, a bit north of there.'

'We?'

'It's a long story, Rolly. And it seems to be getting longer and longer.'

'Where are you going?' He sounded genuinely concerned.

'Maybe on a wild goose chase,' I said. 'But there's a chance I may have found Cynthia's family.'

'Are you kidding me?'

'No.'

'But Terry, honestly, they must be dead after all these years.'

'Maybe. I don't know. Maybe someone survived. Maybe Clayton.'

'Clayton?'

'I don't know. All I do know is, we're on our way to an address where the phone's listed under the name Clayton Sloan.'

'Terry, you shouldn't even be attempting this. You don't know what you're getting into.'

'Maybe,' I said, then glanced over at Vince and added, 'but I'm with someone who seems to know how to handle himself in tricky situations.'

Unless, of course, just being with Vince Fleming was the tricky situation.

Once we'd crossed over into New York State and had picked up our toll ticket at the booth, it wasn't long before we were at Albany. We both needed something to eat, and to take a pee, so we pulled off at one of those interstate service centers. I bought us some burgers and

Cokes and brought them back out to the truck so we could eat and drive.

'Don't spill anything,' said Vince, who kept the truck pretty tidy. It didn't look as though he'd ever killed anyone in here, or would want to, and I chose to take that as a good sign.

The New York Thruway took us through the southern edge of the Adirondacks once we got a bit west of Albany, and if my mind had not already been occupied with my current situation, I might have appreciated the scenery. Once we were past Utica the highway flattened out, along with the countryside around it. The odd time I'd done this drive, once heading up to Toronto years ago for an educational conference, this had always been the part that seemed to drag on for ever.

We made another pit stop outside Syracuse, didn't lose much more than ten minutes.

There wasn't a lot of conversation. We listened to the radio – Vince picked the stations, of course. Country, mostly. I looked through his CDs in a compartment between the front seats. 'No Carpenters?' I said.

Traffic got bad as we neared Buffalo. It was also starting to get dark. I had to refer to the map more here, advise Vince how to bypass the city. As it turned out, I didn't do any of the driving. Vince was a much more aggressive driver than I, and I was willing to suppress my fear if it meant that we'd get to Youngstown that much quicker.

We got past Buffalo, proceeded on to Niagara Falls, stayed on the highway without taking the time to visit one of the wonders of the world, up the Robert Moses Parkway past Lewiston, where I noticed a hospital, its big blue 'H' illuminated in the night sky, not far from the highway. Not far north of Lewiston, we took the exit for Youngstown.

I hadn't thought, before we left my house, to write down the exact address off the computer under the listing for Clayton Sloan, nor had I printed off a map. I hadn't known, at the time, that we were going to be making this trip. But Youngstown was a village, not a big city like Buffalo, and we figured it wouldn't take that long for us to get our bearings. We came in off the Robert Moses on Lockport Street then turned south on Main.

I spotted a bar and grill. 'They'll probably have a phone book,' I said.

'I could use a bite,' Vince said.

I was hungry, but I was also feeling pretty anxious. We were so close. 'Something quick,' I said, and Vince found a place to park around the corner. We walked back, went inside, and were awash in the aromas of beer and chicken wings.

While Vince grabbed a chair at the counter and ordered some beer and wings, I found a pay phone, but no phone book. The bartender handed me the one he kept under the counter when I asked.

The listing for Clayton Sloan gave the address as 25 Niagara View Drive. Now I remembered it. Handing the book back, I asked the bartender how to get there.

'South on Main, half a mile.'

'Left or right?'

'Left. You go right, you're in the river, pal.'

Youngstown was on the Niagara River, directly across from the Canadian town of Niagara-on-the-Lake, famous for its live theatre. They held the Shaw Festival there, I remembered, named for George Bernard Shaw.

Maybe some other time.

I ripped the meat off a couple of wings and drank half a beer, but my stomach was full of butterflies. 'I can't take this any longer,' I said to Vince. 'Let's go.' He threw some bills on the counter and we were out the door.

The truck's headlights caught the street signs, and it wasn't any time at all before we spotted Niagara View.

Vince hung a left, trolled slowly down the street while I hunted for numbers. 'Twenty-one, twenty-three,' I said. 'There,' I said. 'Twenty-five.'

Instead of pulling into the drive, Vince drove a hundred yards further down the street before turning off the truck and killing the lights.

There was a car in the driveway at Number 25. A silver Honda Accord, maybe five years old. No brown car.

If Jeremy Sloan was headed home, it looked as though we'd gotten here before him. Unless his car was tucked into the separate, two-car garage.

The house was a sprawling one-storey, white siding, built in the sixties most likely. Well-tended. A porch, two wood recliners. The place didn't scream rich, but it said comfortable.

There was also a ramp. A wheelchair ramp, with a very slight grade, from the walkway to the porch. We walked up it, and stood at the door together.

'How you wanna play this?' Vince said.

'What do you think?'

'Close to the vest,' Vince suggested.

There were still lights on in the house and I thought I could detect the muted sounds of a television somewhere inside, so it didn't look as though I was going to wake anyone up. I raised my index finger to the doorbell, held it a moment.

'Showtime,' Vince said.

I rang the bell.

FORTY

When no one came to answer the door after half a minute or so, I looked at Vince. 'Try it again,' he said. He indicated the ramp. 'Might take a while.'

So I rang the bell again. And then we could hear some muffled movement in the house, and a moment later the door was opening, but not wide, not right away, but haltingly. Once it was open a foot or so, I could see why. It was a woman in a wheelchair, moving back, then leaning forward to open the door a few more inches, then moving back some more, then leaning forward again to open the door wider yet.

'Yes?' she said.

'Mrs Sloan?' I said.

I put her age at late sixties, early seventies. She was thin, but the way she moved her upper body did not suggest frailty. She gripped the wheels of her chair firmly, moved herself deftly around the open door and forward, effectively blocking our way into the house. She had a blanket folded over her lap that came down over her knee, and wore a brown sweater over a flowered blouse. Her silver hair was pinned back aggressively, not a stray hair out of place. Her strong cheekbones had a touch of rouge on them, and her piercing brown eyes were darting back and forth between her two unexpected visitors. Her features suggested that she might possibly have been, at one time, a striking woman, but there exuded from her now, perhaps from the strong set of her jaw, the way her lips pursed out, a sense of irritability, maybe even meanness.

I searched her for any hints of Cynthia, but found none.

'Yes, I'm Mrs Sloan,' she said.

'I'm sorry to disturb you so late,' I said. 'Mrs Clayton Sloan?'

'Yes. I'm Enid Sloan,' she said. 'You're right. It's very late. What do you want?' There was an edge in her voice suggesting whatever it was, we could not count on her to be obliging. She held her head up, thrust her chin forward, not just because we towered over her, but as a show of strength. She was trying to tell us she was a tough old broad, not to be messed with. I was surprised she wasn't more fearful of two men showing up at her door late at night. The fact was, she was still an old lady in a wheelchair, and we were two able-bodied men.

I did a quick visual sweep of the living room. Knock-off colonial furniture, Ethan Allen-lite, lots of space between the pieces to allow for the wheelchair. Faded drapes and sheers, a few vases with fake flowers. The carpet, a thick broadloom that must have cost a bundle when it was installed, looked worn and stained in places, the pile worn down by the wheelchair.

There was a TV on in another room on the first floor, and there was a comforting smell coming to us from further inside the house. I sniffed the air. 'Baking?' I said.

'Carrot cake,' she snapped. 'For my son. He's coming home.'

'Oh,' I said. 'That's who we've come by to see. Jeremy?'

'What do you want with Jeremy?'

Just what *did* we want with Jeremy? At least, what did we want to *say* we wanted with Jeremy?

While I hesitated, trying to come up with something, Vince took the lead, 'Where's Jeremy right now, Mrs Sloan?'

'Who are you?'

'I'm afraid we're the ones asking the questions, ma'am,' he said. He'd adopted an authoritarian tone, but he seemed to be making an effort not to sound menacing. I wondered if he was trying to give Enid Sloan the impression he was some kind of cop.

'Who are you people?'

'Maybe,' I said, 'if we could talk to your husband. Could we speak with Clayton?'

'He's not here,' Enid Sloan said. 'He's in the hospital.'

That took me by surprise. 'Oh,' I said. 'I'm sorry. Would that be the hospital we saw driving up here?'

'If you came up by way of Lewiston,' she said. 'He's been there several weeks. I have to take a taxi to see him. Every day, there and back.' It was important, I guessed, that we knew the sacrifices she'd been making on her husband's behalf.

'Your son can't take you?' Vince asked. 'He's been gone that long?'

'He's had things to do.' She inched her chair forward, as if she could push us off the porch.

'I hope it's nothing serious,' I said. 'With your husband.'

'My husband is dying,' Enid Sloan said. 'Got cancer all through him. It's only a matter of time now.' She hesitated, looked at me. 'You the one who phoned here? Asking for Jeremy?'

'Uh, yes,' I said. 'I've been needing to get in touch with him.'

'You said he told you he was going to Connecticut,' she said accusingly.

'I believe that's what he said,' I told her.

'He never told you that. I asked him. He said he didn't tell anybody where he was going. So how do you know about that?'

'I think we should continue this discussion inside,' Vince said, moving forward.

Enid Sloan held on to her wheels. 'I don't think so.'

'Well, I do,' Vince said, and put both hands on the arms of the chair and forced it back. Enid's grip was no match for Vince's force.

'Hey,' I said to him, reaching out to touch his arm. I hadn't planned for us to get rough with an old lady in a wheelchair.

'Don't worry,' Vince said, trying to make his voice sound reassuring. 'It's just cold out on the porch here, and I don't want Mrs Sloan here to catch her death.'

I didn't care much for his choice of words.

'You stop that,' Enid Sloan said, swatting at Vince's hands and arms.

He pushed her inside, and I didn't see that I had much choice but to follow. I closed the front door behind me.

'I don't see any easy way to pussyfoot around this,' Vince said. 'You might as well just ask your questions.'

'Who the fuck are you?' Enid spat at us.

I was taken aback. 'Mrs Sloan,' I said. 'My name is Terry Archer. My wife's name is Cynthia. Cynthia Bigge.'

She stared at me, her mouth half-open. She was speechless.

'I take it that name means something to you,' I said. 'My wife's, that is. Maybe mine too, but my wife's name, that seems to have made an impression.'

She still said nothing.

'I have a question for you,' I said. 'And it might sound a bit crazy, but I'll have to ask you to be a bit patient here if my questions sound ridiculous.'

Still silent.

'Anyway, here goes,' I said. 'Are you Cynthia's mother? Are you Patricia Bigge?'

And she laughed scornfully. 'I don't know what you're talking about,' she said.

'Then why the laugh?' I said. 'You seem to know these names I'm mentioning.'

'Leave my house. Nothing you're saying makes any sense to me.'

I glanced at Vince, who was stone-faced. I said to him, 'Did you ever see Cyn's mother? Other than that one time, going out to the car that night?'

He shook his head. 'No.'

'Could this be her?' I asked.

He narrowed his eyes, focused on her. 'I don't know. Unlikely, I think.'

'I'm calling the police,' Enid said, turning her chair. Vince came around behind it, went to grab for the handles, until I waved for him to stop.

'No,' I said. 'Maybe that would be a good idea. We could all wait here for Jeremy to return home, and ask him some questions with the police here.'

That stopped her wheeling the chair, but she said, 'Why should I be afraid to have the police come?'

'That's a good question. Why should you be? Could it have something to do with what happened twenty-five years ago? Or maybe with more recent events, in Connecticut? While Jeremy's been away? The death of Tess Berman, my wife's aunt? And a private detective named Denton Abagnall?'

'Get out,' she said.

'And about Jeremy,' I said. 'He's Cynthia's brother, isn't he?'

She glared at me, her eyes filled with hate. 'Don't you dare say that,' she said, her hands resting on the blanket.

'Why?' I asked. 'Because it's true? Because Jeremy's actually Todd?'

'What?' she said. 'Who told you that? That's a filthy lie!'

I looked over her shoulder at Vince, whose hands were on the rubber grips of the wheelchair.

'I want to make a phone call,' she said. 'I demand that you let me use the phone.'

'Who do you want to call?' Vince asked.

'That's none of your business.'

He looked at me. 'She's going to call Jeremy,' he said calmly. 'She wants to warn him. That's not such a good idea.'

'What about Clayton?' I asked her. 'Is Clayton Sloan actually Clayton Bigge? Are they one and the same person?'

'Let me use the phone,' she repeated, almost hissing like a snake.

Vince held on to the chair. I said to him, 'You can't just hold her like that,' I said. 'It's like, kidnapping, or confinement, or something.'

'That's right!' Enid Sloan said. 'You can't do this,

you can't barge into an old lady's house and hold her like this!'

Vince let go of the chair. 'Then use the phone, to call the police,' he said, repeating my bluff. 'Forget about calling your son. Call the cops.'

The chair did not move.

'I need to go to the hospital,' I said to Vince. 'I want to see Clayton Sloan.'

'He's very sick,' Enid said. 'He can't be disturbed.'

'Maybe I can disturb him long enough to ask him a couple of questions.'

'You can't go! Visiting hours are over! And besides, he's in a coma! He won't even know you're there!'

If he were in a coma, I figured, she wouldn't care whether I went to see him. 'Let's go to the hospital,' I said.

Vince said, 'If we leave, she's going to call Jeremy. Warn him that we're here. I could tie her up.'

'Jesus, Vince,' I said. I couldn't condone tying up an elderly disabled woman, no matter how unpleasant she seemed. Even if it meant never finding the answers to all my questions. 'What if you just stayed here?'

He nodded. 'That works. Enid and I can chat, gossip about the neighbors, that kind of thing.' He leaned over so she could see his face. 'Won't that be fun? Maybe we can even have some of that carrot cake. It smells delicious.' Then he reached into his jacket, took out the keys to the truck and tossed them my way.

I grabbed them out of the air. 'What room is he in?' I asked her.

She glared at me.

'Tell me what room he's in, or I'll call the cops myself.'

She gave that a moment's thought, knew that once I got to the hospital I'd probably be able to find out anyway, then said, 'Third floor. Room 309.'

Before I left the house Vince and I exchanged cell phone numbers. I got in his truck, fiddled with getting the key into the ignition. A different vehicle always takes a minute or two to get used to. I turned on the engine, found the lights, then backed into a driveway and turned around. I needed a moment to get my bearings. I knew Lewiston was south of here, and that we'd gone south from the bar, but I didn't know whether continuing in a southerly direction would get me where I had to go. So I backtracked up Main, cut east and once I'd found my way back to the highway, headed south.

I took the first exit once I saw the blue H in the distance, found my way to the hospital parking lot, and entered by way of the emergency department. There were half a dozen people in the waiting room; a set of parents with a crying baby, a teenage boy with blood soaking through the knee of his jeans, an elderly couple. I walked right through, past the admissions desk, where I saw a sign indicating that visiting hours had ended a couple of hours ago, at eight, and found an elevator to the third floor.

Chances were good that someone was going to stop me at some point, but I figured if I could just make it to Clayton Sloan's room, I'd be OK.

The elevator doors parted onto the third floor nurses' station. There was no one there. I stepped out, paused a moment, then turned left, looking for door numbers. I found 322, discovered the numbers got bigger as I moved on down the hallway. I stopped, went back in the other direction, which was going to take me past the nurses' station again. A woman was standing with her back to me, reading a chart, and I walked past as noiselessly as possible.

I looked for numbers again. The hallway turned left, and the first door I came to was 309. The door was partly ajar, the room mostly in darkness except for a neon light mounted to the wall next to the bed.

It was a private room, one bed. A curtain obscured all but the foot of the bed, where a clipboard hung on a metal frame. I took a few steps in, beyond the curtain, and saw that there was a man in the bed, on his back, slightly raised, fast asleep. In his seventies, I guessed. Emaciated-looking, thinned hair. From chemo, maybe. His breathing was raspy. His arms lay at his sides, his fingers long and white and bony.

I moved around to the far side of the bed, where the curtain gave me cover from the hallway. There was a chair near the head of the bed, and when I sat down, I was able to make myself even more invisible to anyone passing by the room.

I studied Clayton Sloan's face, searching for something there that I'd been unable to find in Enid Sloan's. Something about his nose, perhaps, a trace of cleft in his chin. I reached out and gently touched the man's exposed arm, and he made a slight snorting noise.

'Clayton,' I whispered.

He sniffed, wiggled his nose about unconsciously.

'Clayton,' I whispered again, rubbing his leathery skin softly back and forth. Inside his elbow a tube ran into his arm. An IV drip of some kind.

His eyes fluttered open and he sniffed again. He saw me, blinked hard a couple of times, let his eyes adjust and focus.

'Wha—'

'Clayton Bigge?' I said.

That not only brought his eyes into focus, but made him turn his head more sharply. The fleshy folds of his neck bunched together. 'Who are you?' he whispered.

'Your son-in-law,' I said.

FORTY-ONE

As he swallowed, I watched his Adam's apple bob along the length of his throat. 'My what?' he said.

'Your son-in-law,' I said. 'I'm Cynthia's husband.'

He opened his mouth to speak, and I could see how dry his mouth was.

'Would you like a drink of water?' I asked quietly. He nodded. There was a pitcher and glass next to the bed, and I poured him some water. There was a straw on the table, and I put it to his lips, holding the glass for him.

'I can do it,' he said, grasping the glass and sipping from the straw. He took the glass with more strength than I expected. He licked his lips, handed the glass back to me.

'What time is it?' he asked.

'After ten,' I said. 'I'm sorry to wake you. You were sleeping pretty good there.'

'No harm,' he said. 'They're always waking you up here anyway, all times of the day and night.'

He took a deep breath through his nostrils, let the air out slowly. 'So,' he said. 'Am I supposed to know what you're talking about?'

'I think you do,' I said. 'You're Clayton Bigge.'

Another deep breath. Then, 'I'm Clayton Sloan.'

'I believe you are,' I said. 'But I think you're also Clayton Bigge, who was married to Patricia Bigge, who had a son named Todd and a daughter named Cynthia, and you lived in Milford, Connecticut, until one night in 1983, when something very terrible happened.'

He looked away from me and stared at the curtain. He made a fist with the hand laying nearest me, opened his fingers, clenched again.

'I'm dying,' he said. 'I don't know how you found me, but let me die in peace.'

'Then maybe it's time to get a few things off your chest,' I said.

Clayton turned his head on the pillow to look at me again. 'Tell me your name.'

'Terry. Terry Archer.' I hesitated. 'What's your name?'

He swallowed again. 'Clayton,' he said. 'I've always been Clayton.' His eyes moved down. He stared at the folds in the hospital linen. 'Clayton Sloan, Clayton Bigge.' He paused. 'Depended where I was at the time.'

'Two families?' I said.

I was able to make out a nod. The things Cynthia told me about her father. On the road all the time. Back and forth across the country. Home for a few days, gone for a few, back for a few. Living half his life some place else.

Suddenly, he brightened as a thought occurred to him. 'Cynthia,' he said to me. 'Is she here? Is she with you?'

'No,' I said. 'I don't . . . I don't know exactly where she is right now. She may be back home now, in Milford, for all I know. With our daughter. Grace.'

'Grace,' he said. 'My granddaughter.'

'Yes,' I whispered as a shadow went by in the hall. 'Your granddaughter.'

Clayton closed his eyes for a moment, as though in pain. But I didn't think it was anything physical.

'My son,' he said. 'Where is my son?'

'Todd?' I said.

'No no,' he said. 'Not Todd. Jeremy.'

'I think he may be on the way back from Milford.'

'What?'

'He's on his way back. At least, that's what I think.'

Clayton looked more alert, his eyes wide. 'What was he doing in Milford? When did he go there? Is that why he hasn't been here with this mother?' Then his eyes drifted shut and he started muttering, 'No no no.'

'What?' I said. 'What's wrong?'

He raised a tired hand and tried to wave me off. 'Leave me,' he said, his eyes still closed.

'I don't understand,' I said. 'Aren't Jeremy and Todd the same person?'

His eyelids rose slowly, like a curtain rising on a stage. 'This can't happen ... I'm so tired.'

I leaned in closer. I hated pushing an old, sick man as much as I hated Vince keeping an old, disabled woman prisoner, but there were things I had to know.

'Tell me,' I said. 'Are Jeremy and Todd the same person?'

Slowly his head turned on the pillow and he looked at me. 'No.' He paused. 'Todd is dead.'

'When? When did Todd die?'

'That night,' Clayton said resignedly. 'With his mother.'

So it was them. In the car at the bottom of the quarry. When the results of the tests comparing Cynthia's DNA to the samples taken from the bodies in the car came in, we'd be getting a connection.

Clayton raised his hand weakly, pointed back to the small table. 'More water?' I said. He nodded. I handed him the glass and he took a long drink.

'I'm not quite as weak as I look,' he said, holding the glass as though it were a major accomplishment. 'Sometimes, when Enid comes in, I make like I'm in a coma, so I won't have to talk to her, she won't complain so long. I still walk a little. I can get to the can. Sometimes I even get there in time.' He pointed to the closed door on the other side of the room.

'Patricia and Todd,' I said. 'So they're both dead.'

Clayton's eyes closed again. 'You have to tell me what Jeremy is doing in Milford.'

'I'm not sure,' I said. 'But I think he's been watching us. Watching our family. I think he's been in our house. I can't say for sure, but I think he may have killed Cynthia's aunt, Tess.'

'Oh my God,' Clayton said. 'Patricia's sister? She's dead?'

'She was stabbed to death,' I said. 'And a man we'd hired to try to find out some things, he's dead, too.'

'This can't he happening. She said he'd gotten a job. Out west.'

'What?'

'Enid. She said Jeremy got a job, in ... in Seattle or some place. An opportunity. Had to go out there. That he'd come back and see me soon. That was why he wasn't coming to visit. I thought ... just not caring, that would be reason enough.' He seemed to drift off a bit. 'Jeremy, he's ... he can't help what he is. She made him what he is. He does whatever she tells him to do. She poisoned him against me from the day he was born. Can't believe she even comes to visit. She says to me, hang on, just hang on a little longer. It's like, she doesn't care if I die. She just doesn't want me to die yet. She's been up to something, I've known it. She's been lying to me. Lying to me about everything, lying to me about Jeremy. She didn't want me to know where he'd gone.'

'Why wouldn't she want you to know? Why would Jeremy have gone to Milford?'

'She must have seen it,' he whispered. 'Found it, something.'

'What? Seen what?'

'Dear God,' he said faintly, and rested his head back on the pillow, closed his eyes. He moved his head from side to side. 'Enid knows. Dear God, if Enid knows ...'

'If Enid knows what? What are you talking about?'

'If she knows, there's no telling what she might do.'

I leaned in closer to Clayton Sloan or Clayton Bigge and whispered urgently inches away from his ear, 'If Enid knows what?'

'I'm dying. She ... she must have called the lawyer. I never intended for her to see the will before I died ... My instructions were very specific. He must have screwed up ... I'd had it all set up ...'

'Will? What will?'

'My will. I had it changed. She wasn't to know ... If she knew ... It was all arranged. When I died, my estate, everything would go to Cynthia ... Enid and Jeremy, they'd be left out, left with nothing, just what they deserve, just what she deserves ...' He looked at me. 'You have no idea what she's capable of.'

'She's here. Enid is here, she's in Youngstown. It was Jeremy who went to Milford.'

'She must have sent him. She's in a wheelchair. She won't be able to do it herself this time ...'

'Do what herself?'

He ignored my question. He had so many of his own. 'So, he's coming back? Jeremy's on his way back?'

'That's what Enid said. He checked out of a Milford motel this morning. I think we beat him back here.'

'We? I thought you said Cynthia wasn't with you.'

'She's not. I came with a man named Vince Fleming.'

Clayton thought about the name. 'Vince Fleming,' he said quietly. 'The boy. The boy she was with that night. In the car. The boy she was with when I found her.'

'That's right. He's been helping me. He's with Enid now.'

'With Enid?'

'Making sure she doesn't call Jeremy and tell him that we're here.'

'But if Jeremy, if Jeremy's already on his way back, he must have already done it.'

'Done what?'

'Is Cynthia OK?' He got a desperate look in his eyes. 'Is she alive?'

'Of course she's alive.'

'And your daughter? Grace? She's still alive?'

'What are you talking about? Yes, of course they're alive.'

'Because if something happens to Cynthia, everything goes to any children ... It's all spelled out ...'

I felt my whole body shiver. How many hours had it been since I'd talked to Cynthia? I'd had a brief chat with her this morning, my one conversation with her since she'd slipped away in the night with Grace.

Did I really know, with any certainty, that she and Grace were alive now?

I got out my cell phone. It occurred to me then that I probably wasn't supposed to have it on within the hospital, but since no one even knew I was here, I figured I could get away with it.

I punched in our home number.

'Please, please have gone home,' I said under my breath. The phone rang once, twice, a third time. On the fourth ring, it went to voice mail.

'Cynthia,' I said. 'If you come home, if you get this, you've got to call me immediately. It's an emergency.'

I ended the call and then tried her cell. It went to voice mail immediately. I left her pretty much the same message, but added. 'You *must* call me.'

'Where is she?' Clayton asked.

'I don't know,' I said uneasily. I considered, briefly, calling Rona Wedmore, decided against it, called another number. I had to let it ring five times before there was an answer.

A pickup, then throat clearing, then a sleepy 'Hello?'

'Rolly,' I said. 'It's Terry.'

Clayton, hearing the name 'Rolly', blinked.

'Yeah, yeah, OK,' Rolly said. 'No problem. I'd just turned out the light. You've found Cynthia?'

'No,' I said. 'But I've found someone else.'

'What?'

'Listen, I don't have time to explain, but I need you to find Cynthia. I don't know what to tell you, or where to have you start. Go by the house, see if her car's there. If it is, bang on the door, break in if you have to, see if she and Grace are there. Start calling hotels, I don't know, anything you can think of.'

'Terry, what's going on? Who have you found?'

'Rolly, I've found her father.'

There was dead silence on the other end of the line.

'Rolly?'

'Yeah, I'm here. I . . . I can't believe it.'

'Me neither.'

'What's he told you? Has he told you what happened?'

'We're just getting started. I'm north of Buffalo, at a hospital. He's not in very good shape.'

'Is he talking?'

'Yeah. I'll tell you all about it when I can. But you have to look for Cynthia. If you find her, she has to call me immediately.'

'Right. I'm on it. I'm getting dressed.'

'And Rolly,' I said. 'Let me tell her. About her father. She's going to have a million questions.'

'Sure. If I find out anything, I'll call.'

I thought of one other person who might have seen Cynthia at some point. Pamela had phoned the house often enough that I'd memorized her home number from the caller ID display. I punched in the number, let it ring several times before someone picked up.

'Hello?' Pamela, sounding every bit as sleepy as Rolly. In the background, a man's voice, saying, 'What is it?'

I told Pamela who it was, quickly apologized for calling at such a terrible hour.

'Cynthia's missing,' I said. 'With Grace.'

'Jesus,' Pamela said, her voice quickly sounded awake. 'They been kidnapped or something?'

'No no, nothing like that. She left. She wanted to get away.'

'She told me, like, yesterday, or the day before

yesterday – God, what day is this? – that she might not come in, so when she didn't show up, I didn't think anything of it.'

'I just wanted to tell you to be on the lookout for her, if she calls you, she has to get in touch with me. Pam, I found her father.'

From the other end of the line, nothing for a moment. Then, 'Fuck me.'

'Yeah,' I said.

'He's alive?'

I glanced at the man in the bed. 'Yeah.'

'And Todd? And her mother?'

'That's another story. Listen, Pamela, I have to go. But if you see Cyn, have her call me. But let me tell her the news.'

'Shit,' Pamela said. 'Like I'm gonna be able to keep a lid on that.'

I ended the call, noticed that the phone battery was getting very weak. I'd left home in such a hurry I didn't have anything to recharge it with, not even in the truck.

'Clayton,' I said, refocusing after all the phone chatter. 'Why do you think Cynthia and Grace might be in danger? Why are you thinking something might have happened to them?'

'Because of the will,' Clayton said. 'Because of leaving everything to Cynthia. It's the only way I know to make up for what I did. It doesn't, I know, it doesn't make up for anything, but what else can I do?'

'But what does that have to do with them being alive?' I asked, but I was already starting to figure it out. The pieces were starting to fall into place, ever so gradually.

'If she's dead, if Cynthia's dead, if your daughter's

dead, then the money can't go to them. It'll revert back to Enid, she'll be the surviving spouse, the only logical heir,' he whispered. 'There's no way Enid'll let Cynthia inherit. She'll kill both of them to make sure she gets the money.'

'But that's crazy,' I said. 'A murder – a double murder – that'd draw so much attention, police would reopen the case, they'd start looking into what happened twenty-five years ago, it could end up blowing up in Enid's face, and then—'

I stopped myself.

A murder would attract attention. No doubt about it. But a suicide. There wouldn't be much attention paid to something like that. Especially not when the woman committing suicide had been under so much strain in recent weeks. A woman who had called the police to investigate the appearance of a strange hat in her house. It didn't get much more bizarre than that. A woman who had called the police because she'd received a note telling her where she could find the bodies of her missing mother and brother. A note that had been composed on a typewriter in her own home.

A woman like that who killed herself, well, it wasn't hard to figure out what that was about. It was about guilt. Guilt she must have lived with for a very long time. After all, how else did one explain her being able to direct police to that car in the quarry if she hadn't known, all these years, that it was there? What possible motive would anyone else have for sending along a note like that?

A woman this overwhelmed with guilt, would it be any surprise if she took her daughter's life along with her own?

Could that be what was in the works?

'What?' Clayton asked me. 'What are you thinking?'

What if Jeremy had come to Milford to watch us? What if he'd been spying on us for weeks, following Grace to school? Watching us at the mall? From the street out front of our house? Getting into our home one day when we were careless, then leaving with the spare house key so he could get in whenever he wanted. And on one of those trips – I recalled my discovery during Abagnall's final visit to our house – tossing the key back into the cutlery drawer so we'd think we'd just misplaced it. Leaving that hat. Learning our e-mail address. Writing a note on my typewriter, leading Cynthia to the bodies of her mother and brother ...

All these things could have been accomplished before we had the locks changed, the new deadbolts installed.

I gave my head a slight shake. I felt I was getting ahead of myself. It all seemed so incredible, so diabolical.

Had Jeremy been setting the stage? And was he now returning to Youngstown to pick up his mother, so that he could take her back to Milford to watch the final act?

'I need you to tell me everything,' I whispered to Clayton. 'Everything that happened that night.'

'It was never supposed to happen like this ...' he said, more to himself than me. 'I couldn't go see her. I promised not to, to protect her ... Even after I died, when Enid found out she was getting nothing ... there was a sealed envelope, only to be opened after I was dead and buried. It explained everything. They'd arrest Enid, Cynthia would be safe ...'

'Clayton, I think they're in danger now. Your daughter, and your granddaughter. You need to help me while you still can.'

He studied my face. 'You seem like a nice man. I'm glad she found someone like you.'

'You need to tell me what happened.'

He took a deep breath, as though steeling himself for a coming task. 'I can see her now,' he said. 'Staying away won't protect her now.' He swallowed. 'Take me to her. Take me to my daughter. Let me say goodbye to her. Take me to her, and I'll tell you everything. It's time.'

'I can't take you out of here,' I said. 'You're all hooked up here. If I take you out of here, you'll die.'

'I'm going to die anyway,' Clayton said. 'My clothes, they're in the closet over there. Get them.'

I started for the closet, then stopped. 'Even if I wanted to, they're not going to let you leave the hospital.'

Clayton waved me over closer to him, reached out and grabbed my arm, his grip firm and resolute. 'She's a monster,' he said. 'There's nothing she won't do to get what she wants. For years, I've lived in fear of her, did what she wanted, scared to death of what she might do next. But what do I have to fear any more? What can she do to me? I've so little time left, maybe, with what I have, I can save my Cynthia, and Grace. There are no limits to what Enid might do.'

'She won't be doing anything now,' I said. 'Not with Vince watching her.'

Clayton squinted at me. 'Did you go to the house? Knock on the door?'

I nodded.

'And she answered it?'

I nodded again.

'Did she seem afraid?'

I shrugged. 'Not particularly.'

'Two big men, coming to her door, and she's not afraid. Didn't that seem odd?'

Another shrug. 'Maybe. I suppose.'

Clayton said, 'You didn't look under the blanket, did you?'

FORTY-TWO

I got out my cell again, called Vince's. 'Come on,' I said, feeling awash in anxiety. I couldn't raise Cynthia, and now I was panicking that something had happened to a guy who only yesterday I viewed as a common thug.

'Is he there?' Clayton said, moving his legs over to the edge of the bed.

'No,' I said. After six rings, it went to voice mail. I didn't bother to leave a message. 'I need to get back over there.'

'Give me a minute,' he said, inching his butt closer to the edge.

I went over to the closet, found a pair of pants, a shirt and a light jacket. 'You need help?' I asked, laying the clothes out on the bed next to him.

'I'm OK,' he said. He seemed a bit winded, caught his breath, and said, 'Did you see some socks and underwear in there?'

I took another look in the closet, found nothing, then checked the bottom cabinet of the bedside table. 'In here,' I said, taking out the clothes and handing them over.

He was ready to stand up next to the bed, but if he was going to leave the room he was going to have to disengage himself from the IV. He picked away at the tape, pulled the tube from his arm.

'You sure about this?' I said.

He nodded, gave me a weak smile. 'If there's a chance to see Cynthia, I'll find the strength.'

'What's going on in here?'

We both turned our heads to the door. A nurse was standing there, a slender black woman, mid-forties, a look of wonderment on her face.

'Mr Sloan, what on earth do you think you're doing?'

He had just dropped his pajama bottoms and was standing before her, butt naked. His legs were white and spindly, his genitals shrunken away to almost nothing.

'Getting dressed,' he said. 'What's it look like?'

'Who are you?' she asked, turning on me.

'His son-in-law,' I said.

'I've never seen you here before,' she said. 'Don't you know that visiting hours are over?'

'I just got into town,' I said. 'I needed to see my father-in-law right away.'

'You're going to have to leave right now,' she told me. 'And you get back into bed, Mr Sloan.' She was at the foot of the bed now, saw the disconnected IV. 'For heaven's sake,' she said. 'What have you done?'

'I'm checking out,' Clayton said, pulling on his white boxers. Looking at him, in his condition, the words held a double meaning. He steadied himself against me as he bent down to draw them up over his legs.

'That's exactly what you'll be doing if you don't get hooked up to that again,' the nurse said. 'This is absolutely out of the question. Am I going to have to call your doctor in the middle of the night?'

'Do what you have to do,' he said to her.

'My first call's going to be to security,' she said, turning on her rubber-soled shoes and sprinting from the room.

'I know this is a lot to ask,' I said. 'But you're going to have to hurry. I'm going to see if I can find a wheelchair.'

I went into the hall, spotted a vacant chair up by the nurses' station. I ran up to get it, spotted our nurse on the phone. She finished her call, saw me heading back to Clayton's room pushing the empty chair.

She ran over, grabbed hold of it with one hand and my arm with the other. 'Sir,' she said, lowering her voice so as not to wake the other patients, but maintaining her authority. 'You cannot take that man out of this hospital.'

'He wants to leave,' I said.

'Then he must not be thinking too clearly,' she said. 'And if he can't, then you have to do it for him.'

I shook her hand off. 'This is something he has to do.'

'Says you?'

'Says him.' Now I lowered my voice and became very serious. 'This may be the last chance he ever has to see his daughter. And his granddaughter.'

'If he wants to see them, he can have them visit him right here,' she countered. 'We could even bend the rules some about visiting hours if that's a problem.'

'It's a little more complicated than that.'

'Ready,' said Clayton. He had made it to the door of his room. He'd slipped on his shoes without socks, and had not yet buttoned up his shirt, but his jacket was on, and he appeared to have run his fingers through his hair. He looked like an aged homeless person.

The nurse wasn't giving up. She let go of the chair and went up to Clayton, got right in his face. 'You cannot leave here, Mr Sloan. You need to be discharged by your physician, Dr Vestry, and I can assure you he would not be allowing this to happen. I have a call in to him right now.'

I brought the chair up so Clayton could drop himself into it. I spun him around and headed for the elevator.

The nurse ran back to her station, grabbed the phone, said, 'Security! I said I needed you up here now!'

The elevator doors parted and I wheeled Clayton in, hit the button for the first floor and watched the nurse glare at us until the doors slid shut.

'When the door opens,' I told Clayton calmly. 'I'm going to be pushing you out of here like a bat out of hell.'

He said nothing but wrapped his fingers around the arms of the chair, squeezed. I wished it had a seatbelt.

The doors opened, and there was about fifty feet of hall separating us from the emergency-room doors and the parking lot just beyond them. 'Hold on,' I whispered, and broke into a run.

The chair wasn't built for speed, but I pushed it to the point where the front wheels began to wobble. I feared it would suddenly veer left or right, that Clayton would spill out and end up with a fractured skull before I could get him to Vince's Dodge Ram. So I put some weight down on the handles and tipped the chair back, like it was doing a wheelie.

Clayton hung on.

The elderly couple that had been sitting in the waiting room earlier were shuffling across the hall. I shouted ahead, 'Out of the way!' The woman's head whipped around and she pulled her husband out of my path just in time as we went racing past.

The sensors on the sliding emergency room doors

couldn't react fast enough, and I had to put on the brakes so I wouldn't send Clayton through the glass. I slowed down as fast as I could without pitching him forward and out of the wheelchair, and that was when the someone I assumed had to be a security guard came up behind me and shouted, 'Whoa! Hold it right there, pal!'

I was so pumped up on adrenaline I didn't stop to think about what I was doing. I was working on instinct now. I spun around, using the momentum that seemed to be stored in me from moving so quickly down the hall, forming a fist in the process, and caught my pursuer square in the side of the head.

He wasn't a very big guy, maybe 150 pounds, five-eight, black hair and a moustache, must have figured that the gray uniform and big black belt with the gun attached would get him by. Fortunately, he hadn't yet pulled his weapon, assuming, I guess, that a guy pushing a dying patient in a wheelchair didn't pose much of a threat.

He was wrong.

He dropped to the emergency room floor like someone had cut his strings. Somewhere, a woman screamed, but I didn't take any time to see who it was, or whether anyone else was going to be coming after me. I whirled back around, got my hands on the wheelchair handles and kept pushing Clayton out into the parking lot, right up to the passenger door of the Dodge.

I got out the keys, unlocked it with the remote, opened the door. The truck sat up high, and I had to boost Clayton to get him into the passenger seat. I slammed the door shut, ran around to the other side, and caught the wheelchair with the right front tire as

I backed out of the spot. I heard it scrape against the fender.

'Shit,' I said, thinking about how pristine Vince kept the vehicle.

The truck tires squealed as I tore out of the lot, heading back for the highway. I caught a glimpse of some people from the ER, running outside to watch as I sped off. Clayton, already looking exhausted, said, 'We have to go back to my house.'

'I know,' I said. 'I'm already heading there. I need to know why Vince isn't answering, make sure everything's OK, maybe even stop Jeremy if he shows up, if he hasn't already.'

'And there's something I have to get,' Clayton said. 'Before we go see Cynthia.'

'What?'

He waved a weakened hand at me. 'Later.'

'They're going to call the police,' I said of the people we'd left behind at the hospital. 'I've practically kidnapped a patient and I've decked a security guard. They'll be looking for this truck.'

Clayton didn't say anything.

I pushed the truck past ninety on the way north to Youngstown, glancing constantly in my mirror for flashing red lights. I tried Vince again with my cell, still without success. I was nearing the end of my battery.

When the turnoff to Youngstown came, I was hugely relieved, figuring I was more vulnerable, more noticeable, on the highway. But then, what if the police were waiting for us at the Sloan house? The hospital would be able to tell them where their runaway patient lived, and they'd probably stake the place out. What terminal patient doesn't want to go home and die in his own bed?

I drove the truck down to Main, hung a left, went south a couple of miles and turned down the road to the Sloan house. It looked peaceful enough as we drove up to it, a couple of lights on inside, the Honda Accord still parked out front.

No police cars anywhere to be seen. Yet.

'I'm going to drive the truck around back where it can't be seen from the street,' I said. Clayton nodded. I wheeled the truck onto the back lawn, killed the lights and engine.

'Just go on,' Clayton said. 'See about your friend. I'll try to catch up with you.'

I leapt out, went to a back door. When I found it locked I banged on it. 'Vince!' I shouted. I looked through the windows, didn't see any movement. I ran around the house to the front, looking up and down the street for police cars, and tried the main door.

It was unlocked.

'Vince!' I said, stepping into the front hall. I didn't immediately see Enid Sloan, or her chair, or Vince Fleming.

Not until I got to the kitchen.

Enid wasn't there, and nor was her chair. But Vince lay on the floor, the back of his shirt red with blood.

'Vince,' I said, kneeling down next to him. 'Jesus, Vince.' I thought he was dead, but he let out a soft moan. 'Oh God, man, you're still alive.'

'Terry,' he whispered, his right cheek pressed to the floor. 'She had a … she had a fucking gun under the blanket.' His eyes were flirting with rolling up under his lids. There was blood coming out of his mouth. 'Fucking embarrassing …'

'Don't talk,' I said. 'I'm going to call 911.'

I found the phone, snatched the receiver into my hand and punched in the three numbers.

'A man's been shot,' I said. I barked out the address, told the operator to hurry, ignored all her other questions and hung up.

'He came home,' Vince whispered when I knelt down next to him again. 'Jeremy ... she met him at the door, didn't even let him come in ... said they had to go right then. She phoned him ... after she shot me, said step on it.'

'Jeremy was here?'

'I heard them talking ...' More blood spluttered out of his mouth. 'Going back. She wouldn't even let him come in and take a piss. Didn't want him to see me ... Didn't tell him ...'

What was Enid thinking? What was going on in her head?

At the front door, I could hear Clayton shuffling his way into the house.

'Fuck, it hurts ...' Vince said. 'Fucking little old lady.'

'You're going to be OK,' I said.

'Terry,' he said, so softly I almost couldn't hear. I put my ear closer to his mouth. 'Look in ... on Jane. OK ...?'

'Hang in there, man. Just hang on.'

FORTY-THREE

Clayton said, 'Enid never answers the door without a gun under her blanket. Certainly not when she's home alone.'

He'd managed to make it into the kitchen and was using the counter for support as he looked down at Vince Fleming. He was taking a moment to catch his breath. The walk from the truck, around to the front of the house and inside had worn him out.

Once he had a bit of strength back, he said, 'She can be easy to underestimate. An old woman in a wheel-chair. She'd have waited for her moment. When he had his back to her, when he was close enough that she knew she couldn't miss, she'd have done it.' He shook his head. 'No one ever really stands a chance against Enid.'

I still had my mouth close to Vince's ear. 'I've called for an ambulance. They're coming.' Soon, I hoped, be-cause I had few skills to help someone this badly hurt.

'Yeah,' Vince said, his eyelids fluttering.

'We have to go after Enid and Jeremy. They're going after my wife, and my daughter.'

'Do what you gotta do,' Vince whispered.

To Clayton, I said, 'He said Jeremy came home, that Enid wouldn't even let him in the house, made him turn around and head back right away.'

Clayton nodded slowly. 'She wasn't trying to spare him,' he said.

'What?'

'If she didn't let him see what she'd done, it wasn't to spare him from an ugly scene. It was because she didn't want him to know.'

'Why?'

Clayton took a couple of breaths. 'I need to sit down,' he said. I got up off the floor and eased him into one of the chairs at the kitchen table. 'Look in the cupboard over there,' he said, pointing. 'There may be some Tylenols or something.'

I had to step over Vince's legs and detour around the gradually expanding pool of blood on the kitchen floor to reach the cupboard. I found some extra-strength Tylenols in there, and in the cupboard next to it were glasses. I filled one with water and worked my way back across the kitchen without slipping. I opened the container, took out two tablets and put them into Clayton's open hand.

'Four,' he said.

I was listening for an ambulance siren, wanting to hear it, but also wanting to get out of there before it arrived. I shook out two more tablets for Clayton, handed him the water. He had to take them one at time. Getting the four pills down seemed to take him for ever. When he was done, I said, 'Why? Why wouldn't she want him to know?'

'Because if Jeremy knew, he might get her to call it off. What they're planning to do. With him here, shot, with you heading off to the hospital to see me, you knowing who he really is, he'd realize it's all starting to come apart. If they're off to do what I think they're going to do, there isn't much hope now of getting away with it.'

'But Enid has to know all that too,' I said.

Clayton gave me a half-smile. 'You don't understand Enid. All she can see is that inheritance. She'll be blinded to anything else, any problems that might deter her. She's somewhat single-minded about these sorts of things.'

I glanced up at a wall clock, its face made to look like the cross-section of an apple. It was 1.06 a.m.

'How much of a head start do you think they've got?' Clayton asked me.

'Whatever it is,' I said. 'It's too much.' I glanced over at the counter, saw a roll of Reynolds Wrap, a few brown crumbs scattered about. 'She's packed the carrot cake,' I said. 'Something for the road.'

'OK,' Clayton said, gathering his strength to stand. 'Fucking cancer,' he said. 'It's all through me. Life's just nothing but pain and misery, and then you get to finish it off with a mess like this.'

Once he was on his feet, he said, 'There's one thing I have to take with me, but I don't think I have the energy to go downstairs to get it.'

'Tell me what it is.'

'In the basement, you'll find a workbench. There's a red toolbox sitting on top of it.'

'OK.'

'You open up the toolbox, there's a tray in the top you can lift out. I want what's taped to the bottom of the tray.'

The door to the basement was around the corner from the kitchen. As I reached for the light switch at the top of the stairs I called over to Vince.

'How you holding up?'

'Fuck,' he said quietly.

I descended the wooden steps. It was musty and cool down there, and the place was a mess of storage boxes and Christmas decorations, bits and pieces of disused furniture, a couple of mousetraps tucked into a corner. Along the far wall was the workbench, the top of it littered with half-used tubes of caulking, scraps of sand-paper, tools not put away, and a dented and scratched red toolbox.

A bare bulb hung over the bench and I pulled the string dangling from it so I could see what I was doing. I unlocked the two metal clasps on the toolbox, opened the lid. The tray was filled with rusty screws, broken jigsaw blades, screwdrivers. Turning the tray over would make a hell of a mess, not that anyone would notice. So I raised the tray up just above my head to see what was under it.

It was an envelope. A standard letter-sized envelope, dirtied and stained, held in place by some yellowed strips of Scotch tape. With my other hand I peeled the envelope off. It didn't take much.

'You see it?' Clayton called down wheezily from the top of the stairs.

'Yeah,' I said. I set the freed envelope on the bench, put the tray back into the toolbox and relocked it. I picked up the sealed envelope, turned it over in my hands. There was nothing written on it, but I could feel what seemed to be a single piece of paper folded inside.

'It's OK,' Clayton said. 'If you want to, you can look inside.'

I tore open the envelope at one end, blew into it, reached in with my thumb and forefinger, gently pulled out the piece of paper and opened it.

'It's old,' Clayton said from above. 'Be careful with it.'

I looked at it, read it. I felt as though my last breath was slipping away.

When I got to the top of the stairs, Clayton explained the circumstances surrounding what I'd found in the envelope, and told me what he wanted me to do with it.

'You promise?' he said.

'I promise,' I said, slipping the envelope into my sport coat.

I had one last conversation with Vince. 'The ambulance has to be here any time now,' I said. 'Are you going to make it?'

Vince was a big man, a strong man, and I thought he had a better chance than most. 'Go save your wife and girl,' he said. 'And if you find that bitch in the wheelchair, shove her into traffic.' He paused. 'Gun in the truck. Should have had it on me. Stupid.'

I touched his forehead. 'You're going to make it.'

'Go,' he whispered.

To Clayton, I said. 'That Honda in the driveway. It runs?'

'Sure,' Clayton said. 'That's my car. I haven't driven much since I took sick.'

'I'm not sure we should take Vince's truck,' I said. 'The cops are going to be looking for it. People saw me drive away from the hospital. The cops'll have a description, a license plate.'

He nodded, pointed to a small decorative dish on a buffet near the front door. 'Should be a set of keys there,' he said.

'Give me a second,' I said.

I ran around to the back of the house and opened up the Dodge pickup. There were quite a few storage compartments in the cab. In the doors, between the seats, plus the glove box. I started looking through all of them. In the bottom of the center console unit, under a stack of maps, I found the gun.

I didn't know a lot about guns, and I certainly didn't feel confident tucking one into the waistband of my pants. I already had enough problems to deal with without adding a self-inflicted injury to the list. Using Clayton's key, I unlocked the Honda, got into the driver's seat and put the gun in the glove compartment. I started up the car, drove it right up onto the lawn, getting the car as close to the front door as I could.

Clayton emerged from the house, took tentative steps towards me. I leapt out, ran around the car, got the passenger door open, and helped him get inside. I pulled out the seatbelt, leaned over him and buckled it into place.

'OK,' I said, getting back into the driver's seat. 'Let's go.'

I drove right across the yard and onto the road, turned right onto Main, heading north. 'Just made it,' Clayton said. An ambulance, followed closely by two police cars, lights flashing but sirens silent, sped south. Just past the bar where I'd stopped earlier, I headed east to get us back on the Robert Moses Parkway.

Once on the highway, I was tempted to floor it, but was still worried about getting pulled over. I settled on a comfortable speed, above the limit, but not high enough to attract that much attention.

I waited until we were past Buffalo, heading due east to Albany. I can't say that by then I was relaxed, but once we'd put some distance between ourselves and Youngstown, I felt the likelihood of getting pulled over for what happened at the hospital, or what the police found at the Sloan home, diminishing.

That was when I turned to Clayton, who'd been sitting very quietly, his head resting back on the headrest, and said, 'So let's hear it. All of it.'

'OK,' he said, and cleared his throat in preparation.

FORTY-FOUR

The marriage was predicated on a lie.

The first marriage, Clayton explained. Well, the second one, too. He'd get to that one soon enough. It was a long drive back to Connecticut. Plenty of time to cover everything.

But he talked about his marriage to Enid first. A girl he'd known in high school, in Tonawanda, a Buffalo suburb. Then he went to Canisius College, the one founded by the Jesuits, took business courses with a sprinkling of philosophy and religious studies. Wasn't that far away, of course, he could have lived at home and commuted, but he got a cheap room just off campus, figured even if you didn't go far away for college, you at least had to get out from under your parents' roof.

When he finished, who was waiting for him in the old neighborhood but Enid. They started dating, and he could see that she was a strong-willed girl, used to getting what she wanted from those around her. She used what she had to her advantage. She was attractive, possessed a terrific body, had a strong sexual appetite, at least during their early courtship.

One night, teary eyed, she tells him she's late. 'Oh no,' Clayton Sloan says. He thinks first of his own parents, how ashamed they will be of him. So concerned about appearance, and then something like this, their boy, getting a girl pregnant, his mother would want to move out so she wouldn't have to hear the neighbors talking.

So there wasn't much else to do but get married. And right away.

A couple of months after that, she says she's not feeling well, says she's making an appointment to see her physician, Dr Gibbs was his name. She goes to the doctor alone, comes home, says she lost it. The baby's gone. Lots of tears. One day, Clayton's in the diner, sees Dr Gibbs, goes over to him and says, 'I know I shouldn't be asking you this here, that I should make an appointment, but Enid, losing the baby and all, she'll still be able to have another one, right?'

And Dr Gibbs says, 'Huh?'

So now he has an idea what he's dealing with. A woman who'll say anything, tell any kind of lie, to get what she wants.

He should have left then. But Enid tells him she's so sorry, that she thought she was pregnant, but was afraid to go to the doctor to have it confirmed, and then she turned out to be wrong. Clayton doesn't know whether to believe her, and again, worries about the shame he will bring on himself and his family by leaving Enid, starting divorce proceedings. And for a while there, Enid takes sick, is bedridden. Real, or feigned. He's not sure, but knows he can't leave her when she is like this.

The longer he stays, the harder it seems to be to leave. He learns quickly that what Enid wants, Enid gets. When she doesn't, there's hell to pay. Screaming fits, smashing things. One time, he's sitting in the bathtub, Enid's in there with her electric hair dryer, starts joking around about dropping it into the water. But there's something in her eyes, something that suggests that she could do it, just like that, wouldn't have to think twice.

He puts his business education to use, gets a job in

sales, supplying machine shops and factories. It's going to have him driving all over the country, a corridor running between Chicago and New York that skirts past Buffalo. He's going to be away a lot, his prospective employer warns him. That's the clincher for Clayton. Time away from the harping, the screaming, the odd looks she sometimes gives him that suggest the gears inside her head aren't always meshing the way they're supposed to. He always dreads the drive home after a sales trip, wondering what list of grievances Enid will have prepared for him the moment he walks through the door. How she doesn't have enough nice clothes, or he's not working hard enough, or the back door squeaks when you open it, it's driving her mad. The only thing that makes returning home worthwhile is seeing his Irish setter, Flynn. He always comes running out to greet Clayton's car, like he's been sitting on the porch from the moment he left, waiting for the second he returns.

Then she becomes pregnant. The real deal this time. A baby boy. Jeremy. How she loves that boy. Clayton loves him, too, but soon realizes it's a competition. Enid wants the boy's love exclusively, and when Jeremy is barely walking, begins her campaign to poison the father's relationship to his son. If you want to grow up strong and successful, Enid tells him, he'll need to follow her example, that it's too bad there's no strong male role model under this roof. She tells him his father doesn't do enough for her, and how it's a sad thing that Jeremy has his looks, but that's a handicap he can learn to surmount, with effort and time.

Clayton wants out.

But there's something about Enid, this darkness about

her, that to even hint at the subject of divorce, even some kind of separation, there's no predicting how she'll handle it.

Once, before leaving on one of his extended sales trips, he says he needs to talk to her. About something serious.

'I'm not happy,' he says. 'I don't think this is working out.'

She doesn't cry. She doesn't ask what's wrong. She doesn't ask what she could do to help the marriage, to make him happy.

What she does is, she gets up close to him, looks deep into his eyes. He wants to look away, but can't, as though mesmerized by her evil. Looking into her eyes, it's like looking into the soul of the devil. All she says is, 'You will *never* leave me.' And walks out of the room.

He thinks about that on his trip. We'll see about that, he tells himself. We'll just see.

When he returns, his dog does not run out to greet him. When he opens the garage door to put away the Plymouth, there is Flynn, a rope drawn tightly around his neck, hanging from the rafters.

All Enid says to him is, 'Good thing it was just the dog.'

For all she loves Jeremy, she's willing to let Clayton believe the boy's at risk should he ever decide to leave her.

Clayton Sloan resigns himself to this life of misery and humiliation and emasculation. This is what he's signed on for, and he's going to have to make the best of it. He'll sleepwalk through life if that is what he has to do.

He works hard at not despising the boy. Jeremy's

mother has brainwashed him into thinking his father is unworthy of his affections. He sees his father as useless, just a man who lives in the house with him and his mother. But Clayton knows Jeremy is as much a victim of Enid's as he is.

How can his life have turned out like this, he wonders.

There are numerous occasions when Clayton considers taking his own life.

He's driving across the country in the dead of night. Coming back from Chicago, rounding the bottom of Lake Michigan, doing that short stretch through Indiana. He sees a bridge abutment up ahead, and bears down on the accelerator. Seventy miles an hour, then eighty, ninety. The Plymouth begins to float. Hardly anyone wears seatbelts, and even if they did, he's unbuckled his, thereby assuring that he'll go through the windshield and perish. The car eases over onto the shoulder, spewing gravel and dust behind it, but then, at the last minute, he veers back onto the highway, chickens out.

Another time, a couple of miles west of Battle Creek, he loses his nerve, steers back onto the road, but at that high speed, when the front right tire catches the ridge where shoulder meets pavement, he loses control. The car veers across two lanes, right into the path of a tractor trailer, plows into the central barrier, coming to a stop in high grass.

What usually makes him change his mind is Jeremy. His son. He's afraid to leave him alone with her, for the rest of his life. However long that might be.

He has to make a stop in Milford one time. On the prowl for some new clients, new businesses to supply.

He goes into a drugstore to buy a candy bar and there

is a woman behind the counter. Wearing a little name tag that says 'Patricia'.

She is beautiful. Reddish hair.

She seems so nice. So genuine.

There's something about her eyes. A gentleness. A kindness. After spending the last few years trying so hard not to look into Enid's dark eyes, to now see a pair so beautiful, he feels lightheaded.

He takes a long time to buy that chocolate bar. Makes small talk about the weather, how only a couple of days earlier he'd been in Chicago, how he's on the road so much of the time. And then he says something before he's even aware he's said it. 'Would you like to have some lunch?'

Patricia smiles, says if he wants to come back in thirty minutes, she gets an hour off.

For that half hour, as he wanders the shops of Milford's downtown, he asks himself what the hell he's doing. He's married. He has a wife and a son and a house and a job.

But none of it adds up to a life. That's what he wants. A life.

Patricia tells him over a tuna sandwich in a nearby coffee shop that she doesn't go to lunch with men she's just met, but there's something about him that intrigues her.

'What's that?' he asks.

'I think I know your secret,' she says. 'I get a feeling about people, and I got a feeling about you.'

Good God. Is it that obvious? Can she divine that he's married? Is she a mind reader? Even though when he first met her, he'd been wearing gloves, and now has his wedding ring tucked into his pocket?

'What sort of feeling?' he asks.

'You seem troubled to me. Is that why you're driving back and forth across the country? Are you looking for something?'

'It's just my job,' he says.

And Patricia smiles. 'I wonder. If it's led you here, to Milford, maybe it's for a reason. Maybe you're driving all over the country because you're supposed to find something. I'm not saying it's me. But something.'

But it is her. He's sure of it.

He tells her his name is Clayton Bigge. It's like he has the idea before he actually knows he has the idea. Maybe, at first, he was just thinking about having an affair, and having a fake name, that wasn't a bad plan, even for an affair.

For the next few months, if his sales trips only take him as far south as Torrington, he drives the extra distance south to Milford to see Patricia.

She adores him. She makes him feel important. She makes him feel as though he has some worth.

Driving back on the New York Thruway, he considers the logistics.

The company was rejigging some of the sales routes. He could get the one that ran between Hartford and Buffalo. Drop going to Chicago. That way, at each end of the run ...

And there's the money question.

But Clayton's doing well. He's already been taking extraordinary measures to conceal from Enid how much money he has tucked away. It would never matter how much he made, it would never be enough for her. She'd always belittle him. And she'd always spend it. So he might as well tuck some aside.

It might be enough, he thinks. Just enough, for a second household.

How wonderful it will be, for at least half the time, to be happy.

Patricia says yes when he asks her to marry him. Her mother seems happy enough, but her sister Tess, she never warms to him. It's as though she knows there's something off about him, but she can't put her finger on just what it is. He knows she doesn't trust him, that she never will, and he is especially careful around her. And he knows that Tess has told Patricia how she feels, but Patricia loves him, genuinely loves him, and always defends him.

When he and Patricia go to buy rings, he maneuvers her into picking a wedding band for him identical to the one he has in his pocket. Later, he returns it to the store, gets his money back, and is able to wear the one ring he already has, all the time. He fraudulently fills out applications for a variety of municipal and state licenses, everything from a driver's license to a library card – it's a lot less tricky then than in a post 9/11 world – so he can bamboozle the marriage license office when the time comes.

He must deceive Patricia, but he tries to be good to her. At least when he is home.

She gives him two children. A boy, first. They name him Todd. And then, a couple of years later, a baby girl they christen Cynthia.

It is an astonishing juggling act.

A family in Connecticut. A family in upstate New York. Back and forth between the two.

When he's Clayton Bigge, he can't stop thinking about when he will have to return to being Clayton Sloan. And when he's Clayton Sloan, he can't stop thinking about hitting the road again so he can become Clayton Bigge.

Being Sloan is easier. At least that's his honest-to-God name. He doesn't have to worry so much about identification. His license, his papers, they're legitimate.

But when he's in Milford, when he's Clayton Bigge, husband to Patricia, father of Todd and Cynthia, he's always on his guard. Doing the speed limit. Making sure there's money in the meter. He doesn't want anyone running a check on his license plate. Every time he drives to Connecticut, he pulls off the road some place secluded, takes off the orangey-yellow New York plates, puts a stolen blue Connecticut plate on the back of the car in its place. Puts the New York plates back on when he returns to Youngstown. Has to always be thinking, to watch out where he makes long-distance calls from, to make sure he doesn't buy something as Clayton Sloan and give his Milford address without thinking.

Always uses cash. No paper trail.

Everything about his life is false. His first marriage is built on a lie told by Enid. His second marriage is founded on lies he's told to Patricia. But despite all the falsehoods, all the duplicity, has he managed to find any true happiness, are there any moments when he . . .?

'I have to pee,' Clayton said, stopping his story.

'Huh?' I said.

'I gotta take a leak. Unless you want me to go right here in the car.'

We'd recently passed a sign promising a service center. 'There's something coming up,' I said. 'How you feeling?'

'Not so good,' he said. He coughed a few times. 'I need some water. And I could use some more Tylenols.'

I'd grabbed the Tylenols from the house, but hadn't thought to bring any bottles of water. We'd been making pretty good time on the thruway; it was nearly four in the morning and we were closing in on Albany. The Honda, as it turned out, needed gas, so a pit stop was a good idea all around.

I helped Clayton shuffle into the men's room, waited for him to do his business at the urinal, assisted him back to the car. The short trip drained him. 'You stay here and I'll get some water,' I said.

I bought a six-pack of water, ran it back out to the car, cracked open the plastic cap on one of them and handed it to Clayton. He took a long drink, then took the four Tylenols I'd put into his hand one at a time. Then I drove over to the gas pumps and filled up, using nearly all the cash in my wallet. I was worried about using a credit card, fearful that police had figured out who'd taken Clayton out of the hospital, and that they'd be watching for any transactions by my credit card.

As I got back into the car, I thought that maybe it was time to let Rona Wedmore know what was going on. I felt, the more Clayton talked, the closer I was getting to the truth that would, once and for all, end Wedmore's suspicions about Cynthia. I dug around in the front pocket of my jeans and found the card she'd given me during her surprise visit to the house the previous morning, before I'd gone looking for Vince Fleming.

There was an office and cell number, but not a home phone. Chances were she'd be asleep this time of the night, but I was betting she kept her cell next to the bed, and that it was on all the time.

I started the car, pulled away from the pumps, but pulled over to the side for a minute.

'What are you doing?' Clayton asked.

'I'm just going to make a couple of calls.'

Before I tried Wedmore, however, I wanted to give Cynthia another try. I called her cell, tried home. No luck.

I took some comfort from that, strangely enough. If I didn't know where she was, then there was no way Jeremy Sloan or his mother could, either. Disappearing with Grace turned out to be, at this moment, the smartest thing Cynthia could have done.

But I still needed to know where she was. That she was OK. That Grace was OK.

I thought about calling Rolly, but figured that if he knew anything, he would have called, and I didn't want to use the phone any more than I had to. The battery barely had enough charge left for one call.

I entered Detective Rona Wedmore's cell phone number. She answered on the fourth ring.

'Wedmore,' she said. Trying very hard to sound awake and alert, although it came out more like, 'Wed. More.'

'It's Terry Archer,' I said.

'Mr Archer,' she said, already sounding more focused. 'What is it?'

'I'm going to tell you a few things very quickly. I'm on a dying cell. You need to be on the lookout for my wife. A man named Jeremy Sloan, and his mother, Enid Sloan, are heading to Connecticut, from the Buffalo area. I think they intend to find Cynthia and kill her. Cynthia's father is alive. I'm bringing him back with me. If you find Cynthia and Grace, hold on to them, don't let them out of your sight until I get back.'

I had expected a 'What?' or, at the very least, 'Huh?' But instead, I got, 'Where are you?'

'Along the New York Thruway, coming back from Youngstown. You know Vince Fleming, right? You said you did.'

'Yes.'

'I left him in a house in Youngstown, north of Buffalo. He was trying to help me. He was shot by Enid Sloan.'

'This isn't making any sense,' Wedmore said.

'No shit. Just look for her, OK?'

'What about this Jeremy Sloan and his mother? What are they driving?'

'A brown . . .'

'Impala,' Clayton whispered. 'Chevy Impala.'

'A brown Chevy Impala,' I said. To Clayton, I said, 'Plate?' He shook his head. 'I don't have a plate number.'

'Are you coming back here?' Wedmore asked.

'Yes. In a few hours. Just look for her. I've already got my principal, Rolly Carruthers, looking for her too.'

'Tell me what—'

'Gotta go,' I said, folded the phone shut and slipped it into my jacket. I pulled the automatic transmission back to Drive, and got back on to the thruway.

'So,' I said, taking us back to where Clayton had left off before we got off the highway. 'Were there moments when you were happy?'

Clayton took himself back again.

If there are moments of happiness, they only ever happen when he is Clayton Bigge. He loves being a father to Todd and Cynthia. As best he can tell, they love him in return, maybe even look up to him. They seem to respect him. They aren't being taught, each and every day, that he's worthless. Doesn't mean they always do as they're told, but what kids do?

Sometimes, at night in bed, Patricia will say to him, 'You seem some place else. You get this look, like you're not here. And you look sad.'

And he takes her in his arms and he says to her, 'This is the only place I want to be.' It isn't a lie. He's never said anything more truthful. There are times when he wants to tell her, because he doesn't want his life with her to be a lie. He doesn't like having that other life.

Because that's what life with Enid and Jeremy has become. That's the *other* life. Even though it's the one he started with, even though it's the one where he can use his real name, show his real license to a police officer if he's pulled over, it's the life he can't bear to return to, week after week, month after month, year after year.

But in some strange way, he gets used to it. Used to the stories, used to the juggling, used to coming up with fanciful tales to explain why he has to be away on holidays. If he's in Youngstown on 25 December, he sneaks off to a pay phone, weighed down with change, so he can call Patricia and wish her and the kids a Merry Christmas.

One time, in Youngstown, he finds a private spot in the house, sits down, and lets the tears come. Just a short cry, enough to ease the sadness, take the pressure off. But Enid hears him, slips into the room, sits down next to him on the bed.

He wipes the tears from his cheeks, pulls himself together.

Enid rests a hand on his shoulder. 'Don't be a baby,' she says.

Looking back, of course, life in Milford was not always idyllic. Todd came down with pneumonia when he was ten. Came through that OK. And Cynthia, once she was in her teens, she started to be a handful. Rebellious. Hanging out with the wrong crowd at times. Experimenting with things she was too young for, like booze and God knows what else.

It fell to him to be the disciplinarian. Patricia, she was always more patient, more understanding. 'She'll get through this,' she'd tell him. 'She's a good kid. We just have to be there for her.'

It was just that, when Clayton was in Milford, he wanted life to be perfect. Often, it came close to being that way.

But then he would have to get back in the car, pretend to head off on business, and make the drive to Youngstown.

From the beginning, he wondered how long he could keep it up.

There were times when the bridge abutments looked like a solution again.

Sometimes, he'd wake up in the morning and wonder where he was today. Who he was today.

He'd make mistakes.

Enid had written him out a grocery list once, he'd driven down to Lewiston to pick up a few things. A week later, Patricia is doing the laundry, comes into the kitchen with the list in her hand, says, 'What's this? I found it in your pants pocket. Not my handwriting.'

Enid's shopping list.

Clayton's heart is in his mouth. His mind races. He says, 'I found that in the cart the other day, must have been the last person's list. I thought it was kind of funny, comparing what we get to what other people buy, so I saved it.'

Patricia glances at the list. 'Whoever they are, they like shredded wheat same as you.'

'Yeah,' he says, smiling. 'Well, I didn't figure they were making all those millions of boxes of it just for me.'

There evidently was at least one time when he put a clipping from a Youngstown area newspaper, a picture of his son with the basketball team, into the wrong drawer. He clipped it because, no matter how hard Enid worked to turn Jeremy against him, he still loved the boy. He saw himself in Jeremy, just as he did in Todd. It was amazing how much Todd, as he grew up, looked like Jeremy at similar stages. To look at Jeremy and hate him was to hate Todd, and he couldn't possibly do that.

So, at the end of one very long day, after a very long drive, Clayton Bigge of Milford emptied his pockets and tossed a clipping of his Youngstown's son's basketball team into the drawer of his bedside table. He kept the clipping because he was proud of the boy, even though he'd been poisoned against him.

Never noticed it was the wrong drawer. In the wrong house, in the wrong town, in the wrong state.

He made a mistake like that in Youngstown. For the longest time, he didn't even know what it was. Another clipping, maybe. A shopping list written out by Patricia.

Turned out to have been a phone bill for the address in Milford. In Patricia's name.

It caught Enid's attention.

It raised her suspicions.

But it wasn't like Enid to come straight out and ask

what it was about. Enid would conduct her own little investigation first. Watch for other signs. Start collecting evidence. Build a case.

And when she thought she had enough, she decided to take a trip of her own the next time her husband Clayton went out of town. One day she drove to Milford, Connecticut. This was back, of course, before she ended up in the wheelchair. When she was mobile.

She arranged for someone to look after Jeremy for a couple of days. 'Going to join my husband on the road this time,' she said. In separate cars.

'Which brings us,' Clayton said, sitting next to me, parched and taking another sip from his water bottle, 'to the night in question.'

FORTY-FIVE

The first part of the story I knew from Cynthia. How she ignored her curfew. Told her parents she was at Pam's house. How Clayton went to look for her, found her in the car with Vince Fleming, brought her home.

'She was furious,' Clayton said. 'Told us she wished we were dead. Stormed up to her room, never heard another peep out of her. She was drunk. God knows what she'd had to drink. Must have fallen asleep instantly. She never should have been hanging around with a guy like Vince Fleming. His father was nothing but a common gangster.'

'I know,' I said, my hands on the wheel, driving on through the night.

'So, like I say, it was quite a row. Todd, sometimes he enjoyed it when his sister got into trouble, you know how kids can be? But not this time. It was all pretty ugly. Just before I'd come back with Cynthia, he'd been asking me or Patricia to take him out to get a sheet of Bristol board or something. Like every other kid in the world, he'd left some project to the very last minute, needed a sheet of this stuff for some presentation. It was already late, we didn't know where the hell we could get something like that, but Patricia, she remembered they sold it at the drugstore, the one that was open twenty-four hours, so she said she'd take him over to get it.'

He coughed, took a sip of water. He was getting hoarse.

'But first, there was that thing Patricia had to do.' He glanced over at me. I patted my jacket, felt the envelope inside it. 'And then she and Todd left, in Patricia's car. I sat down in the living room, exhausted. I was going to have to leave in a couple of days, hit the road, spend some time in Youngstown. I always felt kind of depressed around those times, before I had to leave and go back to Enid and Jeremy.'

He looked out his window as we passed a tractor trailer.

'It seemed like Todd and his mom were gone a long time. It had been about an hour. The drug store wasn't that far. Then the phone rang.'

Clayton took a few breaths.

'It was Enid. Calling from a pay phone. She said, "Guess who?"'

'Oh God,' I said.

'It was a call that I guess, in some way, I'd always been expecting. But I couldn't have imagined what she'd done. She told me to meet her in the Denny's parking lot. She told me I'd better hurry. She said there was a lot of work to be done. Told me to bring a roll of paper towels. I flew out of the house, drove over to Denny's, thought maybe she'd be in the restaurant, but she was sitting in her car. She couldn't get out.'

'Why?' I asked.

'She couldn't walk around covered in that much blood and not attract attention.'

I suddenly felt very cold.

'I ran over to her window, it looked at first like her sleeves were covered in oil. She was so calm. She rolled down the window, told me to get in. I got in, and then I could see what was all over her, that it was blood. All over the sleeves of her coat, down the front of her dress. I was screaming at her. "What the hell have you done? What have you done?" But I already knew what it had to be.

'Enid had been parked out front of our house. She must have gotten there a few minutes after I came home with Cynthia. She had the address from the phone bill. She would have seen my car in the driveway, but with a Connecticut plate on it. She was putting it all together. And then Patricia and Todd came out, drove off, and she followed them. By this point, she must have been blind with rage. She'd figured out that I had this whole other life, this other family.

'She followed them to the drugstore. Got out of her car, followed them into the store, pretended to be shopping for stuff herself while she kept an eye on them. She must have been stunned when she got a good look at Todd. He looked so much like Jeremy. That had to be the clincher.'

Enid left the store before Patricia and Todd. She strode back to her car. There were hardly any vehicles in the lot, no one around. Just as Enid, in later years, kept a gun at hand in the case of an emergency, back then she kept a knife in the glove compartment. She reached in and got it, ran back in the direction of the drugstore, hid around the corner, which, at that hour, was shrouded in darkness. It was a broad alleyway, used by delivery trucks.

Todd and Patricia emerged from the store. Todd had his sheet of Bristol board rolled up into a huge tube and was carrying it over his shoulder like a soldier carries a rifle.

Enid emerged from the darkness. She said, 'Help!'

Todd and Patricia stopped, looked at Enid.

'My daughter!' Enid said. 'She's been hurt!'

Patricia ran over to meet her, Todd followed.

Enid led them a few steps into the alley, turned to Patricia and said, 'You wouldn't happen to be Clayton's wife, would you?'

'She must have been dumbstruck,' Clayton told me. 'First this woman asks for help, then, out of the blue, asks her something like that.'

'What did she say?'

'She said yes. And then the knife came up and slashed her right across the throat. Enid didn't wait a second. While Todd was still trying to figure out what happened – it was dark, remember – she was on him, slashing his throat as quickly as she'd slashed his mother's.'

'She told you all this?' I said. 'Enid.'

'Many, many times,' Clayton said quietly. 'She loves to talk about it. Even now. She calls it reminiscing.'

'Then what?'

'That's when she found her way to a nearby phone booth, called me. I show up and find her in the car, and she tells me what she's done. "I've killed them," she says. "Your wife, and your son. They're dead."'

'She doesn't know,' I said quietly.

Clayton nodded silently in the darkness.

'She doesn't know you also have a daughter.'

'I guess,' Clayton said. 'Maybe there was something about the symmetry of it. I had a wife and son in Youngstown, and a wife and son in Milford. A second son, who looked like the first one. It all seemed so perfectly balanced. A kind of mirror image. It led her to make certain assumptions. I could tell, the way she was talking, that she had no idea that Cynthia was still in the house, that she even existed. She hadn't seen me come home with her.'

'And you weren't about to tell her.'

'I was in shock, I think, but I had that much presence of mind. She started up her car, drove over to the alley, showed me their bodies. "You're going to have to help me," she said. "We have to get rid of them," she said.'

Clayton stopped for a moment, rode the next half a mile or so without saying a word. For a second, I wondered if he had died.

Finally, I said, 'Clayton, you OK?'

'Yes,' he said.

'What is it?'

'That was the moment when I could have made a difference. I had a choice I could have made, but maybe I was in too much shock to realize it, to know what was the right thing to do. I could have put an end to things right there. I could have refused to help her. I could have gone to the police. I could have turned her in. I could have put an end to all the madness then and there.'

'But you didn't.'

'I already felt like a guilty man. I was leading a double life. I'd have been ruined. I'd have been disgraced. I'm sure I would have been charged. Not in the deaths of Patricia and Todd. But being married to more than one woman, unless you're a Mormon or something, I think they have laws against that. I had false ID, that probably constituted fraud or misrepresentation somewhere along the line, although I never meant to break the law. I always tried to live right, to be a moral man.'

I glanced over at him.

'And of course, the other thing was, she could probably tell what I was thinking, and she said if I called the police, she'd tell them she was only helping me. That it was my idea, that I forced her to go along. And so I helped her. God forgive me, I helped her. We put Patricia and Todd back into the car, but left the driver's seat empty. I had an idea. About a place where we could put the car, with them inside. A quarry. Just off the route I often took going back and forth. One time, heading back to Youngstown, I started driving around aimlessly, not wanting to go back, found this road that led to the top of the cliff that looked down into this abandoned gravel pit. There was this small lake. I stood there for quite a while, thought about throwing myself off the edge. But in the end, I continued on. I thought, given that I'd be falling into water, there was a chance I might survive.'

He coughed, took a sip.

'We had to leave one car in the lot. I drove Patricia's Escort, drove the two and a half hours north in the middle of the night, Enid following me in her car. Took a while, but I found that laneway again, got the car up there, jammed a rock up against the accelerator with the car in neutral, reached in and put it in Drive and jumped back, and the car went over the edge. Heard it hit the water a couple of seconds later. Wasn't much I could see. Looking down, it was so dark I couldn't even see the car disappear beneath the surface.'

He was winded, gave himself a few seconds to catch his breath.

'Then we had to drive back, pick up the other car. Then we turned around again, both of us, in the two cars, headed back to Youngstown. I didn't even have a chance to say goodbye to Cynthia, to leave her a note, anything. I just had to disappear.'

'When did she find out?' I asked.

'Huh?'

'When did Enid find out she'd missed one? That she hadn't totally wiped out your other family?'

'A few days later. She'd been watching the news, hoping to catch something, but the story wasn't covered much by the Buffalo stations or papers. I mean, it wasn't a murder. There were no bodies. There wasn't even any blood in the alley by the drugstore. There was a rain storm later that morning, washed everything away. But she went to the library – there wasn't the Internet then of course – and started checking out-of-town and out-of-state papers, and she spotted something. "Girl's family vanishes" I think the headline was. She came home, I'd never seen her so mad. Smashing dishes, throwing things. She was completely insane. Took her a couple of hours to finally settle down.'

'But she had to live with it,' I said.

'She wasn't going to at first. She started packing, to go to Connecticut, to finish her off. But I stopped her.'

'How did you manage that?'

'I made a pact with her. A promise. I told her I would never leave her, never do anything like this again, that I would never, ever, attempt to get in touch with my daughter, if she would just spare her life. This is all I ask, I said to her. Let her live, and I will spend the rest of my life making it up to you, for betraying you.'

'And she accepted that?'

'Grudgingly. But I think it always niggled at her, like an itch you can't reach. A job not done. But now, there's an urgency. Knowing about the will, knowing that if I die before she can kill Cynthia, she'll lose everything.'

'So what did you do? You just went on?'

'I stopped traveling. I got a different job, started up my own company, worked from home or just down the road in Lewiston. Enid made it very clear that I was not to travel anymore. She wasn't going to be made a fool of again. Sometimes, I'd think about running away, going back, grabbing Cynthia, telling her everything, taking her to Europe, hiding out there, living under different names. But I knew I'd screw it up, probably end up leaving a trail, getting her killed. And it's not so easy, getting a fourteen-year-old to do what you want her to do. And so I stayed with Enid. We had a bond now that was stronger than the best marriage in the world. We'd committed a heinous crime together.' He paused. 'Till death do us part.'

'And the police, they never questioned you, never suspected a thing?'

'Never. I kept waiting. The first year, that was the worst. Every time I heard a car pull into the drive, I figured that was it. And then a second year went by, and a third, and before I knew it, it had been ten years. You think, if you're dying a little each day, how does life manage to stretch out so long?'

'You must have done some traveling,' I said.

'No, never again.'

'You were never back in Connecticut?'

'I've never set foot in that state since that night.'

'Then how did you get the money to Tess? To help her look after Cynthia, to help pay for her education?'

Clayton studied me for several seconds. He'd told me so much on this trip that had shocked me, but this appeared to be the first time I'd been able to surprise him.

'And who did you hear that from?' he asked.

'Tess told me,' I said. 'Only recently.'

'She couldn't have told you it was from me.'

'She didn't. She told me about receiving the money, and while she had her suspicions, she never knew who it was from.'

Clayton said nothing.

'It was from you, wasn't it?' I asked. 'You squirreled some money away for Cynthia, kept Enid from finding out, just like you did when you were setting up a second household.'

'Enid got suspicious. Years later. Looked like we were going to get audited, Enid brought in an accountant, went through years of old returns. They found an irregularity. I had to make up a story, tell them I'd been siphoning off money because of a gambling problem. But she didn't believe it. She threatened to go to Connecticut, kill Cynthia like she should have years ago, if I didn't tell her the truth. So I told her, about sending money to Tess, to help with Cynthia's education. But I'd kept my word, I said. I never got in touch with her, so far as Cynthia knew I was dead.'

'So Enid, she's nursed a grudge against Tess all these years, too.'

'She despised her for getting money she believed belonged to her. The two women she hated most in the world, and she'd never met either one of them.'

'So,' I said. 'This story of yours, that you've never been back to Connecticut, even if you didn't actually see Cynthia, that's bullshit then.'

'No,' he said. 'That's the truth.'

And I thought about that for a while as we continued to drive on through the night.

FORTY-SIX

Finally, I said, 'I know you didn't mail the money to Tess. It didn't show up in her mailbox with a stamp on it. And you didn't FedEx it. There'd be an envelope stuffed with cash in her car, another time she found it tucked into her morning newspaper.'

Clayton acted as though he couldn't hear me.

'So, if you didn't mail it, and you didn't deliver it yourself,' I said, 'then you must have had someone do it for you.'

Clayton remained impassive. He closed his eyes, leaned his head back on the headrest, as though sleeping. But I wasn't buying it.

'I know you're hearing me,' I said.

'I'm very tired,' he said. 'I normally sleep through the night, you know. Leave me alone for a while, let me catch a few winks.'

'I've one other question,' I said. He kept his eyes shut, but I saw his mouth twitch nervously. 'Tell me about Connie Gormley.'

His eyes opened suddenly, as though I'd jabbed him with a cattle prod. Clayton tried to recover.

'I don't know that name,' he said.

'Let me see if I can help,' I said. 'She was from Sharon, she was twenty-seven years old, she worked at a Dunkin' Donuts, and one night, twenty-six years ago, a Friday night, she was walking along the shoulder of the road near the Cornwall bridge, this would be on Route Seven, when she was hit by a car. Except it wasn't exactly a hit-and-run. She was most likely dead beforehand and the accident was staged. Like someone wanted it to look like it was just an accident, nothing more sinister, you know?'

Clayton looked out his window so I couldn't see his face.

'It was one of your other slips, like the shopping list and the phone bill,' I said. 'You'd clipped this larger story about fly-fishing, but there was this story down in the corner about the hit and run. Would have been easy to snip it out, but you didn't, and I can't figure out why.'

We were nearing the New York-Massachusetts border, heading east, waiting for the sun to rise.

'Did you know her?' I asked. 'Was she someone else you met touring the country for work?'

'Don't be ridiculous,' Clayton said.

'A relative? On Enid's side? When I mentioned the name to Cynthia, it didn't mean anything to her.'

'There's no reason why it should,' Clayton said quietly.

'Was it you?' I asked. 'Did you kill her, then hit her with your car, drag her into the ditch and leave her there?'

'No,' he said.

'Because if that's what happened, maybe this is the time to set the record straight. You've admitted to a great many things tonight. A double life. Helping to cover up the murder of your wife and son. Protecting a woman, who by your account, is certifiable. But you don't want to tell me what your interest is in the death of a woman named Connie Gormley, and you don't want to tell me how you got money to Tess Berman to help pay for Cynthia's education.'

Clayton said nothing.

'Are those things related?' I asked. 'Are they linked somehow? This woman, you couldn't have used her as a courier for the money. She was dead years before you started making those payments.'

Clayton drank some water, put the bottle back into the cup holder between the seats, ran his hands across the tops of his legs.

'Suppose I told you none of it matters?' he said. 'Suppose I acknowledge that yes, your questions are interesting, that there are some things you still do not know, but that in the larger scheme of things, it's not really that important?'

'An innocent woman gets killed, then her body's hit by a car, she's left in a ditch, you think that's unimportant? You think that's how her family felt? I spoke to her brother on the phone the other day.'

Clayton's bushy eyebrows rose a notch.

'Both their parents died within a couple of years after Connie. It's like they gave up on life. It was the only way to end the grieving.'

Clayton shook his head.

'And you say that it's not important? Clayton, did you kill that woman?'

'No,' he said.

'Did you know who did?'

Clayton would only shake his head.

'Enid?' I said. 'She came to Connecticut a year later to kill Patricia and Todd. Did she come down earlier, did she kill Connie Gormley, too?'

Clayton kept shaking his head, then finally spoke.

'Enough lives have been destroyed already. There's no sense in ruining any more. I don't have anything else to say about this.' He folded his arms across his chest and waited for the sun to come up.

I didn't want to lose time stopping for breakfast, but I was also very much aware of Clayton's weakened condition. Once morning hit, and the car was filled with light, I saw how much worse he looked than when we'd fled the hospital. He'd been hours without his IV, without sleep.

'You look like you need something,' I said. We were going through Winsted, where Highway 8 went from a winding, two-lane affair to four lanes. We'd make even better time from here, the last leg of the journey to Milford. There were some fast-food joints in Winsted, and I suggested we hit a drive-through window, get a McMuffin, something like that.

Clayton nodded wearily. 'I could eat the egg. I don't think I could chew the English muffin.'

As we sat in the drive-through lineup, Clayton said, 'Tell me about her.'

'What?'

'Tell me about Cynthia. I haven't seen her since that night. I haven't seen her in twenty-five years.'

I didn't entirely know how to react to Clayton. There were times when I felt sympathy for him, the horrible life he'd led, the misery he'd had to endure living with Enid, the tragedy of losing loved ones.

But who was to blame, really? Clayton had made the point himself. He'd made his choices. And not just the decision to help Enid cover up a monstrous crime, and to leave Cynthia behind, to wonder her whole adult life what had become of her family. There were choices he could have made earlier. He could have stood up to Enid, somehow. Insisted on a divorce. Called the police when she became violent. Had her committed. Something.

He could have walked out on her. Left her a note. 'Dear Enid: I'm out of here. Clayton.'

At least it would have been more honest.

It wasn't as if he was looking to me for sympathy, asking about his daughter, my wife. But there was something in his voice, a bit of, 'Poor me.' Haven't seen my daughter for two and a half decades. How terribly sad for me.

There's the rear-view mirror, pal, I thought to myself. Twist it around, take a look. There's the guy who has to carry a lot of the load for all the fucked-up shit that's been going on since 1983.

But instead, I said, 'She's wonderful.'

Clayton waited for more.

'Cyn is the most wonderful thing that's ever happened to me,' I said. 'I love her more than you could ever know. And as long as I've known her, she's been dealing with what you and Enid did to her. Think about it. You wake up one morning, and your family is gone. The cars are gone. Everyone fucking gone.' I felt my blood starting to boil and I gripped the wheel more tightly in anger. 'Do you have any fucking idea? Do you? What was she supposed to think? Were you all dead? Had some crazy serial killer gone through town and killed all of you? Or had the three of you decided, that night, to go off and have a new life somewhere else, a new life that didn't include her?'

Clayton was stunned. 'She thought that?'

'She thought a million things! She was fucking

abandoned! Don't you get it? You couldn't have gotten word to her somehow? A letter? Explained that her family met with a horrible fate, but at least they loved her? That they hadn't just upped and fucking walked out on her one night?'

Clayton looked down into his lap. His hands were shaking.

'Sure, you cut a deal with Enid to keep Cynthia alive by agreeing to never see her again, to never get in touch. So maybe she's alive today because you agreed to live out the rest of your life with a monster. But do you think that makes you some kind of fucking hero? You know what? You're no fucking hero. If you'd been a man, from the get go, maybe none of this shit would ever have happened.'

Clayton put his face into his hands, leaned against the door.

'Let me ask you this,' I said, a kind of calm coming over me. 'What kind of man stays with a woman who's murdered his own son? Can someone like that even be called a man? If it'd been me, I think I'd have killed her myself.'

We were at the window. I handed the guy some cash, took a bag with a couple of Egg McMuffins and hash browns, plus two coffees. I pulled ahead into a parking slot, reached into the bag and tossed a breakfast sandwich into Clayton's lap.

'Here,' I said. 'Gum this.'

I needed some air and to stretch my legs for two seconds. Plus, I wanted to call home again, just in case. I took my cell out of my jacket, opened it up and glanced at the screen.

'Fuck,' I said.

I had a message. I had a goddamn voice-mail message. How was that possible? Why had I not heard the phone ring?

It had to be after we got off the Mass Pike, when we were driving south of Lee, down that long, winding stretch of road. Cell reception was terrible through there. Someone must have called me, couldn't get through and left a message.

This was the message:

'Terry, hi, it's me.' Cynthia. 'I tried to call you at home, and now I'm trying your cell, and God, where are you? Look, I've been thinking of coming home, I think we should talk. But something's happened. Something totally unbelievable. We were staying at this motel, and I asked if I could use the computer in the office? To see if I could find any old news stories, anything, and I checked my mail, and there was another message, from that address, with the date? You know. And this time, there was a phone number to call, so I decided, what the hell. So I called, and Terry, you're not going to believe what's happened. It's the most amazing thing. It's my brother. My brother Todd. Terry, I can't believe it. I've talked to him! I called him and I spoke to him! I know, I know, you're thinking it's some crank caller, some kind of nut. But he told me he was the man at the mall, the man I thought was my brother. I was right! It was Todd! Terry, I knew it!'

I was feeling dizzy.

The message continued:

'There was something in his voice, I could tell it was him. I could hear my father in his voice. So Wedmore was wrong. That must be some other woman and her son in the quarry. I mean, I know we don't have my test in yet, but this tells me something else happened that night, maybe some kind of mix-up. Todd said he was so sorry, that he couldn't admit who he was at the mall, that he was sorry about the phone call, and the e-mail message, that there was nothing I had to be forgiven for, but that he can explain everything. He was working up his nerve to meet with me, tell me where he's been all these years. It's like a dream, Terry. I feel like I'm in some sort of dream, that this can't be happening, that I'm finally going to see Todd again. I asked him about my mom, about dad, but he said he'd tell me all about it when I see him. I just wish you were here, I always wanted you to be there if something like this ever happened. But I hope you understand, I just can't wait, I have to go now. Call me when you get this. Grace and I are heading up to Winsted to see him now. My God, Terry, it's like a miracle has happened.'

FORTY-SEVEN

Winsted?

We were *in* Winsted. And Cynthia and Grace were *coming* to Winsted? I checked to see how long ago she'd left the message. Nearly three hours. So she'd made the call even before we'd got off the Mass Pike, probably when we were in one of those valleys between Albany and the Massachusetts border.

I started doing the math. There was a very good chance Cynthia and Grace were already in Winsted. They could have been here as long as an hour, I guessed. Cynthia probably broke every speed limit on the way up, and who wouldn't do the same anticipating a reunion of this nature?

It made some sense. Jeremy sends the e-mail, maybe before he even leaves Milford, or maybe he's got a laptop or something, waits for Cynthia to call his cell. She reaches him while he's en route, and he suggests Cynthia heads north for a rendezvous. Gets her away from Milford, saves him having to drive all the way back.

But why here? Why lure her up to this part of the state, other than to save Jeremy a bit of driving?

I punched in the numbers for Cynthia's cell phone. I had to stop her. She was meeting with her brother, of course. But not Todd. It was the half-brother she never knew she had: Jeremy. She wasn't on her way to a reunion. She was walking into a trap.

With Grace along for the ride.

I put the phone to my ear and waited for the call to go through. Nothing. I was about to redial when I realized what the problem was.

My phone was dead.

'Shit!' I looked around for a pay phone, spotted one down the street and started running. From the car, Clayton called out wheezily, 'What?'

I ignored him, reaching for my wallet as I ran, digging out a phone card I rarely used. At the phone, I swiped the card, followed the instructions, dialed Cynthia's cell. Not in service. It went immediately to voice mail. 'Cynthia,' I said. 'Don't meet with your brother. It's not Todd. It's a trap. Call me – no, wait, my phone's dead. Call Wedmore. Hang on, I've got her number.' I fumbled around in my pocket for her business card, found it, recited the number. 'I'll check in with her. But you have to trust me on this. Don't go to this meeting! Don't go!'

I replaced the receiver, leaned my head against the phone, exhausted, frustrated.

If she'd come to Winsted, she might still be around.

Where would be an easy place to rendezvous? The McDonald's, where we were parked, certainly. There were a couple of other fast-food joints. Simple, modern, iconic landmarks. Hard to miss.

I ran back to the car, got in. Clayton hadn't tried to eat anything. 'What's happening?' he asked.

I backed the Honda out of the spot, whipped through the McDonald's lot, looking for Cynthia's car. When I couldn't find it there, I got back on the main road and sped down the street to the other fast-food outlets.

'Terry, tell me what's going on,' Clayton said.

'There was a message from Cynthia. Jeremy called her, said he was Todd, asked her to meet him. Right here, in Winsted. She probably would have gotten here an hour ago, maybe not even that long.'

'Why up here?' Clayton asked.

I pulled into another lot, scanned it for Cynthia's car. No luck. 'The McDonald's,' I said. 'It's the first big thing you see when you come off the highway coming north. If Jeremy was going to arrange to meet any place, that would have to be it. It's the most obvious choice.'

I spun the Honda around, sped back down the street to the McDonald's, jumped out of the car with the engine running, ran over to the drive-through window, cutting in front of someone trying to pay.

'Hey, pal, you can't be there,' the man at the window said.

'In the last hour or so, did you see a woman in a Toyota, she'd have had a small girl with her?'

'You kidding me?' the man said, handing a bag of food to a motorist. 'You know how many people go through here?'

'You mind?' said a driver as he reached for the bag. The car sped out, the side mirror brushing against my back.

'What about a man with an elderly woman?' I said. 'A brown car?'

'You have to get away from this window.'

'She'd have been in a wheelchair. No, there might have been a wheelchair in the back seat. Folded up.'

A light went on. 'Oh yeah,' he said. 'Actually, that does kind of ring a bell, but it was a long time ago, maybe an hour. Kind of tinted windows, but I remember seeing the chair. They got coffees, I think. Pulled over there.' He pointed in the general direction of the lot.

'An Impala?'

'Man, I don't know. You're in the way.'

I ran back to the Honda, got in next to Clayton. 'I think Jeremy and Enid were here. Waiting.'

'Well, they're not here now,' Clayton said.

I squeezed the steering wheel, let go, squeezed again, banged it with my fist. My head was ready to explode.

'You know where we are, right?' Clayton asked.

'What? Of course I know where we are.'

'You know what we passed on the way down. North of here, few miles. I recognized the road when we went past it.'

The road to the Fell's Quarry. Clayton knew, from my expression, that I had figured out what he was talking about.

'Don't you see?' Clayton said. 'You'd have to know how Enid thinks, but it makes perfect sense. Cynthia, along with your daughter, she finally ends up in the place Enid believes she should have been all these years. And maybe, this time, Enid doesn't even care if the car and bodies inside get found right away. Let the police find them. Maybe people'll think Cynthia was distraught, that somehow she felt responsible, was in despair over what had happened, the death of her aunt. So she drives up there and goes right over the edge.'

'But that's crazy,' I said. 'That might have worked at one time, but not now. Not with other people knowing what's going on. Us. Vince. It's insane.'

'Exactly,' Clayton said. 'That's Enid.'

I nearly rammed the car into a Beetle as I drove out of the lot, heading back in the direction we'd come from.

*

I had the car going over ninety, and as we approached some of the hairpin turns heading north to Otis, I had to slam on the brakes to keep from losing control. Once I had us through the turns, I put my foot to the floor again. We nearly killed a deer that ran across our path, almost took off the front end of a tractor as a farmer came out the end of his driveway.

Clayton barely winced.

He had his right hand wrapped tight around the door handle, but he never once told me to slow down or take it easy. He understood that we might already be too late.

I'm not sure how long it took us to get to the road heading east out of Otis. Half an hour, an hour maybe. It felt like forever. All I could see in my mind's eye were Cynthia and Grace. And I couldn't stop picturing them in a car, plunging over the side of the cliff and into the lake below.

'The glove box,' I said to Clayton. 'Open it up.'

He reached forward with some effort, opened the compartment, revealing the gun I'd taken from Vince's truck. He took it out, inspected it briefly.

'Hang on to that till we get there,' I said. Clayton nodded silently, but then went into a coughing fit. It was a deep, raspy, echoing cough that seemed to come all the way up from his toes.

'I hope I make it,' he said.

'I hope we both make it,' I said.

'If she's there,' he said. 'If we're in time, what do you think Cynthia will say to me?' He paused. 'I have to tell her I'm sorry.'

I glanced over at him, and the look he gave me suggested he was sorry that there was nothing more he could do than offer an apology. But I could tell from his expression, that no matter how late it would be in coming, how inadequate it might be, his apology would be genuine.

He was a man who needed to apologize for his entire life.

'Maybe,' I said, 'you'll have a chance.'

Clayton, even in his condition, saw the road to the quarry before I did. It was unmarked, so narrow, it would have been easy to drive right past it. I had to hit the brakes, and our shoulder straps locked as we pitched forward.

'Give me the gun,' I said, holding the wheel with my left hand as we rolled down the laneway.

The road started its steep climb up, the trees began to open up, and the windshield was filled with blue, cloudless sky. Then the road started leveling out into the small clearing, and there, ahead of us, the back ends of the brown Impala on the right, and Cynthia's old silver Corolla on the left.

Standing between them, looking back at us, was Jeremy Sloan. He had something in his right hand.

When he raised it, I could see that it was a gun, and when the windshield of our Honda shattered, I knew that it was loaded.

FORTY-EIGHT

I slammed on the brakes and threw the car into Park in one fluid motion, undid my seatbelt, opened the door and dived out. I knew I was leaving Clayton to fend for himself, but at this point, I was thinking only of Cynthia and Grace. In the couple of seconds I'd had to survey the situation, I'd been unable to spot either of them, but the fact that Cyn's car was still on the precipice, and not in the lake, seemed to me a hopeful sign.

I hit the ground and rolled into some high grass, then fired wildly into the sky. I wanted Jeremy to know I had a gun, too, even if I had no skill with it. I came to a stop and maneuvered myself around in the grass so that I was looking back at where Jeremy had been, but now he was gone. I looked about frantically, then saw his head poking out timidly from around the front bumper of the brown Impala.

'Jeremy!' I shouted.

'Terry!' Cynthia. Screaming. Her voice was coming from her car.

'Daddy!' Grace.

'I'm here!' I shouted.

From inside the Impala, another voice. 'Kill him, Jeremy! Shoot him!' Enid, sitting in the front passenger seat.

'Jeremy,' I called out. 'Listen to me. Has your mother told you what happened back at your house? Has she told you why you had to leave so fast?'

'Don't listen to him,' Enid said. 'Just shoot him.'

'What are you talking about?' he shouted back at me.

'She shot a man in your house. A man named Vince Fleming. He'll be in the hospital by now, telling the police everything. He and I went to Youngstown last night. I figured it out. I've already called the police. I don't know how you originally planned this to go. Make Cynthia look like she was going crazy is my guess, make it look like she might even have had something to do with her brother and mother's deaths, then she comes up here, kills herself. Is that it, more or less?'

I waited for answer. When none came, I continued, 'But the cat's out of the bag, Jeremy. It's not going to work any more.'

'He doesn't know what he's talking about,' Enid said. 'I told you to shoot him. Do what your mother says.'

'Mom,' Jeremy said, 'I don't know ... I've never killed anyone before.'

'Suck it up! You're about to kill those two.' I could make out the back of Enid's head, see her motioning to Cynthia's car.

'Yeah, but all I have to do is push the car over. This is *different*.'

Clayton had the passenger door of the Honda open and was slowly getting to his feet. I could see under the car, spotted his shoes, his sockless ankles as he struggled to stand. Granules of windshield glass fell from his trousers to the ground.

'Get back in the car, Dad,' Jeremy said.

'What?' Enid said. 'He's here?' She caught sight of him in the passenger door mirror. 'For Christ's sake!' she said. 'You stupid old coot! Who let you out of the hospital?'

Slowly, he shuffled his way toward the Impala. When he got to the back of the car, he placed his hands on the trunk, steadied himself, caught his breath. He appeared to be on the verge of collapse. 'Don't do this, Enid,' he wheezed.

Then Cynthia's voice: 'Dad?'

'Hello sweetheart,' he said. He tried to smile. 'I can't tell you how sorry I am about all this.'

'Dad?' she said again. Incredulous. I couldn't see Cynthia's face from my position, but I could imagine how shocked she must have looked.

Evidently, while Jeremy and Enid had somehow managed to abduct Cynthia and Grace and get them up here above the quarry, they had not bothered to bring them up to speed.

'Son,' Clayton said to Jeremy. 'You have to put an end to this. Your mother, she's wrong to drag you into this, make you do all these bad things. Look at her.' He was telling Jeremy to look at Cynthia. 'That's your sister. Your *sister.* And that little girl, she's your niece. If you help your mother do what she wants you to do, you'll be no better a man than me.'

'Dad,' said Jeremy, still crouched around the front of the Impala. 'Why are you leaving everything to her? You don't even know her. How could you be so mean to me and Mom?'

Clayton sighed. 'It's not always about the two of you,' he said.

'Shut up!' Enid snipped.

'Jeremy!' I called out. 'Get rid of the gun. Give it up.' I had both hands wrapped around Vince's weapon, lying there in the grass. I didn't know the first thing about guns, but I knew I needed to hold onto it as tightly as I could.

He rose up from his hiding spot in front of the Impala, fired. Dirt kicked up just to my right, and I instinctively rolled left.

Cynthia screamed again.

I heard fast moving steps along the gravel. Jeremy was running, closing in on me. I stopped rolling, aimed up at the figure closing in on me, fired. But it went wide and before I could shoot again Jeremy kicked at the gun, the toe of his shoe slamming into the back of my right hand.

I lost my grip. The gun flew off into the grass.

His next kick caught me in the side, in my ribcage. The pain shot through me like a bolt of lightning. I'd barely registered that pain when he rammed his foot into me again, this time with enough force that I rolled over onto my back. Bits of dirt and grass stuck to my cheek.

But that still wasn't enough for him. There was one last kick.

I couldn't catch my breath. Jeremy stood over me, looking down with contempt, as I gasped for air.

'Shoot him!' Enid said. 'If you won't do it give me back my gun and I'll do it myself.'

He still had the gun in his hand, but he just stood there with it. He could have put a bullet in my brain as easily as dropping a coin into a parking meter, but the resolve was not there.

I was starting to get some air into my lungs, my breathing was returning to normal, but I was in tremendous pain. A couple of cracked ribs, I was sure of it.

Clayton, still using the trunk to support himself, looked at me, his eyes filled with sadness. I could almost read his thoughts. We tried, he seemed to be saying. We gave it our best shot. We meant well.

And the road to hell is paved with good intentions.

I rolled over onto my stomach, slowly got to my knees. Jeremy found my gun in the grass, picked it up, tucked it into the back of his trousers. 'Get up,' he said to me.

'Are you not listening?' Enid screamed. 'Shoot him!'

'Momma,' he said. 'Maybe it makes more sense to put him in the car. With the others.'

She thought about that. 'No,' she said. 'That doesn't work. They have to go into the lake without him. It's better that way. We'll have to kill him some place else.'

Clayton, using his hands, one over the other, was moving up along the side of the Impala. He still appeared on the verge of collapse.

'I . . . I think I'm going to pass out,' he said.

'You stupid bastard!' Enid shouted at him. 'You should have stayed in the hospital and died there.' She was having to move her neck around so much, trying to keep track of what was going on, I thought it might snap. I could see the handles of her wheelchair rising above the sills of the back door windows. The ground was too bumpy, too uneven, to bother getting it out so she could move around.

Jeremy was forced to choose between keeping an eye on me, or running over to help his father. He decided to attempt both.

'You don't move,' he said, keeping the gun pointed in my direction as he backstepped over to the Impala. He was about to open the back door so his father could sit down, but it was filled with the wheelchair, so he opened the driver's door.

'Sit down,' Jeremy said, glancing from his father to me and back again. Clayton shuffled the extra couple of steps, then slowly dropped himself into the seat.

'I need some water,' he said.

'Oh, stop complaining,' Enid said. 'For Christ's sake. It's always something with you.'

I'd managed to struggle to my feet now, and was coming up alongside Cynthia's car, on the driver's side, where she sat, Grace next to her. I couldn't quite tell from where I was standing, but they were sitting so rigidly, they had to be tied in somehow.

'Honey,' I said.

Cynthia's eyes were bloodshot, her cheeks streaked with dried tears. Grace, on the other hand, was still crying. Damp lines ran down her cheek.

'He said he was Todd,' Cynthia told me. 'He's not Todd.'

'I know,' I said. 'I know. But that is your father.'

Cynthia looked to her right at the man sitting in the front of the Impala, then back to me.

'No,' she said. 'He might look like him, but he's not my father. Not any more.'

Clayton, who had heard the exchange, let his head fall toward his chest in shame. Without looking at Cynthia, he said, 'You're entitled to feel that way. I know I would, if I was you. All I can tell you is how sorry I am, but I'm not so old and foolish as to think you'll forgive. I'm not even sure you should.'

'You get away from the car,' Jeremy warned me, coming around the front of Cynthia's Corolla, the gun pointed my way. 'You stand back over there.'

'How could you do it?' Enid said to Clayton. 'How could you leave everything to that bitch?'

'I'd told the lawyer you weren't to see it before I died,' Clayton said. He nearly smiled, and said, 'Guess I'm going to have to look for a new lawyer.'

'It was his secretary,' Enid said. 'He was on vacation, I dropped by, said you wanted to take another look at it, up in the hospital. So she shows it to me. You ungrateful son of a bitch. I give up my whole life for you and this is the thanks I get.'

'Should we do it, Mom?' Jeremy asked. He was standing by Cynthia's door, preparing, I figured, to lean in through the window, turn the ignition, slap it into Drive, or Neutral, pull himself back through the window and watch the car roll over the edge.

'Hey, Mom,' Jeremy said, more slowly this time. 'Shouldn't they be untied? Won't it look funny if they're tied up in the car? Doesn't it have to look like my ... you know ... like she did it on her own?'

'What are you blathering on about?' Enid shouted.

'Should I knock them out first?' Jeremy asked.

I couldn't think of much else to do but rush him. Try to grab his gun, turn it on him. I might end up getting shot myself, would probably end up dead, but if that meant saving my wife and my daughter, it didn't seem like that bad a deal. Once Jeremy was out of the way, there wouldn't be anything Enid could do, not without the use of her legs. Eventually, Cynthia and Grace would be able to free themselves, get away.

'You know what?' Enid said, ignoring Jeremy and turning her attention to Clayton. 'You never appreciated anything I did for you. You were an ungrateful bastard from the moment I first met you. A miserable, useless, good for nothing. And on top of that, unfaithful.' Enid shook her head disapprovingly. 'That's the worst sin of all.'

'Mom?' Jeremy said again. He had his hand on Cynthia's door, the other still pointing the gun at me.

Maybe, when he leaned in, I thought. He'd have to turn his back to me, at least for a second. But what if he managed to knock Cynthia and Grace out, put the car into gear before I got to him? I might get the drop on him but not in time to stop the car from rolling off the edge.

It had to be now. I had to rush him—

And then I heard a car starting.

It was the Impala.

'What the hell are you doing?' Enid screamed at Clayton, sitting in the driver's seat. 'Turn that off!'

But Clayton wasn't paying any attention to her. He turned, calmly, to his left and looked at Cynthia's Toyota. He had a small smile on his face. He looked almost serene. He nodded at his daughter and said, 'I never, ever stopped loving you, or ever stopped thinking about you, and your mother, and Todd.'

'Clayton!' Enid screamed.

And then Clayton looked at Grace, her eyes just visible above the door. 'I wish I could have gotten to know you, Grace, but I know without a doubt that with a mother like Cynthia, you are very, very special.'

Then Clayton gave his attention to Enid. 'So long, you miserable old cunt,' he said, dropped the car into gear and hit the gas.

The engine roared. The Impala bolted forward toward the edge.

'Momma!' Jeremy screamed and ran around the front of Cynthia's car and into the path of the Impala, as if he thought he could stop it with his own body. Maybe Jeremy thought at first that the car was only rolling, as if Clayton had shoved it by accident into Neutral.

But that wasn't the case at all. Clayton was trying to see how fast he could go from zero to sixty in the thirty feet he had between himself and the quarry's edge.

The car threw Jeremy up onto the hood, and that's where he was when the Impala, with Clayton at the wheel and Enid screaming in the seat next to him, shot out over the edge.

It was about two seconds before we heard the splash.

FORTY-NINE

I had to move Clayton's windshield-shattered Honda out of the way to make room to get out of there in Cynthia's Toyota. She got in the back so she could sit with her arms around Grace for the long drive back south to Milford.

I knew we should probably have called the police, waited there at the top of the quarry for them to arrive, but we thought the most important thing was to get Grace home, where she would feel the most safe, as quickly as possible. Clayton and Enid and Jeremy weren't going anywhere. They'd still be at the bottom of that lake when we gave Rona Wedmore a call.

Cynthia wanted me to get to a hospital, and there was no doubt in my mind that I needed one. Both my sides were in intense pain, but it was mitigated by an overwhelming sense of relief. Once I had Cynthia and Grace home, I'd head over to Milford Hospital.

We didn't talk a lot on the drive back. I think Cynthia and I were on the same page – that we didn't want to go over what had happened, not just today but twenty-five years ago – in front of Grace. Grace had been through enough. She just needed to get home.

But I did manage to get the rough details of what had happened. Cynthia and Grace had driven to Winsted, met Jeremy at the McDonald's lot. He had a surprise, he told them. He had brought along his mother. The inference being, of course, that he had brought along Patricia Bigge.

Cynthia, dumbstruck, was taken over to the Impala, and once she and Grace were in the car, Enid held her gun on Grace. Told Cynthia to drive the car to the quarry, or she'd kill Grace. Jeremy followed in Cynthia's car.

Once on the precipice, Cynthia and Grace were tied in to the front seats of Cynthia's car in preparation for their trip over the side.

Then Clayton and I arrived.

Almost as briefly, I told Cynthia what I'd learned. About my trip to Youngstown. Finding her father in hospital. The story of what happened the night her family disappeared.

Vince Fleming getting shot.

I would call, the moment I got home, to see how he was doing. I didn't want to have to go into school and face Jane Scavullo, tell her that the only man in years who'd been decent to her was dead.

As far as the police were concerned, I hoped to Christ Wedmore believed everything I was going to tell her. I don't know that I would have, if it hadn't actually happened to me.

Something still wasn't quite right. I couldn't shake the memory of Jeremy standing over me, gun in hand, unable to pull the trigger. He certainly hadn't shown that kind of hesitation where Tess Berman was concerned. Or Denton Abagnall.

They'd both been murdered in cold blood.

What was it that Jeremy had said to his mother while he stood over me? 'I've never killed anyone before.'

Yeah, that was it.

When we passed through Winsted again we asked Grace whether she wanted something to eat, but she shook her head no. She wanted to go home. Cynthia and I exchanged worried glances. We would take Grace to see a doctor. She'd been through a traumatic incident. She might be suffering from mild shock. But before long, she was asleep, and gave no indication that she was having nightmares.

A couple of hours later, we were home. As we made the turn into our street, I saw Rona Wedmore's car in front of our house, parked at the curb, with her behind the wheel. When she spotted our car she got out, eyeing us sternly with arms folded as we turned into the driveway. She was waiting for me by the car when I opened my door, ready, I suspected, to start peppering me with questions.

Her expression softened when she saw me wince as I slowly got out of the driver's seat. I hurt like hell.

'What happened to you?' she asked. 'You look awful.'

'That's pretty much how I feel,' I said, touching one of my wounds gingerly. 'I took a few kicks from Jeremy Sloan.'

'Where is he?' Wedmore asked.

I smiled to myself and opened the back door and, even though a couple of my ribs felt as though they were about to snap, took a sleeping Grace into my arms to carry her into the house.

'Let me,' Cynthia said, now out of the car herself.

'It's OK,' I said, taking her to the front door as Cynthia ran ahead to unlock it. Rona Wedmore was trailing us into the house.

'I can't carry her anymore,' I said, the pain becoming excruciating.

'The couch,' Cynthia said.

I managed to set her down there gently, even though I felt I was going to drop her, and despite all the jostling and talking, she didn't wake up. Once she was on the couch, Cynthia tucked some throw pillows under her head and found an afghan to drape over her.

Wedmore was still just watching, courteously giving us a moment. Once Cynthia had tucked the afghan around Grace the three of us moved into the kitchen.

'You look like you need to see a doctor,' Wedmore said.

I nodded.

'Where's Sloan?' she asked again. 'If he assaulted you, we'll have him arrested.'

I leaned up against the counter. 'You're going to need to call in your divers again,' I said.

I told her pretty much all of it. How Vince had spotted what was wrong with that old newspaper clipping, how that had led us to Sloan and Youngstown, my finding Clayton Sloan in hospital, Jeremy and Enid's abduction of Cynthia and Grace.

The car going over the cliff and down into the quarry, taking Clayton and Enid and Jeremy along for the ride.

There was only one small part I'd left out, because it was still troubling me, and I wasn't sure what it meant. Although I had an inkling.

'Well,' Rona Wedmore said. 'That's quite a story.'

'It is,' I said. 'If I were going to make something up, trust me, I'd have come up with something more believable.'

'I'll want to talk to Grace about this, too,' Wedmore said.

'Not now,' Cynthia said. 'She's been through enough. She's exhausted.'

Wedmore nodded silently. Then, 'I'll make some calls, see about the divers, be back later this afternoon.' To me, 'You get over to Milford Hospital. I could drop you off if you like.'

'That's OK,' I said. 'I'll go in a little while, call a cab if I have to.'

Wedmore left, and Cynthia said she was heading upstairs to try to make herself look half respectable again. Wedmore's car had only been gone half a minute when I heard another one pull into the drive. I opened the front door as Rolly, wearing a long jacket over a blue plaid shirt and blue slacks, reached the step.

'Terry!' he said.

I put a finger to my lips. 'Grace is sleeping,' I said. I motioned for him to follow me into the kitchen.

'So you found them?' he said. 'Cynthia too?'

I nodded as I went hunting for Advils in the pantry. I found the container, shook some out into my hand and ran a glass of cold water from the tap.

'You look hurt,' Rolly said. 'Some people will do anything to get a long-term leave.'

I almost laughed, but it hurt too much. I popped three pills into my mouth, had a long drink of water.

'So,' Rolly said. 'So.'

'Yeah,' I said.

'So, you found her father?' he said. 'You found Clayton?'

I nodded.

'That's amazing,' he said. 'That you found him. That Clayton's still around, still alive, after all these years.'

'Isn't it, though,' I said. I held back telling Rolly that while Clayton had been alive all these years, he was no longer.

'Just amazing.'

'Aren't you wondering about Patricia, too?' I asked. 'Or Todd? Aren't you curious to know what happened to them?'

Rolly's eyes danced. 'Of course, yes, I am. I mean, I already know they were found in the car, in the quarry.'

'Yeah, that's true. But everything else, who killed them, I figure you must already know about that,' I said. 'Otherwise, you'd have asked.'

Rolly's look grew grim. 'I just, I don't want to bombard you with questions. You've only been home a couple of minutes.'

'Do you want to know how they died? What actually happened to them?'

'Sure,' he said.

'Maybe in a minute.' I took another drink of water. I hoped the Advils would kick in soon. 'Rolly,' I said. 'Were you the one who delivered the money?'

'What?'

'The money. For Tess. To spend on Cynthia. It was you, wasn't it?'

He licked his lip nervously. 'What did Clayton tell you?'

'What do you think he told me?'

Rolly ran his hand over the top of his head, turned away from me. 'He's told you everything, hasn't he?'

I said nothing. I decided it was better for Rolly to think I knew more than I actually did.

'Jesus Christ,' he said, shaking his head. 'The son of a bitch. He swore he'd never tell. He thinks it was me that somehow led you to him, doesn't he? That's why he's reneged on our arrangement.'

'Is that what you call it, Rolly? An arrangement?'

'We had a deal!' He shook his head in anger. 'I'm so close. So close to retirement. All I want is some peace, to get out of that fucking school, to get away, to get out of this goddamn town.'

'Why don't you just tell me about it, Rolly. See if your version matches Clayton's.'

'He's told you about Connie Gormley, hasn't he? About the accident.'

I didn't say anything.

'We were coming back from a fishing trip,' Rolly said. 'It was Clayton's idea to stop for a beer. I could have done the drive home without stopping, but I said OK. We went into this bar, we were just going to have a beer and go, and this girl, she starts coming on to me, you know?'

'Connie Gormley.'

'Yeah. I mean, she's sitting with me, and she's had a few beers, and I ended up having a few more. Clayton, he's kind of taking it easy, tells me to do the same, but I don't know what the hell happened. This Connie and I, we both slip out of the bar while Clayton's taking a leak, end up out back of the bar in the backseat of her car.'

'You and Millicent, you were married then,' I said. It wasn't really a judgment, I simply wasn't sure. But Rolly's scowl made clear how he'd taken it.

'Once in a while,' he said. 'I'd slip.'

'So you slipped with Connie Gormley. How'd she end up going from that backseat to that ditch?'

'When we ... when we were done, and I was heading back to the bar, she asked me for fifty bucks. I told her if she was a hooker she should have made that clear from the outset, but I don't know if she even was a hooker.

Maybe she just needed the fifty. Anyway, I wouldn't pay her, and she said maybe she'd look me up some time, at my home, get the money from my wife.'

'Oh.'

'She started scrapping with me by the car, and I guess I shoved back, a little too hard, and she tripped and her head came down right on the bumper, and that was it.'

'She was dead,' I said.

Rolly swallowed. 'People had seen us, right? In the bar? They might remember me and Clayton. I figured, if she got hit by a car instead, the police would think it was some sort of accident, that she'd gone walking, that she was drunk, they wouldn't be looking for some guy she picked up in the bar.'

I was shaking my head.

'Terry,' he said. 'If you'd been in that situation, you'd have been panicking, too. I got Clayton, told him what I'd done, and there was something in his face, like he felt he was as trapped by the situation as I was, he didn't want to be talking to any cops. I didn't know then about the kind of life he was living, that he wasn't who he claimed to be, that he was living a double life. So we put her in the car, took her down the highway, then Clayton held her up at the side of the road, tossed her in front of the car as I drove past. Then we put her in the ditch.'

'My God,' I said.

'Isn't a night goes by I don't think about it, Terry. It was a horrible thing. But sometimes, you have to be in a situation to appreciate what has to be done.' He shook his head again. 'Clayton swore he'd never tell. The son of a bitch.'

'He didn't,' I said. 'I tried to get him to, but he didn't

give you up. But let me see if I can guess how the rest of this goes. One night, Clayton and Patricia and Todd, they disappear off the face of the earth, nobody knows what happened to them, not even you. Then one day, a year later, maybe a few years later, you get a call. It's Clayton. Quid pro quo time. He covered up for you, for killing Connie Gormley, now he wanted you to do something for him. Be a courier, basically. Deliver money. He'd send it to you, maybe to a postal box or something. And then you'd slip it to Tess, drop it in her car, hide it in her newspaper, whatever.'

Rolly stared at me.

'Yeah,' he said. 'That's more or less what happened.'

'And then, like an idiot,' I said, 'I told you what Tess had revealed to me. When we had lunch. About getting the money. About how she still had the envelopes and the letter, the one warning her never to try to find out where the money came from, to never tell anyone about it. How, after all these years, she'd saved them.'

Now Rolly had nothing to say.

I came at him from another direction. 'Do you think a man who was prepared to murder two people to please his mother would lie to her about whether he'd ever killed anyone before?'

'What? What the hell are you talking about?'

'I'm kind of thinking out loud here. I don't think he would. I think a man who was about to kill for his mother, I don't think he'd mind admitting to her if he'd already killed before.' I paused. 'And the thing is, up until the moment the man said it, I was convinced that he'd already killed two people.'

'I have no idea what you're driving at,' Rolly said.

'I'm talking about Jeremy Sloan. Clayton's son, from the other marriage, with the other woman, Enid. But I suspect you know about them. Clayton would have probably explained it when he started sending you money to deliver to Tess. I figured Jeremy had killed Tess. And I figured he'd killed Abagnall. But now, I'm not so sure about that anymore.'

Rolly swallowed.

'Did you go see Tess after I told you what she had told me?' I asked. 'Were you afraid that maybe she'd figured it out? Were you worried that maybe the letter she still had, the envelopes, that maybe they might still carry some forensic evidence linking them to you? And that if that happened, then you'd be linked to Clayton, and he wouldn't be obliged to keep your secret any longer?'

'I didn't want to kill her,' Rolly said.

'You did a pretty good job of it, though,' I said.

'But I thought she was dying, anyway. It wasn't like I'd be stealing that much time from her. And then, later, after I'd done it, you told me about the new tests. About how she wasn't dying after all.'

'Rolly . . .'

'She'd given the letter and the envelopes to the detective,' he said.

'And you took his business card from the bulletin board,' I said.

'I called him, arranged a meeting, in the parking garage.'

'You killed him and took his briefcase with the papers inside,' I said.

Rolly cocked his head a bit to the left. 'What do you think? Do you think my fingerprints would still have been on those envelopes, after all these years? Saliva traces, maybe, when I sealed them?'

I shrugged. 'Who knows,' I said. 'I'm just an English teacher.'

'I got rid of them just the same,' Rolly said.

I looked down at the floor. I wasn't just in pain. I felt a tremendous sadness. 'Rolly,' I said. 'You've been such a good friend for so many years. I don't know, maybe even I'd be willing to keep my mouth shut about a horrible lapse in judgment more than twenty-five years ago. You probably never meant to kill Connie Gormley, it was just one of those things. It'd be hard to live with, covering that up for you, but for a friend, maybe.'

He eyed me warily.

'But Tess. You killed my wife's aunt. Wonderful, sweet Tess. And you didn't stop with her. There's no way I can let that go.'

He reached into the pocket of the long coat and pulled out a gun. I wondered if it could be the one he'd found in the schoolyard, among the beer bottles and crack pipes.

'For crying out loud, Rolly.'

'Go upstairs, Terry,' he said.

'You can't be serious,' I said.

'I've already bought my trailer,' he said. 'It's all set. I've picked out a boat. I've only got a few weeks to go. I deserve a decent retirement.'

He motioned me toward the stairs, followed me up them. Halfway up, I turned suddenly, tried to kick at him, but I was too slow. He jumped back a step, kept the gun trained on me.

'What's going on?' Cynthia called from Grace's room.

I stepped into the room, followed by Rolly. Cynthia,

over by Grace's desk, opened her mouth when she saw the gun but no words came out.

'It was Rolly,' I said to Cynthia. 'He killed Tess.'

'What?'

'And Abagnall.'

'I don't believe it.'

'Ask him.'

'Shut up,' Rolly said.

'What are you going to do, Rolly?' I asked him, turning around slowly by Grace's bed. 'Kill both of us, and Grace, too? You think you can kill that many people, and the police won't figure it out?'

'I have to do something,' he said.

'Does Millicent know? Does she know she's living with a monster?'

'I'm not a monster. I made a mistake. I had a bit too much to drink, that woman provoked me, demanding money that way. It just happened.'

Cynthia was flushed, her eyes wide. She must not have been able to believe what she was hearing. Too many shocks for one day. She lost it, not unlike the time when the phony psychic dropped by. She screamed and charged at him, but Rolly was ready, swinging the gun into her face, catching her across the cheek, knocking her to the floor by Grace's desk.

'I'm sorry, Cynthia,' he said. 'I'm so sorry.'

I thought I could take him at that moment, but he had the gun back on me. 'God, Terry, I hate to have to do this. I really do. Sit down. Sit on the bed there.'

He took a step forward, and I moved back a foot, sat down on the edge of Grace's bed. Cynthia was still struggling to get up off the floor, blood running down toward her neck from the gash in her cheek.

'Toss me a pillow,' he said.

So that was the plan. Put a pillow over the muzzle of the gun, cut down on the noise.

I glanced over at Cynthia. She had one hand slightly under Grace's desk. She looked at me, and she nodded ever so slightly. There was something in her eyes. Not fear. Something else. She was saying, 'Trust me.'

I reached for a pillow at the top of Grace's bed. It was a special one, with a design of the moon and the stars on the pillowcase.

I tossed it to Rolly, but I made my throw just a bit short, and he had to take half a step forward to catch it.

That's when Cynthia got to her feet. Sprung would be a better word. She had something in her hand. Something long and black.

Grace's piece-of-crap telescope.

Cynthia first swung it back over her own shoulder, giving her a chance to build up some speed, then she came at Rolly's head with her famous backhand, putting everything she had into it, and a little bit more.

He turned, saw it coming, but he never had a chance to react. She caught him across the side of his skull and it didn't sound much like something you'd hear at a tennis match. It was more like the crack of a bat hitting a fastball.

It was a home run.

Rolly Carruthers dropped like a stone. It was a wonder Cynthia didn't kill him.

FIFTY

'OK,' said Cynthia. 'So you know the deal?'

Grace nodded. She had her backpack ready. Her lunch was in there, her homework, even a cell phone. A pink cell phone. Cynthia had insisted and I put up no argument. When we first told Grace our plan, she said, 'Will it have text messaging? It *has* to have text messaging.' I'd like to tell you Grace is the only kid in fourth grade with a cell phone, but I'd be lying. Such is the world today.

'So what do you do?'

'When I get to school, I call you.'

'That's right,' said Cynthia. 'What else?'

'I have to get the teacher to say hi, too.'

'That's right. I've already set it up with her. She'll be expecting it. And she's not going to do it in front of the class, so you won't have to be embarrassed.'

'Am I going to have to do this every day?'

I said, 'Let's just take it a day at a time, OK?'

Grace smiled. That was fine with her. Being able to walk to school unescorted, even if you had to call home when you got there, made the deal pretty attractive to her. I don't know which, of the three of us, was the most nervous, but we'd had a long talk about it a couple of nights earlier. There was a consensus that we all needed to move forward, to reclaim our lives.

Walking to school alone was at the top of Grace's agenda. We were surprised, frankly. After what she'd been through, we thought she might actually be happy with an escort. The fact that she still wanted her independence seemed to me and Cynthia a hopeful sign.

We both gave her hugs goodbye, and we stood in the window watching her as long as we could, until she turned the corner.

It seemed like we were both holding our breath. We hovered over the phone in the kitchen.

Rolly was still recovering from one hell of a concussion. He was in hospital. That made him easy to find when Rona Wedmore showed up to charge him in the deaths of Tess Berman and Denton Abagnall. The Connie Gormley case had been reopened too, but that one was going to be a bit trickier to prove. The only witness, Clayton, was dead, and there was no physical evidence, like the car Rolly had been driving when he and Clayton staged the hit. It was probably rusting away in an automobile graveyard some place.

His wife Millicent phoned and screamed at us, said we were liars, that her husband hadn't done anything, that they were just getting ready to move to Florida, that she was going to get a lawyer and sue our asses off.

We had to get a new number. Unlisted.

It was just as well. Just before we did, we were getting several calls a day from Paula Malloy at *Deadline*, wanting to do a follow-up story. We never returned her calls, and when we saw her through the window standing on the front step, we didn't answer the door.

I had to get my ribs all taped up, and the doctor says Cynthia will probably need plastic surgery on her cheek. As for emotional scars, well, who knows.

Clayton Sloan's estate is still being sorted out. That could take a while, but that's OK. Cynthia's not even sure she wants the money. I'm working on her about that.

Vince Fleming was transferred from the hospital in Lewiston to the one here in Milford. He's going to be OK. I visited him the other day and he said Jane better end up with straight As. I told him I was on it.

I promised him I'd keep tabs on Jane's academic career, but I might be doing it from a different school. I'm thinking of putting in for a transfer. It's not many teachers end up getting their principal charged in two murders. It can get a bit awkward in the staff room.

The phone rang. Cynthia had the receiver in her hand before the first ring finished.

'OK ... OK,' she said. 'You're OK? No problems? OK ... Let me talk to your teacher ... Hi, Mrs Enders. Yeah, no, she sounds fine ... Thank you. Thank you so much ... Yes, we have been through a lot, it's true. I think, I might still go over and meet her after school. At least today. OK ... Thanks. You too ... OK ... Bye.'

She hung up. 'She's OK,' she said.

'That's what I figured,' I said, and we both shed a couple of tears.

'You OK?' I said.

Cynthia grabbed a tissue, dabbed at her eyes. 'Yeah. You want some coffee?'

'Sure,' I said. 'Pour us some. I have to get something.'

I went to the front hall closet, dug into the pocket of the sport coat I'd been wearing that night when everything happened, and pulled out the envelope. I came back into the kitchen, where Cynthia was sitting with her coffee, a mug sitting across the table at my spot.

'I already put your sugar in,' she said, and then she saw the envelope. 'What's that?'

I sat down, holding on to it.

'I was waiting for the right time, and I think this is it,' I said. 'Let me give you some background.'

Cynthia had the look you get when you're expecting bad news from your doctor.

'It's OK,' I said. 'Clayton, your father, he explained this to me, wanted me to explain it to you.'

'What?'

'That night, after you had that big fight with your parents, and you went up to bed, I guess you kind of passed out. Anyway, your mom, Patricia, she felt bad. From what you've said, she didn't like it when things were bad between the two of you.'

'No, she didn't,' Cynthia whispered. 'She liked to smooth things over as soon as she could.'

'Well, I guess that was what she wanted to do, so she wrote you ... a note. She put it out front of your door, before she left to take Todd to the drugstore.'

Cynthia couldn't take her eyes off the envelope in my hands.

'Anyway, your father, he wasn't feeling quite so conciliatory, not yet. He was still pretty pissed about having to go out and look for you, finding you in that car with Vince, dragging you home. He was thinking it was too soon to smooth things over. So, after your mother left, he went back upstairs and he took the note that she'd left for you, and stuffed it into his pocket.'

Cynthia was frozen.

'But then, given what happened over the next few hours, it turned out to be more than just some note. It was your mom's last note to her daughter. It was the last thing she'd ever write.' I paused. 'And so he saved it, put it in this envelope, hid it in his toolbox at home, taped under the tray. Just in case, someday, he'd be able to give it to you. Not a goodbye note, exactly, but worth having just the same.'

I handed the envelope, already torn open at one end, across the table to Cynthia.

She slid the paper out of the envelope, but didn't unfold it right away. She held it a moment, steeling herself. Then, carefully, she opened it up.

I, of course, had already read it. In the basement of the Sloan house in Youngstown. So I knew Cynthia was reading the following:

Hi Pumpkin:

I wanted to write you a note before I went to bed. I hope you haven't made yourself too sick. You did some pretty stupid things tonight. I guess that's what being a teenager is about.

I wish I could say these are the last stupid things you'll do, or that this is the last fight you'll have with me and your father, but that wouldn't be the truth. You'll do more stupid stuff, and we'll have more fights. Sometimes you'll be wrong, sometimes maybe even we'll be wrong.

But here's the one thing you have to know. No matter what, I will always love you. There's nothing you could ever do that would make me stop. Because I'm in this for the long haul with you. And that's the truth.

And it's always going to be that way. Even when you're on your own, living your own life, even when you've got a husband and kids of your own (imagine that!), even when I'm nothing but dust, I'll always be watching you. Someday, maybe you'll think you feel someone looking over your shoulder, and you'll look around and no one's there. That'll be me. Watching out for you, watching you make me so very, very proud. Your whole life, kiddo. I will always be with you.

Love,
Mom

I watched Cynthia as she read it to the end, and then I held her while she wept.